Praise for *Court of Lies*

"Gerry Spence electrified the courtroom every time he argued a case. Now, the legendary lawyer makes his crime novel debut, and lightning strikes again. *Court of Lies* is a stunning drama filled with characters as smart and surprising as Spence himself, and brilliant plotting that twists and turns to an ending you'll never see coming. I loved it!"

—Linda Fairstein, *New York Times* bestselling author of *Killer Look*

"Witty and fast-paced, this novel is filled with tension, suspense, and sharply drawn characters."

—William Martin, *New York Times* bestselling author of *Bound for Gold*

"Classic noir. A roller-coaster ride through a courtroom case by one of America's foremost lawyers. Terrific book—can't wait for the movie." —David Black, recipient of three Edgar nominations, two Emmy nominations, and a Writers Guild Award, and author of *Fast Shuffle*

"An easy novel to read and a difficult one to put down."
—*Booklist*

"Enthralling . . . witty and insightful." —*Publishers Weekly*

"Spence's prose is as polished as his final summation to the jury, helping to make the case that he belongs alongside John Grisham and Scott Turow as the foremost legal thriller writers of our time." —*The Providence Journal*

ALSO BY GERRY SPENCE

COURT OF LIES

GERRY SPENCE

A TOM DOHERTY ASSOCIATES BOOK
NEW YORK

This is a work of fiction. All of the characters, organizations, and events portrayed in this novel are either products of the author's imagination or are used fictitiously.

COURT OF LIES

Copyright © 2019 by G. L. Spence and Lanelle P. Spence Living Trust

All rights reserved.

A Forge Book
Published by Tom Doherty Associates
120 Broadway
New York, NY 10271

www.tor-forge.com

Forge® is a registered trademark of Macmillan Publishing Group, LLC.

ISBN 978-1-250-22460-6

Our books may be purchased in bulk for promotional, educational, or business use. Please contact your local bookseller or the Macmillan Corporate and Premium Sales Department at 1-800-221-7945, extension 5442, or by email at MacmillanSpecialMarkets@macmillan.com.

First Edition: February 2019
First Mass Market Edition: April 2020

Printed in the United States of America

0 9 8 7 6 5 4 3 2 1

*I dedicate this book to
my dear good friend Dr. Teddy Goldstein,
whose enduring love of his fellow humans and his
patients sets the standard for us and his profession.*

COURT OF LIES

CHAPTER 1

KILLING IS A part of living.

A man kills a deer with those soft, innocent eyes the size of large black cherries. He kills the plodding, harmless steer standing knee-deep in manure in the stockyards waiting to be slaughtered. He kills young men in religious wars over a god who was nailed to a cross. He kills whole cities with a single bomb, the children splayed and gutted and burned and the dead mothers' breasts drained empty on the pavement. And when the landlady said we couldn't keep all of the kittens that our cat deposited one night in her bed at the far corner of the kitchen, my father put all but the black kitten in a sack full of rocks and threw them in the river. Seven kittens. My mother said he had to. My mother said he cried, but I never saw my father cry.

The people of Jackson Hole are my people. The people know I'm a killer, and although some claim I have kind eyes and a good sense of humor, nevertheless, down where life and death meet I can be on the side of death, and the color of my robe—black—admits that. The people may smile at me and nod when we pass, but they know that given certain facts I can kill them, and that I will kill them. I hope they understand. I'm not a killer at heart. I kill only out of duty.

A winter in Jackson Hole feels as if time were caught on a snag in an eternally frozen river. Sometimes the temperature drops to forty below. The people burn their woodstoves twenty-four hours a day, and the smoke settles down on the valley in a dark gray ground-hugging blanket. In the winter, the ranchers hitch up a team of good horses to their hay wagons and feed their stock the hay they've put up in the summer. Used to do some feeding myself when I worked after school for old Henry Johnson. A good team knew its path. You tied the reins to the wagon's front, and the team plodded on while you forked off the hay to the cattle, and as I've always said, in the winter the sweat of a man at work reduced the cold to good medicine.

In winter the people dress to challenge the climate. Men wear those Converse leather-legged rubber boots and woolen socks with their Levi's tucked in, and they cover their bodies with sheepskin coats, the buffered raw wool still on the hide. Some women also wear jeans and boots. And some wear long dresses to make a decent attempt at hiding their feminine proportions and "to keep their knees warm." The countrywomen here often fulfill the role of a hired man. A good wife knows how to plant and hoe the garden and milk the cow and gather the eggs and ax the head off a frying chicken for Sunday supper. She cooks over a woodstove, the kindling for which she's likely also chopped.

"Out there," as we placid people of Jackson Hole refer to the remainder of the world, the people are panicked. The government is encouraging our women to do what we've always done here in the Hole—to keep a good stock of canned goods on hand, and in a safe place store

a tub full of dried beans, and another tub full of wheat. The people out there are told they'd better have a bunch of flashlights and half a truckload of batteries, because all power sources may be demolished. "Look what a couple of A-bombs did to the Japs," the people say to one another. All the while, Elvis Presley is banging out rock and roll, and the people are jumping and jerking as if their last jerk were close at hand.

Then the one night the world came crushing in on me. I was in deep sleep. I stumbled to the ringing phone and recognized the voice immediately. The caller said, "He's dead, Judge Murray."

"What do you mean, 'He's dead'?" I asked.

"He's dead. Dead."

I knew the caller. I loved her like a father loves his child. "And they've charged me with his murder," she said. And that's all she said before I heard the phone click dead.

CHAPTER 2

EVERY WORKDAY MORNING, the town fathers gathered at the Big Chief Café for breakfast. Hardy Tillman claimed the joint hadn't been hosed out since the big fire in '47. "This place even smells like the Old West, and I mean the Old West," Hardy said. He ran the Main Street filling station in Jackson Hole. He sported a budding beer belly, but everybody in those parts admitted Hardy was tough. Nobody tried Hardy Tillman.

Generations of spiders had spun their webs between the horns of mounted elk heads that stared down with glass eyes from the once-whitewashed walls, now smoke-stained and, near the kitchen, darkened to bay-horse brown from the blowout of scorched pans and flaming grills. Under half an inch of dust and grease, a rusted musket lay across the antlers of a mule deer's head, the trophy of a forgotten hunter.

Posters of current movies starring Doris Day as Calamity Jane, and the fast-gun hero John Wayne in *Hondo,* curled at their corners, as if struggling to roll up in slumber. The floor was covered with linoleum that was mopped daily, and the hard boots of workingmen had worn away its original redbrick design except in the far corners of the café.

Each morning, two waitresses, Mary Johnson and Molly Hocks, rushed the men's orders to the kitchen, bounced back to fill their coffee cups, empty or not, and shortly, like gastronomic midwives, delivered their breakfasts steaming hot and laden with grease.

"How's my darling doing? I dreamed about you all night, honey," Molly Hocks cooed.

"Don't give that line again, honey," Harry Halstead, part-time mountain guide and part-time bartender, said. "That's what you told me yesterday and I tipped you the last two dimes in my pocket, which'll have to do you for today, since you're still giving me that same old dream."

Peaks of hilarity bounced off the café walls and comingled with the jangle of pans and kettles from the kitchen and the hollering of the cooks and waitresses—the racket reaching the raging uproar of an orchestra gone mad.

A potpourri of appetizing aromas escaped from the kitchen—of ham, bacon, and frying sausage, of fresh coffee and pancakes hot off the griddle. The odor of workmen in their overalls of dirt and sweat mixed with the scent of a few business types, their hair shiny in Brylcreem and radiating a smell akin to lilacs and bug spray. As each waitress whisked by, she was trailed by a wake of fragrance perhaps attributable to a dab of something called Seven Winds, "for the woman who wants to be loved," or a spray of Nostalgia, which "turns my lamb into a wolf."

Over the ruckus and racket, the men at Lester McCall's table were talking in high shouts about Lillian Adams. She'd been charged with the murder of her husband, Horace Adams III. His friends called McCall "Too Tall" McCall. He was six and a half feet tall, and he said, "I don't give a damn what they call me as long as they call me for supper." His voice reverberated from the walls like the um-pah-pah of a bass horn in a high school marching band.

"Well, I knew Lillian as a kid," McCall bellowed through the tumult. "She always did whatever she damn well pleased and got whatever she damn well wanted. But it sounds like she went a little too far this time. Old Adams had more money than I got gravel in my gravel pit, and, at that *pre*cise moment before she pulled the trigger, he was all that was standin' between her and it."

"I don't think she did it," Harold Farmer, the town's mayor, said. His head was bald, but he displayed an undisciplined beard in order to show some hair, of some kind, someplace. "She wasn't the kind to go killing for money. When we were kids in high school, I took her rabbit hunting one Saturday. I wasn't figuring to just hunt rabbits. I wanted to bag me a bunny, if you get my meaning." He laughed. "But she wouldn't let me shoot even a cross-eyed jackrabbit. She said, 'I'm on the rabbit's side.' But I will say one thing for her: She sure could outshoot me."

"Don't have to be much of a shot to hit somebody with your gun shoved up against his head," Harv Bailey said as he took a big bite out of a glazed doughnut and a swig of coffee to help wash it down. He owned the local men's store, with his typewriter shop in the back. He was wearing the latest banded jacket, jodhpurs, and hiking boots that laced up to just below the knees. He wore his mop of black hair in a cowlick, the product of a careful application of hair coloring that contrasted with a sprinkle of white in his three-day-old beard. He took out a pack of Lucky Strikes and offered one to Ben Mays, the Teton County assessor.

"I'm trying to quit," Mays said as Bailey lit their cigarettes. Some called him "Magpie" Mays. His habitual plumage was a black suit, a white shirt, and a black tie—put a person in mind of a magpie. "The judge should've taken himself off the case. She isn't related to him by blood, I'll give you that, but the judge and Betsy haven't got any kids except her, and they always saw her as belonging to them. I know for a fact the Adams dame had the judge's number couple of times in the past. And I hear she's still pretty much running things up there in the courtroom."

"I wonder how come old Judge Murray let her outta jail with practically no bond at all. Fifty thousand is nothing to her," Henry Green said. "Should've been ten mil at least. She probably had a little meeting with the judge in his chambers, if ya know what I mean."

"You're full a shit," Hardy Tillman said. He and Judge Murray had been best friends since grade school. Hardy stood up and spit his words into Henry Green's face again. "I said you're full a shit."

Henry Green looked down, blew on his coffee, and sat tight in his chair.

CHAPTER 3

HASKINS SEWELL, THE Teton County prosecutor, was a joyless man of indeterminate age. He stood straight, lean, and gray as a prairie bone. Some called him "a walking stiff." Some referred to him as "the man in gray." He was never to be seen except in a gray three-piece suit with a white shirt and a matching gray tie. His skin and his slicked-down shelf of thin hair were the same shade of gray. He claimed it a sinful vanity to spend even a minute of one's life concocting an outfit each day that met the supercilious whims of the New York fashion gurus. Sewell's gray eyes were dead set in concrete on one immutable goal—the conviction of Lillian Adams for the murder of her husband.

Haskins Sewell's father, Joseph Sewell, sold mules he imported from neighboring states, and on one such a trip he'd met Henrietta Housely at a picnic in the Jackson Hole Square. She was the only daughter of the Baptist preacher, John Housely, and soon she and Joe were tumbling desperately, helplessly in love, the towering Teton Mountains providing a glorious background for their delirium. However, before the Reverend Housely gave his consent to their marriage, he demanded that Joe be baptized in his church.

"Do you take Jesus Christ as your Lord and Savior?" the Reverend John Housely shouted into the baptismal waters of Jackson Lake.

Joe Sewell looked over at the budding Henrietta and replied, "Yes, Jesus, sir!" And thereupon, the Reverend Housely dipped Joe in the chilling waters of the lake and held him under, some thought a bit too long, while reciting Matthew 28:19: "I baptize you in the name of the Father and of the Son and of the Holy Spirit." Nine months after their marriage, Henrietta bore the couple a son. They named him Haskins after Lord knows who, or why. But soon Joe's frequent and careless wanderings outside the marital boundaries led to the couple's divorce. Henrietta moved into her parents' home in Jackson, where her son was reared, and where he was also dipped in the same baptismal waters of Jackson Lake.

Haskin Sewell's mother taught what she held out as simple truths: "You can never trust someone who says they love you. When you hear that, you know they're lying, for the only true love is the love of Christ." She taught that survival is the overriding virtue of all virtues, and that only the blind, the ignorant, and the foolhardy are given to trust one another.

"You know how your father was," his mother often reminded him. "He'd give a bum his last nickel and then run off with the first woman who gave him the look. Women!" she moaned. "They'll take if all if given half a chance."

To ensure that her son would not follow his father's faithless footsteps, and for minor infractions, Henrietta often whipped poor Haskins's back and buttocks—thirty-nine times ("forty lashes *less one*," according to the law of Moses that proclaimed forty lashes would kill, but one less than forty was, accordingly, maximum punishment). Once, after catching him masturbating behind the outhouse, she flogged poor Haskins until he passed out. She viewed dating and dancing as satanically inspired.

Haskins's grandfather, the Reverend John Housely, sent Haskins to the Southwestern Baptist Theological Seminary in Fort Worth, Texas, to prepare him for the ministry. But Haskins proved to be a man with a vision of his own. After he graduated from the seminary with decent grades, he enrolled in the seminary's parent school, Baylor University on the Brazos River in Waco, Texas, where he studied law, after which he returned to Wyoming, took the bar, and went to work for the local prosecutor, Warren Garrison.

Sewell learned that in the unforgiving world of the courtroom, victory and breathing were equally essential to life. In the world beyond the courtroom, the rule was the same: kill or be killed, the corollary of which was that if one were in charge one might avoid loss, injury, death, and, in the end, perhaps damnation.

Sewell believed rules were the folly of losers and were merely bothersome fences that society put in place to placate the public, a congregation of ignorant dolts who'd been spoon-fed the troublesome language of the Declaration of Independence and all that other patriotic blather about the rights and privileges of an American citizen.

Although prosecutor Sewell had never experienced the love of a woman, he was fully capable of loving his little dog. Most often he carried the little bug-eyed beast wherever he went and it snapped at anyone who approached, all except, of course, Haskins Sewell.

Haskins Sewell's life's work was destined for the courtroom. The courtroom is a distant cousin of a church's room of worship. Both have hard pews for the audience and high ceilings that suggest consequential carryings-on therein. In the courtroom "the bar" is a short, usually wooden divider behind which the lawyer and the jurors and other court functionaries sit. As in a church where the clergy is elevated to the pulpit (closer to God) so in the courtroom the judge sits above all at "the bench." From there the judge peers down on the humanoids below. So it was in the courtroom of the District Court of Teton County.

Prosecutor Haskins Sewell approached the jury box and surveyed the jurors with a skeptical eye. They returned the same. He cleared his throat to begin his opening statement without offering the customary salutation of "Ladies and gentlemen of the jury."

"Lillian Adams is a murderer," Haskins said in his flat gray voice. "She killed in cold blood. She tried to cover the killing with a forged suicide note she attributed to her dead husband. He was an extremely wealthy individual, and she shot him as he was begging for mercy. You will see his last plea frozen as a death mask on his face. This is a soulless, calculating woman with a long history of violence—"

"I object!" Timothy Coker shouted. He wore thick glasses that magnified his green eyes and provided an owlish presence. He stumbled toward the bench. "Mr. Sewell knows better than to open up that subject."

"Approach the bench," the judge ordered. "And keep it down."

The judge turned to Sewell. "As you know, Mr. Sewell, Lillian Adams's past legal history is prejudicial and cannot be cited in the presence of the jurors."

"On behalf of my client, Lillian Adams, I move for a mistrial," Coker cried in naked anger.

Judge Murray turned to the jurors and said with

unyielding firmness, "Ladies and gentlemen, Mr. Sewell has just made a statement concerning the alleged history of the defendant. It was an improper statement. You are instructed to disregard it completely."

Coker, still at the bench, shot further argument at the judge, "You can't unring the bell that Sewell just rang."

"Proceed," the judge ordered. "And I shall use every means to keep all improper utterances at a minimum."

Sewell glared at Coker. "Ladies and gentlemen, I will prove beyond a reasonable doubt that Lillian Adams is guilty of murder, and I will ask you, good citizens, sworn under your duty to do justice, to return a verdict of murder in the first degree. That, indeed, will be justice." He returned to his chair at the counsel table.

The judge turned to Coker, who was fumbling through a stack of papers. "You may make your opening statement," Judge Murray said.

"The defendant, Lillian Adams, reserves her opening statement until after the state rests its case," Coker announced, and sat down.

Judge Murray looked at Coker in shock and disbelief. "I beg your pardon?" the judge said. Competent defense attorneys rarely, if ever, reserved their opening statements. Standard wisdom held that the defense must begin raising reasonable doubt at the first opportunity. But Coker remained silent, his eyes focused on the east courtroom wall, which, so far as the judge could see, was off-white and blank.

Finally, the judge turned to Sewell. "Call the state's first witness, Mr. Prosecutor."

"The state calls Sergeant Harold Illstead," Sewell announced.

Shrapnel on Omaha Beach had left the right side of Illstead's face deeply scarred, and the right side of his mouth drooped. His right eye was covered with a black patch. When Illstead took the stand, he was still wearing an "I Like Ike" button on his lapel.

Illstead had been retired from the Jackson Hole sheriff's office, but when the Lillian Adams murder case called for expert testimony, Illstead was summoned to duty by Sewell and he was offered to the jury as the county's expert witness. Illstead once attended a short course in crime-scene investigation conducted by the FBI, after which he'd been anointed as the county's "criminalist."

Illstead settled stiffly into the witness chair.

Sewell provided the jury with Illstead's qualifications as an expert. He then asked: "I suppose, Sergeant, that you examined the deceased for powder burns?"

"Yes," Illstead replied. He opened his briefcase, extracted a pile of papers, and began fumbling through them. At last, he withdrew an eight-by-ten-inch photograph and held it close to his good eye for inspection. In the photograph, the deceased was shown seated in a desk chair, his face grotesquely contorted as it rested on the desktop in a large pool of blood. The blood had begun to dry around the edges. Sewell marked the photograph as an exhibit and offered it into evidence.

With old watery eyes, Judge Murray glared hard at defense attorney Timothy Coker. Surely he got the judge's message. Why hadn't Coker objected to such a prejudicial photograph? The photograph's only relevance was to prove Adams's death, and Coker had already admitted Adams was killed by a contact bullet wound through the skull.

Coker could usually be counted on to raise all sorts of hell over such tactics. Coker was competent, all right—often too aggressive. He'd been well versed in "the school of hard knocks," as Coker liked to refer to his years of experience. If an accused was charged with a crime—any crime, from a bad check to a bar fight, even murder—Timothy Coker was the lawyer for the case. People had come to expect that along the way he'd pull something out of his bag of tricks to convince the jury to acquit, and sometimes he'd been successful. Why, the judge wondered, did Coker sit there like a dead frog on a rotting log and not object to the bloody exhibit? The judge had no choice but to allow its admittance.

Sewell handed the photograph to the juror, Harmony Biernstein, a Realtor. She glanced fleetingly at the photograph and passed it on to the next juror, Helen Griggsley, a piano teacher, who let out a small gasp and shoved it quickly to William Witherspoon, a craggy-faced rancher who was never repelled by blood. Over a lifetime he'd castrated and butchered a trainload of cattle. He regarded the photograph for a minute or more before finally passing it on to the banker, James P. Smithson, the jury foreman. Smithson examined the photograph as if he were adding columns on a balance sheet. Then he passed it on.

Meanwhile, prosecutor Sewell marked as an exhibit a close-up of the deceased's head, and offered it into evidence, and again it was admitted without objection from Coker. Illstead, with permission from the judge, stepped cautiously down from the witness chair, turned the easel bearing the photograph toward the jurors, and took the pointer Sewell handed him. "This is a photograph of the deceased's head taken later in the mortuary," Illstead said. "The blood has been cleaned away to reveal the bullet's entry wound in his forehead. You can see the star-shaped lacerations around the black entry wound there." He pointed. The jurors, fascinated with the unfolding drama, leaned forward.

Illstead continued: "When the end of the gun's barrel is flush against the skin and the gun is fired, the released gases blast into the subcutaneous tissues and cause those star-shaped injuries. Here you can also see the grayish discoloration from the gunshot residues, sometimes referred to as 'powder burns.'"

The judge glanced at the defendant, Lillian Adams. Yes, she'd been a handsome woman. She was a couple inches taller than Coker. Her black hair was done up in a tight bun on the back of her head. She was wearing a plain black dress that extended well below the knees. She wore a string of inexpensive pearls. Small tracks of sweat glistened on her forehead.

Judge Murray and his wife, Betsy, had loved Lillian Adams since she was a small child. She wasn't their blood child, but she was the closest thing to a daughter they'd ever have. Yes, the judge knew he was in conflict. But he argued to himself that he was frequently in conflict. In this small berg he might one day have his doctor in court, and the next day his banker or Betsy's best friend. But such was the challenge of every judge in thousands of small one-horse towns across the land. If they called in a new judge every time a conflict made its appearance, the county would be required to pay the new judge, and there was no budget or money for such as that.

Still, in every trial, by rule, each side had the right to disqualify one judge in a timely manner. Why had Coker left Judge Murray on the case? For Coker, the question had been simple: Would his defense of Lillian Adams go better in front of Judge Murray or with another judge who'd be selected by Judge Murray if he stepped down? Although in the past Coker and the judge had had their issues, they'd also enjoyed a long history as close friends and partners. Coker trusted the judge's integrity.

On the other hand, Sewell knew that meticulous fairness was most important to Judge Murray, and Sewell would play on it. And he had other plans that would explode in the judge's face down the line.

Sewell turned back to his witness, Illstead: "When you were at the scene, did you check the hands of Mrs. Adams for traces of gunshot residues?"

"Yes. I swabbed her hands and did the standard testing."

"What was the result?"

"She was positive for gunshot residues." Illstead's disfigured face lent a macabre credibility to his testimony.

"And what does that mean?"

"It means that she either fired a weapon that night or that she was very close to one."

"When you arrived at the scene, did you observe a weapon?"

"Yes, next to the deceased's right hand on the desktop was a revolver."

"What else did you observe, Sergeant Illstead?"

"I saw a handwritten note at the far end of the desk. It supposedly bore the signature of the deceased."

"Did you examine the pistol, State's Exhibit forty-three?"

Illstead put his good eye close to the weapon. "Yes, I examined this pistol."

"And were you able to discern any fingerprints on the gun?"

"No, I wasn't."

"What does that mean to you?"

"It means that the gun was fired by someone wearing gloves, or that the prints had been wiped off."

Sewell handed Illstead a photograph marked "Exhibit 9." "What is this?"

"This is a photograph I took that night. It shows the floor of the den."

"What did you intend to reveal with this photograph?"

"That there was blood on the floor where the body had been dragged."

"Dragged?"

"Dragged."

"Did you take fingernail scrapings from the defendant, Lillian Adams?"

"Yes."

"How did you acquire them?"

"I simply took them from Mrs. Adams at the same time that I swabbed her hands for gunshot residues—standard police procedure."

"And what did you discover from an examination of her fingernail scrapings?"

"As reported by the FBI, she had traces of blood underneath her nails that matched the blood type of the deceased."

The judge had given Coker another hard look, inviting his objection. The FBI's report was hearsay. But Coker remained inexplicably silent. Lillian Adams, who sat next to Coker, glanced at her nails and then looked quickly away.

"What other evidence did you take from Mrs. Adams, the defendant?" Sewell asked.

"I saw what appeared to be blood on her white slacks. She also had blood on her high-heeled pumps. At my direction she went to her bedroom, changed clothes, and returned the bloody clothes to me, as I requested. The FBI reported that both her slacks and shoes contained blood splotches that matched the blood type of her deceased husband." Sewell offered the exhibits into evidence. Coker made no objection.

"At the time you were at the scene, did you have a conversation with Mrs. Adams?"

"Yes."

"Who was present?"

"Just myself and Mrs. Adams."

Suddenly, Coker came alive. "Just a minute. Your Honor, we need to approach the bench."

At the bench, Coker whispered to the judge, "Your Honor, Sewell is attempting to elicit from Sergeant Illstead what Mrs. Adams *said* to Illstead, and that's protected by the Fifth Amendment."

The judge turned up the volume on his hearing aid. "Mr. Sewell, would you state what you expect your witness's answer will be?"

"Yes," Sewell whispered back. "Sergeant Illstead will testify that he asked Mrs. Adams what happened and she told him she came home at about midnight and found Mr. Adams dead at his desk, and she called the police."

"I see nothing objectionable with that testimony," the judge ruled. "You may proceed."

Sewell, still standing stiff and straight, returned to the podium. "During your investigation, Sergeant, what conversation did you have with Mrs. Adams?"

"I asked her if she could tell me what happened, and she said no, that she had gotten home about midnight and found him dead at his desk."

"I see," Sewell said.

Illstead continued: "Then I said, 'I have to clear the record, Mrs. Adams. Did you have anything to do with this?'"

Coker shouted, "This is in gross violation of my client's—"

"Hold it right there, Mr. Coker," the judge said, interrupting him. "I sustain your objection."

Illstead, seeming to ignore the judge's warning, replied. "She said she wanted to talk to her attorney."

Coker bounded to his feet. "Again, I move for a

mistrial. This is outrageous. This is a blatant violation of Mrs. Adams's rights. Sewell knew what the sergeant would say, and he knows that any statement concerning Mrs. Adams's request to see her attorney is protected."

"Mr. Sewell, what do you have to say for yourself?" Judge Murray asked, glaring down at the prosecutor.

"Well, Your Honor," Sewell replied under a cloak of innocence, "I had no idea he was going to tell us she wanted to talk to her lawyer."

"I'll bet not!" Coker said. "Once more, I demand a mistrial."

"I'll take care of it," the judge said. The judge turned to the jurors: "Ladies and gentlemen, you are to totally disregard the testimony of this witness concerning Mrs. Adams's wanting to talk to her attorney. She has an absolute right to make such a request. Indeed, we should all talk to an attorney concerning all legal matters. Moreover, Sergeant Illstead should have advised her that she had a right to talk to her attorney. That a citizen seeks legal advice must not be construed in any way as evidence of that citizen's guilt or innocence. It has no bearing on this case whatsoever, and it was wrong for Sergeant Illstead to testify to anything in that regard." He turned to the lawyers. "Proceed, gentlemen."

Coker rushed to the edge of the judge's bench.

"Back off, Mr. Coker," the judge warned, slamming his gavel. "I said, 'Back off'!"

Coker took a step back, his arms swinging wildly in the air, his fists clenched as if he were in the throes of a boxing match. "Your admonition to the jury will not cure this intentionally committed error. It cannot be cured," Coker hollered.

The judge pounded his gavel in response. Then the judge, along with the lawyers, the court reporter, and

Lillian Adams, adjourned to the judge's chambers. "All right, Mr. Coker," the judge said in chambers, "let's see if you can address the court in a civil manner."

Coker detonated again. "Sewell has just won his case by another of his sleazy tricks. Despite your instruction to the jurors, there isn't a juror sitting there who believes an innocent person would need to talk to her lawyer. The jurors will now believe that Mrs. Adams killed her husband and wanted a lawyer to protect her."

Yes, the judge thought, it was a typical sleazy Sewell trick. "Mr. Sewell, you are skating on very thin ice here. Any more little surprises like this and I may be forced to grant Mr. Coker's motion for a mistrial. Do you understand?"

"Yes, of course." Sewell tendered the judge a small, pained smile.

Was Sewell attempting to force the judge to declare a mistrial? If he declared a mistrial, Lillian might be set free due to the constitutional prohibition against double jeopardy. What scheme was Sewell devising?

Judge Murray turned to the prosecutor. "Mr. Sewell, as you know, my job here is very much like that of the referee in a boxing match. You might get away with one low blow, maybe two, depending on how severe. But if you keep this up, you may forfeit the fight on a foul. Do you get the picture?"

"Yes, Your Honor, of course," Sewell said. He worked up another painful smile and announced he would have no more questions for the witness.

CHAPTER 4

THE JUDGE ORDERED the jurors be returned to the courtroom, and Timothy Coker headed to the podium for his cross-examination of Sergeant Illstead.

"Let's shed some honest light on your testimony, Sergeant. You claim that your Exhibit nine reveals drag marks of blood on the floor. Did you test those stains on the floor to determine if, indeed, they were from blood?"

"No, I didn't."

"Why not?"

"I didn't believe it was necessary."

"Not necessary? Can we now go to the scene of this homicide and make any tests to determine if the stains you saw on the floor were actually blood?"

"Of course not," Illstead said. "The scene has been cleaned up."

"The jurors must now accept your beliefs rather than the results of any scientific tests, isn't that true?"

"I suppose."

"Don't you agree that a competent death-scene investigator would have determined what those stains on the floor were?"

"No."

"Is it all right with you that we guess?"

No answer.

"Well?"

Still no answer—except the sergeant's one-eyed glare at Coker.

"Well, Sergeant, you want the jury to guess this lady into a murder conviction?"

Sewell: "Objection. This is argumentative."

Judge Murray: "Sustained."

"Now let's deal with another issue here," Coker said. "Did you attempt to determine who owned the revolver that you discovered at the scene of this death?"

"Yes, I did."

"Why did you do that?"

"Standard investigation."

"Why do you say it is standard?"

Illstead was silent.

"It's good to know who owns the weapon that was supposedly involved in the homicide, isn't that true?" Coker asked.

"Yes."

"Who owned the pistol involved here?" As Coker waited, he hung his thumbs in his suspenders.

"I assume Mr. Adams."

"You assume? *You assume?*"

No answer.

"To whom was it registered?"

"The pistol was unregistered."

"You mean that the gun that supposedly killed Mr. Adams was not registered to him?"

"Yes."

"Anyone with an unregistered gun could have dropped that gun there, isn't that true?"

"I suppose."

"Is 'I suppose' a yes answer, or is it a no answer?"

No answer from the sergeant.

"Did you determine if the bullet that killed Mr. Adams was fired from that gun?"

"No."

"Why not?"

"The bullet not only went through the skull of Mr. Adams, it also lodged in the wall behind him. I had to dig it out of the plaster. The bullet was so thoroughly scarred that no comparison could be made so as to tie it to the firearm in question."

"You are not equipped to make that comparison, are you?"

"No."

"You would ordinarily send both the revolver and the bullet to the FBI for such comparisons, isn't that true?"

"Yes."

"Did you send the gun and the bullet to the FBI to see if, in fact, they could match the bullet to the gun?"

"No, I didn't."

"So what we have here is another of your assumptions—namely, that the FBI couldn't have matched the bullet to the gun—isn't that true?"

"The bullet was too scarred, as I've testified."

"No one from the FBI said so, did they?"

"No."

"It's you, who took a six-week course somewhere in crime-scene investigations, who is now telling us what the FBI can or can't do?"

No answer.

"Sir?"

No answer from the deputy—only the hostile glower from his one good eye.

"And you can't testify that the bullet you dug out of the wall was fired from the unregistered pistol that you found at the scene?"

"No, I can't. But it was obvious."

"'Obvious' means you guessed again, because both the bullet and the revolver were found at the scene, isn't that true?"

"Both were at the scene, yes."

"Now, you testified that you found what you took to be gunshot residues on Mrs. Adams's hands?"

"Yes."

"You don't know that Mrs. Adams ever fired a gun, do you?"

"I know she had gunshot residues on her hands."

"I would appreciate an answer to my question, Sergeant. You don't know that Mrs. Adams ever fired a gun."

"I don't know."

"Even though you don't know if she ever fired a gun, you want the jury to believe she did, isn't that true?"

"I want the jury to know the facts."

"Would the facts include your assumptions?"

No answer.

"Well, Sergeant Illstead, do you want the jury to believe your assumptions?"

Sewell: "Objection, Your Honor. He's arguing with the witness again."

Judge Murray turned to Illstead. "Do you want the jury to believe your assumptions, Sergeant?"

"It's up to them," Illstead replied.

Coker continued: "You don't know if Mrs. Adams ever fired the gun in question, or any other gun, do you?"

"I can't say."

"She could get gunshot residues on her hands by simply picking up a recently fired gun, isn't that true?"

"Yes." His good eye narrowed and began roving the courtroom.

"If she touched the deceased, she could get gunshot residues on her hands as well as blood on her clothing and under her fingernails."

Illstead looked over to Sewell for help.

"You can't get your answer from Mr. Sewell, Sergeant. You'll have to answer my question yourself."

"Yes, gunshot residues and blood are transferable."

"Thank you," Coker said. "Now that wasn't too hard, was it?"

Sewell came alive. "He's badgering the witness."

Judge Murray: "Do you feel badgered, Sergeant?"

No answer. Only his one-eyed glare.

"And did you test Mr. Horace Adams the Third's hands for gunshot residues?"

"I did."

"You didn't tell us that before. Was this a secret between you and Mr. Sewell?"

"I wasn't asked."

"Did you talk with Mr. Sewell about the facts of this case before you took the stand here?"

"Yes."

"Where?"

"In his office."

"Did you tell Mr. Sewell about testing Mr. Adams's hands for gunshot residues?"

"No."

"No?" Coker took a single step closer to the witness. "No? Was that just your secret in this case?"

"Mr. Sewell didn't ask me."

"The result of that test is an important fact in this case, isn't that true?"

"Yes, it was standard."

"And you learned that in your schooling?"

"Yes."

"Do you follow a rule that says if the prosecutor doesn't ask you, don't tell?"

"Not that I know of."

"Well, I'm asking you. What were the results of the test on Mr. Adams's hands?"

"He was positive for gunshot residues, as well."

"Which means?"

"That he either fired a weapon that night or was close to one when it was fired."

One could hear the gasping and high whispered exclamations from the front row occupied by the press. The *Casper Star Tribune* reporter hurried to the door. "Got a headline here!" he said aloud to the reporter from *The Denver Post*. "Gotta make my deadline." The *Rocky Mountain News* reporter also jumped up and rushed toward the back of the courtroom.

"Order!" The judge gaveled repeatedly.

When the courtroom was cleared of reporters, Coker continued: "A man who sticks a gun up to his forehead and pulls the trigger is going to have gunshot residues on his hands, isn't he?" Coker asked.

"Probably."

"No, not probably, Sergeant Illstead, not probably, but absolutely. Can you think of any circumstance when that wouldn't be true?"

"If he was wearing gloves."

"Was Mr. Adams wearing gloves?"

"No."

"So why don't you turn to the jury and tell them the truth. I will help you. Say to the jurors, 'Ladies and gentlemen, if Mr. Adams shot himself by placing his pistol to his head, and he pulled the trigger, there would absolutely be gunshot residues on his hands.' Can't you just turn to the jurors and say that simple truth?"

Sewell jumped to his feet. "Objection, Your Honor. Mr. Coker is not permitted to put words in the witness's mouth."

"This is cross-examination," the judge ruled. He turned to the witness. "Sergeant Illstead, do you agree with what Mr. Coker just said?"

"Well . . . yes, there would likely be gunshot residues on one or both of his hands. But nothing is absolutely certain."

"Sergeant Illstead, have you been reading a lot of *True Detective* magazine lately?"

"That is utterly out of order!" Sewell screamed. "I move that Mr. Coker be admonished."

The judge turned to Coker and in a flat, unconvincing voice said, "You are admonished, Mr. Coker."

"And I want the jury instructed to disregard Mr. Coker's gratuitous remark," Sewell insisted.

"Move along, Mr. Coker."

Sewell looked over at the judge, his face etched with anger. "I want to approach the bench." He slammed his notebook on his table. The elderly woman juror in the front row let out a small, startled yelp.

The judge rapped his gavel. The woman jumped again. "It's time for a recess," the judge said. "I'll see counsel in my chambers."

CHAPTER 5

IN CHAMBERS, SEWELL addressed the judge angrily. "You mean to tell me, Your Honor, that Coker can tell this jury that my case is nothing more than something dragged out of a pulp magazine?"

"Keep your voice down," the judge said. "These walls are not totally soundproof. I've ruled, Mr. Sewell."

"You certainly have. And your rulings are impeding justice."

"You're verging on contempt," the judge said.

"Are you threatening me?"

"I am reminding you of the consequences of judicial disrespect."

"Well, I have something to say," Coker said. "This prosecutor withheld the fact that gunshot residue tests were taken from the hands of Horace Adams the Third, and that those tests were positive. If I hadn't stumbled onto that fact in my cross-examination, the jury would believe that the only person in this case whose hands were contaminated with gunshot residues was Mrs. Adams. That was a sure road to conviction, and both Illstead and Sewell knew this."

Sewell shrugged, indifferent to the assertion.

"This prosecutor," Coker continued, shaking his finger at Sewell, "knows he had the duty to provide the defense with that exculpatory evidence before trial, and he hid it from us. I ask that Mr. Sewell be admonished and the jury be instructed that this prosecutor has intentionally withheld evidence favorable to Mrs. Adams, and that this is a violation of his duty under the law."

"I will reserve my ruling on that, Mr. Coker. If there are further incidents of this nature, I will give your motion renewed consideration."

"Your Honor," Coker pressed, "Mr. Sewell had the further duty to tell us before trial that this gun was unregistered, and that he did not send the bullet and the gun to the FBI for comparison as is standard procedure."

"Yes, Mr. Sewell. Why wasn't Mr. Coker so advised?"

"The revolver was found at the fingertips of the deceased. The ownership of the gun is irrelevant to the question of who fired it."

"I see," the judge said. "That may or may not be so. But these very troublesome facts can certainly be argued by Mr. Coker to the jury."

"I must observe that the weaker the prosecution's case becomes, the more Mr. Sewell pursues his case by impropriety and dirty tricks," Coker said.

Sewell turned to Coker. "This is off the record. If you weren't such a senile old bastard, I'd personally show you a trick or two." He started to unbutton his coat.

Coker jerked his glasses off and dropped them on the judge's desk. "This is off the record, too. Give it a try, you lying piece of shit."

Shocked, Lillian Adams retreated to the far wall.

"There's nothing off the record, here," the judge yelled. "Stop this unprofessional conduct this minute!" The judge was looking for his gavel. He'd left it on the bench. He turned to the clerk. "Call the sheriff, Mr. Clerk."

"I don't have to take that insult from anybody," Sewell said. "As you can see, he's attacking me. I want that on the record."

"Back off," Coker warned Sewell. "You smell like dog shit, and that can go on the record."

"I find you both in contempt," Judge Murray yelled, "and that is definitely on the record. Both of you take your seats immediately. Mr. Clerk, call the sheriff!" the judge ordered again.

The two lawyers plopped down in their chairs like obedient but angry schoolboys.

"I've already called the sheriff twice," the clerk hollered back.

The sheriff burst into the room. "What's going on here?"

The judge was holding the left side of his chest with both hands.

"They're in contempt of court," the clerk said, trying to be helpful. "Did you get that, Madam Reporter?"

The court reporter sobbed, "I can't get this all down. Everybody's screaming at once."

"I find both of these lawyers . . . in con . . . tempt," the judge said in halting words.

"That's what I said," said the clerk.

"I order the sheriff . . . to forthwith lock both these alleged lawyers up . . . until further order of this court."

"Well," the sheriff said, "we got more'n a full house. You want 'em dumped in with the drunks and the pukes?"

"I'll appeal this order," Sewell said.

"In the meantime, Mr. Sheriff, these men are not to be released without my prior order, do you understand?"

"Yes, Your Honor."

The judge was still holding his chest. "And if you disobey, Mr. Sheriff, you will join them in your own establishment. Do you understand?"

"Yes, of course, Your Honor. But we only have that one vacant cell—the padded one."

"That's not my problem," the judge said.

"Come on, boys," the sheriff said to Coker and Sewell in his standard preamble to an arrest. "You comin' peacefully like gentlemen, or do you want to come the hard way?"

The clerk called Betsy Murray, who arrived at the courthouse shortly after the sheriff had departed with his two subjects. She wanted to take the judge home.

"I'm all right," the judge insisted to Betsy. "One thing for sure, I am not going to let a couple of common thugs, who've somehow been admitted to practice in my court, to put this court into a vulgar shambles. I'm not in jeopardy." He pulled his hands away from his chest. "What's in jeopardy is their license to practice law. And that, too, Madam Reporter, can go on the record."

The next morning, the judge, seated at his desk in chambers, called the sheriff.

"Both your favorite people are alive and well this morning," the sheriff reported. "They spent a night together in our padded cell."

"What? And they didn't kill each other?"

"Men will not fight in the absolute dark," the sheriff said. "They can't see to hit each other, and they can't see to defend themselves. And when men fight, they secretly expect that somebody will break up the fight and stop them from killing each other."

The judge shook his head, astonished.

"And, to make sure, I took away their only remaining weapons."

"Weapons?"

"Yes, their shoes. They spent the night in the dark, barefooted. You can't kick a man to death with bare feet without breaking a toe."

"I must remember that," the judge said, shaking his head.

"And both are so out of shape, they didn't have enough energy to hurt each other anyway."

"What did they do in there all night?"

"Don't know. I had Deputy Huffsmith sit near their cell with his ear to the door. He said there was a lot of cussing going on for a while, and then it was totally quiet the rest of the night."

A small smile crept onto the judge's face. "Give the prisoners a decent breakfast. Then bring them to my chambers."

Shortly, the sheriff ushered prosecutor Haskins Sewell and defense attorney Timothy Coker into the judge's chambers. Their suits were a disheveled mess, their ties hanging at half-mast, their shirt collars pushing out over the lapels of their coats, their pants rumpled top to bottom. Coker's belt was unbuckled and his pants were held up by one suspender.

"You two look like a couple of old horses that've been 'rode hard and put up wet,'" Judge Murray said. Suddenly, he felt sorry for them, their bravado fled, their anger retreating to embarrassment. "Gentlemen, are we prepared to proceed?"

"I move the court for a recess," Sewell said in a quiet voice. "I need to go home and change."

"I object to a recess," Coker said. "Let's get this

bullshit—strike that last word—this miserable trial over with."

Silence.

Coker spoke again in a strangely subdued voice. "I do not want anyone to know that I slept with a prosecuting attorney, much less one named Sewell. It would forever damage my reputation for both chastity and sanity."

"I will keep our cohabitation a secret, I can assure you," Sewell said. "I wouldn't want anyone to know the torment I've suffered spending the night with you."

"The court will take up again at one-thirty this afternoon," the judge said. "That should give you both time to rearrange yourselves into fresh clothes so you can appear to be proper members of the bar, even though your past conduct supports the opposite conclusion."

CHAPTER 6

JOHN MURRAY HAD been in private practice nearly ten years when Timothy Coker, fresh out of law school, and a recent survivor of the Wyoming Bar Examination, came bursting into Jackson Hole like a sudden spring-time thunderstorm. Murray thought the kid had style, the swagger and a cock-of-the-walk attitude, and he sure wasn't some pretty boy who'd turn off the men on a jury. Coker had done some fighting both in and out of the ring. A middleweight, he'd won a few and lost a few. The scar over his left eye and his nose, which bent slightly to the left, commemorated a short-lived campaign as a prospect. His black hair had already given up its roots at the front of his head. His green eyes looked owlish through his thick glasses. He favored pinstriped suits, and he'd marched into town in a pair of black-and-white wingtip shoes he'd ordered from Sears, Roebuck.

Coker wanted work. Murray looked him over, sat back, and said, "You selling Fuller brushes door-to-door or what?"

"I came to help you out," Coker said.

"Help me? What makes you think I need help?"

"My uncle Les Simpson told me about you. He said you must be needing help bad because it took 'a couple trips of the Earth around the Sun,' as he put it, to get the first thing done in your office."

"Why would someone like you come to a nothin' burg like Jackson Hole?" Murray asked. "You look like you'd be more at home pimping call girls in L.A."

The kid looked down. "That hurt my feelings," he said. He waited for an apology. Finally, he said, "My uncle Simpson told me the same thing. He said, 'You need to dress down a little. People don't cater to fancy dudes in this little town. But I told my uncle, 'I hear that Mr. Murray is a very intelligent man. He'll understand that a person has to dress to please himself.'" Then in a confidential tone, the young lawyer said, "I'm not trying to please anybody except me, Mr. Murray. You have to be okay with yourself before you can ask anybody to be okay with you, don't you agree?"

"I never gave that much thought," Murray said. "But—"

"My uncle claims we'll be a perfect match. You need a lot of help, and I need to learn a lot. He says you're the best all-round lawyer this side of the Mississippi and a good man. That's exactly how he put it."

Later, Murray said he never fully understood what happened after that, but before the kid left his office, he'd taken Timothy Coker in as a partner, not a full partner to begin with, but with the idea that one day down the line they might become equal partners. Equal partners in what—a practice that seemed destined to lead them to the poorhouse before they could find the courthouse?

Murray made his decision without asking Coker the first word about his history. He argued that you could ask people to tell you who they are, and down where the truth hangs out, they don't know. They only knew whom they shouldn't be like: "Don't be a smart-ass like Willie." Or they'd been told they should be like Uncle Jim, who, no matter what, always had a smile welded to his face. Or they thought they should emulate some tough-guy movie star like Humphrey Bogart. Murray argued that most folks were long lost and never found themselves. Murray trusted his instincts about people.

Over the years that followed, Murray learned a lot about his partner. He learned that Coker had grown up in a small coal-mining town called Acme, a desperate company town that housed desperate men with busted bodies who lived their lives like slaving moles in a dangerous hole, men who came up from the underground mine shafts after twelve hours of hell picking at the coal seams and loading it into those little coal wagons on tracks, all in the dark and the dust and with their faces and lungs black, because working in the mines was all the work there was, and it was better than the family starving—barely better.

"Jesus, I'd rather shovel shit from the chicken house all day, every day, for the rest of my life than go into the mines," Coker said. "Look what it did to the old man. He was coughing up pieces of lung and he was only forty, and he coughed out the rest of his lungs before the year was over. We buried him in the Acme graveyard alongside of Uncle Luke and all the others."

After his father died, Coker's mother moved in with her parents in Sheridan, Wyoming. His grandfather, Pete McGinnis, worked as a mechanic in the Chevy garage. In Sheridan, "Little Timmy" Coker, as he was called, then about ten, sold his mother's hot fresh cinnamon rolls to the whores up in the Rex Rooms above the Bison Bar. And he sold sweet peas that he raised in his grandmother's garden to the cafés, two bouquets for a quarter, all done up pretty with asparagus ferns. His mother made him save the money to go to college. That's what she said: "You have to go to college, or you'll end up coughing up your lungs like your father."

Coker said he grew up scared. He was always scared. But he was scared to be scared, because being a coward was like wearing a big sign that read I'M A FULL-FLEDGED CHICKENSHIT, and he'd rather be dead than be a full-fledged chickenshit. Then he read somewhere that you couldn't be a hero without being a coward first, and that idea helped. One day, he stood up to Martin Sheldon, the school bully, and got his ass kicked good, knocked out a front tooth. He had to work all summer in the hay fields behind a team of old Percheron horses to save enough to pay for the dental bridge. After that, the bridge became his symbol of honor, and he took up boxing as a sport.

He was still scared, but he'd learned that being afraid helped him from getting his ass kicked, and if he fought with all he had and lost, he was still an acceptable human being, and strangely he began to look for a fight. It relieved his need to run. He'd probably never be a hero, but he'd learned how to deal with being afraid and survive. "Just bow your neck and fight till ya drop."

After high school, he dutifully marched off to the University of Wyoming at Laramie, worked as a night bellman in the town's only hotel, and later he'd labored nights in the local cement plant, sweat out those long hours under the kiln or cleaned up under the ball mill, where the noise was so damned deafening that you couldn't hear a man screaming an inch away from your ear, and his ears rang for a week. At the end of the day, he and the other workers filled out a time card reporting their work for the shift. Then the rebellious side of the kid took over because he knew no one ever read the time card. He wrote things like "Seducing the canine, ten hours," and if some asshole up in the front office read it, he was probably too dumb to know that Coker meant "Fucking the dog," even though some nights he worked until exhaustion won the night. He'd learned to laugh at himself. How did he get that tired "fucking the dog"?

He decided to be a lawyer, because trial lawyers like Clarence Darrow were fighters. And Coker was a fighter. He graduated at the top of his class. It wasn't that he was so smart, he told Murray. He was scared he'd flunk out. "What the hell would I do then? Sell vacuum cleaners door-to-door? Work the mines? Sleep in the park on a bench and freeze to death in the winter?"

Then he'd become infamous among the law school crowd as being the first honor graduate to flunk the bar. Maybe he was too scared to understand the questions. He couldn't punch a bar exam in the face. Maybe the law wasn't his kind of fight. After he failed the bar, he went to work in the oil fields and, of course, he got into a brawl with a couple of derrick hands there, and when the fight was over, he couldn't work for a week and lost his job.

His mother said he should take the bar exam again. She said he shouldn't be a coward and run from it. Her coward talk got to him, all right, and when he walked in to take the exam, he was mad. He hadn't studied for it this time. He was taking the damn bar to satisfy his mother, to quiet her down—and damned if he didn't pass it.

But there weren't any practicing lawyers hiring lawyers out there in the boonies of Wyoming. Nobody needed lawyers. Seemed like nobody sued anybody in Wyoming. You needed a lawyer to examine an abstract before you bought a piece of real estate—sixty-dollar fee for a title opinion, and somebody might need a lawyer to draw up a will. If a drunk ran over you, well, the drunk went to jail and somehow you got by, and that was about it. There were a couple of shysters who sued for injured people, but in Wyoming, only the lawyers who represented corporations and big money were respected.

So there he was, this Timothy Coker with a license to practice law and he'd never seen the inside of a courtroom. Didn't know the first thing about drawing a contract or trying a case. They didn't teach lawyers anything in law school except how to read a case and write a brief. Some lawyers never went to law school. They studied under a practicing lawyer, often without pay, and some years later they took the bar, and some passed the bar "by reading the law," as they called it.

Coker approached finding a job as a lawyer the same way that he'd sold his mother's sweet rolls. He came knocking at Murray's door with his good smile. He'd been up and down the state, in Wyoming's big towns (which were really little more than villages) and the tiny burgs like Jackson. Unfortunately, no practicing lawyer needed a young lawyer still wet behind the ears to help him, and he was about ready to go back to the oil fields when he came upon John Murray in Jackson.

Then something magical happened. Neither of them knew what the magic was, but it grabbed them, not like love, but like when two men meet and right off they both feel better in each other's company than they feel alone. "I was tired of talking to myself," Murray said, "and Tim Coker seemed like a man who heard me. It wasn't quite like that," Murray said, "but it was something like that."

Over the ensuing decade and under the guidance of Murray, and with a relentless dedication to the art of the trial, Timothy Coker became a talented advocate. And they did become equal partners. Standard doctrine on the frontier held that real men never exhibited feelings of closeness. If they felt it, they didn't talk about it. But one time when they were celebrating a verdict they'd won for an old lady who'd slipped on the ice in front of the grocery store and broke her ankle, and after a couple of brews and some laughs, Murray heard himself saying to Coker, "You're the best thing that's happened to me for a long time." Coker just smiled and raised his bottle of beer in response.

As for romance, Murray said, "I've had a few flings, all right, but I've come to the conclusion that falling in love is nothing more than an annoying chatter of the testicles."

"That's because you're too intellectual," Coker said. "You can't make it with a woman by trying to explain the meaning of life. That either frightens 'em or bores 'em."

"I've heard you claim more than once that falling in love is just another form of insanity," Murray said. Coker had survived some passing flings, all right, one with a hairdresser who thought she could dig down to where the "warm and fuzzy stuff was buried," as Coker liked to call it, and another who started waiting tables at the Big Chief Café and, as Coker was soon to discover, was seeking someone to pay the rent on her house and the loan on her car. And she had a couple of kids to feed.

"And how about that nurse at the hospital who got turned on by your so-called pugnacious personality?" Murray chided.

"I was too kind to her," Coker said. "I was trying to treat her like a nice, sweet guy, and I guess I got a little bit too gentle for what the dame had in mind."

But that was before Murray met Betsy Thompson at the lily pond. How could he confess to his partner that he was no longer a free man, that his heart had been captured, that he'd fallen helplessly, hopelessly, irretrievably in love with Betsy Thompson?

One night at quitting time, after a couple of beers, it all came bursting out. "Jesus Christ," Murray said, "it's like I've walked around all of my life with only one shoe. Then one day I found the other shoe, and it fit. Perfectly."

"Betsy's like your shoe? You really got it bad," Coker said. "Like you told me a hundred times, fallin' in love is just Mother Nature using your nuts to play her dirty tricks."

"Yeah. But this is different."

"Remember how ya told me 'When those chemicals in the gonads get to boiling, you can mistake it for what you call love.' You told me it has to do with the survival of the species. 'If people were as uninspired about sex as they are about doing the dishes after supper, the human race would soon become extinct.' Those were your exact words."

"But this is different," Murray insisted. "I used to be happy and safe hanging out in my intellectual self. What did I care about poetry? Now I'm writing it! Before Betsy, I couldn't carry a tune in a chamber pot. Now I sing getting up and going to bed."

"Before Betsy!" Coker said. "B.B., and save me from your poetry and your singing. You never could carry a tune. That's gonna take a lot more than Betsy."

"She teaches art to grade-school kids," Murray said.

"I always knew there was something wrong with our educational system!" Coker said. He slammed shut the shaky door between their small offices but then opened it again. "I'm pulling my load, but musically speaking, if you don't get over this and start bringing in a little do-re-mi, they're going to throw our asses out in the street." He slammed the door shut again.

A little later, Coker, feeling guilty for being such a hard-ass, brought in a couple of cold ones. Murray was staring out the window. Coker popped the beers and shoved one over to his partner. True, his partner needed a little guidance now and then when he went off on one of his infamous head trips. But this time it was a heart trip—and that kind was a lot more dangerous. Murray had been meeting Betsy at the lily pond.

"What the hell do you want outta life?" Coker asked.

Murray kept gazing out the window. Finally, he said, "I want peace."

"A piece a what?" Coker said. "There's no peace in our business. We gotta work harder. I always forced myself to do one more lap when I was training for a fight, even if I fell flat on my face from pure exhaustion. Work is the key, man. Keep your head down and work!"

"Well, I don't want to go on suing a bunch of poor bastards who can't pay their bills. Most of 'em haven't even got a job. Most of 'em are as poor as we are. Nothing much going on here except a few crazies trying to kill themselves climbing the Tetons, and some cowboys who think that God created the world from the back of a horse."

"Yeah," Coker added. "The honest people never sue anybody. They just hunker down and work harder and pay their bills and die in the shadows."

Finally, after a couple more dead soldiers, Murray heard himself saying, "I agree. I am crazy. And I like being crazy. You can either hang in with a crazy partner or go it alone. Your choice." Murray was bluffing.

"Well, to hell with it," Coker said. "I'm up against the

ropes, I'll admit. But if you got it that bad, I suppose I'd better stick around to make sure you don't hurt yourself. And I'll say one thing: You could have done a hell of a lot worse than Betsy."

And that seemed to settle it.

John Murray and Betsy Thompson continued to meet at the lily pond, each offering various excuses for arriving at the tip of the morning. Betsy, the teacher, the painter, claimed, "I've resolved to capture on canvas every mood, every variation of this pond if it takes the rest of my life."

"Well, I understand," Murray said. "I've spent a major part of my life studying the art of fly-fishing, hoping that someday I would become an expert. But that seems to be a long way off, considering all the variations a fisherman encounters. And I am also studying the most intelligent and wondrous of all birds, the Canada goose."

One day in the early fall, Murray found himself shyly proclaiming to Betsy that the souls of two wild geese had settled on them, and without warning she grabbed him in her arms and accidentally smeared him with blue and yellow paint as she kissed him. They melted to the cushioning short grass on the bank. The grass was damp under their bodies, and the early air smooth and sweet. Resting on their elbows, they stared into the pond, the water as clear and smooth as window glass. "I wonder where the ripples have all gone?" he mused.

"They're in us," she said.

"Where are my geese?" he whispered.

"They're still across the way," she said softly.

He listened. He heard their strange soft songs, the goslings nearly old enough to leave the nest.

"The world has suddenly changed," he said. "We are the same, but the world has changed."

"Yes," she said.

Later, in mid-October, while the aspens and cotton-woods were still golden, Murray and Betsy stood in front of the local Episcopal priest. They'd dressed for the occasion, the groom in his old go-to-court blue suit, middle button hanging loose, a blue shirt, and a dark blue tie with red stripes. He'd shined his black shoes and furnished them with new black laces.

She argued that no marriage should begin on a misrepresentation, with the bride wearing a virgin white dress. Her dress was a rich, deep cream color, trimmed just below the knees with a gay little ruffle of lace that bounced as she walked. She wore her mother's turquoise necklace, pieces of blue-green stone the size of large grapes. Her ivory-colored shoes were round-toed and comfortable. Her black braid was curled into a bun high on the back of her head. Her grandmother's large shell hairpins held it in place, along with a single red rose.

He swore, not to her, not to any preacher, but to himself, that she was so beautiful to his heart's eye that he would spend the rest of his life striving to be worthy of her. He admitted it: He'd fallen into a pit occupied by those he'd always scorned—those maudlin romantics, those fools who claimed they were insanely in love.

Yes.

He was insane.

And he cherished his insanity.

Betsy told Murray, "I grew up wondering why I didn't have a father like other kids. My mother never spoke of my father. One time I said, 'Mom, where is my father?' and she said, 'We do not talk about him. And if we don't talk about him, it's like an iron door, and he can't get through and hurt us anymore.'"

"I see," Murray said.

"I was afraid that maybe my father was a murderer and he would come and kill us if he could get through the iron door."

Murray's eyes were sad.

"I grew up behind the iron door, and somehow I felt safe behind it until I met you." She teared up and ran to the stove, as if to keep the pot from boiling over. But there was no pot on the stove.

"My mother worked at the laundry. She had those terrible varicose veins in her legs—her legs were almost purple—and when she came home at night after standing on those legs all day, she was too tired and too full of pain to cook supper. I cooked for us from the time I was old enough to light the stove."

They'd wanted children of their own. But she was forty-two, and the doctor said it wasn't her fault, nor Murray's.

Murray said, "Well, honey, we've got each other, and as you already know, I'm the biggest baby a woman ever had." And he tried to laugh, and she laughed with him.

Before they had exchanged vows, the Episcopal priest had sat the couple down on the hard oak pews of the old log church where the north window framed the Tetons—a holy place that any passing god would have chosen as his residence in chief. The air was pure. A mountain bluebird was chirping away outside the window. Even the sky was a gentle, inviting blue and promised eternal peace.

The smells inside the chapel were of old wood, the faint remnants of women's perfume, and the Sunday shaves of men. Comingled was the faint smell of horse manure from the boots of generations of cowboys who occasionally attended church for the wedding or the funeral of some poor devil who got kicked in the head by the love beast or by a nasty bronco.

"I see here you want to marry a teacher," the Reverend Matthew Hamondtree said to Murray. He'd been inspecting the marriage license. "Well, let me tell you, I'm married to one, and she keeps on teaching me." He laughed. "Why are you marrying this woman?" the priest asked Murray. He wore the Episcopal priest's garb—the black top and the white round collar. He was a man of middle age whose height, breadth of shoulders, and no-nonsense demeanor reminded Murray of a former tackle on some college football team.

"I have no choice," John Murray said with surrendered eyes at Betsy.

"What do you mean you have no choice? I don't see anyone with a pistol at your head."

"I can't live another day without her," John Murray said.

"I see," said the priest, with a look at Murray that questioned his competence.

"She's standing on the shore with a life preserver," Murray said. "Don't you see her there? She is saving me by marrying me. Otherwise, I will drown in an empty life."

"Drown in an empty life?" the priest asked aloud. He thought for a moment. "Yes," he said, "a person can drown in an empty life."

Then the Reverend Hamondtree turned to Betsy Thompson. "And why, my dear, are you marrying this madman?"

"I'm a little mad, too," she said. "I must have this madman. Look at him. He loves birds. He tries to talk to geese; he fishes and throws most of the fish back; he defends people who have committed sin; he writes poetry about the snow, and about spring grass, and about me. And he loves me. Doesn't that prove he is quite mad?"

"Yes," said the priest. "Quite. I find there is no logical basis for this marriage, and therefore it's a good match. Are you ready?"

Then the priest, not risking further inquiries, and in the simple glory of the old log chapel, led them through their vows, and each put a gold ring on the other's finger, and thereupon he pronounced the painter and the fisherman, both from the lily pond, husband and wife.

Some say one should always be mindful of the lurking occult. Not to be doubted, mystical powers rose out of the quiet waters of the lily pond. As the mirror reflects in reverse, so, too, did the forces at play at the pond.

One morning just at sunup in the late fall, and at Betsy's suggestion, Murray visited the mirrored waters of the pond to catch a mess of trout for dinner. He was about to whip his fly back for a second cast when he saw the figure of a man across the way mostly hidden in the cattails. He was packing a shotgun.

At that moment, Murray heard the noisy, happy honking of low-flying Canada geese, the goslings nearly grown, the flock returning to their home, where they'd been safe all spring and summer. In horror, Murray saw the hunter pull down on the lead goose and fire. He saw the bird fall and flap crazily in the water. The man stood calmly by, waiting until the goose offered no further movement, its one good wing pointing skyward, the surrounding water stained red. Then he waded out, picked up the bird by its head, and, like a lion trainer cracking his whip, gave the goose a quick snap to break its neck.

The hunter headed to Murray's side of the pond, his twelve-gauge shotgun in one hand and, in cadence with his steps, the dead goose limply swinging from his other.

"What the hell do you think you're doing?" Murray hollered.

Surprised, the hunter asked, "You talking to me?"

"Why would you shoot an innocent goose?"

"It's goose season," he replied.

"If you'd kill a beautiful goose, you'd kill anything and anybody," Murray said. "Don't you know that geese mate for life? Listen, for Christ sakes, listen!" He pointed to the single circling goose overhead that was calling.

Calling.

Calling.

The hunter stood staring at Murray.

"Geese don't kill one another like us humans," Murray said. "You must be one rotten son of a bitch."

The man with the dead goose dangling in his hand stood glaring, silent, deciding whether or not he was in imminent danger at the hands of this lunatic with a fly rod in his hands.

The circling goose mate was calling.

Calling.

Calling.

"Surely you feel shame," Murray said.

As if to prepare for an attack, the man transferred the dangling dead goose to his left hand and took the shotgun in his right. He cocked a fresh shell into the gun's chamber. Then he said, coldly, calmly, "I have the same rights here as you, pal. Up yours, and your talking geese." With that, he left Murray standing at the pond's edge, his pole in his hand.

The man's name was Haskins Sewell.

CHAPTER 7

SOME MONTHS LATER, Haskins Sewell found work as an assistant to Warren Garrison, who'd held the prosecutor job in Teton County for more than twenty years. He hired young Sewell with the encouragement of the county commissioners. Garrison was suffering from a terminal illness and needed help. The commissioners hoped he would train his successor to ensure that an uneventful succession would take place. Garrison resigned the following year. Sewell was appointed and sworn in to complete Garrison's term.

"One thing you should always remember in Teton County," Garrison counseled Sewell before departing the office. "The ranchers have the land, the money, and the power. Keep the ranchers happy, and you'll keep the job as long as you want it."

Sewell's first case was the prosecution of an alleged hay thief by the name of Ezra Mills—at least that's the name he went by, "a filthy ignoramus," as Sewell called him, or, at times when Sewell felt more charitable, "a walking garbage can."

The district judge, Robert R. Rose, let Ezra out on

bond secured by his only asset, his team of old draft horses. He lived on twenty barren, rented acres, the grass bitten to the ground and clawed to the roots by his hungry horses. He made a few dollars in the spring plowing gardens and pulling a ditch or two.

True to the advice of Garrison, Sewell set out to bestow on the ranchers of Teton County the benefit of his prosecutorial powers. He directed the sheriff to bring Ezra in for interrogation. Later, none of the law-enforcement gang would talk about it, but it seems Ezra was treated with such a vicious series of assaults that he limped for a month from a police baton across his right knee.

Ezra was with it enough to conclude that his rights had been violated, and he contacted John Murray and Timothy Coker to represent him. "They beat me till I couldn't see no more. And that guy Sewell was there, and once he told them to kick me in the belly, and that deputy kicked me, and I puked and I passed plumb out."

"We can't just turn our backs on this," Coker said.

"Well, we got them to drop charges against Ezra, and he's out there probably stealing more hay from his neighbor," Murray said.

"But we can't have a member of the bar, much less the prosecutor, taking part in such inhumane conduct. If we don't stop this, none of us will be safe." Coker gave his partner a long, hard look, and waited.

Finally, Murray said, "Well, if we go to the bar association for his license, we may be starting something we'll wish we never started."

There were a couple of prosecutors on the bar committee, and the committee split, the prosecutors arguing that since Sewell dropped all charges against Ezra, even though Sewell's conduct was unethical, it did not affect the outcome of the case. The other members of the bar argued that such inhumane conduct could not be con-

doned in the state of Wyoming, and that the bar had a
duty to protect the reputation of the profession by issuing
a severe punishment, if not disbarment. The committee
finally agreed on a confidential reprimand of Sewell.

As Sewell left the hearing, Murray and Coker were
following behind. Suddenly, Sewell stopped short. He
turned to Murray, his face frozen in anger. "If it takes
me the rest of my life, I will make you two curse the day
you first heard my name."

Two years later, Judge Rose retired and Haskins
Sewell filed as a nonpartisan candidate for the judgeship.

"We can't let that dried-up piece of dog shit take
over the judgeship," Coker said to Murray. "You're a
fair man, John, the kind who ought to be a judge. You
have compassion, and you aren't in this business for the
money—that's for sure."

"I don't want to be a judge," Murray said. "I really
never wanted to be a lawyer, either."

"What do you mean?" Coker asked.

"I told you before. I don't like all the fight and hate
and hurt that comes with the legal business. Somebody
wins. Somebody loses in every case. Somebody on one
side of a case or the other always feels wronged."

"Somebody has to do it," Coker said.

"And somebody has to bury the dead."

"Well, the dead are gonna be us for sure if Sewell gets
elected."

Murray was fixed on the ceiling, calculating his response. Finally, he said, "If I were given a second life,
I'd never go to law school. I'd keep our cabin in the
woods and study the language of birds. They have a language, you know, and . . ."

Coker laughed. "Yeah, like a rooster crows when he's
looking for a little piece of feathered pussy."

"Yes," Murray said, still looking up. "Chickens have the exact same feelings as we, and they talk about it. A hen sitting on her eggs actually growls words if you try to take her eggs out from under her, and she'll fight you. A hen clucks certain words to call her chicks to where the corn's on the ground. She has a warning call when there's danger. Yes, and the rooster crows his joy to the rising sun."

"God Almighty, John," Coker said. "You know more about chickens than you do about people." A few mornings later, Coker bumped up against the door to Murray's office and the door swung open. Coker looked like he hadn't slept; his eyes were red, his face hard. "We gave it a fair shot," he said.

"What's the matter?" Murray asked.

"John, we've been starving here for years. We're like those chickens of yours, scratching in the chicken yard, where there's nothing left to eat but chicken shit."

"I'm getting used to it," Murray said. He got up and walked over to his partner to console him.

"If it wasn't for Betsy's teaching, you'd have starved a long time ago. And I've used up everything my father left me. It's all gone, John. All."

Murray put a hand on his partner's shoulder. "It's got to get better. Can't get worse. We've hit the nadir."

"Yeah, like Ezra's case," Coker said. "That was the last damned straw."

Then Coker got head-to-head with Murray. "There isn't enough in this business for both of us. Besides, it's your duty. If you let Sewell take the judgeship, he and the sheriff are going to run this county, and it's not going to be pretty for anybody. Either you run for the judgeship or I'm getting the hell out of Dodge. Sewell's been laying in wait for us. One day, he's going to get one or both of us. Mark my word."

"Why don't you run?" Murray asked. But he knew better. His partner, with his quick temper and yearning for combat, had not been gifted with a judicial temperament. Coker only had the temper.

Sewell understood county politics. The ranchers, the strongest political contingent in the county, considered hay stealing and cattle thievery on a par with rape and murder. The sheriff, a former rancher, bankrupt from the last drought, threw his support to Sewell for judge, as did the clergy of the Baptist church where Sewell claimed membership.

True, a few of the townspeople urged John Murray to run, even a rancher who'd strayed from the flock. And Coker kept the pressure on Murray to throw his hat in the ring. Murray resisted. Finally, Coker put it to his partner straight: "Run for judge, or I'm vacating the premises."

Murray felt as if he were being drafted into a war he didn't want to fight. He complained to Betsy. "Fate is dragging me into a corner and spitting in my eye. I don't want to be a judge."

"You'd be a good judge," she said. "You're a fair man—at least most of the time." Sounding like a judge herself, she added, "The question comes down to this: You get to be judge and we stay put, or Sewell gets to be judge and you'll never win another case. In fact, he'll probably find a way to get you disbarred or jailed, or worse."

On the last day, John Murray filed for the judgeship, and the next week Sewell and Murray met in a debate sponsored by the Lion's Club Youth Betterment Committee held in the high school auditorium. The town was suffering what many of the townsfolk considered a rash of juvenile crime—mostly kids raising hell for lack of something better to occupy their time. There'd been a street fight one Saturday—mostly for entertainment. One kid got drunk and ran his parents' cars into an irrigation ditch, and another kid got the mayor's daughter pregnant.

"No babying these kids," Sewell argued to a nearly empty room of fewer than a hundred seats. Sewell was on a roll and his high nasal voice was sharp enough to scrape paint off the ceiling. "Get 'em out of our town so they can't hurt innocent people again. If they're going to be babied, let 'em be babied at the Boys' Reformatory in Worland." He got a good hand on that from a couple of retired ranchers sitting in the front row. "We're in harm's way as much from criminal juveniles as we are from criminal adults." With a small, tight smile on his stony face, he bowed to the several clapping hands.

"Well, that may be so," Murray said when it was his turn. "But I don't want to give up on our kids, even those who go astray and commit crimes. We only have one real chance to save them, and that's now."

Silence from the front row.

"Once they're behind bars, we've lost that chance," Murray argued, "and when they get out, they'll be worse than when they went in. I say guidance and caring always trump punishment." He heard a single person clapping in the back. It was Betsy.

Timothy Coker and a handful of friends did a door-to-door campaign for John Murray. Sewell hadn't let the ranchers forget that Murray had represented the convicted hay thief, Ezra Mills, and he put a couple of ads in the local paper about being tough on criminals, young and old. The ranchers and the church came down solidly for Sewell, but John Murray beat him by twenty-three votes. He thought they were probably Betsy's friends. Everybody loved Betsy.

CHAPTER 8

LILLY MORTENSEN WAS seven when Betsy first encountered her in the second grade. "This child is touched with genius," Betsy told the judge. Betsy viewed the girl as one might have viewed the young Mozart, who at five was already proficient at both the keyboard and the violin.

"What do you mean, 'genius'?" the judge asked Betsy. "That's a careless word people use about those whose native gifts differ from the rest of ours."

"It's like meeting a wizard in the closet," Betsy said. "She's already painting, while the rest of her classmates scribble with their crayons. And sometimes the child frightens me—what she paints is so beautiful, so wild and unseen. Yesterday she was standing over her painting, which she'd laid on the floor. She was looking down at it and crying. 'Why are you weeping, Lilly?' I asked."

She didn't answer, but kept slashing at the canvas with purple paint.

"What are you painting?"

"I don't know," she finally said.

Depending on the psychological stew of the viewer,

the emerging face on Lilly's painting could be seen as a demon or as an old man about to recite his daily prayers.

As an art teacher, Betsy claimed she was an accomplice in aiding the child to pry open the locked door of the self. "What right do any of us have to declare that when the child's inner self comes rolling out, screaming out, weeping or laughing out on the canvas, it is not art?"

Over the years, Betsy had become attached to the child, as if, at last, the daughter she'd always missed had finally come home. Jim and Helen Mortensen, Lilly's parents, were elated that their daughter was often with Betsy after school, or in the evenings at the Murrays' house. Jim Mortensen usually came by to pick her up, or Betsy drove her home before bedtime.

"Mothers need daughters like fathers need sons," Betsy said more than once. Now Betsy had Lilly. During the summers, the child began to accompany Betsy to the pond, where, in the early morning, they painted together. She often brought Lilly home to the judge, who, infected by Betsy's love for Lilly, soon found himself also captured by the child. "Well, fathers need daughters, too," the judge proclaimed one day.

The judge, Betsy, and the gifted but somehow disturbing Lilly were gathered at the dinner table on an early-summer evening.

"So, you are going to be a great painter?" the judge asked Lilly matter-of-factly.

"I already am one," she said.

By this time, Betsy and the judge had completed an emotional adoption of Lilly "by order of the heart," as the judge termed it.

"I've heard that great painters have special eyes," the judge once said. "They see what ordinary people do not see. What do your eyes see that mine do not?"

"I see pretty diamonds up there. Look!" She jumped from the table and ran to the window. "See them?"

"I don't see them," he said.

"They are all colors. They're beautiful. They're hanging from those trees over there."

"Ah, yes," the judge finally said. "I see them. They are raindrops. It rained this afternoon."

"No," Lilly said. "They're diamonds, and we are all very rich." Then she laughed, and the judge, unable to resist, pulled the child to him and kissed her lightly on the top of her head.

Years later, on a crisp, clear early-spring evening, the judge arrived at the cabin with a fresh cutting of pussy willows, faint green life shyly showing through furry, silvery buds. They grew wild along the road. "I had Lilly in Juvenile Court today," the judge said offhandedly, handing Betsy the bouquet. Lilly was sixteen.

Betsy, stunned, stood frozen, the willow branches clutched in her hands.

"Don't worry," he said. "Lilly's just temporarily insane. She's in love." He took the bouquet from Betsy and settled the wickers into a slender green vase on the kitchen table. "She's been charged in my juvenile court with stealing her father's car. What am I supposed to do with her? She's fallen in love for the first time. She demonstrates all the classic signs of libidinal insanity."

"Were we insane?" Betsy asked.

"Yes," he said. "I thought Lilly made a decent argument. She said, 'There's no law against being in love. It ought to be the other way around: Everybody should be required to fall in love. And if they refuse, send 'em to jail. The world isn't safe with people running around who can't fall in love.'"

"She's got something there," Betsy said. "My God, what are we going to do?"

"We're going to do nothing," the judge replied. "This is the time in Lilly's life when she has to find her own way. Everybody, including us, has to let go and make room, and hope."

"And pray," Betsy added.

Lilly Mortensen left the court with her parents, but that same night she ran back to Billy. She dropped out of high school and got a job at Ralph's City Cleaners, doing hand-spotting. She learned to iron and to sack up the suits for delivery. She and Billy got married, rented a basement apartment in the west end for thirty dollars a month and skipped along, laughing, through life, their noses lifted at the boring townsfolk, whom they believed knew nothing of love and, therefore, nothing about life. And in the evenings while Billy was pumping gas, Lilly studied the masters from a book that Betsy had lent her, and she painted over a dozen portraits of her love, Billy Banister, one in the style of van Gogh's *Portrait of Armand Roulin,* and one reminiscent of Thomas Gainsborough's *The Blue Boy.*

In the heat of August, and on the couple's first anniversary, Lilly's boss at the dry cleaner's gave her the afternoon off to celebrate. Lilly had picked a bouquet of late-blooming purple iris that grew in the shade of an abandoned shack once occupied by an old Irish couple, both now long buried. With flowers in hand, she rushed into the apartment to surprise Billy, only to find her love mate in bed with the landlady, an overnourished forty-year-old with poor teeth and pumpkin orange hair.

Lilly jerked a brass vase off the bed stand. "Honey," Billy muttered, "I—" But before she allowed another word to escape his adulterous lips, she struck him—the dull, ominous sound of the hard metal against his skull, the blood rushing from the wound above his left temple. She then threw the bouquet of iris at his head.

The landlady, naked and screaming, threw herself in front of Billy's lifeless body to ward off Lilly's continued assault. The landlady ducked another wide wild punch, and with Lilly at her heels, she ran up the stairs to her bedroom, slammed the door shut, and turned the lock as Lilly beat at its splintering wood with the brass vase. The landlady called the police from her bedroom phone.

Within a few minutes, two officers arrived with their guns drawn.

"You'd better be careful," the landlady screeched to the officers through her bedroom door. "That bitch out there is crazy."

When Lilly saw the officers with their guns, she turned back to face them, as if injected with a magical elixir of tranquillity. She donned a girlish pout and a hard-to-reject innocent face. "I'm glad you came," she said to the lead officer. She was still panting. "I would have killed her, too," she added, pointing to the landlady, who had just inched out of her bedroom.

The first officer ran down the stairs to the apartment. He found Billy bleeding and seemingly dead, but, discovering a weak pulse, he radioed for an ambulance. "What went on here?" the first officer asked the landlady.

"I was down there checking out a noise on the furnace. I thought the rattle I heard come from their bedroom. I come into the bedroom just as she come home, and her husband was in bed, and she thought something was going on."

"You lying bitch!" Lilly jumped up to renew her attack. The younger cop shoved her back down into the chair. Lilly screamed, "You were in bed with him, and naked. Naked! I suppose you usually do your housecleaning naked, and I suppose you were vacuuming under the blankets."

"I don't give a good Wyomin' damn who's doin' who," the first officer said. "You can't brain people with heavy objects for screwing."

Prosecutor Haskins Sewell charged Lilly in the Juvenile Court with two counts of assault with a deadly weapon, both felonies. At her court hearing, Lilly was accompanied by both of her parents and seemed solid, smiling, and sane. She profusely apologized to the lead officer.

Judge Murray turned to Lilly. "You almost killed your husband, and then you'd be here on a murder charge."

"What would you do if you came home and found Betsy in bed with one of your neighbors?"

"I'm not here to answer your questions, young lady," the judge said, as if she were a stranger. "Do you realize the seriousness of the charges?"

"Well, sometimes people have to hurt people," Lilly said. The sound of innocence arguing such violence surprised the judge.

"Where, young lady, have you ever heard such things?" the judge asked.

"My daddy was in the war, and he shot a lot of people." Jim Mortensen looked down at his work-roughed hands. "My daddy says that sometimes you have to stop people to protect the family."

"Violence is against the rules in every civilized society, Mr. Mortensen," Judge Murray said.

James P. Mortensen had served in the Second World War as a paratrooper in the Eighty-second Airborne and landed in Normandy on D-day, June 6, 1944. He was a sergeant and "the point man," the soldier up front, leading his squad in battle. He spoke straight from a straight mouth. He was handsome in the way outdoor men with hard histories are handsome.

Finally, the judge said, "Mr. Mortensen, fathers have a powerful influence over their children. You obviously have had considerable influence over your daughter. Perhaps we have the wrong person in court here this morning." The judge aimed a raised eyebrow at Mortensen.

"You can send me to jail," Mortensen said. "I'll take the blame."

At last, prosecutor Sewell spoke up. He'd been sitting at the counsel table, open amusement leaking onto his bony gray face. "Isn't it pretty obvious, Your Honor, that we have very little to work with here? This is the second time this juvenile has been before this court. She comes from a home that shows little respect for the law. I should think it a grave mistake to send her back to the likes of Mr. Mortensen."

Judge Murray did not know what to do. He had always cared deeply for this girl. What good would come from incarcerating her? What would he have done had he caught someone in bed with Betsy and a baseball bat had been handy? At times, he thought the natural law was more in tune with justice than those cold strictures in bloodless, loveless, soulless legal books. He slammed his law book closed.

"I'm ready to render my decision," Judge Murray said. He didn't know what he was going to say, but he heard his own voice clearly speaking the words. He turned to Lilly. "If I see you in here one more time, young lady, you can't imagine how tough I can be. You're a fine young woman with good parents who love you. But you have to control your temper and live by the rules of society. Those rules, for your information, do not include assaulting anyone who angers you. Do you understand?"

"Yes, Your Honor." Lilly's words sounded sincere.

"Is that your position as well, Mr. Mortensen?"

"Yes, Your Honor."

Then the family walked out together, Lilly holding on to her father's arm and clutching her mother's hand.

With his upper lip curled, Haskins Sewell spoke in a loud whisper that was clearly audible to the judge. "Today it's assault with a deadly weapon and resisting arrest. Tomorrow it will be murder. Then who will be responsible? You will, Your Honor."

The judge made no response, but at the judge's chamber door, Sewell stopped and faced the judge. "Frankly, Your Honor, I've considered impeachment. Your decision was both biased and irresponsible." He waited at the door.

"Do what you have to do," the judge said. "Just get the hell out of my chambers."

Sewell left the room, but in the silence that followed, the judge knew Sewell was right.

CHAPTER 9

NEARLY TWENTY-FIVE YEARS had passed since Lilly caught Billy Banister in bed with the landlady and had smashed in his head as his reward. Haskins Sewell had seen it all too clearly: Although she did not succeed in killing Billy, it wasn't for lack of trying. Lilly was capable of extreme violence, and those murderous chickens had now come home to roost. Lilly just had been arrested for the murder of her husband, Horace Adams III.

When Officer Hollister led her to the jail's padded cell, the only accommodation the county maintained to house a woman prisoner, he slammed the door. He slammed the door on all prisoners. The sound sent an authoritative message.

The following morning, the portly deputy in charge, Arthur Huffsmith, hitched up the pants of his blue police uniform, lumbered to the cell, unlocked it, and pulled the door open. Lillian threw her hands up to shield her eyes against the light. Huffsmith led her to the phone for her one permitted call. It was, of course, to Timothy

Coker. Huffsmith then led her back to the dark padded cell.

When Coker arrived, Sewell was already addressing the judge. "As I predicted, Your Honor, we're all gathered together here with your little family because Lillian has killed her husband."

"You haven't forgotten have you, Mr. Sewell, that at this point in the case you can petition to disqualify me?"

"No, I haven't forgotten, and if I detect bias in your rulings, I will do just that."

Yes, Sewell was setting him up for impeachment. The judge knew he had no business in the case—knew it to the marrow of his bones. He was biased in Lillian's favor. He should recuse himself. But he could not abandon Lillian. Sewell would employ every dirty trick in the book to send her to the chair. The judge could not trust the young woman to Sewell's untender mercies.

Sewell had him trapped. If the judge stayed on, he might very well be charged with a serious violation of the canons of ethics. But he had no choice. He was risking his judgeship, his reputation, perhaps his freedom, but he had to stay on. If Lillian were guilty, well, he'd face it.

Yes, face it.

And what about Sewell's threat of impeachment? The judge had no doubt that at some point the bastard would file charges against him.

Well, he'd face that when it came, too.

When the bond issues had been settled, the sheriff finally authorized Deputy Huffsmith to transfer Lillian to the sheriff's office, where Coker was waiting. She stumbled by Coker, again blinded by the light of day after her long stay in total darkness. Huffsmith helped her into a chair in the corner of the room. A couple of deputies sat at their desks, laughing, paying no attention to them. Phones were ringing.

"You must have had a damn hard night," Coker said to Lillian in a soft voice.

"It was totally dark in there," she said.

When a door slammed, Lillian jumped.

"You're all right," Coker said, patting her shoulder. "I'll take you home."

He led her to his old Chevy, opened the passenger door, and helped her get settled. They drove in silence.

Her face was ashen. Her mascara was smeared under her eyes. She stared, unseeing, at her feet. Finally, she said in a faraway voice, "I want you to know the truth."

"Don't tell me anything right now," Coker said. "Let's just talk about you." At his first meeting with a client charged with a serious crime, Coker refused to discuss the facts. If a false story were to be offered, it was the client's decision, not his, and it would be the client's story that dictated his defense.

But what if his client went to the death house because the truth failed to convince the jury? If a lawyer faithfully followed all the canons of ethics, the result, too often, was injustice. The judge could not live with that.

"If they send me to prison, who'll take care of my daughter, Tina?" Lillian asked.

Coker remained silent.

"I could never send her to my folks. They're old, and my father doesn't know how to deal with children."

"He dealt with you."

"Not really. My father locked me in a closet once," Lillian said. "I wouldn't do my homework, and he thought being locked in a closet would make homework

seem like fun, but I'm still afraid of the dark. I always
sleep with a night-light on. And that jail cell . . . my
God." She began to shake. She spoke as if no one were
present to hear her. "He always thought he was doing
right. He loved me, but he didn't know how to deal with
children."

"You want me to plead you insane?" Coker's remark
was only half-serious.

"Sometimes I think I am insane. One night the
man you love is dead, and you see the blood. . . ." She
couldn't say the rest. "And you're shocked and sick with
grief, and before you can unravel it all, you're charged
with his murder. That . . . is insane."

"Sewell couldn't wait to charge you; he has his
agenda," Coker said.

"I despise that man."

"You may be shocked to learn that Sewell's feelings
for you are identical."

"Why? I've never done anything to him."

"Well, for one, the judge cares about you, and Sewell
hates anybody the judge cares about."

"He's supposed to protect our rights. He's the prosecutor."

"He's been waiting a lotta years to get to you. He
thinks the judge should have sent you to the reformatory
when you were a teenager. He thinks you've bamboo-
zled the judge. The man is short on compassion, vindic-
tive as hell, and long on memory." The car groaned as he
shifted gears for the hill leading to the Adams family's
residence, an old log ranch house that Horace Adams
had purchased and restored.

"I don't cast spells."

"We have something in common, Lillian. It hasn't
been especially uplifting to spend half of my adult life

in court against the likes of Sewell. More than once, I've thought I'd like to kill the bastard."

She looked blankly up the road.

What is this woman feeling? Coker asked himself. When some murderers emerged from their psychic holes, they felt guilt. Others were racked with fear. Pathological killers often felt neither shock nor remorse. Nothing. What did an accused feel who'd been wrongly charged with murder? Some felt terror, some felt outrage, some thrashed against drowning in a sea of helplessness, and some gave up, surrendered, as if delivering their lives to the prosecutor would appease the gods and would leave them a small vestige of their former lives.

He glanced over at his passenger. Her eyes were focused on her hands. Guilty or innocent, she was entitled to a fair trial. If she'd murdered her husband, Sewell's legal burden was to prove her guilt beyond a reasonable doubt.

But what if she was innocent and he lost? The loss would grind him to pieces and never let up. And Sewell would wear that smirk on his face, as the sheriff slapped the cuffs on her, and then Sewell would say to Coker, "I been waiting for this a long, long time," and Lillian would look back at Coker with her "Why didn't you save me when you knew I was innocent?" eyes.

And if she were guilty and the jury turned her loose? That was Sewell's problem, not his. He liked to say that the system had to lose a case now and then to keep it honest.

Lillian, twisting her wedding ring, asked, "Can't you stop him?"

"Only a jury can stop him," Coker said.

"Can't the judge stop him? The judge knows I'm innocent."

"How would the judge know?"

"My God," she blurted. "He knows I'm innocent. He's known me since I was a child. He loves me. I shouldn't be putting him through this."

Then they were silent, and Coker's car bounced over the rocky, rutted road.

"If it takes money . . ." Lillian finally said.

"Money won't help except to pay my fee," he said with an apologetic smile. "But if it's any comfort, Sewell has hated me longer than he's hated you."

"Should I hire a lawyer he doesn't hate?"

"That's up to you," he said.

"I can't think. It's like I can't wake up from a nightmare. And my husband is dead?"

"Yes, Horace Adams the Third is dead."

"I loved him, but I must not have loved him enough." She looked into her hands again. Suddenly, she grabbed at her purse, opened it, and began scratching around in it. "Oh God," she said. "I am going crazy. I'm looking for a cigarette, and I haven't smoked for ten years. Do you have a cigarette?"

"Don't smoke," he said.

"Jesus, I need a smoke."

She gathered herself. "I didn't understand Horace," she said. "Sometimes he was innocent as a child, and sometimes he had a childlike wisdom. He was brilliant at times, and he was one of the strongest, most self-reliant men I've known. I felt safe with him. But he was losing his memory, and it worried him, and the doctors said he was in the first stages of some sort of senile dementia. But he wasn't old enough for that. Even then he was a comfort to me. I don't know if I can go on without him."

Coker pulled up in front of the old log house Lillian called home. A couple of long-eared black-and-white springer spaniels came bounding out and were scratching at the car door for attention.

"I think it took courage for Horace to do what he did," she said. She turned from Coker, as if showing tears were bad manners. "Once he said, 'I have to value each day. I don't have too many left. And I want to spend them all with you.' I tried to laugh it off. 'Oh, come now, darling, you'll outlive me,' I said. And he just looked away."

Coker patted her hand like a kindly father. "Let's talk about the judge. Should Judge Murray sit on this case, knowing what he knows about you?"

Silence.

"I mean, you're like a member of his family."

"Yes," she said, "the judge cares about me. And I'd hate to become an emotional burden to him. He doesn't deserve that. If it hadn't been for him and Betsy, Sewell would have sent me off to the girls' reformatory, and I'd have come out as spoiled goods."

"It'll cause the judge a shitpot full of trouble if he stays on the case," Coker said.

"The Murrays taught me to appreciate who I could be," Lillian said. "Betsy taught me to speak the English language correctly. She was always after me, saying I couldn't get anywhere in the world if I sounded like a hillbilly." Searching for more words, she finally said, "I'm very tired. I feel beaten up. I can't even cry."

She seemed not to hear the spaniels' whining.

"Betsy always talked about 'a worthy life.' They don't teach anything about 'worthy lives' in school," she said.

Coker tried to imagine how she would have looked at the moment she'd been insane enough to kill. The vision wouldn't crystalize.

"No one except Betsy ever told me about 'a worthy life.' Then I met Horace, and that's all he wanted to talk about."

She started to open the car door.

"I love Betsy Murray," she said. "And the judge is like the father I don't have. The judge and Betsy were proud of me. That made a difference. All my father knows is the killing he learned in the war, and that's killing him and my mother, too."

She opened the car door, stepped out, and gave an automatic acknowledging pat to the spaniels. "I'd invite you in, but I have to go. Tina will be crazy with worry. The poor child's been at Sylvia Huntley's place all night. She's my best friend." Lillian took several cautious steps toward the house.

"Fine painter, Sylvia," Coker said, getting out. "I'll see you to the door."

"I never became the fine painter that Betsy hoped for," Lillian said as they walked. "Sometimes my paintings scared me. I saw things that other people didn't see." She stopped and turned to face Coker. "Can we win?"

"You never know what a jury will do," Coker said. "I don't know what facts Sewell thinks he has—or that he'll make up. He has an insatiable need to punish. He can't decide whom he wants to hurt the most, the judge, you, or me. And he has the memory of a pissed-off elephant."

"Can you win?"

"Don't know the facts yet," he said. "But before Sewell convicts you, he'll have to kill me."

CHAPTER 10

AFTER LILLY CAUGHT Billy Banister with the land-lady, she asked her father to annul the marriage. He was only too happy to oblige. "Finally, you've come to your senses," he said.

But Lilly also wanted out of Jackson Hole, out of its judgments, its memories, its barbed-wire borders, and its invisible ceiling that hurled back any who asked questions or embraced change. The message was clear: Do not step over this line. You know the line. Those on the other side of the line do not belong to us and will be banished.

She couldn't walk down the street without meeting someone who knew about her past life with Billy Banister, who by this time had taken up residence with a cocktail waitress in Buffalo, Wyoming. Lillian had a "reputation," and anywhere she went, her infamous past was never far behind. She was friendless.

One day, standing in line at the grocery store, she heard some guy refer to her as "the mad bitch of Jackson Hole." Her father, Jim Mortensen, told her that the only way out of hell was for her to get an education. She said she wanted to go into the design business. He asked her, "What do you mean, 'design business'?"

"I want to make things. Pretty things. Things that people have never seen," she said.

Jim Mortensen said, "Well, you can't make a living just fluffin' around. And don't forget: Artists starve to death, and you always liked to eat," and that's all he had to say.

"Well, she's different, Papa," and that's all her mother would say.

Judge Murray and Betsy grieved over her going. "She has to find her way," the judge said. "If you try to hold her back, she'll rebel and break loose. People could get hurt in the process."

Betsy finally relented and gave Lillian her mother's turquoise necklace—the one Betsy had worn when she and the judge were married.

"If you wear this, you'll find yourself the love of your life," Betsy told Lillian. "It's got great power. Look what it brought me." She nodded to the judge, holding back tears. He gave Lillian the hundred dollars he'd saved up for a new fly rod, and Jim Mortensen gave her another hundred from his pension, and then the Mortensens and the Murrays saw her off at the bus depot, and after that the four of them went down to the Ramshorn Saloon and had a beer in the middle of the day.

They didn't know what to talk about or how to talk about it.

Lillian found work as a waitress in a small diner that put her in mind of the Big Chief Café in Jackson Hole. Sharing a room with a couple of other waitresses, she found better jobs in better restaurants, made friends, and eventually worked as a draftsperson at a several ad agencies, where her creative talents, including her ability with a paintbrush, were salable.

She took night courses at New York University in a curriculum she labeled "AAA"—art, advertising, and administration—and after seven years she'd worked her way up to the top rungs at the Belmont Advertising Agency on Madison Avenue. Management had its collective eyes on her as their next chief executive.

For years, beginning with Horace Adams II, the Horace Adams Brewing Company of Milwaukee had been one of the Belmont Advertising Agency's major clients. Top management there proposed an ad campaign starring dancing bottles of Horace Adams beer, accompanied with bouncy, giggly music. When Ronald Summers, the agency's president, presented the campaign to Horace Adams III, he responded, "Who this side of hell wants to watch beer bottles dance?"

But Ronald Summers argued that the ads told a subliminal story that sold. "It's the reptilian brain that these ads stimulate—the most primitive part of the stem, which governs appetite, fear, lust, and aggression." He twisted his mouth into an uneven smile. "The more recent parts of the cranium overlie the reptilian core, but the core is always in charge. 'Give me what I want,' it demands."

"For Christ sakes," Adams replied, "we're selling beer to people, not to reptiles."

Adams pulled his baseball cap down low. His face was a tangle of hard lines, but his nose was straight, his eyes were brown and clear, and there was a hint of humor tucked into the corner of his mouth.

"People don't know why they buy what they buy, Mr. Adams," Summers said. "Think of it this way: The bottles are empty. They bear the Horace Adams label. We cannot overtly claim that drinking beer makes you happy. The whole damn antibooze crowd would be down on us overnight. But the hidden story is that the bottles were once full, and even now that they're empty, they're still happy. It's that simple. And bottles doing their dance thing is funny."

"Our customers can get their laughs at the movies," Adams said. "We're selling beer, not bottles. My father had me working in the brewery from the time I was boy. I grew up alongside of the men, including summers during my time at Harvard. I hated Harvard students, their phony airs, their high-flying intellects. I went back to work at the brewery. I lived with our guys a lot of years. I laughed, cried, and sweated with them. I think I have some idea what workingmen want. And it's not a bunch of beer bottles dancing." He started for the door.

"Please wait a moment, Mr. Adams," Summers said.

Adams's hand was on the doorknob. "The price of bullshit has reached an all-time high here. I'm tired of it."

"Well, I understand, but don't judge us too quickly, Mr. Adams. I'd like you to talk to our motivational expert." Before Adams could push the door open, Summers called on the intercom for Lillian Mortensen.

When she entered, she walked straight to Adams with the confidence of a burgeoning universe, in which he was but a wandering, solitary star.

"Miss Mortensen has been working on an entirely new campaign for Horace Adams beer," Summers announced.

Adams took in the tall, admirably proportioned woman with jet black hair and bright blue eyes.

"You're a busy man," Lillian said. "Let me repeat what you already know. To sell anything, the buyer's needs, real or imagined, must be satisfied. So the question is, Does your beer fill those needs on any level?"

What he saw got in the way of her question.

"So tell me," she continued. "What would make Horace Adams beer number one?"

She waited for his response.

"No ideas?" she asked, prodding with a slightly forgiving smile. "If anyone should know why a Horace Adams beer should be preferred over every other beer in the world, wouldn't that be you?"

Summers let out a muffled cough, a signal for Lillian to lighten up, but she charged on.

"Coors uses the Rocky Mountains to sell its—well, call it what you want. Horace Adams will open a brewery in Jackson, Wyoming, home of the Teton Mountains, the most magnificent mountains in America."

"You want me to retreat to the boondocks?" Adams finally asked.

"You're already trapped as the number-seven beer in the country, and you've been stuck there for a decade. You're either happy there or you want to get the hell out," she said. "How about advancing to numero uno? Or could you stand the shock?"

Summers stood up to further signal that she should wrap it up.

Lillian Mortensen cemented her focus on Adams. "The Tetons make the Rocky Mountains of Coors look like molehills," she said. "*Grand tétons* is French for breasts—actually, big breasts. Men respond to that image. Or hadn't you noticed?"

"I noticed," he said, quickly lowering his eyes to her white silk blouse and holding them there an instant past an accidental glance.

"Studies show that seventy-three percent of adult males look at a woman's chest first, then her face."

"Women don't have chests," he said.

"And what do they have?"

"Tetons," he said, and laughed.

"Exactly!" she said. "You're a very fast study. The French trappers weren't slow to name what they admired—and longed for."

A hint of lust leaked through his smile.

"I can create an ad campaign that'll rock the world. After my campaign for your beer, there'll never be a woman's breast seen or dreamed of that won't bring on a thirst for a Horace Adams beer—'the beer brewed under the shadow of the Tetons.'"

As if it had been his idea in the first place, he said, "We can probably build a plant in Jackson Hole in less than two years. It took us seven years to build our last one in Milwaukee, but we got caught up in a lot of local beer politics."

"You made up your mind about my proposal in less than thirty seconds. Why did it take you so long?" She was laughing.

"You are a distraction, madam," he said.

"You'll find the Tetons to your liking," she replied.

Adams hired Lillian Mortensen away from the Belmont Advertising Agency to supervise the advance work for his new brewery in Jackson Hole. They both moved to that nearly vacant valley under the Tetons. She was coming home. People knew she'd "made it big-time," and people have a way of altering their memories when a person makes it big-time. He would trust no one but Lillian to manage his latest project. Along the way, she authored the slogan for the new Horace Adams beer: "Under the Tetons, the beer that knows what you want."

Lillian and Horace worked out of the company's temporary Jackson Hole office, a twenty-foot mobile home. They spent their days on the construction site and their evenings together in a local café, or at one or the other's apartment, planning the work for the next day. He was in charge of the construction crew. She was generous with her advice, kept the inventory of construction materials, and made sure that the specialists as well as the workingmen were available as needed. "This little gem in the Tetons is going to put to shame our home brewery in Milwaukee," Horace said.

Sometimes, Lillian was gone for several weeks at a time, solving material hang-ups or working out agreements with the subcontractors who provided the multiple systems of a modern brewery—the grinding system, the heating system, the brewhouse system, the fermentation system, the cooling system, the cleaning system, and the control system, all of which included endless tanks, pumps, fixtures, and fittings, not to mention the establishment of fuel sources and storage.

Once, Lillian remarked, "I could build a rocket to the moon easier than putting together a goddamned brewery." But she was quick to admit she loved the work, and she soon became an expert at the fabrication of a brewery.

They wanted their new beer to embody the reflected excitement of the Tetons. Adams ordered the brewmaster in Milwaukee to join in their search for a perfect flavor, and every two or three weeks the brewmaster airshipped his latest recipe to Horace and Lillian for their responses. A sample might be "too tart," or "too bitter," or "too sweet," or "not crystal like fresh snow," or "too flat," or it didn't have that "little pop at the end of a swallow," whatever that meant.

"We can call our new beer 'Horace's Teton High,'" he said. "'Give me a Horace's High' will become the cry of America!"

"Great!" she exclaimed. "It's the beer that made Jackson Hole famous."

"I trust your taste," Horace said. "We'll not be satisfied until our recipe makes you swoon."

"I'm already swooning," she said, and they drank another round.

"I wish I could bottle up how I feel about you," he said one night. And on that night, Horace burst open the door to the outside porch and whispered in her ear, "Let us swoon to the moon."

One evening under the persuasion of the brewmaster's latest recipe, Horace said, "Imagine the power! We can sit here and adjust the taste of beer for millions." Then suddenly, he grew serious. "What if we had the power to change the souls of people instead of their taste for beer?"

"For God's sake," Lillian said. "We're selling beer, not Jesus."

"Jesus would have liked our beer," he said. "He would have served it at the Last Supper."

Before Lillian, Horace had lived a solitary life in Milwaukee. "Weren't you lonely living up there all by yourself in that city?" Lillian asked.

"How could I be lonely? I lived every day with the most interesting person I know."

"Who would that be?"

He pointed to himself. He opened a couple more bottles of the latest recipe for Horace's High and handed one to Lillian. "After years of being alone, loneliness gets lonely and flees."

"Where does it go?" she asked.

"It disappears into the cosmos and becomes a star."

"There must have been a lot of lonely people. I've never been lonely," she said.

Horace wondered why he'd ended up marrying Rebecca Jordan Jones—"Cupcake," he called her. Something had amused him about her childlike innocence—the way she wrapped up in her imitation of worldly sophistica-tion. And she was a true performer in bed. After the daily, depleting drudgery of running a brewery and the cutthroat competition for the "beer dollar," he'd sought simple pleasure and release. Cupcake had provided that, but he'd never felt loved.

One morning, Horace woke to take stock of his mar-riage. Cupcake insisted she was a direct descendant of John Paul Jones, the American Revolution's naval hero. He realized that his entertainment from her predictable but laudable accomplishments under the covers had already become old hat. And after he'd listened to the same war stories about John Paul Jones over and over, yes, over and over, he decided that John Paul as well as Cupcake were history, and he wasn't a history buff.

Preempting their five-million-dollar prenuptial agree-ment, he wrote a check to Cupcake for seven million. "Peanuts," he told Lillian. "Besides, she deserved it, having to live with the likes of me." He shook his head, amused at himself. "Maybe I'd been testing my beer too often when I decided to marry her."

"Maybe we'd better lay off our beer tasting," Lillian said.

"That woman," Horace said, referring to Rebecca Jordan Jones, "loved to parade her skinny rump on the ramp of the Junior Women's Club style show they put on for the poor girls of Milwaukee. Thank God for Milwaukee's poor little girls. If it weren't for them, the country club women couldn't show off their bony butts to raise money for those poor little girls. I offered to give them twice the net that the style show was collecting for poor girls if the rich women would stop their obscene parading for the poor, but Cupcake said I was too stodgy to understand."

Horace was growing on Lillian. Yes, he was shamefully wealthy, but his values sharply detoured from those of the imperial moneyed society.

"And those women all have perfect snow white teeth," he said. "Yours aren't perfect."

"I hoped you hadn't noticed. My folks couldn't afford an orthodontist. My teeth got straight on their own, all except this canine tooth on the right, which is a metaphor for my life."

He was too busy in his reverie to ask what she meant.

"Do you want any more children?" he suddenly asked one evening.

She didn't answer.

He continued, as if her silence had been her answer. "Think of all the politicians and movie and sports types who lay it all down for a little sex on the side, and it ends up destroying 'em."

"You sound like a preacher, not a beer salesman."

"Sex makes even the most ardent atheist a believer. Otherwise, why, at that precise moment of orgasm, do they always holler for God? 'Oh God, oh God!'"

He laughed.

She laughed.

Then she asked, "Why are you talking about other women? Am I so boring?"

Finally, he said, "I don't know how to talk about us."

"What do you mean?"

"I don't know how to talk to somebody like you about . . ."

"You don't need to talk," Lillian said. She took one of his hands in each of hers and with her tongue lightly kissed their palms. Then she pulled them to her breasts. "Tetons," she whispered, and at first she only brushed his mouth with her lips.

CHAPTER 11

"PRAISE GOD YOU'RE finally here," Jenny Winkley said like a mother whose lost child had just returned home. "They've been waiting for you in there for hours, and they're hollering so loud at each other, I thought I'd have to call the sheriff."

Judge Murray handed his old mackinaw to his secretary, a middle-aged woman who looked like a rounded-out retired rodeo queen with a bunch of red hair piled up on her head. She wore those rhinestone-framed cat's-eye glasses and an off-red long-sleeved cotton dress imprinted with images of white roses and other posies. Her dress hung well below her knees. Still in her mother mode, she inspected the judge as if he were her child about to march off to his first day in school.

She opened the door to Judge Murray's small inner office, referred to in the profession as his "chambers." Both lawyers jumped to their feet. The judge spoke without looking at either of the lawyers. "I understand you gentlemen are engaged in an attempt to settle all pending matters in a professional manner. What concessions have you been able to make?"

"Sewell won't even agree to the standard 'reasonable doubt' instruction," Coker said. He was red-faced in anger and sweating, as if he'd just survived the fifteenth round of a championship boxing match.

"I'm perfectly willing to agree to the standard 'reasonable doubt' instruction," Haskins Sewell replied. "But Coker won't agree we can introduce evidence of Lillian Adams's past violent conduct under Rule 404b."

"I filed a motion in Limine this morning against that irrelevant and prejudicial evidence," Coker snarled. He handed a copy of his motion to the judge.

"Keep it down, gentlemen. My hearing aids are working perfectly. Let's get to business." The judge leaned back in his worn leather chair to listen.

"Let me refresh your memory, Your Honor." Coker's voice began rising again. "Lillian Adams's 'bad conduct,' as Mr. Sewell likes to call it, was with her first husband, and she was a mere juvenile. She never—"

"No need to holler," the judge said.

"She was never convicted. You sent her home to her father. She has no criminal record. Her conduct as a juvenile cannot be entered against her these many years later. She is protected under the law. According to *State v. Hammond*, a juvenile—"

"I know the case," the judge said.

"Well, she wasn't a juvenile when she stabbed her second husband with that pen," Sewell said.

"If we prosecuted every woman who took after her old man with a pen or table knife, we'd have most women in prison. Maybe even Betsy," Coker said. He lifted his eyebrow at the judge, as if he knew something.

Sewell started to speak, but the judge interrupted.

"Mostly, Lillian Adams hurt her second husband's pride," the judge said, "a man named Gordon Ford, as I recall. She testified that he was beating their dog and wouldn't stop. Said she couldn't live with a dog-beater. I'll admit, there's nothing in the statutes that allows a judge to grant a divorce for dog abuse. But I gave her husband all the money and gave her custody of their child, Tina, and the dog. I remember her saying that she didn't want a dirty dog-beater's money."

"I'll admit that one who beats a dog is entitled to little mercy," Sewell said. "But this woman is charged with murder, and her history of violence is admissible under the rules." Then he added words touched with poison: "It's too late for me to disqualify you, but you should disqualify yourself."

"Why didn't you file for a new judge when you had the chance?" the judge asked.

"No reasonable person would have guessed that a fair judge would rule as you have in this case." Sewell said through his usual curled-up top lip, "nor, given your obvious conflict, could a reasonable person have foreseen that any judge burdened with such disabilities would remain on this case."

The judge studied the face of the prosecutor, his skin drum-tight over his skull, his eyes hard, almost yellow. So Sewell wanted to present evidence of Lillian's past violence? Another judge would likely agree. Then Lillian would have to take the stand to defend herself. The judge could already hear Sewell's cross-examination:

"You struck your first husband with a brass vase, knocked him unconscious, and tried your best to kill him, isn't that true?"

"He was naked and in bed with the landlady," Lillian would protest.

"So, Ms. Adams, you believed it was your right to take the law into your own hands and render the death penalty to your first husband, isn't that true?"

It would make no difference how she answered.

Lillian's willingness to kill would become a fact in the case.

But Sewell would just be beginning. Then he'd ask, "And after you thought you'd killed your husband, you tried to kill the police officer who came to stop your killing, isn't that true?"

She might respond, "I was a just a teenager. I was upset."

"Yes," Sewell would reply, taking in the jurors with his long, imperious look. "You are willing to kill when you get upset, isn't that true?"

"No, sir."

"And," Sewell would continue, "you stabbed your second husband with a pen, isn't that true?"

"Yes, he was beating our dog and wouldn't stop."

"And so your remedy to stop his beating the dog was to kill him?"

Sewell knew all the tricks to transform the understandable, the forgivable, even simple habit, into evil. "He exercised the devil's power," the judge had often called it.

The judge cleared his throat, as if to open an entrée to his decision. "The years have provided me with enough enmity against both of you to pretty much even things out." He smiled first at Coker and then at Sewell. "Yes, gentlemen, I will treat both sides with equal respect and fairness, given the state of my underlying animosity toward both of you and toward all of mankind in general." He smiled again to confess his humor, but neither attorney smiled back.

Sewell shook his head in disbelief. "When she beat her first husband nearly to death, you sent her home to her father. Killing runs in that family. You let her off for stabbing her second husband, and you're going to sit on this case in which she is charged with the murder of her third husband? With all due respect, I again insist you have no business whatever in this case."

"Well, gentlemen," Judge Murray said, "I am getting too old for this kind of unprofessional fiddle-faddle. I am going to give my standard 'reasonable doubt' instruction—you've both heard it many times, and Mr. Sewell, if you have competent evidence of Lillian Adams's violence that's admissible under Rule 404b, and that evidence isn't more prejudicial than probative, I'll let it in."

"Lillian Adams is like a daughter to you and your wife, Betsy, and you're still sitting on this case?" Sewell's voice was ominously low, almost a whisper. "How can that happen in an American court of law?"

"Perhaps the better question is, Why did you waive your disqualification of me in the first place?" the judge asked. "It appears you've played a little game and now you believe you made a mistake, and you want me to correct it."

"No, I just wanted the record to show that I reminded you of your impropriety, for later reference at an appropriate time." His threat was clear.

Impeachment.

Then as if nothing untoward had occurred, the judge proceeded to conduct the pretrial conference in his standard way. "Gentlemen, have you arrived at any stipulated facts?"

Coker said, "Yes, I will stipulate that Mr. Adams was shot once in the head. The shot entered the forehead and exited the back of his head, killing him instantly." Coker started to sit down. Instead, he began pacing, all the while jabbing his finger at Sewell. "And I want this man ordered to stop calling this death a murder. That's for the jury to determine."

"I've offered Mr. Coker's client a plea to first-degree

murder, with the possibility of parole after thirty years," Sewell stated. "It was a cold-blooded, premeditated killing. I hope you recall, Your Honor, that I predicted years ago that Lillian Adams would come to no good end."

"First off," Coker replied, "Sewell has no business making any reference to our discussion concerning a plea bargain. That's privileged and he knows it. He's up to his dirty tricks again. . . ."

"All of us in this room know the woman's proclivity toward violence," Sewell said. "She's playing Coker like she's played all of you all these years, if you don't mind my saying so, Your Honor."

"I mind it," the judge said. "And I remind you to be professional. You demand that my personal feelings, whatever they might be, should not be visible here. So both of you are bound by the same rule of conduct. Remember that nearly sacrosanct rule of law: What's good for the goose is good for the gander, as it were."

Sewell said, "Coker has been hoodwinked by his client. But then he's ready prey for her kind."

Coker glared at Sewell and took a menacing step toward him.

"Sit down, Mr. Coker!" the judge ordered. "Your boxing days are over."

Coker slowly slumped into his chair.

"As you can plainly see," Sewell said, "Lillian Adams has bewitched what little common sense Mr. Coker has left."

Coker sprang to his feet again.

"That will be enough," the judge said to Sewell. "There's plenty of space in that nice concrete room for lawyers who can't conduct themselves in a professional manner. Mr. Coker, you remember the last time you stepped over the edge. That goes for you, as well."

After the judge dismissed the lawyers for the day, he sat

alone in his chambers. He could see it all very clearly. He must keep watch over the law in the same way he would protect the public from a schizophrenic killer.

The law, too, was a killer.

Yes, he thought. The law itself is like a person suffering from what the psychiatrists call a "blunted affect"—a person who feels no emotional response to real-life situations that bring on pain, anger, sorrow, and the whole agglomeration of human feelings experienced by normal people. The law is a cold, emotionless, lifeless killer, and it sweeps away all human emotions like dead houseflies.

Even a jury's rare acquittal meant only that the prosecutor had failed to prove the defendant's guilt beyond a reasonable doubt, not that the accused was innocent. We are all guilty, the judge thought. We were all born in sin. Ask Jesus. Ask the Pope. Ask any Baptist preacher. Ask the law. The judge heard himself saying aloud, "I should have studied the discourse of birds. When birds are joyous, they know how to sing. I've never seen a judge singing."

And he remembered what Betsy preached to him every morning: "You have a duty to both of us just this once. Lillian is like the daughter we never had. Please don't forget that."

As Judge Murray gazed blankly out the window of his chambers, he saw Haskins Sewell take fast, measured steps to his car. He carried his small, hairless gray dog under his right arm. Yes, the judge thought, the birds are wiser. Most fly south in the winter, but I'm trapped in Jackson Hole with Haskins Sewell, and I'll never escape.

One evening, Horace and Lillian were dining in the town of Jackson at the Howdy Pardner Café, a joint locally famous for its buffalo T-bone steaks—probably steaks hacked off a grass-fed steer but called "buffalo" on the menu. The tourists would pay an extra half buck for the experience. Yeah, they'd been in old Wyoming. They'd even eaten buffalo steaks. Horace chopped at the meat with his steak knife. No one complained that the steaks were tough. They were buffalo.

"I sort of grew up without parents," Horace told Lillian. "My mother left my father when I was seven. I was told my mother was a hopeless alcoholic and ran off with a beer salesman who worked for my father. My father said she was insane. I don't know if she was or not. But it became an established fact in the family history. Growing up, I worried she might kill me, you know, like you think crazy people will kill you."

Horace was gazing off into the room's dense fog of smoke, which drifted in from the open kitchen and melded with the smoke of the diners' cigarettes. "When I was still seven, my mother sneaked into our house on Christmas Eve and crept into my room. I thought she was drunk. I was terrified. She saw I was afraid, and she tried to entice me with a box of Cracker Jacks. She said. 'Honey, your father is crazy, and he'll kill me if he catches me here.' She was looking every which way and her eyes were wild."

He struggled to say more. Finally, he said, "Her skin was white and her hair was long and shaggy, like old rope. I tried to get away, but she cornered me and kissed me, and told me she loved me, and after that I never saw her alive again. I was handled by a string of nannies."

Lillian reached across the small table for his hand. It was large and strong and felt safe.

"I ate the caramel corn in the Cracker Jack box, and inside there was always a little toy. That time, it was a play cigar made of dark brown paper with red and white painted fire at the end. I treasured it—the only thing my mother ever gave me. I have it today. I keep it and the empty Cracker Jack box in my safe and take the box out sometimes and talk to it. I get comfort from that." He looked away. "Maybe insanity runs in the family." Then he added, "At her funeral, my father made me walk by her open coffin and say good-bye. She was pretty in her casket."

She felt his hand tighten.

"I like being with you because you hear me," he said. "Everyone can listen. But hearing is an art."

"Yes," she said, "hearing can break a hole through a wall."

"I know about hearing through walls," Horace said. "My father was always hollering. You could hear him no matter where you were in the house. I used to pile the pillows over my head so I couldn't hear him. He ran around hollering when no one was in the house. He hollered about the goddamned farmers who supplied our barley, or the goddamned railroad that shipped it, and he hated his goddamned competitors like one hates thieves. He hated the goddamned Democrats who were 'wannabe Commies,' as he called them. He lived a life fueled by hatred."

Lillian had discovered that Horace was a man, all right, and she was "man-sensitive," as she called it. Every kind and nature of man inhabited the planet, each as different from the other as their fingerprints. Some were indolent, some aggressive, some nutty, and some even toxic to the touch. Some were empty boxes with a smile inscribed across the front of the box, and a few, she thought, were potentially trustworthy, and fewer still even marginally engaging.

"At this stage in my life, I'm attracted to very few men," she said. "Still, I don't see myself as a full-blown 'misandrist.'"

"I'm glad of that," he said, "whatever that means." They both laughed, and he lifted his wineglass in a quick salute.

"But I've had enough of those little side trips with certain subtypes who call themselves men," she said. Horace not only made her feel safe; he had his own mind, which often wandered, but he wanted to share himself with her, and his trust endeared him to her. No secrets? We all have secrets, she thought. Most people only tell the secrets they need to tell to create trust. And you don't find out a person's real secrets until the door's been closed and locked after the "I dos." Then their secrets can come bursting out in every imaginable queer quirk, hang-up, and horror.

As for his gifts as a lover, she thought that Horace was no physical athlete under the covers, nor was he a bag full of tricks. He led her into deeper waters, where the experience was often dark but also inviting and exciting. And frightening. She told Sylvia Huntley, "He makes me feel loved in places I didn't know existed."

Horace was still carrying on with his life's story. "When I was twenty-three and in Harvard Business School, my father started showing signs of losing it; the doctors called it 'senile dementia.' He'd forget where he was. Sometimes he thought he was still living with my mother, and he'd be screaming at her, accusing her of running around on him with 'that asshole jerk,' the beer salesman.

"I was never allowed to enter his office. I wondered if the room hid some horrible secret. One night when I was eighteen, I decided to investigate this forbidden chamber. The old man was attending the annual brewers' convention in Chicago, where Clark Gable was the guest of honor. After ten minutes of my hollering and pounding on the office door, the watchman, Hank, came stumbling to the door. I started for the hallway leading to my father's office. Hank stepped in front of me."

Horace said that with both hands he shoved the watchman aside and with one thrust he kicked in the door, and there he stood for the first time inside his father's office, surveying the forbidden. The lights were on. They were always on.

"Hank came staggering into the room. He grabbed me by the back of my collar and jerked me toward the door. All it took was a single punch to the belly, and old Hank crumbled."

Horace said he stepped into the middle of the room, walked around a long, wooden, beaten-up conference table, and started shuffling through the papers. In the bottom drawer of a large adjoining chest, he came upon a series of old yellowed newspaper clippings. They were stories about a starlet known as Colatta Connley, "the future Irish queen of the screen." He wouldn't have recognized his mother except for those vacant eyes and a mouth that appeared to be constantly saying no.

"Do you know what happened to my mother, Hank?" Horace asked.

"I'm going to lose my job," Hank pleaded. "I let the boss's kid break into the old man's office. Me and my wife are raising our grandkids and all." He started for Horace again.

"Don't," Horace warned. "Stay put." Then he asked, "What happened to my mother?"

Hank stood stone-statue mute. Finally, he said, "Some claim the old man beat her to death. I happen to know that ain't so. She died down there in the park. A couple days before she died, I seen her wanderin' around. They found her body there on a park bench. She probably froze to death."

Horace held up a photograph of a nude woman.

"Do you know who this is, Hank?"

"It's one a them autopsy pictures."

"Who is it, Hank?" Horace was in the man's face.

"It's your ma, Horace."

Horace slipped the photograph into his jacket pocket. Then he and Hank worked at straightening things up. They were able to get the door locked again by lifting it slightly by the knob until the lock fell into place.

"This hasn't been the perfect crime," Horace said. "But neither one of us knows anything about this, right, Hank?"

"That's for damn sure," Hank said. "And by the way, if you want to get into boxing, I know some people. You got one hell of a right." Then he added, "But it was a lucky punch."

Horace was still sharing his life's story with Lillian. "One night, my father fell down the stairs in our house. I'd been out with some workers from the brewery and got home about two in the morning. I found him dead, bunched up against the door at the bottom of the stairs like a pile of old bloody rags. I felt guilty. I thought if I hadn't been out drinking, I might have saved him. But in a way, I was glad it was over for him. He was losing his mind. I had to take over the business. That's been punishment enough."

Horace looked off to some distant place, and his words stalled.

"What?" she prompted.

"I was thinking about his funeral. Before they closed the coffin lid, I dropped the autopsy photo of my mother inside so that it rested on my father's dead heart."

His eyes clouded.

Then he proceeded. "The workers got half an hour off to attend the funeral," he said. "No one cried. Not even me."

After his father died, Horace, then thirty-seven, took over the brewery. He'd been working at various jobs there, from laborer on up to his latest job, in marketing. As his first official act as head of the company, he tore everything out of the old man's office and sent it to the dump. He hired a decorator, who brought in the painters and had the walls painted in bright, living colors. "I want this room gone. There are going to be new times for the Horace Adams Brewing Company and new times for the workers, as well."

Horace and Lillian retreated from their day's work to her cabin in Jackson Hole. She dumped a log into the small fireplace, retrieved a bottle of Cabernet from the top shelf of her cupboard, popped the cork, and poured them each a glass. They were quiet for a time, content in the warmth of the room, the fire snapping and the wine good.

Finally, Horace broke the silence. "I have—what do they call it?—certain peculiarities."

"Like what?" she asked. "Is this confession time?"

He looked down at the top of one hand, then the other, embarrassed. "The preachers would laugh if they heard the head of a brewery say he wanted to live a worthy life. They'd say, 'Go set that evil place of yours on fire, or turn it into a home for street urchins. That would be doing good.'"

"What's a worthy life?" she asked.

"I don't know. I'm afraid I'll die before I can answer that question."

"That's why the rich write a check to provide a new wing to some hospital. That's worthy. And they get a tax write-off, and the new wing is named after them," she said.

Finally, Horace said, "I didn't want to run the business."

"What did you want to do?"

"I wanted to be a chef—I wanted to cook."

Horace started cooking, a "fancy dish," as he called it. It turned out to be spaghetti and meatballs, but he insisted his spaghetti sauce was classic. He peeled an onion and, with the pizzazz of a celebrated chef, chopped it into small square chips, mashed the garlic with the chef's knife, minced a carrot, slipped in a couple teaspoons of olive oil, some canned tomatoes and tomato paste, after which he added oregano, fresh basil, and, at last, a teaspoon of sugar, half a cup of red wine, and a pinch of crushed red pepper.

He formed the meatballs like a kid creating small snowballs. He quickly tossed one to Lillian. "Think fast," he said, and, to his surprise, she caught it and tossed it back.

"Think fast," she said, and they both laughed.

"This will be good. Very good."

She walked over to the stove. He was still stirring the sauce, and she kissed him dearly.

"I been thinking of the workers," he said. "Maybe doing 'good' is when everyone makes a profit, including the workers."

"Your father would have disowned you as a filthy Commie."

"And good is when you make a great marinara brimming with joy and meatballs."

CHAPTER 12

COKER'S DEFENSE WAS founded on his belief that whether or not Lillian killed Horace Adams III, she was entitled to a fair trial, and it was Coker's job to see that she got it. He'd lay it all down to save her and, beyond pure perjury, he'd set no boundaries.

Few would understand that at times even a judge must be brave. Judge Murray's time had arrived. His vow of fidelity to the law and his oath of neutrality were the commands of his office, but they were at odds with his unequivocal promises to save Lillian. He knew he must create a record in the trial that would be scrutinized by the "pesky, peering, peeping appellate judges," as he liked to call them. With them, the revered, so-called appearance of justice would be the test. Things had to look right on the record.

The law itself was tilted toward conviction. The judge knew that if he didn't intervene from time to time, and at the right time, and carefully, Lillian would go down.

But what if she were innocent? She could be facing the gas chamber. She wouldn't be the first innocent person who'd died gasping inside that chamber from hell, and at this point, execution appeared to be the most probable outcome.

Days before the trial, there'd been the usual talk among the townsfolk. During coffee time at Hungry Jake's grocery store, Herman Sikora, the horseshoer, said, "She probably wouldn't give him what he wanted. She is one piece, if you know what I mean, and he probably said, 'Well, up yers, then, and the horse you rode in on,' and she said, 'Well, up yours,' and pulled out her gun, and whambo! She's a multimillionaire, just like that, and he's a poor dead sumbitch. Would you shoot the old bastard for a couple hundred mil?"

"Don't ask me no questions, and I'll tell you no lies," Bill Wimpenny said. He and his wife had just sold their ranch and were planning to tour "the good old US of A." "But I'll tell you one thing: She damn near killed her first husband. Killing's in her blood."

"Sure be a waste of good pussy to send her off to them lezzies that'll be waiting fer her in the pen," Sikora said. "I hear that even the guards there are queer. They got me called for jury duty on Monday."

"Aren't you the lucky one?" Harmon Watson said. He was the foreman of the telephone company's line crew. "Who's she got for her mouthpiece?"

"I seen by the paper that old Coker is representing her," Sikora said.

"He'd dance a hula dance with a rattlesnake if you offered him a dime. I hear he got that guy off who works for the Bar Double X ranch. He was charged with screwing his own daughter. Jesus save us! His own daughter!" Sikora exclaimed.

"Yeah, well, if you're guilty, you'd better get old Coker

to represent you. I'll say that much." It was Wimpenny again.

"Well, if you wasn't guilty, who would you get to represent you?"

"Coker," Wimpenny said.

The *Jackson Hole Post* called Lillian "the Queen of the Hill, who looked down from her antique log home on high." The townsfolk wanted to see the queen wiggle and squirm on the witness stand, hear her counterfeit excuses, see Sewell cut her to ribbons, see her beg for mercy, see her get her comeuppance, and some wanted to see Coker's latest tricks. This would be an honest-to-God murder trial like in the movies, and it was happening in their own little burg of Jackson.

CHAPTER 13

JUDGE JOHN MURRAY walked to the bench as sure and straight as his old legs permitted. The clerk ordered the audience to rise, the customary acknowledgment of respect for the law as personified in His Honor, the judge. In response, the judge donned his standard judicial mask. It was not a face to take to a dinner party.

The judge was unaccustomed to feeling fear in his own courtroom. The accused on trial were often terrified. And at times the lawyers themselves were soaked in fear, especially as they awaited the jury's verdict. He hoped his attempt at a stern, implacable demeanor would grant him some protection. He banged his gavel harder than usual and gazed out at the audience.

The clerk, Benjamin Breslin, announced the case: "*State of Wyoming v. Lillian Mortensen Adams.*" Breslin was a man who exposed no known sins, nor did he advertise any virtues. He was chiefly without a palpable persona. "Is the state ready?" Breslin asked like a sleepy preacher at a funeral.

"More than ready!" Sewell replied in his near-soprano

voice, which prevailed when his adrenaline was running high.

"Is the defense ready?" Breslin asked.

"The defense is as ready as we can be considering the refusal of the state to fulfill its discovery obligations." Coker believed Sewell, as usual, was hiding evidence, which the law required him to reveal before trial.

Coker's eyes locked on each prospective juror as the juror was called and walked to his or her assigned seat. "We can lie with our words, but we can't lie about how our lives have formed us," Coker claimed. The jurors would expose themselves by the sounds of their voices, how they carried themselves, their facial expressions, their body language, and how they dressed—often more reliable clues as to who the jurors were than what the jurors said.

Coker wanted jurors who strode to the box with a dutiful, painful resolve, who didn't want to serve on a jury. A prospective juror who was eager to serve was a juror equally eager to judge, and too often such judgments were retaliatory—that is to say, the juror was ready to even things up for the bad luck, the bad parents, or the bad decisions the juror had suffered. Or the juror had simply been born with an overload of mean genes.

The clerk spun the jury drum, a six-inch-diameter canister on a spindle. He reached in, withdrew a slip of paper containing the name of a prospective juror, opened the folded paper, and announced the name: "Margaret Reed Smith."

The Smith woman was a plump grandmother type in her early sixties with a broad motherly face, and she let out a small, surprised gasp when her name was called—as if she'd just won in bingo. She wore a long multiflowered silk dress with a purple collar, and a matching belt. She walked in quick, proper steps, with her thighs squeezed tightly together.

The clerk drew the name Harvey Bottomsley. A scrawny middle-aged man in a pink T-shirt and faded blue jeans hurried to the jury box. He was a reclusive artist who still lived with his mother. His paintings weren't in demand, but he hadn't given up. He looked at the Smith woman for reassurance.

William Witherspoon, a tall, well-built cowboy in his fifties, was called. He clomped to the jury box with bowed legs and turned-over heels on his scuffed, never polished cowboy boots. His sun brown face was heavily wrinkled. His forehead was white, having been protected from the sun by his hat.

Then Mary Lou Livingston's name was drawn. A waitress in the Buckhorn Coffee Shop, she had a hip-swinging walk, which earned a lot of attention as she poured coffee and served breakfast, and she'd learned how to convert the propositions dumped on her every morning into decent tips. She had kids at home to feed. She gave the cowboy in the jury box a friendly wink as she took her seat next to him.

The clerk called George Hardesty, a plumber, who strode to the jury box with heavy feet. He was wearing his wrinkled Sunday suit absent a tie, but his denim shirt was buttoned to the top. He kept twisting his head back and forth in response to the tightness around his neck. Coker knew those jokes about the hot housewife who was always calling the plumber to fix something. Hardesty didn't fit the mold. He took his seat next to the waitress and gave a small nod of recognition.

Tom Mosley's name was drawn. He was fat, bald, middle-aged, and dour. He owned the Best Bargain Pawn Shop. He watched where he put each foot, making sure no hidden impediment threatened. He sat down stiffly next to the plumber.

When the clerk called Louise Greenwood, she hollered, "I can't serve on this jury. I have kids at home and nobody to care for them. I gotta go."

The judge said, "Stop right there."

She stopped.

"You are excused," Judge Murray said. "For us to insist that mothers leave their children unattended to serve on a jury would make us accomplices to the crime of child neglect. My respects." He hit his gavel to underscore his decree.

Next called was Helen Griggsley, a piano teacher. She was tall, stately, and wearing a modest navy blue dress. No jewelry. She bore a resemblance to George Washington on the one-dollar bill. She wore her gray hair in his style, as well. She walked with resolute steps in black low-heeled shoes. She favored the community with her students' annual recital in the basement of the Methodist church, an event that was usually attended only by parents and grandparents trapped behind the high fence of duty.

Henry Harris, a car salesman, was called. He approached the jury box with a leisurely stroll to emphasize his cool. He nodded at Tom Mosley, the pawnbroker. He wore a leather jacket over a blue cotton shirt open at the neck. His tinted glasses obscured his eyes. He looked the jury panel over, as if to identify the easy mark, and took his seat.

Melvin Myorga, a man approaching his late sixties, plowed gardens in the summer and did snow removal in the winter. When the clerk called his name, he got up with some effort, and walked bent over. He fought his discomfort with a small lurch to the right after each step. He wore a newly pressed and starched pair of bib overalls. He took his seat in the jury box as if entering enemy territory.

Norman Etsomovich, of middle age, the local roofer, wore his work clothes—blue jeans and a blue jean jacket. He prided himself that he'd been on the roofs of nearly every householder in Jackson Hole and from that vantage point knew more about the secret carryings-on of the townsfolk than even the local priest. He walked with all due care—a man who needed to be sure of his footing. He nodded to Myorga as he sat down. Myorga gave a reluctant nod back.

James P. Smithson was the vice president of the local bank. He was blond, youngish, and a man on his way up. He was already a leader in the local Chamber of Commerce. Part of his job was to paste a good public image on his bank. He displayed a pliable face, one that molded itself in ways that were either marginally attractive or slightly offensive. He wore a blue suit with a white shirt and a red checkered tie. He walked with authority, his toes pointed straight ahead, but he lifted his right leg slightly with each step, suggesting his need to accommodate the heavy burden he carried below the pockets.

Harmony Biernstein was the twelfth juror drawn by the clerk. Biernstein was in the real estate business. She wore her blond hair bunched up high in a schoolteacher's bun. She was decked out in a dark burgundy business suit, along with black shoes with medium-high heels. She shot the judge her standard business smile when her name was called, and walked with eager steps to the jury box.

With the first twelve prospective jurors seated, the judge nodded to Sewell. "You may examine the jurors, counsel."

Sewell wasted no time. "Ever been in court before?" he asked Henry Harris, the car salesman.

"Once for no license plates. I was using our dealer plates on my private car and got caught." He tried to laugh aside his confession.

"Ever know Lillian Adams or anybody who does?"

"Yeah. I know her daddy. He's a hardworking man, and a guy who never took nothing from nobody."

"Ever hear anything about her?"

"A guy hears a lot of stuff in a town like this."

"What have you heard?"

The other prospective jurors leaned forward to catch Harris's answer.

"Your Honor," Coker interjected, "may this juror accompany counsel and Your Honor to your chambers?"

In chambers and with the court reporter alongside, Coker erupted. "Did you see what Sewell just tried, Your Honor? He wanted to poison the whole panel against my client by asking what Mr. Harris had heard about Lillian Adams."

"What did you hear about Lillian Adams, Mr. Harris?" the judge asked.

"I heard she was one tough little lady. I heard she could put you to the mat and bust you up pretty good." The juror laughed. "Something like that."

"I ask that the juror be excused," Coker said.

"Are you challenging for cause?" the judge asked.

"Yes."

"On what grounds?" the judge asked. "I've known tough women who could bust you up pretty good who were good citizens." Betsy, for one, he thought.

"Could you follow the court's instructions," Sewell asked, "and not permit this mere hearsay to affect your decision in this case?"

"Yeah. Sure."

"Well, how do you go about wiping things out of your mind?" Coker asked Harris. "Do you have a magic brain eraser or something?"

The juror shrugged his shoulders without answering.

"You think she might be a violent type, right?" Coker asked.

"Maybe."

"I ask that this juror be excused," Coker repeated, and sat down.

"I'm going to excuse the juror," the judge said and gave the juror his standard judicial smile, along with thanks for his service.

As the day progressed, prospective jurors were examined and cross-examined on every issue the lawyers could imagine—the movies they'd watched, the books they'd read, their attitude about the sheriff, the prosecutor, and the defense counsel, what they thought about reasonable doubt and the presumption of innocence. They were even asked to identify the bumper stickers on their vehicles.

Norman Etsomovich, the roofer, said, "I know a lot of things about a lot of people, and I get along with all of them." Melvin Myorga agreed.

Harmony Biernstein, the Realtor, said it was the slow time of the year for her and she could sit. But she knew Lillian Adams "from a distance."

"What do you mean, 'from a distance'?" Coker asked. "I know you 'from a distance.'"

"Really!" She laughed. "Did we have a good time?" The courtroom laughed.

"We're both members of the Chamber of Commerce," Coker said.

"You should come to our meetings," she responded with a measure of impudent humor.

"I would, but they're too boring," Coker said.

"That's why you should come," she replied. "You'd liven things up."

"You ever do business with Mrs. Adams?"

"No. But I would like to."

"Do you know Mr. Sewell?"

"Everybody knows him," she said.

"How did you come to know him?"

"I can't remember," she said. "Long time ago. We were kids."

The banker, Smithson, said that his bank did business with Horace Adams III. "He was a good customer of ours."

Coker was on him. "So am I a good customer of yours. You haven't bounced one of my checks for nearly six months." Laughter from the audience. "If you were me, what would you do with a prospective juror like you?" Coker asked.

"I would kick him off the jury."

"Why?"

"He might be prejudiced in favor of Adams. None of his checks ever bounced." He held back his smile.

Coker turned to the judge. "I challenge Mr. Smithson based on his frank assessment of himself."

Judge Murray: "Well what would you say, Mr. Coker, if Mr. Smithson were equally prejudiced against Mr. Sewell?"

"I'd say we should punt."

"Punt?" the judge asked.

"Yes, to put it another way, I think he should get the hell off this jury. I don't think we should have anyone who's prejudiced for or against anyone." Coker was playing his game. He thought Smithson would be a Sewell juror for sure.

"Can you be fair, Mr. Smithson?" Judge Murray asked.

"Depends on how you define *fair*," he said.

"Yes," the judge responded. "I've been attempting to define that word myself for all these years."

Coker was at Smithson again: "You know that your bank's lawyer and I have cases against each other all the time. I try to stop your foreclosures. And I defend a depositor now and then who you claim has made a fraudulent loan application. You must get a little tired of me?"

"That would be correct," Smithson said. "But I have to admit, if the bank was after me, I'd be knocking at your door to defend me."

With that, both sides accepted the banker. The judge thought Coker had made a big mistake. Smithson would have power over the other jurors who were doing business with his bank. He'd likely be elected the jury foreman and could guide the jury to a conviction. Yet, on the other hand, if Lillian were acquitted, she might reciprocate with mammoth deposits in his bank.

No grounds for challenges were uncovered for the piano teacher, Helen Griggsley, or for Mary Lou Livingston, the waitress.

George Hardesty, the plumber, said he'd worked on the Adams place before they bought it. "If they'd bothered to ask me, I could have told them that their cast-iron pipes was about to go and should have been replaced with copper. But they never asked me."

Tom Mosley, the pawnbroker, told Sewell, "I keep my mouth shut on who pawns what for what amount and how often. That's the way I do business."

"Well, you obviously never did business with Lillian Adams or her husband," Sewell said.

"I ain't saying one way or the other. That would be violating a confidentiality." He aimed his determined frown at Sewell.

"Have you done business with any of the prospective jurors here?"

"I ain't saying."

Coker joined the fray: "You're bound by certain state laws that govern how much interest you can charge, isn't that true?"

"Yeah."

"And Mr. Sewell enforces those laws, right?"

"I suppose."

"I challenge Mr. Mosley," Coker said.

Judge Murray interposed: "Mr. Sewell enforces the laws against all of us, Mr. Coker. If you or I commit a crime, it's likely Mr. Sewell's duty to prosecute. Your challenge on that ground is overruled."

In chambers, Judge Murray asked Mosley if he'd done any business with any prospective juror. "How come you ask me that?" he complained. "You never asked Smith, the banker, those questions. And I'm just the poor man's bank."

"I don't ask the questions," the judge said. "Counsel does."

"Well, I ain't answering those questions for you or nobody else."

"I withdraw any questions about his business customers," Sewell said.

"I join," Coker said. Mosley walked out of the judge's chambers and took his seat in the jury box, his chin nearly pointed at the ceiling.

At the noon recess, Jenny Winkley brought the judge a hamburger and some fries and stood over him like an unyielding mother until he took the first bite. "You know the trouble you get into when you don't keep your blood sugar up."

Shortly after lunch the lawyers on both sides waived any unexercised peremptory challenges—each side being entitled to ten—and twelve jurors and two alternates were sworn by the clerk to try the case. Of the original twelve, only Smithson, Biernstein, Mosley, Livingston, Witherspoon, Smith, and Griggsley had survived the lawyers' challenges. Why any of them were still on the jury, the judge couldn't guess. He would have gotten rid of the banker, Smithson, and the "people's banker," Mosley, as well. He believed that bankers habitually distrust people. Biernstein, in the real estate business, was too closely connected to the power structure of Jackson Hole.

And the piano teacher, Griggsley, was a mystery to the judge until he suddenly realized that his animosity toward the woman wasn't toward her. It was toward his childhood piano teacher, whom he'd despised. She would whack his fingers when he missed a chord, and he'd missed them frequently.

The challenged jurors were replaced with other citizens, most of whom didn't read a newspaper, and whose histories were as bland as skim milk. The judge told Betsy that evening, "Some jurors have been hiding so long in their personal gopher holes that the holes have become their whole world."

Four of the last six called were excused, leaving Amos Rogers, the blacksmith, Bertie Hartnett, the secretary to the school district, and Josephine Heller, an unemployed teacher.

Three more prospective jurors were called, along with two alternates. Two of the last three, Manuel Ortega, a plumber, and William Carter, a mechanic, were seated. The alternates were Matt Pollack, a ranch hand, and Symphony Finder, a homemaker.

When all the personality components of the seated

jurors and the lawyers were gathered and dumped into the psychic soup, no rational analysis could predict the collective predisposition of the jury. If the judge had to guess, it would be for a conviction. At the primal core of the human beast was an untethered jealousy of those who by reason of luck or even hard work had scored above them, and now luck had given the juror the chance to even things up against the likes of Lillian Adams.

Before the judge called a recess, he spoke to the chosen jurors. His voice suggested that even his vocal cords were giving up. "It's hard work to find justice," he said with a distant look. "I mean, what is justice? You can't see it. You can't touch it. No one can agree on what it is. What's justice for one person is injustice for another. Just thinking about justice can make a person tired, don't you agree, counsel?"

"Yes, Your Honor," Sewell said. "But it will be very plain to see in this case."

"Plain to the likes of you, but not to anybody else," Coker retorted.

The judge slammed down his gavel hard. A long silence followed. The crowd in the courtroom waited. Finally, the judge said, "What is truth? You must look for the truth here." He was gazing out to the fringes of the firmament. "We cannot guess at truth, or we shall never find it." His voice was dreamy. "But we can never be sure of it. The law says the truth you find must be beyond a reasonable doubt." He looked down at his desktop, expecting an answer. He waited.

Jenny Winkley hurried to him with a piece of paper and pretended to ask a question concerning something she was pointing to. Instead, she whispered, "Are you all right, Judge? Has your blood sugar gone to the basement again?" He seemed not to hear her.

The judge droned on: "What is truly reasonable, as in

'reasonable doubt'? And how can doubt be reasonable or unreasonable? And beyond—as in 'beyond a reasonable doubt'—how far beyond? Two city blocks, fourteen feet, beyond a doubt that the sun will rise tomorrow? I am confused already. But then, this jury will be wiser than I."

"I object to this volunteered, irrelevant rhetoric," Sewell said, rising to his feet. "The law is clear and undisputed. All we are required to prove is that the defendant, Lillian Adams, is guilty beyond a reasonable doubt."

"Yes, of course, Mr. Sewell, I quite agree." The judge shrugged his shoulders, as if any fool would agree.

Then more silence.

Sensing that the judge was in need of assistance, Benjamin Breslin, the clerk, offered lifeless words: "Your Honor, before we recess until tomorrow morning, do you want to admonish the jury?"

In a voice on the margin of a mumble, the judge said, "You are not to read newspapers, or listen to the radio concerning this case, and you are not to discuss this case with anyone, including each other." He gave the clerk his best "Does that satisfy you?" look and dismissed the jury until the following morning.

As usual, the judge drove to Hardy Tillman's tire store and filling station for his evening libation. The shelving on the back wall of the station was composed of twelve-inch planks filled with gallon cans of antifreeze and quart cans of motor oil of various brands. The concrete floor was black with old oil and smelled like rubber, grease, and gasoline.

"One lives by habit, wouldn't you say, Hardy?" The judge eased himself stiffly into the worn-through over-stuffed chair across from his friend.

"What you talking about? You okay?" Hardy opened

the old Sears refrigerator, pulled out a beer, and handed it to the judge. Hardy had scars on both eyebrows. His nose had been broken multiple times and had been patched and repatched, so that it bulged at the top and fell off precipitously to the left. His coveralls, laden with grease as thick as cowhide, were evidence of where he'd spent most of his life—under the bellies of uncounted motor vehicles.

The judge looked at his bottle of beer to absorb its answers. "I mean, you live today like you lived yesterday, which means that life becomes a meaningless redundancy."

"Yeah, I suppose so," Hardy said, "whatever that means." He lifted his bottle. "Here's to Lillian Adams." Then thinking better of it, he said, "I suppose you can't drink to her, you being the judge and all."

The judge took a long draw from the bottle. From the time they were kids in the schoolhouse across Fish Creek, he and Hardy had remained close friends. Hardy had been good at fixing things, shooting hoops, and could whip any kid in his grade and most of the older kids, as well. In those days, Hardy and the judge enjoyed a sort of unspoken pact: Hardy was better at fistfighting than the judge, and the judge excelled in the "book stuff," as Hardy called it. They'd supported each other along the way as circumstance required.

"You got that jury pretty well confused on that 'reasonable doubt' business," Hardy said. "It was pretty smart the way you was working to get a hung jury for Lillian."

"I don't know what you're talking about," the judge said.

"You were talking about justice and all. I say it wouldn't be justice for a woman like her to be took out of circulation."

"Aren't you a little too old for those kind of thoughts?"

"A man is only as old as his genitals," Hardy said. "That being the measure, I'm just short of sixteen."

"Tell me more," the judge said, meaning the opposite.

Then Hardy said, "There's something a little bit strange about a rich bastard like old Adams who has himself a couple billion and then comes to a pissy-ass little burg like Jackson Hole to live. He ain't got no friends here, and they're living in that old log house up on the hill that's been falling apart for Lord knows how long. I say something a little queer was going on there."

"Lillian convinced him to build a brewery here. That's what was going on."

"Well, I suppose." Hardy gave the judge a long look. "You feeling all right about what's going on there in your court?"

The judge was silent. What could he say to his old friend? Should he say it appeared that Sewell was winning? Should he say it would kill Betsy if he let that happen, and that he wouldn't know how he could bear it himself—that he had to stop the conviction, but he didn't know if he could?

"You got to get her out of there," Hardy said. "The world is better off with them kind running free." Then he looked over at the judge to apologize and saw that his old friend seemed to have fallen asleep. When it was time for him to go, he touched the judge lightly on the shoulder, but the judge had been awake. When he opened his eyes, they were sharply focused—on what, Hardy couldn't tell.

"Betsy will be waiting supper for me," the judge said.

CHAPTER 14

IN CHAMBERS, JUDGE Murray slipped his judicial robe over his blue flannel winter shirt. No tie. He brushed the folds of his robe over his "golden-age belly," as he called it. With both hands, he smoothed back the sparse remnants of a once-thick bush of hair, stroked the undisciplined hairs of his gray beard, entered the courtroom from the side door, and faced the three steps upward to the bench as the packed courtroom watched. He took the steps with an imposed steadiness on unsteady legs.

Benjamin Breslin hit his gavel and intoned, "All rise."

The dutiful stood in unison like churchgoers about to sing "Rock of Ages." Joe Morris, a veteran, struggled up on his artificial legs and worn crutches, both legs left at the Anzio beachhead during World War II.

The judge ordered the audience seated, then settled into his chair. The small reading lamp on his bench reflected light across the long, deep valleys of his forehead and the ravines that cut through his cheeks. His mouth was wide and his ears liberal. The weary light reflected a marbled image of an old man whose features lent authority to his thin face.

Squatting lamps with green shades provided thin yellow illumination on each attorney's table. At Coker's table, the lamp reflected a flat, lifeless light on the face of Lillian Adams. Her face was carved in white marble, like a statue at the hands of some nameless ancient Greek sculptor—stonelike, yes, immobile and without expression.

The judge glanced down at the woman whom he'd known since she was a child. He wouldn't have recognized her. He saw the early lines of pain that had begun to form around her eyes—pain from the loss of her husband or from the relentless stabbing of guilt?

While the courtroom waited, the judge began reading the indictment to himself. His lips moved silently at the grinding words of the law that described first-degree murder—a killing with malice aforethought—that Lillian Adams had first planned and then intentionally killed her husband.

The judge began to feel heady. His brain, like an undisciplined hound, had run off. He kept trying to call it back. He motioned to the clerk to come to the bench. He heard himself whisper, "Are we not all waiting for that dreadful moment, Mr. Clerk?"

"What dreadful moment, Your Honor?" the clerk asked. He reached for the water pitcher on the judge's bench and filled the judge's glass. He heard the ambient rustling of the restless crowd impatient for the trial to begin. "Should I call a recess, Your Honor?"

"The murder demon lurks insidiously in all of us, Mr. Clerk, and we deny it with all due vehemence." He looked down at the prosecutor, Haskins Sewell, who glared up at him with a jaw-tight sneer. More than once the judge had said to himself, I ought to kill that man for the good of society. Of course, he would never utter such words aloud, not even to Betsy. Everyone suffered unspeakable fantasies from time to time—fantasies that provided a healthy means by which to render harmless the ever-lurking murder demons.

"You remember what Sewell did to old Joe Skivington?"

The clerk stared at the judge without answering.

"Sewell charged that poor man with a fraud he hadn't committed, and Sewell knew it—you remember Old Joe, who was treasurer of the board of the Farmers' Co-op." The judge's eyes were fastened on Sewell. "Old Joe believed that a man's reputation was all a man had, and he said even if he were acquitted by the jury, he'd never get his good name back. He shot himself in the head, Mr. Clerk. You remember that."

"I remember the case, Your Honor."

"The board audited his books, and they were immaculate to the penny," the judge said.

"I heard that, Your Honor, but we have a case here to try and—"

"Sewell had that audit in his possession all along. He was fighting Old Joe to get on the co-op board. I remember it all. Sewell murdered the man. And when Joe's widow put in for compensation, Sewell contested it, and she had to go on welfare with their three kids."

With obvious concern, the clerk said, "Your Honor, is there something wrong?"

The judge, annoyed, looked down at the clerk. "Something wrong? Yes, of course there's something wrong," he said. "I should have thrown Sewell's case against Old Joe out of court. I could have, you know. I could have," he repeated. "But, Mr. Clerk, there was nothing on the record that would allow me to dump the case. Sewell made a perfect record."

"We could talk about this later, Your Honor," the clerk said. "The people are waiting."

"They will have to wait a long time for justice," the judge said.

"Your Honor, I'm going to call a recess." The clerk turned to the audience. "We will stand in recess until tomorrow morning at nine A.M." The clerk started to help the judge down from the bench, but the judge rejected the clerk's hands. "How are you feeling, Your Honor?"

"I feel fine, Benjamin," the judge said. He patted the clerk on the arm. "I feel very fine." As the crowd of onlookers left the courtroom, the judge continued to sit at his roost on the bench.

My God, the judge thought. I can smell—actually smell—the history of this courtroom. He shook his head in disbelief and felt the pulse in his wrist to make sure he was alive. "Yes, Benjamin, I can actually smell the lawyers who fought their battles in this courtroom. Can't you smell their sweat and their foul cigar breath? Surely you can smell them, Benjamin. The jurors smelled, too, and the accused—oh, Benjamin—the poor accused! I can smell that hideous odor when the jury pronounced its sentence of death. That odor can never be expunged from a courtroom. Never. Surely you can smell that, Benjamin."

The clerk looked hard at the judge and coughed nervously.

"You can draw the names of the jurors in the morning," the judge said.

He carefully stepped down from the bench and turned toward his chambers.

"The jury has already been selected, Your Honor," Breslin said.

"Oh, yes, of course," the judge replied. He took a step toward his chambers. "We should ask the commissioners for funds in next year's budget to repaint the courtroom—that ghastly smell in here, you know."

CHAPTER 15

"I FED YOUR birds," Betsy said as the judge opened the cabin door. She was setting the kitchen table for dinner. He shook the snow from his mackinaw and tossed it on the bench. He was greeted by an inviting smell of something toasting in the oven. The old dog, Horatio, named after Hamlet's most trusted friend, came waggling up for his pat on the head and the judge's scratching under the old dog's collar. "I fed your dog, too," she said.

She opened the oven door and pulled out the roast beef, his favorite. She wore her hair in long gray braids, like a Shoshone Indian woman, and sometimes she hung a beaded breastplate from her neck, one with the red Shoshone rose on a white-beaded background. "How did it go today up in your crazy house?" Same question she always asked. But her worried face exposed a woman asking for an answer she didn't want to hear. She waited.

No answer.

"I should go to the trial," she said. "But it's like the doctor operating on your child. You should be there, but not in the operating room."

"Yes," he agreed. "And if I know you, about the time Sewell said anything against Lillian, you'd be all over him like a herd of cats on a sick rat, and I'd have to send my own wife to jail, and that'd give Sewell grounds to disqualify me. Then what?"

"Everybody thinks Lillian killed her husband," Betsy said, pouring his coffee. "Judy Roberts told me she knows Haskins Sewell, and she says he's an honest, churchgoing Christian man. And he wouldn't charge Lillian if she wasn't guilty."

"He'd charge Jesus Christ if he thought it would get him an advantage," the judge said.

"Judy Roberts told me she was called for jury duty."

He tried to remember: Had Judy Roberts gotten on the jury while he was on one of his excursions?

"Did Judy Roberts get on the jury?" Betsy asked.

He didn't answer, took a sip of his coffee, and hoped she wouldn't ask again.

Concern captured her face, but she didn't press him.

Then he heard himself saying, "Time changes people."

"Not Lillian," Betsy said. "Not in the important ways. Did time change us?"

"I suppose," he said.

"No," she said. "Time didn't change us. I still feel the same about you. It's not so crazy, but I still feel it," she said.

"Have you ever thought of murdering someone?" the judge asked.

"Don't be silly—except when you come home all silent and sullen because things went crazy in your crazy house." She served the roast beef with its steaming gravy over the potatoes and carrots. "Judy Roberts says that everyone knows how violent Lillian Adams can be. I told her she didn't know what she was talking about.

I felt like shooting her. I probably would have if I'd had a gun."

"We all have a little violence in us," he said.

"We're a civilized people, not savages still in the jungle. And Lillian has always been one of the best and the brightest."

"Bright people commit murder."

"You surely don't think she's guilty, do you?"

He didn't answer.

She walked over to the judge and stooped down, her face up close to his face.

"You surely don't believe she's guilty, do you?" she asked again.

"Of course not."

"I've seen inside that girl. We talked on our field trips. Nature has a way of opening doors to deep places in a person. You always said that yourself. She never cared about money. She had enough of her own."

The judge nodded again.

"Can you save her?"

"Yes," he said, but he looked away. He was supposed to be God in his courtroom. Surely God could save her.

He didn't feel like even a demigod. He felt tired and powerless. Often the decisions a judge was required to make came hard. The law was hard—hard to discover, hidden as it was in the tomes of endless cases written by other judges, who wore their political ambitions under their robes. And the law, once discovered, was even often harder to apply.

He was alone. He had no one with whom to share his feelings, nor to discuss his damnable conflicts—not even Betsy. And she needed a strong man—one she could respect. What would she think if he came home and confessed, "Honey, I'm not what you think I am. I'm just a scared old man with extraordinary responsibility, and I'm not qualified to make the decisions I'm required to make"? Almighty God, the ultimate judge, must be very lonely, he thought.

Why couldn't he leave Lillian's fate to the jury? That was another cruel fiction sold to the people—about the collective wisdom of juries, and how they protected the people's rights. The judge decided what evidence the jurors would hear. The judge decided what law would govern the case. The judge decided how he'd display his feelings toward the lawyers and the witnesses and thereby influenced the jurors. Claiming that a jury actually decided the outcome of a case was like arguing that schoolchildren ran the school. They occupied their seats in the classroom and followed the instructions of their teacher and recited what they were taught. Somehow, as powerless as he felt, he would find a way to use his power.

"Sewell knows Lillian's not guilty," Betsy said. "He's the one committing the crime. And he wants your job." She slammed the oven door shut. "He's the one who ought to be shot. In the head."

CHAPTER 16

"CALL YOUR NEXT witness, Mr. Prosecutor," the judge ordered Haskins Sewell.

Momentarily, Dr. Roger Norton entered the courtroom. Norton's gait was straight and steady, and he was absorbed in the business at hand. He brought to mind a banker attending a bothersome foreclosure. He lived in Idaho Falls. Absent a qualified pathologist in the county, he'd been appointed by the Teton County commissioners as the county coroner. He was a small man with stiff, squared shoulders, which gave the appearance of having been framed out by a careful carpenter. His hair, in a military-style crew cut, was graying at the temples. His flat belly reflected one who cared little for the most common pleasures.

The coroner raised his small white hand to be sworn. "Let me see the hands of a man," the judge liked to say, "and often his soul will be revealed." Yes, the coroner's are hands that cut up dead bodies, the judge thought, soft, antiseptic, the nails trimmed to the quick. Then he examined his own wrinkle-laden hands covered with complicated blue veins.

Sewell had met with the coroner the night before in Sewell's office. "Let's go over your testimony one more time," Sewell said. "Let's make sure that Coker doesn't cross you up again like he did the last time, when he got you to admit that the corpse could have been dead thirty-six hours, which made the defendant's alibi stand up."

"I only know what I know," Dr. Norton had said in his lean way.

"And Coker always wants to play the 'possibilities game,' so remember, anything is possible. Tell Coker when he gets into his possibilities bullshit that it's possible a herd of giraffes will come stampeding down Main Street today—that's possible, but not probable."

Once settled in the witness chair, Dr. Norton crossed his legs and slightly pulled up his left pant leg to release the pressure at the knee. He signaled to the prosecutor with a slight nod of his head that he was ready. Sewell's first questions summarized Norton's education and qualifications. Then without a change in pace or sound, Sewell said, "Tell the jurors how you became involved in this case."

"I was summoned to the death scene by the sheriff and found Horace Adams the Third slumped over his desk, the top of which was covered with blood," Norton replied. "Whatever items that had been on the desk at the time of death, Deputy Arthur Huffsmith had already gathered. He was appointed as custodian of the evidence by the sheriff. In short, the deceased suffered a bullet hole in his forehead, through and through."

"Did you examine the body at the scene?" Sewell asked.

"No," Dr. Norton replied. "I didn't make a full examination of the body until my autopsy at the mortuary. It was there that I first closely observed the entry wound."

"What do you mean, 'entry wound,' Doctor?"

"I mean the murderer's bullet entered the front—in the forehead."

"Objection!" Coker hollered. "Objection!"

Judge Murray leaned over the bench toward Coker. "What is the problem, counsel? And please quiet down. You're scaring the rats out of the basement."

Laughter in the courtroom.

Coker glared at Sewell. "You ask what is the problem? This man"—he gestured toward the coroner—"has just told the jury this was murder, when it was suicide!"

"Your objection is sustained," the judge ruled.

"That's not enough, Your Honor." Coker pointed his finger at Dr. Norton. "This same man has just jumped into the jury box with his prejudicial answer. He and the prosecutor probably planned it that way. I move for a mistrial."

"I don't see my witness in the jury box," Sewell said. He shaded his eyes like a captain searching the horizon.

Another rumble of laughter rose from the audience.

Judge Murray hit his gavel. "Enough of this. I instruct the jury that this witness's talk of murder was improper and invades the province of the jury." He nodded at Sewell. "Proceed."

"That's not enough." Coker was again addressing the judge. "This man"—he was still pointing at Dr. Norton— "has intentionally poisoned this jury. He's a pathologist. He commands respect—"

"That's because he tells the truth," Sewell said, interrupting him.

"No, that's because he shines his shoes and wears a clean white shirt to court; we call him 'Doctor' and Teton County pays his exorbitant fees. And, he says what Mr. Sewell has him primed to say."

"I object to those gratuitous comments," Sewell said, striding toward the bench.

"I object to your objections," Coker replied.

"Do you gentlemen know what I'm seeing?" The judge looked out across the courtroom into the unseen distance.

"I couldn't guess," Sewell said.

"I seem to remember a small padded cell that's waiting for lawyers who can't abide by the rules of civility."

Sewell shrugged his shoulders, as if the judge's words prompted no meaning. He turned back to Dr. Norton. "So tell the jury what you observed at the scene."

"I saw blood all over the tabletop and—"

"That's redundant. We know there was blood there," Coker objected.

"Sustained," the judge ruled.

"How large an area did the blood cover?"

"Approximately two and a half square feet."

"What did you observe with respect to the blood?"

"From the dim light of the chandelier, it was difficult for me to come to any conclusions at first glance."

"By observing the blood, could you conclude how long Mr. Adams had been dead?"

"I can only say it was turning dry on the edges, where it had begun to coagulate. I couldn't see the entry wound at that moment because the deceased was facedown, but I could see where the bullet exited the back of the head."

"I object to all of this mention of blood again," Coker said, pounding the air as if to strike Sewell, who stood more than fifteen feet to his left.

"May we proceed with as little blood as possible?" Judge Murray asked.

"Did you observe anything else?" Sewell asked.

"Yes, there was a wide smear of blood on the floor behind the desk."

"On the floor? *On the floor?*"

"Yes, on the floor."

"What do you make of that, Dr. Norton?"

"That calls for a conclusion," Coker objected. "He's trying to put his witness back in the jury box again."

The judge was silent. How far should he enter into this brawl? His continuous ruling in favor of Coker made him uncomfortable. By forcing Coker to object, and after that to object again and again, Sewell was leading the jury to conclude that Coker was trying to hide something from them. But if Sewell had an honest case of murder, why would he be resorting to cheap tricks?

"Your objection is sustained, Mr. Coker," the judge said.

Sewell turned back to Dr. Norton. "Did you perform an autopsy on this gentleman?"

"Yes."

"Would you take us through the autopsy, please."

"We don't need to go through the autopsy," Coker said, immersed in exasperation. "We admit the deceased died as a result of that head wound. This is the prosecutor's continuous attempt to fill this courtroom with more blood and gore."

"I am not responsible for the blood and gore," Sewell snapped back, casting an accusing look at Lillian Adams.

"I'll hear a question or two to see where you're going with this," the judge said.

"Tell us how you examined the brain," Sewell asked.

"Well, using a bone saw, I cut the skull—"

Lillian let out a soft, high whine of deep agony.

"Just a minute," Coker said. "It's one thing to be charged with murder and yet another to endure a description of the mutilation performed on a loved one's body by this coroner. This is a continued and obvious effort to further prejudice this jury."

Sewell responded, "I want the jury to understand the care with which the coroner's examination was made, to remove any doubt as to the authenticity of his opinions."

"We have no quarrel with his opinion as to the cause of death," Coker said.

Sewell turned to his witness. "Doctor, were there any other injuries observed other than the bullet hole through the brain?"

"None."

"Any source of bleeding other than from the head wound?"

"No."

"Do you have an opinion, based on reasonable medical certainty, as to whether the head wound you observed caused instantaneous death?"

"Death was instantaneous."

"Well then, do you have an opinion as to how the deceased got from the floor to the chair?"

"Yes, I do."

"And what is that opinion?"

"Objection!" It was Coker again. But before the judge could rule, the coroner burst out with it, "The body was moved by a person or persons unknown after he was shot and killed."

Coker was charging to the bench.

"We will stand in recess until nine in the morning," Judge Murray said.

CHAPTER 17

THE JUDGE CLOMPED into their cabin like an old horse weary in the harness. When he flopped into his chair, Horatio came sidling up for his pat on the head. The smell of fresh corn bread and chili filled the cabin. The judge liked to quip that Betsy's chili gave him the strength of ten men, and she knew he needed the strength of ten to save Lillian, yes, and them, as well.

"Coker is getting his ass whipped," the judge said. The moment he said it, he realized his thoughtless words would reopen Betsy's wounds.

She pretended not to hear him. She ladled the chili into the bowls and topped it with crumbled bacon and shredded cheddar cheese.

"Eat this," she said, joining him with a small bowl of her own. "You've always said that no one could beat you after eating my chili." She tried to harness her fear.

He took another bite and looked away. "Don't worry. It's going to be all right," the judge said.

Yes, he thought, Sewell had the jury wrapped up in a case dripping with blood—Horace Adams III with a hole through his head—and now it looked like he'd been dragged and put in the chair after he was shot.

"You have to stop Sewell," Betsy said. "You know he makes up his cases." She passed him the corn bread.

"Don't worry. I'm still the judge."

Absently, he buttered his corn bread. "Sewell will never get Lillian. Never. Trust me." He'd never lied to Betsy. But at times, small lies were gifts of kindness.

He ate without tasting. Silence set in. He knew he'd lost control of the lawyers. He had no power over the system. He felt like a warrior without a weapon. Suddenly, he got up, the chili half gone. "Have to let old Horatio out for a run."

That night, restful sleep was stolen from the judge by the ghouls in his dreams. He saw the laughing faces of those sitting on the jury. He admonished them, but they continued to laugh. He threatened them with contempt, but they jeered at him, and some called him an old fool. He summoned the clerk, the man who never laughed. "What is all this insane laughter?" the judge asked his clerk, but the clerk didn't answer. He only laughed.

From a distance, he heard the clerk muttering, "Life has no meaning." How strange, the judge thought, that the clerk should make such a statement as if he'd been immersed in the literature of Kafka. As far as the judge knew the clerk had never read anything.

When the judge wakened in the morning, he was exhausted and confused. He was uncertain about what was real and what had been his nightmares. He stumbled out of bed, and it wasn't until he'd brushed his teeth and examined his face in the mirror that he was able to put the nightmares aside and begin preparing for the day.

"Have you ever dreamed that people were laughing at you?" he asked Betsy as he sipped at his first cup of coffee.

"No. You're probably worried that people are laughing at you because you had one of those spells. Don't worry," she reassured him. "We are all entitled to an occasional detour in our lives."

"A detour," she called it. Nobody would think his spell had been just a detour. He ate an extra egg for breakfast. Protein could help fight against those low blood sugar forays. But he hadn't had any sugar on the day of his spell. Maybe it had been the bread in his sandwich.

When he entered the courtroom after his breakfast, he nodded good morning to the attorneys, the reporter, and the clerk, and after the jurors were seated, he furnished them with his practiced judicial smile. He turned to the clerk. "Where were we, Mr. Clerk, when we adjourned last evening?"

"Your Honor, I believe Mr. Coker was about to cross-examine Dr. Norton."

"Oh, yes, of course. You may proceed, Mr. Coker."

The courtroom was packed, as before. The onlookers eagerly awaited the expected Coker fireworks. Coker's face reflected his raw disdain for the witness, Norton, as he threw his yellow pad with its illegible tracks on the lectern and aimed his first question at the coroner.

"I suppose, Dr. Norton, that before you testified yesterday you had a conference with the prosecutor?" He pointed at Haskins Sewell, who was thumbing through a thick file, his back turned against Coker.

"Yes, I met with Mr. Sewell."

"I wasn't present, was I?"

"Of course not."

"I wasn't invited to hear your secrets."

"We have no secrets."

"And he told you to keep talking about all that blood, didn't he?"

"No."

"He told you to throw in that clever little remark about this being a murder, that poisonous conclusion of yours that the judge told the jury to ignore because it was improper. That's true, too, isn't it?"

"No, it isn't." Dr. Norton glared back.

"I suppose you can't figure out who moved this body, if it was moved."

"That's not my job."

"But you want the jury to believe that the body was moved?"

"It was. The drag marks of blood were clearly discernible on the floor, and his clothing had smears of blood."

"Where are the clothes he was wearing?"

"I don't know."

"What did you do with them?"

"I gave them to Deputy Huffsmith, who attended the autopsy and who was appointed as the custodian of the evidence in this case."

"And I suppose you saved a sample of the so-called blood on the floor?"

"I didn't, no. That would be the job of the criminalist, Sergeant Illstead."

"So you don't know, not even by hearsay, whether the marks you saw on the floor were blood, and if so, whose blood it was, isn't that true?"

"I know blood when I see it," the coroner said.

"Well, what about this?" Coker walked up to the coroner, holding out his sleeve for the witness to examine. "Is this blood?" The witness glanced at the lawyer's sleeve, where a brownish red substance appeared.

"This is improper cross-examination," Sewell objected.

"Is it blood, Dr. Norton?" the judge asked.

"I wouldn't know," the witness said.

"You wouldn't know? How can you say you wouldn't know?" Coker asked.

"It's easy, I wouldn't know."

"Well, well, well. Could it be catsup?"

"Perhaps."

"Could it be red paint?"

"Perhaps."

"Could it be raspberry jam?"

"Probably not."

"But maybe? Maybe it is raspberry jam?"

"An outside chance."

"Do you make your decisions as a scientist on outside chances?"

"I take in all of the facts available, my years of experience, and give my opinions."

"You have had as many years' experience, perhaps more, looking at catsup than at blood, isn't that true? I mean, you eat catsup on your hamburgers, don't you?"

"I don't eat hamburgers."

"A good scientist doesn't base his science on something he assumes, don't you agree?"

"One can assume the obvious."

"So you've forgotten to tell us something, haven't you, Mr. Coroner?" Coker demanded.

"What would that be?"

"You've not told us the time you arrived at the Adams residence and how long the deceased had been dead when you first saw him."

"I wasn't asked."

"I wonder why you weren't asked."

"You would have to ask Mr. Sewell. I only answer the questions I'm asked."

"But you talked about your testimony with Mr. Sewell before you came here today—talked about it behind closed doors in Mr. Sewell's office, isn't that true?"

"Yes."

"And you discussed the time of death, didn't you?"

"I don't remember."

"You don't remember?" Coker's voice was alive with dramatic disbelief.

"How can you tell this jury that you can't remember setting the time of death for the prosecutor, but you can remember every little gory detail about the blood?"

"That is argumentative, purely argumentative," Haskins Sewell objected.

The judge examined his hands, his unattractive, powerless old hands—good-for-nothing hands, except to scratch behind Horatio's ears, and to wave them about in his futile scolding of the lawyers.

"That is argumentative," Haskins Sewell insisted.

The judge seemed absent for the moment.

"Your Honor, please. Please. May we have a ruling?"

"Your objection is sustained." I can still make a correct ruling, he thought, even with the smattering of functional brain tissue that remains in my head.

"So you don't know the precise time of death?" Coker asked.

"The time of death is always an approximation."

"Does that mean it's another one of your guesses?"

"It is an opinion based on reasonable medical probability."

"An 'approximation' is a reasonable medical probability?"

"Yes."

"'Reasonable'?" Coker echoed. "Who says it's reasonable?"

"I say so."

"Very well. You're asking us to just take your word for it?"

"If you put it that way."

"And another expert might ask us to take his word for a different time, even though his opinion varies substantially from yours, and even though he says his opinions are also based on reasonable medical probability, isn't that true?"

"I don't know what another expert would say."

"What did you do, if anything, before you left the death scene to establish the time of death?"

"I checked the body temperature rectally."

"Rectally? You checked it rectally? Why did you do that?"

"It's an established fact that the rectal temperature drops at an average of one and a half degrees per hour."

"So from this measurement, what did you conclude?"

"I concluded that the deceased had been dead four hours by the time I arrived at the Adams residence."

"Now that's another guess you've made, isn't that true?"

"No, it's a reasonable medical opinion."

"Yesss," Coker said. He drew his cynical "yessss" out across the courtroom.

Sewell jumped up. "This sarcasm, this scorn, is inappropriate, Your Honor."

The judge turned to Sewell. "Well, Mr. Sewell, when Mr. Coker says 'Yes' in the record, he's only agreeing with your witness."

"It didn't sound like agreement to me," Sewell said.

"Was it agreement, Mr. Coker?" the judge inquired.

"Hardly."

"You mean that yes means no?" the judge asked, scowling.

A skiff of sniggers from the audience.

"I mean," Coker replied, "that every modern authority on this subject holds that a thermometer up the rectum of a dead person is unreliable for establishing the time of death."

"Ask the witness," the judge said.

Coker pressed on. "Do you argue with the authorities who say that the use of the rectal thermometer is a guarantee of inaccuracy?"

"I wouldn't go that far."

"Don't you agree that a considerable weight of reasonable medical opinion holds that a rectal examination should never be used in suspicious deaths, that no instrument should be inserted into the rectum before trace evidence has been sought?"

"I haven't given that any thought."

"Well, please give it thought. Did you make a rectal examination of the corpse before you took his temperature?"

"No, I did not."

"Let me say it then: You did not follow standard medical procedures, isn't that true?"

"I did what I thought necessary under the circumstances."

Coker rolled his eyes upward to record his dismay. Then he asked, "What is meant by 'the bracket of probability' as it applies to the time of death?"

Norton studied the ceiling. "It means that the time of death falls within a time period—likely not sooner than a certain time and likely not later than a certain time."

"But you've testified to a certain time."

"No, an average time."

"You didn't say it was an average time. You said that the deceased had been dead four hours."

"He is arguing with the witness," Sewell objected.

"Well then," Coker said before the judge could rule, "what time do you guess the deceased died?"

"I arrived at the Adams residence at five A.M. If the deceased died four hours earlier, he would have been alive at approximately one A.M. the same morning."

"What times did you use to arrive at your average?"

"What do you mean?"

"You said four hours was an average time. Between one in the afternoon and nine in the evening makes an average of four hours. Is that how you arrived at the time of death?"

"Of course not."

"Well then, between three in the afternoon and eleven at night is an average of four. Is that how you arrived at the time of death?"

"No."

"You said an average of four hours," Coker repeated. "In the last example, the time of death, averaged between three and eleven, would be seven in the evening. Is that how you decided the time of death?"

The coroner looked up to the judge as if seeking help.

"Is this another example of what you refer to as a 'reasonable medical probability'?" Coker asked this side of a sneer.

No answer.

"You don't know when Mr. Adams died, do you?"

"I've given my best medical opinion."

"Well then, tell us what was the first thing you did at the scene?"

"I took in the scene. I examined the deceased without moving him. I then lifted his head to observe the entry wound. I made notes of my observations."

"Did you talk with the officers who were there?"

"Yes."

"What time did you leave the scene?"

"About an hour later."

"You say you arrived at five A.M.? So you would have left at approximately six A.M.?"

"Yes."

"Were you present when these photographs were taken by Sergeant Illstead?"

"Yes. He took them just before I left."

"I notice by these photographs that the deceased is still fully dressed."

No answer.

"So what you are telling us is that you arrived at the scene, you somehow had the deceased lifted from his chair, you pulled down his trousers and shorts and inserted your thermometer into his rectum, and then you pulled his trousers up again, put him back in the chair, and Sergeant Illstead took these photographs?"

"May I refer to my notes?" Dr. Norton asked. "Yes, I see that I didn't take his rectal temperature until he was at the mortuary."

"What time would that have been?"

"Sometime after six. My notes don't reveal the time."

"That could be one minute or ten hours."

No answer.

"What was the temperature outside at the time?"

"I don't know."

"It was considerably below room temperature, was it not?"

"I suppose."

"Do you know how long the deceased was outside in the cold in the hearse before he was finally removed inside to the mortuary?"

"Not exactly."

"And even the workroom in the mortuary is somewhat below room temperature, isn't that true?"

"I suppose."

"So the longer the deceased was located in cold or cool rooms, the faster his body temperature would have lowered, isn't that true?"

"Yes."

"The one-and-a-half-degrees-per-hour loss of body

temperature is based on room temperature, isn't that true?"

"I suppose so."

"His body would have cooled faster than if it had been kept at room temperature, isn't that true?"

"I suppose."

"As an expert, can't you offer an opinion other than 'I suppose'? 'I suppose' is hardly a scientific conclusion, wouldn't you agree?"

Norton offered only his silent glower to Coker.

"Well, don't you suppose?"

Sewell: "He's badgering the witness, Your Honor."

"I suppose," the judge said. "Sustained."

Coker continued: "Considering that he was out in the cold, and after that in a room below room temperature at the mortuary before you took his rectal temperature, according to your formula he must have died on his way to the mortuary or in the mortuary itself."

"That is ridiculous."

"Yes, isn't it? You don't know when you took his temperature. You don't know the temperatures to which the body was exposed between death and the time you took the temperature reading, and, last, you have no idea how fast or how slowly the temperature of the deceased's body decreased under the circumstances, isn't all that true?"

"I can only testify to my expert conclusion."

"Wouldn't it be your honest testimony that you do not know, and cannot even approximate, the time of death in this case based on the body temperature you took at an unknown time at the mortuary?"

No answer.

"Don't you want to answer my question, Dr. Norton?"

No answer.

"You now admit that you didn't take his temperature at the scene and you don't know what time you took it at the mortuary, isn't that true?"

No answer.

"Would you please answer."

"My notes may be mistaken."

"Something is mistaken here, wouldn't you say, Dr. Norton?"

No answer.

"Perhaps this is why Mr. Sewell didn't ask you any questions about the time of death, don't you agree?"

"I am not able to answer for Mr. Sewell."

"Of course you can't. You know we contend that Mrs. Adams came home about midnight and found her husband dead and sitting at his desk, as shown in State's Exhibit three."

"I don't know what you contend."

The judge had been following his wondering mind. Death does not just sit out there like a bunch of turnips at the grocery store, he thought, because death is beyond the realm, and therefore it cannot be understood, and it ought not be feared, because fear exists only in this realm.

"I'm not afraid of it," the judge heard himself say.

"I beg your pardon, Your Honor," Coker said.

"I said, 'Proceed,'" the judge replied.

Coker blinked half a dozen times, as if to corral his thoughts. Then he started anew. "You talked about the time of death with the prosecutor, didn't you?"

"I said I don't remember."

"And he told you that we have adamantly insisted from the outset that Mrs. Adams was not home at the time of Mr. Adams's death."

"He told me your client claimed she got home about midnight."

"So you knew our contentions here after all, Dr. Norton! And by your guessing and averaging, you attempted to lead this jury to the conclusion that Mr. Adams didn't die until something like one in the morning—an hour after Mrs. Adams arrived home."

"These are not guesses. These are opinions based on—"

"You are quite willing to guess in favor of the prosecution. Couldn't you now guess for the defense? Guess that Mr. Adams was dead five or six hours before you arrived, which would mean he died between eleven and midnight that night, before Mrs. Adams arrived home?"

"No, I don't think I could say that."

"Because this would leave Mrs. Adams's defense still alive and well before this jury?"

"No. There were other matters that I took into consideration," Norton said. "I considered his blood-alcohol level."

"How does this blood-alcohol thing work?" Coker asked Norton, as if he didn't know. He'd defended a hundred drunk drivers and had cross-examined dozens of experts about "this blood-alcohol thing."

Norton spoke directly to the jurors, as if they were a class of medical students. "The amount of alcohol in your bloodstream is referred to as the blood-alcohol level, the BAL, as it were. It's recorded in milligrams of alcohol per one hundred milliliters of blood. For example, a BAL of point ten means that one-tenth of one percent, or one one-thousandth of your total blood content, is alcohol. When you drink alcohol, it goes directly from the stomach into the bloodstream. This is why you typically feel the effects of alcohol quite quickly, especially if you haven't eaten in a while."

"So was Mr. Adams drunk at the time of his death?"

"I would say so. Very. More than twice the BAL for

drunk—he was passed out, or nearly, I would say without hesitation."

"But you don't know when Mr. Adams drank or what he drank, do you?" Coker asked.

"He was drinking scotch."

"Do tell! And so when did you take the blood sample?"

"At the funeral home. As you know, we always do our autopsies at the funeral home. Hopefully, the county will one day provide us with facilities elsewhere." Dr. Norton looked to the jury to solicit their support.

"But at what time did you perform your autopsy?

"About noon."

"Noon the same day? What were you waiting for?"

"It was ungodly early when I was called to the scene." He looked pained. "I went home after my initial examination to catch a few winks. I had a heavy schedule ahead. I got up again about ten-thirty, ate a late breakfast, and went to the funeral home to do the autopsy. I would say about noon."

"You ate before you cut up the corpse?"

A whimper of shock escaped Lillian Adams.

"Objection!" Sewell cried.

"Sustained," the judge ruled in a tired voice before Sewell could state his grounds.

"Do you always eat before you cut up a corpse?" Coker asked. He turned to Sewell, inviting his objection.

"Objection!"

"Sustained," Judge Murray ruled. "You seem not to understand my rulings this morning, Mr. Coker. Should I invite the sheriff to take you on a small trip to you know where?"

"That won't be necessary, Your Honor. I misunderstood your ruling. I thought you ruled that I couldn't ask Dr. Norton if he ate before he cut up the corpse on the day in question. I was asking a totally different question: I wanted to know if he always ate before he cut up a corpse."

"You know better than to play games with me, counsel," the judge said. "The objection is sustained. Proceed if you have any proper questions remaining."

Coker continued, "So, Dr. Norton, if the time of death was one o'clock in the morning, as you guessed it to be, it was eleven hours after death that you finally got around to taking a blood sample, or twelve hours or more if he died at midnight or before?"

"Yes."

"And what did you do with the sample?"

"I sent it to the lab for analysis."

"Yes, of course, but when did the lab get it?" Coker began shuffling through a carelessly arranged stack of papers. "It says here the lab didn't get the sample until five that evening. I suppose you kept the sample in the refrigerator during all that time?"

"I don't remember."

"Is there a refrigerator in the autopsy room?"

"I don't remember one."

"How many times have you done an autopsy in that room?"

"I don't know."

"Hundreds?"

"Perhaps."

"But you can't remember if there's a refrigerator in the autopsy room?"

No answer.

"You certainly didn't take the blood upstairs to the mortician's living quarters and ask his wife to put it in her refrigerator along with the hamburger and pumpkin pie, did you?"

"No."

"Then I take it that this blood sample lay around for five more hours before the lab got it?"

"I wouldn't know."

"Well, something you do know: You know that putre- faction and microbiological fermentation can result in the production of alcohol."

"That's what they say. I never studied that."

"If the deceased died as you guess, at one o'clock that morning, and the blood sample you finally took at noon was left unrefrigerated until it was received by the lab, a total of about sixteen hours elapsed after you claim he died but before the lab received the blood?"

"If you say so."

"And you know that the level of alcohol that can be produced from drawn blood that stands around for a long time before it is tested can be quite high."

"I don't know how high."

Coker looked over at the jury. The jurors seemed con- fused. "That simply means blood can ferment and pro- duce alcohol, the same as grape juice can ferment and produce alcohol, isn't that true?"

"Yes."

"I mean that if you, Dr. Norton, had had a couple of glasses of wine and you were picked up for speeding and your blood sample was taken, what would you say if you learned that the sample sat around for sixteen hours before it was tested for blood alcohol, and you threw a point two BAL, which meant that you were so drunk that you were nearly passed out while driving?"

"I don't drink," the coroner said.

"And you are sworn here to tell the truth, isn't that true?"

"Yes."

"So the deceased may have been sober as the judge at the time of his death, isn't that also true?"

"I only know what the lab reported as to his blood-alcohol level. I do know they found a near-empty bottle of scotch on the desk where he'd been sitting."

"And you don't know whether he, one, drank any scotch, or, two, if he did, whether the bottle was mostly empty when he first drank from it—that's true, isn't it?"

"Yes," he said with an indifferent shrug of his shoulders.

Lillian Adams coughed. Coker leaned down and she whispered in his ear. "I see," Coker said aloud. He turned back to the witness. "Haven't you yet discovered that Mr. Adams despised scotch?"

"That would not be in the realm of my expertise," the coroner replied.

CHAPTER 18

As usual, the judge stopped at Hardy Tillman's station for their evening get-together. "I seen you in court today. You ain't enjoying this case a'tall like you used to." Hardy popped a couple bottles of Horace Adams, "a Whore-ass Adams," the wiseacres liked to call the beer.

"Here's to poor old Horace the Third," Hardy said. "One thing I know for sure: Lillian didn't kill the guy. She might have got pissed and whipped his ass, but a shot through the head—no way!"

"Coker was all over the place today," the judge said. "I couldn't figure out where he was going with his cross-exam on Adams's blood-alcohol level."

"Coker was trying to show that the old boy was sober when he was shot," Hardy said. "The way Sewell's got it, Lillian walked up to a drunk man and shot him while he was passed out, or damn near."

"I would have argued that Adams was intending to kill himself," the judge said, "that it took a lot of bottle courage to do it, that he drank damn near a fifth of scotch to get his courage up, and, drunk, he finally pulled the trigger. That makes more sense."

"Well, I don't know about that," Hardy said. "If I was old Coker, I'd be telling the jury that you couldn't believe a damn thing Sewell told them, that Sewell tried to pawn off a sober man as drunk so he could claim that Lillian shot a drunk man who couldn't protect himself—and that Sewell's whole damn case is a made-up pile a shit."

"Don't know why I missed that," the judge said. He looked tired. "Supposedly, Adams wrote that suicide note," the judge said, reaching into his shirt pocket and extracting a slip of paper. "I copied it. I wanted to give it some thought. Does this sound like a man, drunk or sober, who's about to shoot himself in the head?" He read the note aloud to Hardy:

Thanks for the good ride, Darling. I'm getting out before the roof caves in. This is total proof of my love for you.

Love, always,
Horace Quincy Adams III

"'Good ride'?" Hardy asked. "Maybe a drunk cowboy would have said 'good ride.' But old Adams never was on a horse in his life. And roofs don't cave in for them eastern guys. They live in them stone houses with them tile roofs and all. No, that don't sound like something old Adams would have wrote." Hardy took a long double swig on his beer. "Besides, I hear that old Adams was losing it pretty good. I had an uncle that was like that. Hope it don't run in the family."

"And would a man about to shoot himself in the head sign his name Horace Quincy Adams the Third?" the judge asked. "Wouldn't he just sign it, Horace?"

"You got something there," Hardy said. "On the other

hand, suicide is a pretty formal thing, don't you think? Cause of death and all got to be made clear so nobody else gets blamed for it. I wouldn't want to sign my name just Hardy. I'd want to put my full moniker out there— Hardy Raymond Tillman—so it looked plumb legal."

"I wouldn't have let that supposed suicide note go to the jury, but both parties agreed to it, so I had no choice," the judge said. "Sewell probably wants the jury to see it so that down the line he can prove it's a forgery. He's going to blame Lillian for writing it. And Coker wants it in because he thinks it's a forgery, too, and that Sewell is responsible for putting fake evidence to the jury. That's how I've got it figured." The judge shoved the copy of the note back in his shirt pocket.

"I'll tell you one thing," Hardy said. "You'd better watch out for that Sewell. The rumor's floating around that he's going to run for judge again. He's been wanting that job for as long as I can remember. His term as DA is up this year, and you'll be up for reelection, too."

Judge Murray took another draw on his Horace.

"The guy figures you're an easy mark," Hardy said. "Some out there are saying you shoulda retired a couple years ago. And watch out for that sumbitch Sewell. He's got more balls than a blind lion trainer."

The judge got up and walked toward the door. Hardy followed. "I have to go feed Horatio. Betsy's probably already cooking supper."

"And some are saying, including me, that you and Betsy ought to give up living like a bunch of hermits out there in the woods. You ought to come into town, get yourself a nice little cabin or something, and get civilized." He laughed and patted the judge's back.

"We want to live out there," the judge said. "I like the birds. I like the wild geese on the river. She's got her studio in the back of the cabin. She's—"

"Oh hell," Hardy said. "Wrong again." Then he gave a laugh that sounded like the braying of a musical mule.

That evening, the judge told Betsy how Hardy had mentioned that people were saying the judge was too old and should retire.

"Well," she said, "Hardy always claims a good story needs a little embellishment."

"Yes, but a man has to pay attention to what people are saying. Sewell is waiting for me to make the first mistake."

"You give Sewell too much credit," she said. "You're the judge. You're the one with the power. If he gets out of hand, you can throw him in jail."

"No," the judge said, "he's the only person in the county who can do me in. He can charge me with any crime he and the sheriff decide to make up. I've seen them do it more than once. And even if the jury acquitted me, the people would say I got off because I had a smart lawyer."

"Who would you get to defend you against that lying, rotten weasel?"

He didn't wait to think about it. "Tim Coker, of course."

"It will all be all right," Betsy suddenly said. "I'm having one of my 'all-right feelings,' and they've always been right. They started when I married you."

She walked to a small room on the far side of the cabin. She lifted a canvas off the easel and started to the kitchen with it. She set the painting on a kitchen chair and stepped back to inspect it. Then she said, "I agree. Sewell is a danger to us. But he's always been, and we've made it this far." Betsy stared at the painting as if, in the full light, she were seeing it for the first time.

"Do you remember when I painted this?" she asked. It was a small painting with a bright but disappearing horizon, like the work of the great nineteenth-century English painter J. M. W. Turner, "the painter of light." Instead of sailing ships embattled against a sky exploding in fire, Betsy had painted the lily pond where they'd first met. A tall man and a small woman were silhouetted against the calm waters, also turned to fire. Their shadows covered the full width of the pond and disappeared into the dark bank across the way. He looked at the painting for a long time.

"This must be us," he finally said.

She offered a small, tender smile.

"It has to be us," he said. He turned and walked to the window.

CHAPTER 19

LILLIAN AND HORACE had been out for a stroll on their way to lunch when they came upon an old woman pushing a baby carriage filled with junk and a worn, filthy sleeping bag. She stopped at a garbage can and began sorting through its contents.

"If you want to help somebody," Lillian said to him, "there's the kind that need help."

"They made bad choices," he said, his voice void of pity.

"Just as your mother made a bad choice?" She caught herself. "I'm sorry. I wish I hadn't said that."

He looked at Lillian and then away. "She married my father. She didn't have to."

She saw the pain in his face. "What do we ever really know about the person we marry? Once the 'I dos' are said and the clothes of romance are shed, Lord knows what we'll find underneath."

"I've made bad choices," he said. "You take the leap, like a blind bee smelling the honey. And then the law gets involved where it doesn't really have any business."

"The law?"

"Yes. After you're married, the law sneaks in and whispers in your new wife's ear, 'You have legal rights now, honey. You can screw him without screwing him.'"

"Right," she said. "Or after the 'I dos' are said, he can claim he has the right to screw her anytime he wants because she is his wife, and it's her wifely duty to give it to him whenever his little dick gets hard."

They were watching the old street woman furiously digging in the garbage. Her hair looked like a discarded mop. Her mouth was open. She had no teeth.

Horace turned away. "For Christ sakes, what are we doing? I can't stand to watch that," he said.

Lillian saw the repulsion on his face. "We're all on the same mission," she said.

"We're not on her mission."

"Yes," Lillian replied. A softness took over her voice. "She's looking for something to eat. And we're on our way to lunch at the best restaurant in Jackson Hole, Wyoming, as good as that might be.

"When it came to choosing a father, your father made a very wise choice," Lillian said. "He chose a father who'd already established a successful brewery. And you were really good at choosing a father, too."

Horace's eyes were locked on the old woman.

Lillian nodded toward her. "She's safe. She has nothing that anyone wants."

Suddenly, Horace said, "That's my mother."

"What are you talking about?"

CHAPTER 20

DR. NORTON, THE county coroner, was still on the stand, and Timothy Coker, like a terrier after a cornered rat, continued his cross-examination.

"So you say that Horace Adams the Third was in rigor mortis by the time he arrived at the mortuary?"

"Yes."

"And what is rigor mortis?"

"It is muscular stiffening following death."

Yes, the judge thought, rigor mortis is that morbid phenomenon that leads the vulgar to refer to the dead as "stiffs." Rigor mortis is life's last protest against death.

"What causes rigor mortis?" Coker asked.

"Who knows?" Norton said, his words shaded with boredom. Then, as if anticipating Coker's next question, he said, "The condition results from a chemical change in muscle protein, the precise nature of which is unknown."

"Another guess, I suppose," Coker said. He glanced at the jury for reassurance. The woman in the middle of the front row nodded, but only slightly.

The judge looked down at Lillian Adams. If she killed

her husband, she might have had just cause. But law did not permit the killing of even a helpless, screaming person in the last torturous throes of death begging to be killed.

The species is nourished on killing, craves killing, and is entertained by killing in books, at the movies, and on television. And as jurors, they are joined together as a legally sanctioned mob of twelve to kill.

We're a nation of killers, the judge thought. We send young men off to wars and put medals on their chests for killing other human beings not much different from themselves. We've perfected killing. With a single bomb dropped on a city, we can kill every man, woman, and child, every puppy dog, canary, and goldfish.

"Was Mr. Adams in rigor mortis when you arrived?" Coker asked Dr. Norton in a near whisper.

"Yes. We had to pry him from his chair, and he was taken to the morgue frozen in that position."

Lillian Adams stifled another gasp.

The judge looked down at her again. He thought that in ways her agony enhanced her beauty. He looked quickly away. He tried not to see her as his child, but as just another defendant at the dock, but the image would not come.

Coker moved behind her and gently laid his hand on her shoulder. "What did that condition—namely, rigor mortis—mean to you?"

"It meant that Mr. Adams had been dead about the time I've testified to—about four hours," Dr. Norton replied.

"Have you made any study about how long after death it takes a corpse to freeze into rigor mortis?"

"No. I've made no studies myself."

"Can you name a single study that you've read on this question?"

"No, not offhand."

Coker let surprise take over his face. "Doctor, you're saying you can't name a single study in the entire world that supports your conclusion that the deceased had been dead only four hours?"

"Not offhand."

"How about with two hands?" The lady in the front row covered her mouth to hide an escaping smile.

Sewell cried, "This sarcasm is uncalled for!"

"Really?" Coker responded before the judge had fully awakened to the latest squabble between counsel. "Well, when did you last read any study anywhere of any kind on this subject, Dr. Norton?"

"I wouldn't know," Norton said.

"You've just been guessing again, haven't you, Doctor?"

"No, this is an opinion based on—"

"He is still browbeating the witness," Sewell objected.

"Move along, Mr. Coker," the judge said.

"All right, I will move along. Are you aware of the study conducted by Niderkorn, who examined one hundred and thirteen bodies and found that rigor mortis did not set in on twenty of the bodies until six hours after death"—he was reading from a large textbook—"that eleven did not go into rigor mortis until seven hours, that seven did not go into rigor mortis until eight hours, and several more did not go into rigor mortis until thirteen hours after death. Are you aware of that standard study, sir?"

"In the name of justice, counsel is now testifying!" Sewell cried. "In the name of justice!"

"Sustained," the judge ruled.

"Well, your question refreshes my memory after all," Dr. Norton said. He put his fingers to his temple. "Yes, I believe that study showed that rigor mortis set in, in the greatest number of cases, within four hours. If one is to give an opinion, it should be based on the greatest weight of the facts. That is precisely what I've done here."

"Well, you admit, do you not, that a substantial number of the dead do not go into rigor mortis until six or more hours after death?"

"It's possible. But then, I am not testifying to possibilities. It's possible that tomorrow a herd of giraffes might stampede down the main street of Jackson, but it is not probable. I'm testifying to reasonable medical probability."

"That's a weary cliché we've heard so many times, Doctor. Mr. Sewell told you to talk about giraffes on Main Street, didn't he?"

No answer.

"Didn't he!" Coker insisted, unbuttoning his suit jacket as if readying himself for a fight.

No answer.

"And aren't you aware of the fact that rigor mortis sets in most rapidly in one who has had prolonged muscular activity, for example, exhaustion in battle?"

"I've heard of that."

"And do you think that this two-hundred-fifty-pound man had been engaged in prolonged muscular activity, so that rigor mortis would set in rapidly?"

"Four hours isn't rapidly."

"Four hours is rapid compared to thirteen hours, as reported by Niderkorn, isn't that true?"

"Argumentative," Sewell objected.

"Overruled." The law is in systemic rigor mortis, the judge thought.

"So you really don't know when this man died, do you?" Coker asked.

"I have my opinion."

"Could your opinion be wrong?"

"Perhaps. But not likely."

"Turn to this jury and tell them, 'I know that Mr. Adams was alive when his wife came home on the night in question.'"

"Objection!" cried Sewell.

"Overruled." The judge knew his ruling was wrong, but he wanted to hear how Norton would handle this.

"Well," the coroner began in a slow, almost melodious voice. He moistened his lips with a rapid tongue. "I think I could say that with reasonable medical probability."

"Are you sure?" Coker demanded.

"Nothing is absolutely sure in this world except death."

"Am I to take that as a no?"

"Take it any way you like."

"As a matter of truth, Dr. Norton, we know very little about the passage we call death," Coker said, as if to himself. He waited. A silence settled over the courtroom.

Finally, Judge Murray said in a near mumble, "We have no experience in dying, counsel. We get only one chance at it."

"Yes," Coker said.

The judge looked up at the chandelier again. "How does one focus on taking one's last breath? How does it feel when the heart takes its last beat?"

"I beg your pardon, Your Honor?" said Sewell.

"How can one do a reasonable job of dying without any experience at it?" the judge asked.

"I think that is irrelevant, if I may say so," Sewell said.

"Yes, of course it is," the judge said. He glanced down at Lillian again. She seemed alone and fragile, her lawyer up there wrestling with the coroner. She began to shiver.

"Mr. Bailiff, what is the temperature in here?" the judge asked.

The bailiff toddled to the thermometer on the west wall.

"Are the jurors comfortable?" the judge asked. All nodded in the affirmative except the woman in the back row second on the left who gave no sign one way or the other. He peered down once more at Lillian Adams, who was shaking as if suffering fever chills. His watch told him it was only 11:15 in the morning. "The court will be in recess until nine tomorrow morning." The sudden arrival of his words surprised him.

The judge rose and moved slowly, unsteadily down from the bench. "Mr. Bailiff, please see to the temperature in this courtroom. Perhaps we can thaw justice from these frozen walls."

CHAPTER 21

THEY WATCHED THE old woman hobble, pushing her
baby carriage down the alley.

"There are untold thousands like her, and nobody
sees them," Lillian said.

"They found my mother dead on a bench in the park.
She froze to death. That old woman is going to die in the
same way." His eyes held Lillian's. "How can it be that no
one in the world, not one person out of billions, cared for
my mother?" He said it again. "Not one. Not even me."

"I could have been like her," Lillian said. She looked
at her hands and moved her fingers as if they'd become
strangers. "I wanted to be a painter, but I didn't have
the courage to starve or sleep on the street day after day
with my palette and paintbrushes, hoping that this is the
day I'll be discovered. I didn't have a Theo van Gogh
as a brother, and my father thought painting was just an
excuse for not having a job."

Suddenly his face lit up, and with a voice exploding with
enthusiasm, he said, "Why not set up a charity to fight
Fate? We could call it 'Fate Fighters,' or something. You
want to be a Fate fighter?" His ignited passion surprised

him. "And we could hire qualified lookouts to comb the streets for women who are Fate's favorite victims—like her. Maybe she was a great painter, or dancer, or poet. We could take Fate head-on. Yes, we'll become the founders of the Secret Society of Fate Fighters."

Lillian smiled. "You always practice that uncomfortable art of sentimentality. But it's one of the things I love about you."

"I keep thinking of my mother," he said.

"Your mother gave a gift to mankind and didn't know it," Lillian said. "If it weren't for her, we'd never dream of establishing the Secret Society of Fate Fighters. Sometimes Fate gets fooled."

They walked on.

"Fate!" he yelled, raising a fist in the air as if Fate resided up one of the great Teton canyons. "I'm coming after you. I'm going to cause you a lot of trouble."

She watched, and was moved by his words. Yet her feelings for the man frightened her.

Still hollering at Fate, he said, "But this once, I'm also going to fight you for what I want."

"What do you want?" she asked.

His eyes grew soft and his lips moved, but no words came. She knew what he wanted. "You want to get married," she said.

"How did you know?" he said.

"Will you cook your seared salmon with caramelized onion and—"

"I promise," he said.

"Will you love me as you've loved me—as nobody has ever loved me?"

"I promise," he said again.

"Then I'm in, all in," and they fell laughing into each other's arms. As quickly, he drew back and grew serious.

They were silent again.

"Are you afraid?" she asked.

"Yes," he said. "Are you?"

"Yes. Can we trust Fate?"

"She brought us together," he said. Then in a distant voice, he added, "If I were to lose it, you know, if I were ever to get to the place where I don't know who I am or anything, would you put me out of my misery?"

She looked away.

Then he said, "I will love Tina as if she were my own blood."

Tina.

Lillian was twenty-four when she married Tina's father, Gordon Ford. She met him in New York, "a male debutante," she used to call him. Never worked a day in his life. Why had she married him? Hunger for security? Loneliness? Her first encounter with the glamour of New York's elite? Whatever the reason, after Tina was born, she soon divorced Ford. In ways, she and Tina were two girls growing up together.

By the time she met Horace Adams III, the luster of her work at the Belmont Advertising Agency had faded. She'd become reattached to the Tetons, and although she had no close friends there, the little hamlet of Jackson Hole seemed to call her home. She longed to escape the craziness and crime of the big city, yes, and she thought Jackson Hole was the right place to rear Tina. She was a difficult child, and she needed the security of a solid, isolated mountain community. And both Betsy and the judge had taken to Tina like adoring grandparents. That was the most enduring gift that Jackson Hole could offer.

Betsy taught Tina to cook the judge's favorite chili, and in the summer Tina and the judge visited the lily pond to watch the wild geese and their gay gray goslings, who followed their mother, one gosling after another, like the cars of a child's toy train. But what the judge once experienced there with Tina gave him pause.

"I saw them last night in my bedroom," she said. "How did they get into my bedroom, Grandpa?"

"What did you see in your bedroom, honey?"

"The geese."

The judge saw her eyes tinged with fear. "You were only dreaming, Tina. And your job is to learn how to separate what you dream from what is really happening. I have trouble like that sometimes, too. Do you know how to do that?" he asked.

She shook her head no.

"You jump up and down three times and wiggle your toes. If it's a dream, you do not feel your feet or toes." Then he laughed, and when he laughed, Tina laughed, too.

"Yes," Lillian had said, "let's get married. I think we can live our lives together better than we can live them separately."

Horace wanted to be romantic.

Although at unexpected times Horace displayed an uncanny insight into "the human condition," as he called it, what she liked most about him were his boyish ways. "I love you, and I don't know how to say anything more about it," he'd lament. "I'm not a poet. It's not fair. I have all this money and I can't write even a silly limerick. Poets have all those pretty words, but most can't buy a decent meal. Life isn't fair." Then he said, "But I love you more than any poet would love you."

"The poetry is in your eyes," she said.

Neither of them had obligatory religious leanings,

but they were married by the aged Episcopal priest, the Reverend Hamondtree. He sat Lillian and Horace down on the front pew of the church and began his standard inquiry. "Why are you marrying this woman?"

Horace looked out the north widow to the towering Grand Teton. He struggled for words. "I don't know how to say it."

The old priest waited with a curious frown.

"Frightens me," Horace said. "I've never felt this way before. I am marrying her because . . ." He reached into his pocket, pulled out a folded paper, and began to read his poem to Lillian:

I was a lost person
And you found me.
I saw . . .

He stopped. Then he tore up the paper into small pieces and stuffed the pieces in his pants pocket. "I'm marrying her because I love her and can't live without her. I wish I could say it better." Embarrassed, he offered her an apologetic smile and looked down to the old worn plank floors of the church.

The small birds under the church eaves were singing.

Finally, the priest broke the silence. "A good marriage is a poem, Mr. Adams."

Lillian grabbed Horace and kissed him.

"Hold on!" the priest said. "Save the kissing for after the vows." He turned to Lillian.

"And why are you marrying this man?" the priest asked her.

"I never thought I would marry again," she said. "I want a husband who loves me, and Tina needs a father who loves her." She looked out at the Grand Teton. "Love is hard to find."

"It's everywhere," the priest said.

"It's been hard for me to find," she said. "But he drowns me in his joy, and marrying Horace will not leave blisters on my soul."

They bought the beaten-up old log house on the hill, and on seventeen acres at the edge of town they started the groundwork for building the new brewery for Jackson Hole. Pure water from a generous well. Good barley just over the pass in Idaho.

"I feel like a salmon that's migrated back to the place where it was spawned," Lillian said. "But not to die."

The sound of her words made him afraid. "I'll never let you die," he said.

"Promise?"

"Not as long as I'm alive."

"Then we'll have to die together," she said, and kissed him deeply, and then again.

CHAPTER 22

TINA VIEWED HER mother's romance with Horace as a hostile act. Worse, she thought they were engaged in a conspiracy to abandon her. She referred to him as "that stupid beast."

When Horace and Lillian were dating, Tina said, "Why do you spend so much time with him, Mother? We don't need him." The girl was nearing six feet, with her mother's dark hair, her father's ivory skin. Her large black eyes seemed to be searching for prey, or, at times, beseeching her mother's succor. She presented herself as a confused adolescent warrior ready to attack, but on the edge of crying, her mouth pouty and puckered.

"He's a client," Lillian said.

Tina stuck her head into the bathroom, where Lillian was putting on her morning makeup. "You don't spend time like that with your other clients, Mother. You didn't get home until one this morning. I think you should go see our shrink, Dr. Brady."

"Well, I happen to like Horace," Lillian said. "And I would remind you: You are not my mother."

"Why would you possibly like him, Mother? He's really old and really weird."

Lillian called after her, "Lots of good people seem weird until you get to know them, Tina. Some people probably think we're weird."

Morning was the worst part of Lillian's day—herding Tina through her toiletry, and into her clothes, and all the time fighting off her barrages of insecurity and anger, her begging and blustering, and the nearly physical effort required to launch her off to school, after which Lillian prepared herself to take on demanding clients and a gang of smart-asses at the office. She hurriedly contained her hair in a classic ponytail that confessed she had no time for the frills and fluffs of the vainglorious.

"I hate him, Mother. He acts like I'm not even alive."

"Horace has never had any children. And growing up, you never had a father to speak of. Maybe you could teach each other."

"I don't want him as a father!"

"None of us gets to choose a father. You never chose yours, and I never chose mine." She hastened to blunt any suggestion of disrespect for her own father. "I was lucky," Lillian said. "Your grandfather is a fine man. Whatever strength I have, I got from him."

"I don't want you choosing someone to play being my father," Tina said.

"And I don't want you choosing the men I go with, either. So how are we going to solve this problem?"

"You should choose me first," Tina said. "I've been with you the longest, and I love you the most."

"You don't know him."

"I think he's just a rich, grubby old primate."

"Where did you learn to talk like that?"

"I love you more than he could ever love you," Tina

said, gathering up her homework and stuffing it in her book bag.

"And I love you more than anyone in the world, Tina. It's a mother's love. It's not the same as love for a mate."

Lillian led her to the door and gave her a mother's kiss. Before Lillian could close the door, the girl said, "I saw you kissing him in the car when you came home last night. It made me want to puke."

After Lillian and Horace were married, they flew to Bermuda for a short honeymoon. He had investments there he'd never mentioned. Boring place, Lillian thought—beaches with fat old men and women with unapologetic bulges pretending not to desecrate the pure white sand and the innocent blue sea. Still, she absorbed the sea's silence and felt its nourishing peace, which was interrupted only by the lapping of small, hesitant waves at the shore.

At times, without announcement, Horace would drift off to some undefined island of his own. He said there was nothing awry. He refused to see a doctor. To reassure her, he reached over and kissed her lightly. He said that when he was with her, he was in heaven, and maybe that was where he'd been. She'd come to dismiss those excursions into another place as his "rich inner life," as she'd come to call it.

During their honeymoon, Lillian left Tina with Tina's grandfather, Jim Mortensen. He was eager to teach his granddaughter how to shoot a pistol, just as he'd once taught Lillian. "Women need to know how to take care of themselves," Mortensen proclaimed. "Nowadays most men don't know how to defend themselves or anybody else. They're little frogs that croak and hop, and that's about all. They couldn't protect you, and it's getting dangerous out there." Tina said she and her grandfather were "a unit." They belonged together.

With his pistol in both hands, and with Tina watching carefully, Mortensen held his arm out in shooting position. "You don't lock your arm. Remember, it's got to handle the pistol's kick. And you cradle your shooting hand in your other hand, just like they love each other. See?" He held the empty pistol in both hands to illustrate. Then he stood behind Tina as she pushed the gun in front of her and took aim.

"Keep both eyes open," he said. "Only amateurs and phonies in cowboy movies shoot with one eye closed. You need 'em both open for perspective."

Tina was pointing the pistol at a photo of General George Custer hanging on the living room wall.

"Now there was one hell of a soldier," Jim Mortensen said. "The know-nothing historians make Custer out to be a fool, and praise the Sioux, the Cheyenne, and the rest of those yappin' redskins like they were the heroes. Well, I'll tell you one thing: If I wanted a man to lead a buncha men into battle, it'd be George Custer. He didn't run from nobody, including a thousand whooping injuns on horseback."

Suddenly, Tina turned and threw her arms around her grandfather. "Why can't Mama find a man like you," she cried, "instead of that stupid beast?" She held on to her grandfather as if he were the last man on earth—and the Indians were attacking.

For two years, Tina had been under the care of the renowned New York child psychiatrist Dr. Josephine Brady. The doctor was an avid mountain climber and rented a cabin every year in Jackson Hole. Lillian held nothing back. She told Horace about Tina shortly after they'd discovered they were getting serious, but his response was always the same: "I'll take you, and everything and everybody you love, as part of me, including Tina."

Why was she attracted to this man? He wasn't handsome like the pretty male faces in the magazine ads. He wasn't an accomplished conversationalist. Often he was silent when she expected a response. And as often his naïveté was on the other side of her expectations. His money was an issue that she'd shelved to worry about later. She thought she had enough of her own money. She felt love for the man, but she thought his money might get in the way.

One night at bedtime, Tina was breathing heavily and her eyes were iridescent and wide. Lillian thought she was approaching hysteria. "Mother, I know you wouldn't have married him if he hadn't possessed you like a witch. A witch, Mother!"

Dr. Brady's advice had been, "Do not engage the girl when she's entered that strange land of hers."

"Was it his money, Mother? If it was his money, that was an awful thing to do. He must have possessed you for you to marry him for money. And he's such a weird old man. Can't you see the wrinkles on his face? Are you that blind?"

"He's not an old man. And you don't judge people's age by the number of wrinkles on their faces. You judge them by who they are, and the life they bring into your life."

"Well, he's so old, he gets lost. I went with him to town like you asked, and he got lost—kept driving around, not knowing how to get back home."

"He's always been that way, Tina. You inherited my good sense of direction, but this little town is new to him."

"A three-year-old couldn't get lost here, Mother. Something's wrong with him."

How could Lillian explain her relationship with Horace to Tina? Tina had experienced no close affiliation with anyone but her. True, Horace was strange during those "excursions." Yes, he was older, but his age was a relief and served to protect her from the mob of horny Don Juans out there begging to be serviced. His wisdom provided what had been lacking in her father, and thrown in as a bonus were his romantic ways, as when he'd come home and drown her with pure love in his eyes and with a fistful of flowers.

Later on, she and Sylvia Huntley were talking about "the man-woman thing," as they called it. "At a certain age, we all secretly wanted babies," Lillian said. "We didn't understand it, but that's what our hormones were hollering for. We bred like dogs. We called it love."

"I never wanted babies—not me, kiddo," Sylvia said. She was a woman Lillian's age—lean and athletic, not the delicate artist type. The roots of her short blond hair were dark. Her large canvases of tough men on hard-ridden horses struggling against weather, wilderness, and wild-eyed beasts hung in the galleries in Taos and Santa Fe. "Do you want babies with him?" Sylvia asked.

"No. For God's sake. I don't want any more babies."

"Well then?"

"But I like being loved. And I like not being alone."

"And the sex thing?" Sylvia asked, as if working down a checklist.

"I don't know how to talk about that. He's older, and he's not a sexual athlete. But men—they're all different. And sometimes they bring something out in you that you didn't know was there, and maybe you like it. You can't just try on sex like a pair of shoes in the shoe store. Besides, shoes are just part of the outfit."

"I never wanted to be barefoot very long," Sylvia said. She'd been married three times. "I see men like I see a painting. I finish one, take a break, and then start on the next. I'd hate to do just one painting in a lifetime. And I wouldn't want it hanging on my living room wall forever."

"Two different kinds of art there. One with a brush and one with a bush," Lillian said.

"I used a brush on my first husband once," Sylvia said.

"What color did you paint it?"

"Made a barber pole out of it."

They were drinking in the Bull Moose Bar. They turned down a couple of invitations to dance before they left. "You're not as much fun to go out with anymore," Sylvia said. "I think you got a serious case of 'settlin' down.'"

Tina was a list of contradictions. Her high school teachers, in their frequent conferences with Lillian, described Tina as "brilliant but . . ." It was the *but* that was the problem. The school counselor tried to downplay Tina's unpredictable outbursts, her days of pouting, her lack of interaction with other students, her combativeness, but, at last, he was unable to avoid calling her "deeply disturbed."

Horace's contacts with Tina had been sparing. When he and Lillian were together, Tina wouldn't come out of her room. When Horace phoned Lillian, and if Tina answered, she'd often hang up. Once, after much cajoling, Lillian got Tina to join them for dinner. Tina glared at her plate, never looked up, never spoke a word, and ate nothing. But they'd been patient. They believed Tina was simply jealous of Lillian's affection for Horace and that she'd get over it in time.

"Mother, he is a warlock, you know. I've seen him doing those things?"

"What things, honey?"

"He walks up and down in front of the books in the library and never takes a book out. He just keeps walking back and forth, and sometimes he's mumbling to himself. He's like that polar bear in the zoo. It walks back and forth and back and forth all day, every day, in its cage. They say that no one goes into the bear's cage because it would kill anyone who did."

"He's just looking for a book, honey. You know we moved his whole library here."

Before Horace and Lillian were married, Dr. Brady had diagnosed Tina as borderline schizophrenic. The doctor explained that the disease is often progressive, and that the girl's symptoms had finally manifested themselves to the point where the doctor could make the diagnosis. She assured Lillian that Tina's condition was probably controllable with continued psychiatric supervision and medication.

"My God! What have I done?" Lillian asked Dr. Brady.

"It's not your fault," the doctor assured her. "Some believe the tendency for the disease is inherited, but others think it may be the result of subtle injuries in pregnancy or at birth. No one really knows."

Lillian folded her arms across her chest, as if to protect herself from further assaults of the shocking truth.

"Teenagers with schizophrenia may suffer hallucinations and become delusional. They may withdraw even from those closest to them, and, from time to time, lose all contact with reality."

"She's so afraid I'll leave her. I always let her know exactly where I'll be at any given time."

"As indeed you should," Dr. Brady said.

"And sometimes she acts as if I'm not there at all. I can't get her to look at me or speak to me or acknowledge that I'm even alive."

"Yes," the doctor said knowingly.

"Should I take her out of school? She's having all kinds of trouble there. She gets in fistfights with some of the boys. As you know, she's large, and she's strong. Her father, my second husband, was six and a half feet tall, and I'm no shrimp."

"As long as she stays on her medication, she'll be better off in the small classes where she is, and where she can get individual attention."

"I can hire tutors."

"She needs social contacts," the doctor advised.

The intensity of Tina's refusal to accept Horace as her stepfather, or even as a member of their household, continued to grow. She blamed him for the destruction of "our happy home." Once, she claimed Horace had tried to poison her. She wouldn't eat if he went near the kitchen.

"I try to keep her busy with her schoolwork," Lillian told Dr. Brady. "At times she can do a week's work overnight. She's so quick. And other times I can't get her to open a book, to watch TV, or even to come out of her room."

"A girl her age can't understand the nature of her condition, so it can be a confusing, terrifying experience for her," Dr. Brady said. "Then add all the normal stresses of teenage life and you understand the real meaning of teenage schizophrenia. It's a world of terror, confusion, and loneliness."

One night after Lillian and Horace had been out to dinner, Tina came charging into Lillian's bathroom. Lillian was getting ready for bed.

"He's dangerous, Mother. You don't understand. He is very dangerous. I couldn't sleep, worrying about you. I have to go to school in the morning, you know."

"Yes, and I have to go to work, too. So go to bed."

"I can't go to bed until you kiss me good night."

With that, Lillian held Tina close to her, kissed her, turned her around and pointed her toward the bedroom door, gave her a small pat on the bottom, followed her into her room, kissed her again on the cheek, tucked her in, and handed her daughter her doggy doll. "I love you most of all," Lillian said. "I will always be your mother until the day I die. That's what's important between us. That's the way it will always be." She turned out the light and shut the door before the girl could say more.

Then she heard Tina crying. "Mother, the voices are arguing."

Lillian went back into the bedroom. "What's the argument about?" she asked.

"Some say I should kill him now. But others say I should wait."

"Tina, don't frighten me like that. You are not going to kill anyone, ever. If you do, they'll take you away from me, and we will never be able to be with each other again."

That night after Tina had finally quieted down, Lillian called Sylvia. They met for coffee at the drugstore, as usual. The place was abandoned except for the pharmacist, who was sleeping, and the clerk up front, who was closing down the cash register. Still they whispered over their cups, the steam from their coffee rising between them.

Lillian looked both ways before she said, "I had to talk to someone. Tina's finally gone over the edge."

"What do you mean?" Sylvia asked.

"She locks herself in her room and won't come out. She screams in there night after night, and I go in, make sure she's taken her meds, and sleep with her and calm her down."

"My God, girl, what are you going to do?"

"I don't know what to do. She's getting worse. I keep calling Dr. Brady, and she says we have to be patient. Dr. Brady has been increasing her meds, but it isn't helping. I'm scared to death. I took her out of school. I'm afraid she's going to kill Horace."

"You have to call the police."

"They'll just lock her up. I can't do that. I'm the only one she trusts. Dr. Brady says I'm the only place she can escape from her nightmares. If I call the police, she'll think I've betrayed her, and she'll never trust me again, and never recover. You don't call the police on your own sick child."

"What about Horace?"

"These days, Horace is out of it most of the time. He wants to help, but he doesn't seem to understand, and if he understood, what would he do? Then he falls off into that strange world of his, and sometimes he's in it for days. He doesn't even know me. Once, when he was clear he understood what was happening to him, he made me promise to keep his condition secret. I promised. I had to share it with someone."

"Of course, honey," Sylvia said, "When my grandfather got old, he didn't know where he was or who he was. He nearly destroyed the family. You have to get Horace to a safe home. You need to be safe yourself."

"I know," she said. "I can't handle two people in the same crazy house who are irrational, lost, and afraid of each other."

That night, Lillian returned home to find Tina screaming hysterically over the body of Horace, a pistol in her hand. "He killed himself," Tina screamed. She screamed it over and over. "The witch killed himself."

CHAPTER 23

SEWELL CALLED SYLVIA Huntley as his next witness. With an air of resolve, she walked to the witness box with strong steps. She was dressed in a navy blue business suit absent jewelry. She was handsome in a way that favored neither sex. After she settled into the witness chair, Sewell charged to the point. "You're the best friend of the defendant, Lillian Adams?"

Sylvia nodded and glared at Sewell like one recoiling from something vile on a dinner plate.

"And you're here under subpoena?"

"Yes." She reached into her purse, removed the folded paper, and held it up.

"Prior to the murder of Mr. Adams, you had a conversation with Lillian Adams?"

"Again?" Coker proclaimed. "Again? Again I move for a mistrial."

The judge slammed his gavel on the bench. "Mr. Sewell, the jury will decide if this was a murder, not you. You know that," the judge said. "Mr. Adams's demise will be referred to as 'a death.'"

"You had a conversation with the defendant, Mrs. Adams, the very night her husband died?" Sewell asked.

"I wouldn't answer any questions about that in your office, and I refuse to now."

Sewell turned to the judge. "I represent to the court that this is a hostile witness and that under the rules I'm entitled to cross-examine her."

The judge excused the jury. Behind closed doors in his chambers, he turned to Sewell. "So you think Ms. Huntley is hostile merely because she doesn't want to talk to you?"

"She's doing more than refusing," Sewell said. "She's made a lot of accusations against me personally. She said I knew Lillian Adams was innocent and that I was prosecuting her in order to make a name for myself, which, of course, is preposterous."

Coker rose slowly, unable to conceal his weariness. He pointed at Sewell. "Mr. Dirty Tricks is at it again. This is one of the oldest scams of all. He wants to ask Ms. Huntley a set of poisoned leading questions, like 'Didn't Mrs. Adams tell you that she wanted to go home and kill the old bastard?' The jurors will naturally think that the prosecutor's questions state the truth, and the reason Ms. Huntley won't answer is because she knows his questions state the truth—that Lillian Adams did indeed go home that same night and kill her husband."

The judge turned to Sewell. "Do you have any bona fide basis for asking leading questions that suggest an answer, such as Mr. Coker fears?" the judge asked.

"Yes, I do, Your Honor. But I'm not at liberty to identify the name of the witness who provided this information to me," Sewell said. "As an officer of this court, my representation to you that I possess a bona fide basis for my question ought to be sufficient under the law."

"Lay a foundation for Ms. Huntley's hostility and I will reconsider your right to cross-examine your own witness," the judge ruled.

Back in the courtroom, Sewell took a step toward Sylvia Huntley and carefully aimed his words at her: "On the night of Mr. Adams's death, did you have a conversation with Lillian Adams at the drugstore concerning her husband?"

"I think I've answered enough questions for you, Mr. Sewell. I will not answer your question. I think you are a miserable son of a bitch."

The judge struck his gavel. "You can't use that language in this courtroom, madam! Mr. Sewell, you've satisfied me that this is a hostile witness. So ask your question again."

Impatiently, Sewell asked, "On the night of the death of Horace Adams the Third, did you have a conversation with Lillian Adams at the drugstore concerning her husband?"

"Answer the question," the judge ordered, and when Sylvia Huntley remained silent, he leaned over the bench. "I said, 'Answer the question,' Ms. Huntley."

"I refuse." She crossed her arms.

"I move for contempt against this witness," Sewell said.

The judge turned to Sylvia Huntley. "You understand you've been asked a relevant question by the prosecutor. There are privileges for some relationships, such as priest and parishioner, doctor and patient, lawyer and client, husband and wife. But there is no such privilege for friends. Do you understand?"

Sylvia Huntley said, "I will not be made a victim by

the law. I am an ethical woman. You force me to choose between my loyalty to my friend and what you claim is my obligation under the law. The choice is not hard for me to make."

"So do you refuse to answer Mr. Sewell's question?" the judge asked.

"Yes, I do."

Again the judge excused the jury and met the parties in his chambers.

"Mr. Sewell, make your offer of proof," the judge said.

"I offer to prove that on the night Mr. Adams died, Mrs. Adams told Sylvia Huntley, 'I ought to kill the son of a bitch.'"

"What is the good-faith basis of your offer?" the judge asked.

"As I've said before, I am not at liberty to disclose my witness."

The judge raised his right eyebrow to a threatening arch. "On one hand, you want me to put Ms. Huntley in jail for refusing to answer your question, and on the other, you refuse to answer mine?"

Coker interrupted them. "He wants the jury to believe Lillian Adams said something incriminating, when she probably was complaining about the kind of sex they were having, or something else that would be confidential between women. We should show a simple respect here both for the dead and the living. Fair's fair. The prosecutor won't tell and Ms. Huntley won't tell."

The judge absently reached for a book on his desk, as if to search for the answer. A witness couldn't come into his court and without legal justification refuse to testify. And a courtroom full of gossip-hungry spectators waited, along with the ravenous media, for the big story of the day: The judge tossed Sylvia Huntley in jail for her refusal to testify. "I'll give the matter my full consideration this evening," the judge said, and recessed court for the day.

Betsy was already cooking supper when the judge got home. The decision he had to make might decide the case. It could deliver Lillian to the death house. He fed Horatio, threw the dog's stick twice, then twice more. Then he returned to the cabin and sat down in front of the stove.

"I heard on the radio that Sylvia won't talk," Betsy said. "Good for her."

"Why?" the judge asked. "She's a witness under oath and had a conversation with Lillian the night of the shooting."

"Why should Sylvia Huntley have to reveal secrets between herself and Lillian any more than two close male friends would tell on each other? If Hardy Tillman told you he'd thought he should kill some son of a bitch, and that person was found shot the next day, you wouldn't tell anyone what Hardy told you."

"Right. I'd probably forget what he told me."

"That's lying," Betsy said. "So I suppose it isn't as bad to lie as it is to refuse to tell the truth."

Betsy often nailed him with her damnable common sense. For Christ sakes, the judge thought, why hadn't Sylvia simply forgotten there'd ever been any such conversation? But suppose there'd been a witness in the drugstore who'd overheard the conversation. Why had Sewell refused to identify the witness?

"Are you going to throw Sylvia in jail?" Betsy's face was tight with concern. "You wouldn't, would you?"

"No," he said.

"I didn't think so." Then she kissed him good night.

The judge lay awake. He heard the sounds of the blizzard outside, the wind howling, the winter-stiffened trees groaning in protest. He listened to Betsy's breathing. He heard old Horatio's occasional yelp in his dreams as he was probably chasing the squirrels of his puppyhood. Then the disharmony of sounds in his ears began to take a new form.

"Careful!" Yes, he heard the word clearly. "Careful!"

"What?" he said.

Betsy stirred.

He sat straight up in bed. "Who's there?" he hollered.

"What's the matter, honey?"

"Didn't you hear that, Betsy?"

"It was only the wind in the spruce trees, honey."

He staggered from bed, his eyes wild, Betsy after him. She turned on the light and shook him. "Wake up! Wake up! It's just a bad dream."

"Didn't you hear that, Betsy?"

"You're just having a bad dream," she said.

At last, he slept. In the light of day, the voice had retreated, and in the early morning the answer came to him, but not from anyplace sane or safe.

CHAPTER 24

THE NEXT MORNING, the judge ordered both lawyers, along with the accused, Lillian Adams, the witness, Sylvia Huntley, and the court reporter to his chambers. Sylvia Huntley, prepared to go to jail, was wearing a pair of comfortable blue jeans, a green woolen sweater, and a pair of canvas house shoes.

Judge Murray spoke to her in a kindly voice. "Madam witness, did you reconsider your position over the past evening? Are you ready to answer the question the prosecutor put to you yesterday?"

"I haven't changed my mind, if that's what you're asking. I will not answer that question." Sylvia Huntley looked torn and tortured.

The judge turned to Haskins Sewell with an imposed, disarming smile. "Mr. Sewell, did you reconsider your position last evening? Are you prepared to reveal the name of your informant?"

"My position remains the same," Sewell replied.

The judge cleared his throat and took Sewell in with the eyes of a patient father. "I have given this matter a good deal of thought. I am not going to speculate on whether your said informant might ever take the stand to tell us anything. I abhor speculation and disavow its worth."

Suddenly, as if possessed, the judge thrust out his arms like Moses ordering the seas to part and proclaimed, "If there were a witness who overheard Mrs. Adams and Ms. Huntley conversing in the drugstore, that witness would presumably be available to testify as to what was said. Mr. Sewell has refused to identify the witness. And although I do not impugn the integrity of Mr. Sewell when I ask his source, he says it is confidential. I am not going to demand more of Ms. Huntley than I demand of Mr. Sewell, an officer of my court—namely, a candid revelation of the facts." He shut his notebook. "Your objection, Mr. Coker, is sustained."

The judge turned to Haskins Sewell. "Ms. Huntley will not be required to answer your question unless you identify your secret witness. You may, if necessary, identify him or her to me in private, but the witness must be identified."

"I want to be heard," Sewell shouted.

"You are ordered not to shout, Mr. Sewell," the judge shouted.

Sewell released a screeching verbal typhoon. "I find your decision utterly out of line."

"Having said that, what else do you wish to say, if anything, counsel? I warn you to be circumspect in your choice of words."

"You've just told the world that you don't trust me. All I have is my good name."

"That's a matter in serious question," Coker chided.

For the first time, the judge felt a tinge of pity for Sewell. But no. He couldn't trust Sewell. "Let us try once more," the judge offered. "Mr. Sewell, let me hear once more the exact question you intend to ask Ms. Huntley."

"I intend to ask her if on the night of her husband's death she had a conversation with Mrs. Adams at the drugstore concerning her husband."

The judge turned to Sylvia Huntley. "Madam witness, what would your answer be?"

"I would refuse to answer the question," she said.

The judge turned to Sewell. "And does your offer of proof remain the same—that on the night Mr. Adams died Mrs. Adams told Sylvia Huntley, 'I ought to kill the son of a bitch'?"

"Yes, it does," Sewell said.

"There you have it," the judge said. "You intend to ask that question knowing full well that the witness won't answer, which can leave the jury with but one conclusion— that Mrs. Adams went home and forthwith murdered her husband. If you have a witness who overheard such a statement by Mrs. Adams, I will allow that witness to testify. Otherwise, you are not permitted to cross-examine Ms. Huntley on that matter. Do you understand?"

"Have you lost your mind?" Sewell shouted at the judge.

An intense silence invaded the judge's chambers.

Finally, the judge said, "I'm not certain I heard you." He reached as if to adjust his hearing aid.

"I'll say it as candidly as I can. I think the Adams woman has robbed you of your senses."

"And what is your evidence, Mr. Sewell?"

Sewell stood up and began to pace. His litany of accusations delivered in his flinty voice punctured the hostile air in the judge's chambers. "You let a murderer out on a nothing bond. You turned her loose to cavort around this county, to the embarrassment of law enforcement and to the endangerment of this community, especially considering the facts that establish her guilt beyond a reasonable doubt."

Sewell glared at the seated judge, the prosecutor's eyes hard, his teeth bared. "Your rulings in this case have been a disgrace to the judiciary. Your history with this woman from the time she was a child is a matter of record. You have never, not once, required her to conform to the law or to decent standards of society."

In truth, the judge thought that Sewell had lost his mind.

Sewell shook a finger at the judge. "You will recall that even defense counsel recognized it was improper for you to sit on this case. And now, now, you prevent me from asking this witness proper leading questions on my assurance that I possess a good-faith basis for my questions."

Be patient, the judge thought. Surely no sane lawyer would be talking to a judge like this. Sewell had gone over the edge.

Sewell gathered new breath. "You granted this woman a divorce when she possessed no legal grounds, indeed, because her husband had allegedly beaten some cur. I am a dog lover, but dogs, unfortunately, have no legal rights. You've systematically, habitually, and intentionally stretched the law beyond all recognition on her behalf." Sewell's voice rose to a high single-noted assault. "And now you've besmirched my honesty, in effect asserting that I have no good-faith basis for my cross-examination of a hostile witness who heard Lillian Adams state she ought to kill Horace Adams the Third." With each step, Sewell's leather soles and elevated leather heels beat at the floor like a metronome. "I have the right to press this witness for her truthful answer under cross-examination. She hides relevant, crucial evidence of Lillian Adams's guilt—and you know it."

Judge Murray spoke slowly, evenly. "I repeat, Mr. Sewell, all you need do is reveal your good-faith basis and—"

"We've just traveled that road," Sewell snapped. "I'm expecting a further report by five this evening."

"What do you mean, 'report'?"

"I have the duty to see that the laws of this state are fully enforced. That includes my duty to investigate any judge who's forsaken his oath of office by engaging in improper conduct with an accused who's being tried in his court."

"I beg your pardon?" the judge said, again reaching for his hearing aid.

"This woman has been free from the day she was indicted. What she's been doing between that time and this trial to ensure her acquittal is the question I'm investigating."

Lillian stared at the judge in shock.

"You're going a little far afield here, Mr. Sewell," the judge said. "Do you want me to step down, but before I do, to declare a mistrial? You understand, of course, the operation of double jeopardy could prevent you from retrying Mrs. Adams?"

"No. I am asking you to step down from this case and permit the chief justice of the Wyoming Supreme Court to name a successor—the same as if you had died."

As if he had died?

"So, Mr. Sewell, we've suffered all of this sophistry in support of your agenda to secure a change of judge, even in the middle of a trial?" the judge asked. "How inventive. I know of no precedent for this. And I find your conduct contemptuous."

At last, Coker spoke. "What we have here is a prosecutor who will risk contempt in order to go judge shopping after he discovers that the judge isn't ruling his way."

"That is plain bullshit," Sewell cried.

Coker got up and started toward Sewell.

"Call the sheriff," the judge ordered the clerk. The clerk quickly left the room.

"I'm not through with what I had to say," Coker continued. "What we have here is a prosecutor who, himself, can be replaced. On your order, the attorney general can appoint another prosecutor to take over this case. Mr. Sewell's insufferable misconduct demands it."

Deputy Huffsmith burst though the door of the judge's chambers, his hand in readiness on his holstered .357 Magnum revolver. He looked from the judge to the lawyers and back to the judge again.

"Do you have a vacant cell in your jail, Deputy Huffsmith?" the judge asked.

"We have that same old padded cell, Your Honor," Huffsmith replied.

"I see," the judge said. He turned to Sewell. "You may still purge yourself of contempt with an appropriate apology, Mr. Sewell. Otherwise, you leave me no other remedy." He heard that distant voice again: "Careful, old man."

"You wouldn't dare put me in jail," Sewell hissed. "How would you like to read in the morning paper that District Attorney Haskins Sewell charged Judge John Murray with engaging in improper conduct with the very defendant who's being tried before said judge on a charge of murder, and when the district attorney called the matter to his attention, said judge threw him in jail?"

"You are forcing me, Mr. Sewell. Forcing me. Do you have nothing more to say? I am waiting for an appropriate apology."

Silence.

At last, the judge said in as strong a voice as he could muster, "I find Haskins Sewell in contempt of this court. I order the sheriff of Teton County to take Mr. Sewell into custody and hold him in the Teton County jail until he

has purged himself of his contempt." The judge turned
to the deputy. "Take this man from my chambers."

"You're insane," Sewell snarled, but he held out his
hands to Deputy Huffsmith for cuffing, which the deputy
refused. "This here man is a low-risk prisoner," he said.
Then he led Haskins Sewell from the judge's chambers.

Judge Murray glanced at those remaining in the room.
He saw the court reporter's silent lips moving. He saw
Coker for once bereft of words. He saw Lillian rising
from her chair, her face laced with fear. Sylvia Huntley
ran to Lillian and held her, both women as still as the
silence before the storm.

CHAPTER 25

HE SAT ALONE in his chambers, his blurry old eyes on a photograph of Betsy that sat on his desk. She was laughing her interminably happy laugh. Often she'd warned him against his recklessness.

What have I done? he asked himself. What a fool! No judge in the history of the state had thrown a prosecutor in jail for contempt, and he'd already thrown Sewell in twice. And judges fear prosecutors like people fear rattlesnakes in tall grass. The prosecutor has the power to institute criminal charges against a judge.

Soon the reporters would be writing stories about how he'd thrown the prosecutor in jail for contempt when the prosecutor was only trying to do his job—to convict a woman who many believed had murdered her filthy rich husband. Had money or unidentified favors, or both, captured the presiding judge? The media hadn't made much of the father-daughter relationship between the judge and Lillian. That didn't generate the gasps and excitement that enthralled a readership that was always readily captured by the prurient.

Sometimes when the judge was called upon to pass

sentence on some poor bastard standing in his jail suit looking up at him with bloodshot eyes steeped in fear, a fellow human being without friends, not even another junkie, and his court-appointed lawyer, who wasn't qualified to defend a sick puppy, was pleading him guilty, and the poor bastard would give his right arm for a fix—it was then that the judge experienced those small, disturbing jabs of sympathy, of caring, that as a judge he was required to ignore. His judgment would likely destroy the man's chance at life, as hopeless as it was in the first place. The judge knew he exercised the power of God, and God Himself must surely know He was unqualified to judge that which He had created.

So you've done it, old man! he said to himself. You've destroyed an entire career—a faithful judge who's always served the law, if not the people. Well, as you sometimes used to tell those who stood before you, kick out all that useless self-pity and deal with it. Try to learn from this experience.

He closed his eyes and saw Sewell strutting in victory. The son of a bitch had outsmarted him. Now Sewell would go to jail, but he would also spew his lies to the press, and for Sewell, that was better than winning. He'd become the martyr, and everyone had been taught to worship martyrs.

He could hear Sewell lecturing some reporter: "Although I sit in this cell, I will continue to prosecute those charged with vicious crimes, even if, in the end, I must give up my freedom and my office."

The judge thought he heard a high, sinister cackle in the distance. But it wasn't Sewell. He'd never heard Sewell laugh.

The judge struggled from his chair and threw open the door of his chambers, but in his outer office he found only his secretary, Jenny Winkley, busy at her typing.

"Did you laugh?" he asked.

"Did you eat today?" Jenny demanded like a cranky mother.

He wanted to go home and go to bed. He wanted to slip down deep into the covers, close his eyes, and shut off his yapping mind.

He thought of Sewell in the padded cell. It would be dark in there. There'd be no place for him to lie down except on a filthy floor pad. When Sewell had previously occupied that cell, Coker's presence, even though hostile, had provided the comfort of another human being similarly suffering. The worst punishment of all would be to spend eternity in hell's misery with no other companion but the self.

Perhaps Sewell could yet be saved. But no, the judge concluded. The toxic seed in Sewell would grow and blossom in the dark, and then seed again. He was a man who lived in order to loathe. He loathed Coker. He loathed Lillian. He loathed the citizens he indicted and convicted, innocent or not. And most of all, he loathed the judge. No, Sewell wouldn't change. He'd spend the night planning the judge's fall from grace.

He could see it now. If Sewell couldn't convict Lillian, he'd win by attacking the judge. In fact, the sheriff and Sewell were no doubt in this together.

The sheriff and his deputies were as morally challenged as most of the criminals they hauled in. They merely occupied different sides of the game. If it took a little perjury to convict, they figured, so what? If they didn't have the facts, they made up the facts. So what? They argued that the "subjects" lied, too. It was all part of the game.

Politics was also part of their agenda. The sheriff needed convictions so that people would feel safe. If they felt safe, the sheriff's reelection every four years was ensured. The people believed that good cops got convictions one way or another, and they really didn't care how. The sheriff never forgot that.

Still, the judge thought he should have a heart-to-heart with Sewell. Surely Sewell would understand that things can get distorted under the pressure of a trial. Perhaps he and Sewell could make a joint public statement that would save Sewell's face, and they could go on with the case from there.

But no.

Sewell would simply see him as old and feeble.

But no, it wasn't time to give up. The judge still had some fight left in him.

CHAPTER 26

THE FOLLOWING MORNING, the judge arrived at his chambers at 9:00 A.M. sharp. And, as usual, Jenny Winkley handed him a copy of the *Jackson Hole Press*. "Take a read at this," his secretary said. He fell into his chair and grabbed the paper with both hands, as if to choke it.

PROSECUTOR CHARGES JUDGE, JUDGE JAILS PROSECUTOR

Yesterday district judge John Murray ordered that Haskins Sewell, the Teton County district attorney, be incarcerated in the county jail until he purged himself of contempt. Judge Murray was not available for comment.

Prosecutor Haskins Sewell said in an interview conducted in the county jail that Judge Murray had been "personally and improperly engaged" with Mrs. Horace Adams III, the accused in the murder case before the judge. The prosecutor refused to elaborate but said he had asked the judge to step down.

Sewell said that the judge had failed to issue lawful rulings, which had prevented the prosecutor from fairly presenting the state's case to the jury, and when Sewell called the judge's attention to the judge's past relationship with the defendant, Mrs. Adams, the judge ordered Sewell thrown in jail for contempt.

Prosecutor Sewell said, "I will take such steps as may be necessary to bring about justice in the people's case even if it requires that I be indefinitely jailed by the judge."

Timothy Coker, the well-known criminal defense attorney who is defending Mrs. Adams, had no comment. However, he did say the Wyoming attorney general has the authority to appoint another prosecutor when the district attorney is unable to proceed.

An accompanying editorial by Harvey Bushnell, of the *Jackson Hole Press*, stirred up embers where old fires had burned.

SHOULD JUDGE MURRAY BE IMPEACHED?

Nowhere is impartiality and unbiased judgment more demanded than in a case as critical to justice as a murder trial. Justice cannot prevail when the judge is compromised by improper conduct with the accused. If Judge Murray, who to this moment has maintained a spotless reputation as a good and fair judge, is guilty of any impropriety, he should immediately step down. Indeed, he should resign his position of trust.

On the other hand, we must exercise patience and caution and remain careful of first opinions based solely on the charges of the prosecutor. Hopefully, proof will be made in accordance with the American system of justice, and the presumption of innocence must be granted to Judge Murray, as he has enforced it on behalf of every citizen charged with a crime who has come before him. And if charges are brought against him, they must be proven beyond a reasonable doubt.

The judge crumpled the paper with a vengeance and threw it in his wastebasket. He felt as helpless as the pitiful miscreants who over the years had stood before him, waiting to be devoured by the hungry mouth of the monster called "the law."

"Precedent is the law stumbling over itself, century after century, and never finding the truth," he'd often proclaimed. And verdicts were too often the products of jurors lying to themselves and to one another and finally, by their verdicts, lying to the court. Justice was the bastard progeny of lies. All too frequently the law itself was a lie in truth's clothing.

Sewell had laid that rotten lie on the press. The judge had never been "personally engaged" with Lillian Adams as Sewell meant those words to imply.

"Everybody is lying!" the judge hollered.

Jenny Winkley invaded his solitude with a pile of orders for him to sign. "How dare Sewell claim that an old coot like you would be messing around with a woman young enough to be your daughter. Who's going to believe that?"

"Probably everybody," the judge said.

"Well, did you?" she demanded.

"Jesus Christ sakes, Jenny, why would you ask that?" He was hollering again.

"I know plenty of dirty old men who'd like nothing better than to"—she fumbled for the word—"you know what."

"You know me better than that," he said.

He felt sick. He wished she would disappear. He wished he could.

Jenny waited until he looked up from his desk. "Lillian called here for you."

"What!" He sprang forward from his chair and grabbed at the pain in his back. "Jesus H. Christ, Jenny, what do you mean she called?"

"She calls all the time. Usually calls just after the jury's been excused for the day."

"Doesn't she know better than to call the judge who's trying her case?"

"I told her you couldn't talk to her, but she says she has to talk to you, that it's important. I asked her what it was about, and she said she couldn't talk to me about it."

"Why haven't you told me about her calls before?"

"I try not to disturb you." She looked at the judge from the corner of her eye. "Since this trial started, you've changed."

"For Christ sakes, Jenny, how have I changed?"

"I don't know," she said. "It's like something's missing in the judgment department—you getting yourself into a mess like this, for example."

She's never been a comfort to me, he thought. She'd been single for the last twenty years, divorced from a man she never mentioned. She saw life as a colorless, involuntary endurance test. He'd kept her in his employ these many years mostly out of sympathy. Who else but he would tolerate her interminable pessimism and her unalterable distrust of the species?

Finally, Jenny left.

He picked up the phone and ordered a big bouquet of red roses for her. She deserved them.

"How do you want the card to read?" the woman at the flower shop asked over the phone.

"'To Jenny, for putting up with me these many years.'"

When he walked into the sheriff's office, there sat Sewell, happily visiting with Sheriff Howard Lowe, a steaming coffee cup in his hand, and his feet propped up on the sheriff's desk. At the moment Sewell saw the judge, perfect scorn blossomed on Sewell's face.

"What's going on here, Sheriff?" the judge demanded.

"What do you mean, 'What's going on'?" Then the sheriff laughed. "You mean why is the DA here and not over there in the padded cell? Well, Judge, I got me some trustees. Now there is old Whitey and Jake, who are in here for vagrancy and shoplifting, but they ain't going no place, and there's Henry Yellow Feather, the Indian, who's in for drunk—again—and he ain't goin' no place neither. I got them mopping up the jail." The sheriff arose from his chair, gave a slight bow to the judge, and, with a sweep of his hand toward Sewell, proclaimed, "And this is my latest trustee, Mr. Haskins Sewell. He is giving me legal advice on a number of important issues."

The sheriff's potbelly was covered by his brown sheriff's shirt with the badge over the heart—to stop a bullet, he liked to say. His eyes were hidden behind large shades, his nose was fat with old pockmarks, and his jowls sagged and quivered when he talked.

"I ordered this man in jail until he purged himself of contempt," the judge said. "Have I made myself clear?"

"Oh, yes, you have. Definitely," the sheriff replied. "Should we also put him on a bread and water diet?"

The judge stared at the sheriff for a moment, then turned and walked out. He heard their muffled laughter in the background.

He found no comfort at his desk; the coffee was cold, the room sepulchral. An array of framed certificates stared down from the walls, honors he'd received from the bar association, from the judicial college, and a commendation from the Chamber of Commerce for meritorious service to the community.

Were people everywhere laughing at him? There stood Death, grinning and exercising its jaws with its never-ending joke that no one appreciated—born, struggle, get old, die and take your "eternity leave," as he'd grown to call the dreaded departure. Death, the ceaseless jokester, never tired of the same joke. I'm too bound up in myself, the judge thought. Others depended on him—Betsy, for one, and Lillian. He tried not to admit his concern for her. His paternal feelings for her pounded at the door of guilt. He knew he should disqualify himself this minute.

The bailiff was knocking. "What do ya want me to do with the jury, Your Honor?" The sound of the bailiff's words lacked their usual lilt of esteem and deference.

He didn't answer the bailiff.

"Your Honor?" the bailiff insisted.

"Tell them to go to hell," the judge said.

"I beg your pardon, Your Honor?"

"I asked where Mr. Coker is."

"He's sitting at his table in the courtroom, waiting, Your Honor."

"Go tell the sheriff to bring Mr. Sewell here immediately. And tell Mr. Coker and Mrs. Adams to come in." He would play the cards dealt to him from the stacked deck. But one thing for sure—he would not, no, *not*, step down from the case.

Jenny Winkley stuck her head in the door. "Harvey

Bushnell, from the *Jackson Hole Press,* is out here. He wants an interview," she said.

"He knows better than to interfere in the judicial process."

"Shall I tell him he knows better?"

"What's wrong with you, Jenny?"

"It's not me," she said. "And Lillian called again." She turned toward the door, taking her squeezed-up little steps as if a full-gaited walk were vulgar.

"My God! What did you tell her?" he called after her.

"I told her if it was official business, she couldn't talk to you here. If it wasn't, she should call you at home."

"She shouldn't be calling me anywhere about anything," the judge shouted.

"Well, I'll tell you something, Judge." She turned back. "This is heating up a lot of courthouse gossip."

He flopped down in his chair. "Jenny, did you give her my new phone number at home?" He felt his panic return.

"Betsy must have given it to her. I know for a fact that she and Betsy talk almost every day. And it's better for her to call you at home than here."

By then, the sheriff and Haskins Sewell had entered his chambers. They stood at his desk looking down at him like amused schoolboys. Sewell was wearing a newly pressed suit, a clean, starched white shirt, and his usual gray tie.

Timothy Coker, in his old tweed jacket, appeared with Lillian Adams, who wore a face of pained endurance and the same black dress. "Sit down, everyone," he said. They took chairs.

The judge's anger seemed to clear his head for the moment. "This trial has to continue, Mr. Sewell. I can hold this jury in abeyance for only so long. And I again remind you: If I have to dismiss the case, double jeopardy may well attach, and you may not be able to retry Mrs. Adams. Are you prepared to deal with this, Mr. Sewell?"

"Yes, of course I am, Your Honor," Sewell said.

"And are you prepared to take the ordinary steps required to purge yourself of contempt, Mr. Sewell?"

"If I insulted Your Honor, I am sorry," Sewell said. "But, sir, I have not only the right but the duty to tell the truth, even if the words offend Your Honor."

"Yes, Mr. Sewell, you have the duty to tell the truth." The calm of the judge's own voice surprised him. "You have accused me of personal misconduct with the defendant, who is charged with murder in my court. You have undertaken a witch hunt to prove a false . . ."

He stumbled for the word. A simple word. Both lawyers and Lillian Adams were watching him, waiting. He finally came up with it. ". . . a false . . . accusation.

"This is a witch hunt!" the judge suddenly hollered. "You lied about me to the media. That is defamation of the worst order."

"I believe what I've said is true," Sewell said.

"In that case, I make the following additional orders." The judge nodded to the court reporter. "Be sure to get this right." He spoke slowly. "I find that your contempt is ongoing. I find that you have refused, given the opportunity, to purge yourself of your contempt. I find that your accusations against this court are false and malicious and with the obvious purpose of attempting to disqualify this judge from this case, and I will make an appropriate report to the bar. However, under these circumstances I have no alternative but to order you to continue in the prosecution of this case, but under the direction and supervision of this court."

The judge turned to the sheriff. "Let the record show that Sheriff Howard Lowe is present in my chambers. Sheriff Lowe, I hereby order you to keep Mr. Haskins

Sewell, the district attorney, in custody whenever court is out of session. He is to be lodged in the county jail until further order of this court. Do you understand, Sheriff Lowe?"

"Yes, of course, Your Honor."

"That doesn't mean that he is to be allowed to lounge around in your office like a playmate, drinking coffee, but that he be confined in a cell until my further order. Is that clear?"

"Oh, yes, very clear," the sheriff parroted.

"Just a minute, please," said Timothy Coker. "The strategy of the prosecutor is too frigging obvious. He's attempting to force the court to dismiss this case for his own political gain. He'll argue that you ought to be thrown out of office because you turned a vicious murderer loose without a trial. Simply put, Your Honor, he is using this case to get your job."

"Where's your evidence?" Sewell shouted.

"You must remember, Mr. Coker, who your client is," the judge said. "I'm not your client. Are you going to move that this case against Lillian Adams be dismissed?"

"No," Coker said. "If you dismissed the case, Mrs. Adams would go through life with people saying she got away with murder. We both want a jury to hear her case, and if a reasonable jury in a fair trial hears her case, she will be acquitted."

Scowling at the judge, Sewell said, "You wouldn't dare dismiss this case. I am advising you on the record that I can produce evidence in this court that your relationship with Lillian Adams is much more than casual."

The judge thought that if he weren't the judge, he'd take a swing at Sewell himself.

"Gentlemen," the judge said at last, "we'll proceed with the case. Mr. Sewell, be prepared to call your next witness first thing tomorrow morning."

Yes, the judge thought, Sewell has checkmated me. If he petitioned the attorney general to appoint a new prosecutor from another county, it might take the lawyer a couple of weeks to familiarize himself with the facts and law of the case, and the judge probably couldn't hold the jurors that long. If he ordered Sewell removed, the bastard would probably take an emergency writ to the Wyoming Supreme Court, and who could predict how those old judges up there might view matters through the lens of their high-and-mighty but provincial myopia.

If he dismissed the case, he could never defend himself against the prosecutor's accusations that he'd been guilty of improper conduct. If he let the case go forward, Sewell would try to poison the case with perjured testimony or smother justice with unethical strategies that could turn the jury against Lillian. Her life was at stake. He had no choice but to continue with the case and see that Lillian got a fair trial. Sewell could take care of himself.

He left the courthouse and, as usual, dropped by Hardy Tillman's for an early beer. Hardy was changing the fan belt on a 1951 Studebaker two-door sedan. Hardy saw him coming, wiped his greasy hands on a rag, and marched into his back office with a wide, naked smile for the judge, exposing an empty upper left gum—all three molars missing.

"This must be Old Codger's Day," Hardy said, his eyes brightening at the sight of the judge.

"What do you mean, 'Old Codger's Day'?"

Hardy gave him a spongy laugh. "Well, I got up this morning and took a close look at myself in the mirror and decided that looking at myself was cruel and unusual punishment. As a guy gets older, everything on him grows—his ears gets bigger, and his feet grows a couple of sizes, and his nose gets longer, an' his belly pops out. The only thing that don't get bigger is his peter."

He laughed and popped a couple of beers. "I keep thinking about how I'd like to catch me one of them sweet young things with that real fine duck fuzz on her skin, and then I realized that I ain't about to catch me one of them, and anything I could catch, I wouldn't want. That there is an old codger's kind a day."

"You got that right," the judge said.

"Then my friend here gets himself mixed up with Jolly Girl," Hardy said. "Now there's one that's got an ass on her like—"

"I'm not mixed up with Lillian," the judge said. "You know that."

"I wouldn't blame you none. Every man is entitled to something like that at least once in his lifetime."

"You know me better than that, Hardy. She's like a daughter to Betsy and me."

"Trouble with you is you're too damned straight. Ain't no room in a civilized society for honest men. They just get pushed around. Why, them politicians would screw their own mother out of her Social Security check. And don't get me started on the bankers. This here country is founded on what I call the 'three C's.'" The judge had heard it a hundred times. "Crime, cheats, and chiselers."

"I ought to give it all up and go home and watch the birds," the judge said.

"Jesus save us. You're just feelin' sorry for yourself again. You want me to go kick the shit out of Sewell? I always wanted to kick the shit out of one of them retarded dipshit monkeys that ought to be made extinct."

"No, Hardy. Save him for me," the judge said.

The judge arrived at the cabin in his old truck. The plows had piled up three feet of snow on the side of the driveway, and the house was cold. He let old Horatio out, emptied the ashes from the wood burner, put in a little pitch-wood kindling, added larger pieces of new wood, and lit the stove. He poured a new supply of seeds and a chunk of suet in the bird feeder. The chickadees got what was left after the magpies, and the magpies got what was left after the ravens. And the defendant in a criminal case got what was left after the prosecutor, the defense attorney, the judge, and, at last, the jurors each got what was required to satisfy their respective agendas.

Judgment.

He needed judgment. Judgment was his business. He couldn't shoot at every moving target out there—Sewell, the sheriff, the damn newspaper, and, yes, the voters.

He needed to talk to Betsy. Where was she?

He thought about putting something on the stove for supper, but Betsy didn't want him near the stove. When the phone rang, he recognized the voice right off. "Judge Murray, I know I shouldn't be calling you, but I have to talk to you."

"You can't talk to me, Lillian," he said, and hung up.

It was as if the woman he'd known and loved all these years had become a witch. Yet he understood her fear, her defenselessness, and, yes, he was also aware that she was a woman with few peers.

He put another slab of wood on the fire to make sure the kitchen would be warm for Betsy when she got home.

CHAPTER 27

.LILLIAN HAD HURRIED straight home after the court recessed to find Tina standing in the kitchen with a butcher knife in her hand. The girl was wild-eyed, like a kitten caught in the corner by a pack of mad dogs.

"Tina!" She ran to the girl and grabbed the knife from her hands.

"They're going to come after us, Mother, and I won't let them." She was screaming in the high, wild voice of a terrorized child. "Mother, Sewell is going to kill you! The voices told me. We have to leave!"

Lillian tried to comfort the girl, held her close and patted her softly, like a mother with a child just taken from her breast.

"You can hear the voices, too, can't you, Mother? Listen to the voices!"

"No, darling, there aren't any voices. They're just bad sounds in your head."

She continued to pat Tina. At last, Lillian put on some canned soup. The only way she could coax the girl to eat was to feed her a spoonful at a time, and with gentle, persistent coaxing, she got her to swallow the pill

Dr. Brady had prescribed to quiet her and to encourage sleep. "Sleep can cure," the doctor had said. "She needs sleep." So did Lillian.

It was late in the evening when Lillian called Sylvia Huntley. Tina was finally in bed, her medication having at last taken hold. Sylvia heard Lillian's panic-stricken voice and rushed to the house. When she arrived, she found Lillian struggling on the cliff's edge of hysteria, her hair a tangle and heavy circles under her eyes.

Lillian burst out with it. "Coker won't listen to me. With Coker, it's all about tactics and ethics and the law. I can't talk to my father. He's threatening to kill Sewell and has my mother scared to death. She's calling me all the time. I tried to talk to the judge. He won't talk to me. I have to talk to somebody."

"Of course," Sylvia said, reaching for Lillian's hand.

"All of this has to always, *always,* be just between us," Lillian said.

Sylvia nodded, followed Lillian to the living room sofa, and waited for her to begin.

"You remember our last meeting at the drugstore? When I got home that night, I found Tina in Horace's study. She was screaming, 'The witch killed himself. The witch killed himself.' I was terrified." Lillian's eyes were wide and frightened at the memory.

"I tried to be calm. I thought I was insane—Horace lying in all that blood, and Tina screaming, with a gun in her hand."

"Oh my God," Sylvia whispered.

"Then later that night, Tina changed her story. She said Horace was going to kill her. Tina said she picked up the gun, put it to Horace's head, and shot him." Lillian began to weep.

"Oh my God," Sylvia whispered again.

"Tina said he fell down on the desk and was shaking

all over, just like her grandpa said they all do when you shoot somebody in the head."

Lillian tried to gather herself. Her eyes were wild. "I grabbed the gun from Tina. Then I put my arms around her and held her. She was screaming and repeating over and over, 'I had to kill him. He was going to kill us both.'

"Then I remembered what Dr. Brady said—that when they're sick like that, they can blame themselves for things they didn't do. I tried to explain that to Tina, but she kept insisting, 'I did it, Mother. I had to kill him.'"

Sylvia held tight to Lillian's hand.

Lillian was still breathing heavily. "I wiped the prints off the gun. Then I put the gun back on the desk by Horace's hand. My hands were bloody. Blood everywhere. I had blood on my clothes. I ran to the bathroom and washed as well as I could. Then I called the sheriff."

Sylvia sat shocked and silent.

"I gave Tina the sedative that Dr. Brady had prescribed in case of an emergency, and thank God she quieted down. Then the deputies came, and the coroner. I kept Tina locked in her room. Finally, hours later, they took Horace's body, and they all left.

"After everybody left, Tina finally wakened and started crying hysterically, and I held her until she fell asleep again." Lillian was speaking barely beyond a whisper. "I called Dr. Brady and asked her what to do. I remember the doctor saying, 'No one knows yet where the truth lies. Tina hated your husband, and if she walked into the room at the moment he shot himself, she could easily be experiencing a transference of guilt and has come to believe she killed him. In Tina's hysteria, she might have picked up the gun where he dropped it, and that's when you walked in.'"

"Could be, honey," Sylvia said.

"Dr. Brady said, 'My advice is to say nothing to

anyone. Let the law work it out.' She said I should continue to keep Tina sedated and feeling as secure as possible."

"What was Tina doing in Horace's study?" Sylvia finally asked.

"She said she went in there looking for me. She thought I was home."

"What about the suicide note?"

"I never saw one. Somebody must have planted it later on."

Finally, Sylvia said what she'd wanted to say all along. "You can't take care of Tina if you go to prison."

"I know." The long silence again.

"What are you going to do?"

"I don't know. What should I do?"

"I don't know."

"I wish I could talk to the judge. He always knows what to do."

Dr. Brady increased Tina's medications, and the doctor spent many hours with the girl. If she was delusional about killing her stepfather, she nevertheless continued to insist she'd killed him.

"Dr. Brady wants me to send Tina to a hospital. I can't abandon Tina to a hospital. If I put Tina in a hospital, she'll never get out. She'll die there. If she killed Horace, she did him a favor."

Lillian struggled against more tears. "I think Horace solved it for all of us. He dealt with it in the only way left for him." She stopped to gather herself. "He must have thought he was saving me from the hell he went through with his father. He was always thinking of me."

"What about Tina?"

"I've hired Roberta Clemmins, a psychiatric nurse from Salt Lake City. She'll join with Mrs. Houseman, who does foster care for troubled children, and the two of them can watch over Tina. Dr. Brady will look in on them. As long as Tina's on her meds, she gets along very well with Mrs. Houseman. And I've hired a couple of tutors to help Tina with her homework. But she's not able to respond to them right now. I know in my heart she didn't do this. But if she did, she was an angel of mercy." The two women held each other with their eyes. Suddenly, Lillian said, "I had no choice. I'm her mother."

"She may be dangerous, Lillian. She could kill you in one of her episodes. She's as strong as a strong man."

"She would never do that. If she were sick with cancer, I'd fight for her to the end. She has a sickness of the mind. I have to stand by her in the same way. I never realized how much I would miss Horace. You never know how much you love somebody until they're gone."

"In a way, I envy you," Sylvia said. "I never had that."

"Well, sweetheart," Betsy said to the judge when she got home, "Nancy Honaker at the grocery store—you know her; you kept her out of jail that time she tried to shoot Carl Middleford for beating up on her youngest son—you remember her?"

"No." He couldn't remember all his cases.

"Well, Nancy told me she didn't believe a thing that Haskins Sewell said about you."

"You saw the paper?" he asked.

"I know you're not messing around with Lillian, for God's sake. I know you both too well. What are you going to do?"

"I don't know."

"You should keep Sewell in jail. Teach him something."

"I'm not his teacher. I'm going to sleep on it." He needed sleep, and he'd learned long ago that good decisions were never the product of a weary mind.

"There's a lot of people out there who'll support you," Betsy assured him. "You haven't been a judge here all these years without people growing to respect you. You have a lot of friends."

"Yes, and a trainload of enemies. Every time I hold against somebody, or they go to jail, I win a new enemy, and all of their family members become enemies, and all of the family's friends and the friends of their friends."

"The good people will come forward," she said. "They always do."

That was Betsy all right. But the judge thought the law spoke with dead lips. In the minds of most, a prosecutor's charges were synonymous with guilt.

The judge looked off into the black-and-white landscape of winter, as if the answer lay buried there in three feet of snow.

CHAPTER 28

GILDED HIGHLIGHTS DANCED on the snow, the work of the sun and its filigreed fingers. A great gray owl perched on a post, waiting for a hungry mouse searching for its breakfast, a seed from a late-summer dandelion.

The judge hadn't slept much. Why should I feel afraid? he'd asked himself. I'll deal with Sewell head-on. I can be hurt only if I fall prey to my own fears.

Betsy fed him his usual breakfast of two soft-boiled eggs, a couple of crisp bacon slices with half a piece of buttered whole wheat toast. As usual, he put on his old mackinaw over his black suit with its frayed cuffs and bulging knees, his blue shirt, and the black necktie that he slipped over his head, the knot always tied and ready to be pulled into place. And, as usual, he took along a thermos of coffee.

At the door, he said, "Honey, everything's going to be all right. I promise," and he gave Betsy his usual good-bye peck on the cheek. Then he walked out the door with a slight limp—on the left side.

He tried to focus on the beauty of the day. He could see it mechanically. Yes, he saw the beauty of the early-morning frost and its painted magic on leaf and limb, but he felt only fear chewing at his belly.

Hope.

"Live with hope" had been his advice to those lost souls who were hauled before him every day, and who were buried alive in their own baggage of misery.

Horatio had followed him out of the cabin. The judge lifted the old dog up and into the passenger seat of his pickup. Horatio loved a trip to the office, and the judge decided this would be Old Dogs Day—yes, hopefully.

Horatio was a celebrity in the courthouse. He stopped for a pat on the head from every passerby and returned the gift with a vigorous wag of his tail. Benjamin Breslin and the clerk's assistants made a fuss over him, as if he were the judge's only child, and even Jenny Winkley smothered him with her baby talk, a kiss on the side of his broad head, and a dog cookie from the box she kept in her bottom desk drawer.

As usual, Jenny Winkley was sitting behind her desk, but for the first time he could remember, she was wearing lipstick and a pink silk dress he'd never seen. She'd arranged the spray of red roses he'd sent her in a quart Kerr canning jar to serve as a vase.

Then Hardy Tillman called. His voice was ragged and filled with excitement. "Judge, I maybe shouldn't 've called you. But I figured Sewell, knowing we was friends, knew I'd call and rat on him. That rat bastard wasn't in jail at all. He stopped by the station here and filled up with gas about fifteen minutes ago, just to make sure I noticed. His tank only took four gallons."

"What do you mean, you thought you shouldn't call me?"

"I didn't just fall off the turnip truck. He probably wanted me to rat on him so you and him could have another one of your famous showdowns."

"Well, you did rat on him."

"Yeah, but that's what you do to a rat, even if the rat wants to be ratted on."

The judge thanked his friend, hung up, and ordered the bailiff to have the sheriff as well as both attorneys and Lillian Adams in his chambers at once. He took off his robe, loosened his tie, and made sure the bottom button on his shirt was fastened. Betsy had often warned him, "You can't command respect as a judge if your naked belly is hanging out." A sudden surge of adrenaline began to crowd out his fear, readying him for the coming combat.

As Sewell made his appearance, he stopped to examine the plaques and photographs on the judge's wall. He seemed most interested in a photo of Coker and the judge with their arms around each other's shoulders. They were standing behind a string of cutthroat trout about eighteen inches long, and both were holding up the weapons of conquering warriors—their fishing poles.

The judge motioned to Sewell and the sheriff to approach him.

"Sheriff, did you follow my direction to incarcerate Mr. Sewell until further order of this court?"

"I did, Your Honor."

"Was he in your custody and control at all times?"

"Of course."

The judge turned to Haskins Sewell. "What do you have to report in this regard?"

"I had to go to my house for a change of clothes. I was gone half an hour. The sheriff was kind enough to grant me trustee status."

Be careful, old man, the judge thought.

"If Mr. Sewell requires attention outside your jail, Mr. Sheriff, you're ordered to arrange for his needs," the judge said to Sheriff Lowe. "He is not to leave your physical custody until I order him released. Do you understand?"

"Of course."

"And, Mr. Sheriff, you say that Mr. Sewell was in your custody and control at all times. Yet you allowed him to go unattended to his home in order to change clothes? It appears you haven't been candid."

The sheriff was quick to answer: "I didn't think you'd want Mr. Sewell to appear in your court in the suit he slept in all night. Therefore, I permitted him to get into a fresh suit of clothes. Technically speaking, he was in my custody and control." The sheriff's accompanying laugh was void of mirth.

They are still taunting me, the judge thought, but he would not fall for the ploy. He turned to Sewell. "Are you prepared to proceed?"

"Yes," Sewell said, rising from his chair. He walked toward the judge's exit door. "My next witness is Hamilton Widdoss, the renowned handwriting expert."

"And for what purpose are you calling him?" the judge asked.

"To establish that the alleged suicide note was a forgery."

Coker leaned in toward the judge's desk. "The dirty little secret is that handwriting analysis is mostly voodoo. One expert says a document is forged and another, depending on who's paying him, says the opposite. It's not a science. It is bull—" He stopped short.

"I must say that Mr. Coker is being a bit cavalier about this," Sewell said. "I have a study conducted by a world-famous expert who reports that in ninety-six percent of all cases the writer of a given sample could be positively identified."

The judge thought that Sewell's handwriting expert constituted an inescapable danger to Lillian. If the judge let Widdoss testify, he'd swear that the suicide note was a forgery. He might even claim that Lillian was its author. On the other hand, if the judge ruled that Widdoss couldn't testify, Sewell would accuse the judge of illegally withholding evidence from the jury. He might even suggest that the judge was part of a criminal conspiracy to protect Lillian. Yet the judge thought Coker was right. Handwriting experts testified according to who hired them, and over the years the law, by its own ill-advised precedent, had propped open the door to potential scams.

"Lay your foundation, Mr. Sewell," the judge ordered, "and we'll see where this takes us." Whereupon the two attorneys and Lillian Adams returned to the courtroom and the judge to his bench.

Hamilton Widdoss took the stand. He was middle-aged, black-bearded, and beginning to gray. He wore round spectacles perched at the end of a long, inquiring nose and a black suit with vest, a white shirt, and a red bow tie.

Sewell took the man's history: Widdoss had been a forensic handwriting analyst for the Chicago Police Department for twenty-three years. "I've examined over five thousand questioned documents and signatures. I was trained by the FBI," the witness said, speaking to one juror at a time to personalize his credibility. "As an expert, my opinions have been accepted in seventeen state courts as well as in numerous federal courts around the country."

The jury seemed mesmerized. The woman in the front row nodded with every phrase that slid from the witness's mouth.

"Is handwriting analysis an exact science that can be tested?" Sewell asked.

"Of course." Widdoss smiled up at the judge. "We

undertook such a study at the department in Chicago. We gathered fifteen hundred unknown signatures and compared them with fifteen hundred known signatures, and my individual rate of error was less than three-tenths of one percent. The national average is about five-tenths of one percent." He looked at each of the jurors with an inviting smile, as if he'd just asked them to join him for a drink at a local saloon.

"Have you examined the questioned document in this case, Mr. Widdoss?" Sewell asked.

Coker interrupted. "Hold on there. I wish to voir dire the foundation for this witness's testimony." Coker hurried to the witness stand and aimed his sights on Widdoss. "You claim to be an expert in handwriting analysis?"

"Just a minute," Sewell interrupted. "I ask the court to order Mr. Coker to step back from the witness. He has no call to tower over Mr. Widdoss in an attempt to intimidate him."

"Are you intimidated?" Coker asked Widdoss.

"Step back, Mr. Coker," the judge ordered.

Coker took two steps back and began again. "So, like a doctor or an accountant, you went to college to study handwriting analysis?"

"There is no such discipline offered."

"You mean there is no college or university in this country where I can be trained as a qualified handwriting expert?" Coker asked in feigned amazement.

"You could go to the FBI's school if you could get in the FBI." He smiled at Helen Griggsley, the piano teacher. She seemed on the rim of rapture, as if listening to a Mozart piano concerto.

"Tell us how long you went to school at the FBI in order to be qualified as a handwriting expert."

"It's a six-week course."

"You mean that in six weeks any person with average intelligence could go through that school and claim to be an expert?"

"I worked after that under well-known experts in the field."

"Like who?" Coker asked.

"I can't recall all of their names."

"I suppose these 'well-known experts' went to school for six weeks, as well?"

"They are professionals who have examined thousands of documents and handwriting exemplars."

"Well, Mr. Widdoss, the fact that someone who taught you has examined even millions of documents doesn't mean that person was even competent at it. It may mean he has looked at them in the same wrong way a million times, don't you agree?"

"They were good at it."

"How do you know that?"

"They had spotless reputations in the Bureau."

"That means, I suppose, that they put a lot of people in prison as a result of their testimony." Before Sewell could object, Coker asked, "Were any of your findings ever tested against established standards?"

"I don't know what you mean." Widdoss pulled the glasses off his nose.

Coker also pulled the glasses off his nose. "Are there any standards against which to test the conclusions of a handwriting analyst?"

"I don't know what you mean."

"Of course you don't," Coker said. "How could you know the standards if there are none?" He fought back an emerging sneer. "Who tested you?"

"We did the test at the department," Widdoss said.

"Who tested you?" Coker asked again.

"We gathered fifteen hundred unknown signatures and compared them with fifteen hundred known signatures, and my individual rate of error was—"

"The question is, who tested you?"

"The department."

"The department is not a person. Who tested you?"

"It was done by a committee."

"Who were the committee members?"

Sewell, seeing his witness in trouble, said, "Objected to as irrelevant."

"Overruled," the judge.

"I don't remember. That was over ten years ago."

"Did you get a diploma with a gold seal on it to verify your expertise?"

"That's argumentative," Sewell objected.

"Did you get a diploma?" the judge asked.

"No."

"I suppose you belong to the National Organization of Forensic Handwriting Analysts, better known as the NOFHA?"

"Yes, I do."

Coker was still on him like a hound barking at a treed cat. "Well, sir, did you pass an examination in order to belong to that organization?"

"You have to have the necessary credentials to become a member."

"Did you pass any examination?" Coker insisted.

"You have to have been employed in the—"

"I'm sorry to interrupt you, Mr. Widdoss, but did you pass an examination?"

"No. But you—"

"I suppose that if one of our jurors decided to become a handwriting expert, put his or her name in the phone book as an expert, and paid the required dues to NOFHA, he or she could be a member, isn't that true?"

Widdoss's durable smile had faded. He was holding on to the arms of the witness chair, as if to launch himself in an assault against Coker.

"And this committee at the police department is composed of persons with substantially the same education in handwriting analysis as yours—that is, each with their six-week course?"

"I don't know what their education had been," Widdoss said.

"So you don't even know that the regulating committee itself is qualified. Sort of the blindfolded pinning the tail on the donkey, right?"

"That is argumentative, Your Honor," Sewell said.

"Sustained."

"Would you say that handwriting analysis is an art or a science?"

"I would say it's a little of both."

"How do you test art?" Coker waited. Finally, he added, "I mean, what is, or isn't, art is in the eye of the beholder, isn't that true?"

"I wouldn't know how to answer that."

"And have there been any set standards by any scientific body known to you by which the science of handwriting analysis has been tested?"

"NOFHA has a committee that has set standards for testing."

"But NOFHA isn't a scientific body, is it?"

No answer.

"And even the members of that so-called committee, whoever they are, and whatever their education, did not examine you for your qualifications, isn't that true?"

"It does not examine. It sets standards."

"And, of course, you can tell us what those standards are, can't you?"

"Not offhand. However, I can assure you that the

comparison I did here would meet those standards in every way."

Long pause. Then Coker asked, "Doesn't it seem strange to you that you should tell this jury that your work can meet those standards when you can't tell us what those standards are?"

"I know them. I just can't quote them verbatim."

Coker turned to Judge Murray. "I object to any testimony from this witness concerning the suicide note of Horace Adams the Third on the grounds—"

"I object to Mr. Coker's characterizing the note as a 'suicide note,'" Sewell interrupted. "This note is a forgery, as can be established by this fully qualified witness."

The judge interposed. "I've heard enough, gentlemen. I will take your arguments in chambers."

When Coker arrived in chambers, Sewell was already pacing the floor, his shiny, black, leather-heeled shoes beating their angry cadence. "I want to make an offer of proof," he began. "Mr. Widdoss will testify that the document, Exhibit five, the alleged suicide note, supposedly written by Horace Adams the Third, is a blatant forgery. I offer to show that Mr. Widdoss has examined that document and has analyzed the handwriting and concludes beyond a reasonable doubt that the document was not written by Adams."

"Is that all?" Coker asked.

"No. I will further prove by this witness that he has examined a number of known exemplars of Lillian Adams's handwriting and has concluded that the document in question, the supposed suicide note, was likely written by her."

Lillian let out a small, pinched cry. "That is a horrible lie!"

The judge hit his gavel to bring order.

"I object to Mr. Sewell's offer of proof on two

grounds," Coker said. "First, handwriting analysis cannot be tested against any known standards, and, second, this witness himself has never been tested by his peers against any known standards. This man is nothing but a bogus bunch of . . . I ask the court's pardon for the forbidden word I was about to employ."

The judge needed time to think this through. "I will excuse the jury and take this matter under advisement. The weekend will provide needed relief for all concerned and, indeed, I will add Monday, as well. You are each ordered to provide me with your brief of authorities by eight-thirty Tuesday morning."

"Pray tell how I am going to research this supposedly difficult question if I am locked in my cell?" Sewell asked.

"The sheriff can accompany you to the county library," the judge replied. "Such an exposure to further learning will not endanger the sheriff's reputation as a man whose life has been dedicated to a search for the truth."

Old Horatio had followed Sewell out of the judge's chambers, the smell of the prosecutor's small hairless lapdog having invited Horatio's canine curiosity. He was trailing behind Sewell when Undersheriff Bromley, renowned for his unmitigated hatred of dogs, came hurrying down the same hallway. He charged up behind the old dog. "Get out of here, you goddamned cur," Bromley hollered. He kicked Horatio in his ribs, and Horatio let out a yelp. "I oughta shoot the son of a bitch. Damn dog's got no business in this courthouse."

Sewell turned on Bromley. "That's the judge's dog."

"I don't give a shit whose dog it is," Bromley snapped. He started again for the old dog, who was cornered at the end of the hall.

"Let the dog alone," Sewell said.

Sewell reached behind him and gave Horatio a reassuring pat on the head. Then he said to Bromley, "A man who'll kick a friendly dog is a man who'll kick a friendly man as quickly."

Bromley spun back around and stomped back down the hall.

Sewell took old Horatio by the collar and led him to the judge's chambers. "Here's the judge's pal," Sewell said to Jenny Winkley. "He got lost."

"I keep telling the judge he shouldn't bring that dog here," Jenny said. "I hope he didn't cause any trouble." She offered Horatio another doggy cookie.

"No, he was no trouble at all," Sewell said.

That night, the judge spent late hours seeking some case, any case authored by a respected authority, that would bolster the decision he wanted to make. The law provided no way out. The weight of authority acknowledged handwriting analysis as a science, and he'd have to permit Widdoss's testimony. Widdoss's purchased opinion could convict Lillian Adams. Would Coker call an expert? Probably not.

The judge knew that Coker rarely called experts in his cases. He argued it this way: "You call your expert to prove that the prosecutor's expert is a store-bought whore and the jury figures that you must be guilty or you wouldn't need to call a whore of your own. The jury's always going to believe the prosecutor's expert over yours. I attack the state's whore," Coker said, "and if I can show him for what he is, and I usually can, I win the battle of the experts without taking the chance of calling one."

And Lillian hadn't been around the judge all those

years without learning something about trial dynamics. She'd learned that if she hired a big-time lawyer, the jurors would resent it. Her spending all that dough for a fancy mouthpiece, one the jurors damn well couldn't afford, would simply mean that she was probably guilty and was trying to buy herself out of prison by hiring some famous foreign shyster. When she hired Coker, the townfolks knew him. He might represent anybody with a dollar and a half to pay him, but he was one of their own, and she wasn't flouncing her money around.

Leaving the courthouse that night, the judge thought that perhaps his judicial answers would come floating up to him from the subterranean caverns of sleep. He'd make his decision Tuesday morning. He was still wrestling with the issue as he walked through the snow to his truck in the courthouse parking lot, old Horatio trotting along, his tail still wagging.

With his bare hand, the judge brushed the snow off the windshield. He pulled open the door on his side of the cab, helped the old dog up, and, grateful for the steering wheel, which he used as a handle, pulled himself up into his truck. Once in, he was suddenly startled by a dark figure sitting next to the door on the passenger's side. He smelled the faint fragrance of a woman's perfume. Horatio was licking the face of Lillian Adams.

CHAPTER 29

ON TUESDAY MORNING at nine sharp, the prosecutor, Haskins Sewell, stood waiting at the door of the judge's chambers with a fistful of papers. Timothy Coker came strolling up, with Lillian at his side. She was pale and still as a statue.

"Well, what is your latest phony flimflam?" Coker asked.

"You'll find out soon enough," Sewell said. At that moment, the door opened, and Judge Murray beckoned them into his chambers.

"I have papers, Your Honor," Sewell said. He handed a copy to both the judge and Coker.

The judge slumped slowly into his chair. "I see," he said. "So what do you propose, Mr. Sewell?"

"As you can see, I've asked the Wyoming Supreme Court to remove you. You are a material witness in this case, and you're severely conflicted. You can voluntarily agree to step down, or you can await the order of the supreme court. It's your choice."

"This is more of his standard bullshit, Judge," Coker said, slapping the papers against his pant leg in disgust.

"I'm going to petition the attorney general to replace this prosecutor on account of his continued harassment and misconduct. There's no end in sight."

"I don't think you'll be making those rash statements when you hear the facts," Sewell said.

"And, pray tell, what are the facts?" Coker demanded.

Sewell turned to the judge. "Do you want to hear the facts now, Your Honor, or would you rather wait until the supreme court holds its hearing?"

The judge grabbed for a breath and sought to focus on the papers in his hands. The allegations were in plain words. The bastard had charged him with carrying on an improper relationship with Lillian Adams. The supreme court had the power to bar him from the case, embarrass him before the townspeople, and perhaps even recommend impeachment.

"Well, Your Honor, what is your pleasure?" Sewell was holding his shivering little lapdog, Honeypot, under his arm, which covered most of the dog's body.

The judge groped for words. None would come.

"Hearing nothing from you, I will present my case to the Wyoming Supreme Court," Sewell said. "You will note that included in the papers is an order for you to appear before that court in Cheyenne at nine tomorrow morning."

Cheyenne. Nine in the morning?

The judge finally heard himself say, "You understand that you have failed to purge yourself of contempt, and that you are to be confined in the county jail until further order of this court?"

"You will note from the papers that the supreme court has stayed that order," Sewell said. "I will see you in court, Your Honor. Have a great day." Sewell patted his small dog lightly on the head and, just this side of a parade step, marched out of the judge's chambers.

Coker pulled Lillian on through the door and shut it behind her.

The door opened again. It was Sheriff Lowe. "Sorry, Your Honor. I forgot something." He reached inside his jacket pocket and extracted a folded legal-size paper. "Here's a subpoena for your appearance as a witness in the case of *State of Wyoming vs. Lillian Mortensen Adams.*" He gave an overlong bow. Then he shut the door behind him.

Sewell had subpoenaed him as a witness in this very case over which he presided—Lillian's case. He called weakly for Jenny Winkley, but there was no answer. He tried to think. He saw Sewell's mocking face. Then he seemed to understand: He should kill that bastard.

He boarded his old pickup and started for the cabin.

When he arrived at the cabin, and for reasons he hadn't considered, he retrieved his pistol, a fully loaded Smith & Wesson .357 Magnum containing six cartridges, all nice and shiny. The manufacturer claimed the gun would shoot through an engine block.

As he held the pistol in his hand, he saw the surprised look that would flash on Sewell's face if he were to blow a hole through the man's head. In his mind's eye, he saw Sewell stagger and fall. Then he walked off and left the bastard, a worthless pile of flesh, by his shiny new Chevy.

He wrote a note to Betsy and left it on the kitchen table:

Don't worry, Honey. Going to Cheyenne. Some business to attend to tomorrow. I'll tell you all about it when I get back.

Love,
John

No reason to get her all riled up when there was nothing she could do except suffer.

In order to arrive at the Wyoming Supreme Court Building in Cheyenne by nine in the morning, he'd have to drive most of the night in his beaten-up truck. When he got there—if he got there—he'd be on trial in the highest court in Wyoming as a common criminal charged with improprieties that were not only shameful but fatal to his reputation. Even if he were acquitted by the high court, which was unlikely, he knew that once charged, an accused could never be innocent again. There'd always be doubts. His legacy was sullied. His professional life was over. He had nothing more to lose.

Snow was falling, and in his headlights he saw Sewell's angry face. Yes, he should kill the bastard. "My God, who am I?" he shouted into the rumble and rattle of the truck's ancient engine. "What am I thinking? How can I be premeditating murder like some depraved killer?"

Let there be reason, he begged.

It was too late. If he stepped down, Lillian, guilty or not, would be convicted. And Betsy believed that as judge he possessed the immutable power to save Lillian. If he failed, Betsy would feel betrayed.

Yes, it was over.

And he didn't know how to defend himself before that arrogant cluster of old drones, the supreme court justices up there on their hallowed judicial thrones.

He stopped at an all-night joint in Rock Springs for something to eat. He had to keep up his strength.

"And what will it be, darling?" a smiling, overweight waitress asked.

"A burger with fries," he said. "Could you grill the onions?"

CHAPTER 30

AT LAST, IN Cheyenne, Judge Murray pulled into the first gas station on his side of the road and filled his tank. He might need a full tank to perfect his escape. In the men's room, he splashed water on his face. He had forgotten to bring a comb, and he smoothed his hair the best he could with his fingers. His suit was wrinkled. He tried to clean off the mustard that had leaked from his hamburger.

The courtroom had those high ceilings. The public seating consisted of dark-stained wooden benches. The judges' high perch, their bench, provided room for five justices, the American flag at one end and the Wyoming flag at the other. Above the tall windows on the west side hung burgundy velvet drapes. The floor was covered with matching carpet.

The judge pushed through the courtroom's doors. Immediately, he saw that Haskins Sewell, Sheriff Lowe, and Undersheriff Jim Bromley were already seated at the long table on the left. The table on the right was obviously reserved for him. He was surprised to see Tim Coker sitting in the front row of the spectators' seats.

And, good Christ, seated next to him was Lillian! It was as if the child had come to witness the execution of the father.

He took his place at the empty table. He was alone. Except for Betsy and Hardy Tillman, he'd always been alone. The bailiff, in a black suit, appeared with a water pitcher. He poured fresh water into the glass pitchers on both tables. The bailiff didn't speak to him or even look at him. One of the court's clerks appeared—a thin, blond, attractive woman of indeterminate age. She, too, didn't look at the judge, but she smiled at Haskins Sewell, handed him some papers, and then disappeared again through the door behind the bench.

Spectators began to enter the room. Some were reporters. He recognized the faces of several lawyers who'd appeared in his court. None even nodded in his direction. They'd come to witness his destruction. Then at nine o'clock sharp, the state supreme court justices marched in.

"All rise," the clerk ordered in a monotone. The judge stood.

He stared at those five old men, most younger than he, their hair thinning or bald, their faces unsmiling, all in their justices' robes. One judge gave a passing squint in his direction, and one seemed on the edge of sleep.

These high court judges had mostly been lower court judges, who'd established conservative records. He used to laugh with Tim Coker, who had quoted some jokester's definition of "a conservative" as one who believed that "nothing should ever be done for the first time."

Chief Justice Beasley called the court to order in the crackly voice of one suffering chronic laryngitis. "Gentlemen, let's get to the matter at hand." He turned to Haskins Sewell. "I understand we have a jury waiting in a murder case. We have, based on your sworn papers, brought this matter forward on an emergency basis. I take it that you possess some evidence you wish to present in support of your petition for the removal of Judge Murray?"

"Yes, I do, Your Honor." Sewell sounded so piously pure and polite.

"Before we hear any testimony, I must say that this matter is of grave concern to this court," Justice Beasley said. "And I might add that Judge Murray is known to us as a good and honest judge who has served the people of this state for many years. We do not take your allegations lightly, Mr. Sewell."

"I am here regretfully," Sewell said. "Still, it is my sad task as the prosecuting attorney of Teton County to faithfully report to this court these very troublesome matters, failing which, I would be derelict in my duties."

Justice Beasley turned to Judge Murray. "Do you wish to say anything before we begin this hearing?"

"No," the judge said.

"Very well, let's begin. Call your first witness, Mr. Sewell."

Jim Bromley, the undersheriff, in full uniform, marched forward. He was sworn by the clerk and took the witness chair. Sewell handed him a file. "What is this, Undersheriff Bromley?"

Bromley replied, "This is a record of the telephone calls received by Judge John Murray from the accused, Lillian Adams, since the beginning of her murder trial, over which Judge Murray has presided. These records are from the receptionist at the courthouse. There are fourteen calls, to be exact, the first beginning the first day of the trial in Jackson and the last on Friday of last week."

"And how did you come by these records?"

"I was informed by Kathy Wright, the courthouse receptionist, that Mrs. Adams was habitually calling the judge. I asked her to make a record of these calls as they came in and to advise me."

"And what did you do as a result?"

Bromley replied, "I informed you of these calls, and you petitioned Chief Justice Beasley for authority to fix a wire interception on Judge Murray's phones, both at home and in his office."

"Was that petition granted by Justice Beasley?"

"Yes, it was."

"Did you then undertake to have the lines of Judge Murray tapped in accordance with the order of Justice Beasley?"

"I did."

"What did you discover as a result of those taps?"

"Mrs. Adams called Judge Murray at his home. He refused to talk to her. I assume he had some knowledge that his phone might be tapped, so later he met with her in person in his pickup."

"How do you know he met with Mrs. Adams in his pickup?"

"I was about to leave the courthouse when I personally observed her entering the judge's pickup. It was a few minutes after court adjourned for the day. The parking lot was almost empty. I waited in the doorway to see what she was up to. Then along came the judge, who got into the pickup from the driver's side."

"And how long, Undersheriff, did they talk together?"

"Several minutes."

"Did you notice anything else?"

"Yes, as Mrs. Adams was exiting the pickup, she leaned over and kissed the judge."

"And what did His Honor do as a result of that show of affection?"

"I couldn't tell."

"And what did she do immediately after having kissed His Honor?"

"Her car was parked nearby. She got in her car and drove off."

"And what did His Honor do?"

"He sat in his pickup for a long time. I couldn't tell what he was doing. Finally, he drove off in the opposite direction of his home."

"Do you know where he went?"

"Yes, I do. He was followed by Deputy Jamison to the home of the defendant, Lillian Adams."

"Thank you, Undersheriff Bromley," Sewell said. "Those are all the questions I have of this witness at this time." Sewell looked up at Justice Beasley with a sorrowful, starched smile stretching his face.

"Do you want to question the witness, Your Honor?" Justice Beasley asked Judge Murray.

Judge Murray struggled to his feet. "I think I should be represented," he said. The sound of his own voice startled him. "Judges, I suppose, are entitled to counsel, the same as any other litigant."

"We can adjourn the hearing several days and give you an opportunity to obtain counsel," Justice Beasley said.

"Your Honors, I'm not sure we can hold the jury that long," Sewell was quick to interject. "I'm concerned about the attachment of double jeopardy, and that the defendant will escape if this case doesn't go forward immediately."

"This is a simple matter, Judge Murray," Justice Beasley said. "Simple. Are you confident you can't ask the necessary questions of this witness so that we may come to an immediate conclusion?" The chief justice's voice was edged with impatience, but his eyes seemed kind enough. "I will, of course, grant you leave to engage counsel—which is your right—if you insist."

"All right," Judge Murray said. "I don't want the case jeopardized by my need for a lawyer. I'll ask some questions."

The judge turned to Undersheriff Bromley, still on the stand, and heard himself ask, "Do you know what was said by Lillian Adams in any of those fourteen calls you claim were made by her to me?"

"No," Undersheriff Bromley said. "The order for the bugs didn't come until just a couple days ago."

"You only know that Kathy Wright, the receptionist at the courthouse, told you the calls were made."

"Yes."

"Do you know if I ever talked to Lillian Adams even once in response to those telephone calls?"

"No, I don't. I assumed you talked to her."

"Assumed! Wouldn't you have taken the trouble to ask my secretary if I ever talked to the woman?"

"I didn't ask your secretary. I figured she'd tell me it was none of my business. After all, she is your confidential secretary."

"You say you assumed I talked to Mrs. Adams. Didn't you know it is improper for a presiding judge to take a call from a litigant who stands charged with a crime in his court?" He felt his strength gathering like water seeping up from an artesian spring.

"Yes. I know that."

"Didn't you consider that I wouldn't have taken those calls because it would be improper for me to do so?"

"I am only reporting what I know."

"What did Mr. Sewell tell you concerning his belief about these circumstances."

"I don't know."

"You did talk to him about it?"

"Yes."

"He did tell you his suspicions?"

"Well, yes. He said he thought you were having some kind of an affair with the woman."

"Did he tell you what evidence he had concerning that?"

"No. He said your rulings in the case were screwy."

"He was upset because I ordered him to jail because of his contemptuous statements, isn't that true?"

Undersheriff Bromley glanced in Sewell's direction, then shrugged his shoulders.

"You took it that Mr. Sewell wasn't very happy about either my rulings in the case or, later, that I had held him in contempt, isn't that true?"

"Yes, I don't think he was very happy with you."

"So there was a tap put on my private phone?"

"Yes, by order of Justice Beasley."

"And you say Mrs. Adams called me once at my home, and that I refused to talk to her?"

"Yes. But Mr. Sewell said he thought that was because somebody told you about the tap."

"Which was a fact not in evidence."

"I don't know."

"Did he say how I would have known about this tap?"

"He said one of the justices on this court might have warned you."

"I object," Sewell said. "That is pure hearsay."

"Overruled, Mr. Sewell," Justice Beasley said.

"And you saw Mrs. Adams come to my pickup after court one day?"

"Yes."

"She got in my pickup before I got there and was waiting for me, isn't that true?"

"Yes."

"Did you know that I leave that old wreck of a truck unlocked at all times and I have left the keys in it for as long as I can remember?"

"The sheriff told me that. He said you hoped that somebody would steal the old wreck." Laughter from the audience and small, repressed smiles on the faces of the justices.

"So you saw Mrs. Adams kiss me?"

"Yes."

"She was waiting in my truck, and when I got in, she said something to me and kissed me?"

"Yes."

"She kissed me on the cheek, didn't she?"

"Yes."

"And do you know what she said to me, and why she kissed me on the cheek?"

"I have no idea."

"Could you make room for the possibility that she said she wanted to tell me something?"

"I don't know what she said."

"Then she left?"

"Yes."

"And I sat there for a long time?"

"Yes."

"Would my inactivity be consistent with one trying to figure out what was the right thing to do?"

"I wouldn't know."

"Then your deputy followed me to the home of Lillian Adams?"

"Yes."

"And did I go into her house?"

"I don't know."

"What did your deputy say?"

Sewell objected. "This is total hearsay," he said.

In an unfriendly voice, Justice Beasley said, "This matter was opened up by your witness, Mr. Sewell. Answer the question, Undersheriff Bromley."

"The deputy said you were met at the door by the maid and that you and the maid had a conversation."

"Did you inquire of the maid what I said to her?"

"Yes, I did."

"And what did I say to her?"

"This is hearsay," Sewell said. Then he sat down before Justice Beasley ruled.

"She said you told her to convey a message to Mrs. Adams."

"Did you ask her what that message was?"

"Yes, you told her to tell Mrs. Adams not to contact you again."

"I have no further questions of this witness," Judge Murray said, and sat down.

He felt slightly buoyed at the power of a decent cross-examination. He looked up at the justices, took them in one at a time, and observed their satisfaction with him and his answers. Or was he only satisfied with himself?

Then Sewell rose to his feet. "I wish to question Judge Murray about this matter, and I call him as my next witness."

CHAPTER 31

CHIEF JUSTICE BEASLEY cleared his throat and scowled down at Haskins Sewell. "The court will be in recess for fifteen minutes. We'll take up your request to examine Judge Murray when we return."

Thoughts swarmed across the judge's mind like competing villains vying for center stage. If the supreme court decided to throw him to the mad dog, Sewell, would he tell "the truth, the whole truth and nothing but the truth"?

The whole truth had no beginning and no end.

No matter what his answer might be, when Sewell pressed him for the whole truth, his life would never be the same. Yes, that night after court when he'd found Lillian waiting in his pickup, she'd confessed to him. "I'm so sorry, Judge Murray, for all the trouble I've caused you." She was crying. "I killed Horace because—" And before she'd been able to say another word, he'd stopped her by raising his hand in front of her face. "Don't tell me anything more, Lillian. And get out of this truck immediately." Then she'd kissed him on the cheek and hurried away.

If Sewell asked what she'd said, he could say she said she was sorry for all of the trouble she'd caused him. That would be the truth. But what if Sewell asked if she had said more? Should he deny that she'd said anything further?

Perjury.

What if he said he didn't remember if she'd said anything more?

Perjury.

For reasons not always clear to him, he loved Lillian Adams as a father loves his child. Did he have any moral right as a surrogate father to lie for his child? If he answered truthfully, she'd be convicted. The death penalty. Her life would rest on his answer. And if they lost Lillian to the gas chamber, Betsy would never recover, and with the loss of both Betsy and Lillian, his life would also be over.

The state floundered in ugly, indefensible hypocrisy. The state itself committed premeditated murder. In rendering the death penalty, the state would murder Lillian. Some ghoul would strap her to the chair in the gas chamber and another would turn the death knob on, and a gallery of ghouls from the media would watch and write their vile stories on how she died a gasp at a time.

The supreme court justices were still in recess. Judge Murray turned to see if Timothy Coker was still sitting behind him. Coker looked sick.

Surely one could lie for just reasons.

Might not circumstances exist when it would be unjust to tell the truth?

Then the justices marched in and the entire courtroom rose as the clerk announced their entry.

Chief Justice Beasley coughed twice and cleared his throat. "We have concluded that you may indeed question Judge Murray in this matter. Proceed, Mr. Sewell."

Sewell thanked the court and waited as Judge Murray walked unsteadily to the witness chair. He raised a shaky hand to take the oath administered by Chief Justice Beasley. "Do you swear to tell the truth, the whole truth and nothing but the truth, so help you God?"

"I do."

Sewell began with his high, flat, stinging voice. "So, Judge Murray, you have known Lillian Adams for many years?"

"Yes."

With steely eyes locked on the judge, and case by case, the prosecutor took the judge though his history as presiding judge in Lillian's cases—from her childhood to the present. "Never once did you hold against Mrs. Adams in any of those cases, isn't that true?"

"Yes."

"And because of that long history, you were asked by both the prosecution and the defense to step down from this case."

"Yes."

"You refused. And after you refused, you had me thrown into jail for contempt because I accused you of an improper relationship with Mrs. Adams?"

"Yes."

"And you refused to permit me to cross-examine Sylvia Huntley on my representation that I had a confidential source who had heard Mrs. Adams say to Ms. Huntley that she, Mrs. Adams, 'should kill the son of a bitch,' referring to Mrs. Adams's late husband, Horace Adams the Third?"

"Yes."

"You've protected her all of these years by your rulings, even now when she is charged with the murder of her husband, Horace Adams the Third, the very wealthy beer magnate."

"Yes."

"I have no further questions," Sewell said.

Judge Murray sat like one battered by repeated blows to the head. His mouth hung open and his eyes were focused on his wrinkled old hands that held on to each other.

"Do you wish to cross-examine?" Chief Justice Beasley asked.

No answer.

"Are you able to proceed?" Chief Justice Beasley asked, his voice betraying concern.

At last, Judge Murray looked up at the justices. "Mr. Sewell claimed he had a witness who heard Lillian Adams tell Sylvia Huntley that she, Lillian Adams 'should kill the son of a bitch,' referring to her late husband." Judge Murray stopped to gather his next words. "In short, if Mr. Sewell had such a witness, who was he? He refused to answer. With the court's permission, I will ask him that question now."

Before the chief justice responded, Judge Murray turned to Sewell, who by this time was seated at his table. "Who was this phantom witness, Mr. Sewell?"

Sewell was quick to respond. "I represented to you then, and I do so now, that the identity of the witness is confidential, and that I had then, and I have now, a good-faith basis for asking that question of Ms. Huntley."

Chief Justice Beasley scowled down. "You either did or did not have a good-faith basis for the question, Mr. Prosecutor. Might you not reveal the identity of the witness to the court?"

"It is confidential."

"It may be confidential, Mr. Sewell, but that does not make it privileged," Chief Justice Beasley said. "We tell each other things every day on a confidential basis. But in a court of law, unless there's an established legal privilege, the fact that a conversation was confidential does not prevent this court from inquiring into it."

"I represent to the court that a good-faith basis existed for my question. That should be sufficient. I am an officer of the court."

"No, Mr. Sewell, the prosecutor has no more protection from revealing confidential communications than any other citizen. What was the good-faith basis for your question to Sylvia Huntley? Who was this supposed witness?"

Sewell looked up at the judges for a long time, and finally, like a petulant child, he said, "I refuse to reveal the source of my information."

"In that case, Mr. Sewell, when you return to the trial, you are precluded from making any inquiry, directly or indirectly, that deals directly or indirectly with the testimony of your claimed confidential witness, do you understand?"

Sewell didn't answer.

Chief Justice Beasley turned to Judge Murray. "You may continue to inquire."

"I would first like the prosecutor sworn," Judge Murray said.

"I object," Sewell said. "I'm the prosecutor, not the witness."

"Yes, of course," Chief Justice Beasley said. "But here at the Wyoming Supreme Court we follow what we have colloquially referred to as our 'bathtub rule'—that is to say, all witnesses are immersed in the same bathtub when we are scrubbing for the truth, as it were. Please take the witness stand, Mr. Sewell."

Sewell looked at Judge Murray with a killer's eye. Then he walked in snappish steps to the stand, where the judge and Sewell changed places.

"Referring to the night of Mr. Adams's death," Judge Murray began.

Sewell waited.

"That night, Lillian Adams had a conversation in the drugstore with her best friend, Sylvia Huntley?"

Sewell nodded, his jaw set, his eyes hard as river rocks.

"And you claim that you had a confidential source who heard Lillian Adams then and there say to Sylvia Huntley that she, Lillian Adams, 'should kill the son of a bitch,' referring to her late husband, isn't that true?"

"Yes."

"Mr. Coker demanded to know who your claimed witness was who supposedly heard Mrs. Adams make such a statement?"

"Yes."

"And you refused to tell him?"

"Yes. It was told to me in confidence by my source."

"But in truth, no such witness existed except as a fiction that you attempted to fraudulently foist on the court, isn't that true?"

"No, it is not true," Sewell said.

"It was all made up by you, isn't that true?"

"No," Sewell barked back.

"Will you tell the chief justice in private who the source of your information was?"

"No, I will not."

"Very well, I have no further questions of this witness or of myself."

"Do you have anything further?" Justice Beasley asked Sewell.

Without answering Sewell stepped down from the witness stand and took his seat at his table.

"The court will stand in recess for ten minutes," Justice Beasley said.

Timothy Coker hurried to Judge Murray's table, where the judge sat alone, waiting for the return of the judges. "Sewell's so-called confidential source was bogus bullshit, and you exposed his lying ass," Coker said.

"If they don't disbar me here, maybe we could get together again, Timmy," the judge replied.

"You still don't know what's going on," Coker said. "You're about to get good news." He walked back and took his seat by Lillian.

Shortly, the judges returned. Chief Justice Beasley cleared his throat to deliver the opinion of the court.

"During this recess we've come to a decision." He turned to Haskins Sewell with an air of exhausted patience. "We've given this matter more attention than it deserves, Mr. Sewell. It appears that you've knowingly taken a set of innocent facts and have presented them to us as evidence of Judge Murray's wrongdoing.

"However"—the justice cleared his throat again—"it is clear to the court that such enmity exists between you and Judge Murray that this case cannot be concluded with all proper safeguards of due process. We've considered replacing you with another prosecutor. But there is not sufficient time for that. Therefore, we have decided that we should replace you, Judge Murray, with Judge Homer Little of Platte County, who advised us by telephone during our recess that he can take over the trial of this case immediately.

"We further order that the contempt orders against Mr. Sewell be vacated in order to ensure a speedy and adequate trial for the state, reserving, however, the right of this court to intervene at any time as may be required should the prosecutor create grounds for disciplinary action.

"We finally find that the petition for the removal of Judge Murray is denied, but we appoint Judge Little to carry on as the judge in this case, not because of any improper conduct by Judge Murray, but solely to expedite the trial of Mrs. Adams, who is entitled to a fair and speedy disposition of her case."

With that, Chief Justice Beasley struck his gavel, and the justices exited the courtroom in single file, black robes billowing behind them like black angels.

As Haskins Sewell walked past Judge Murray, he spit the words from the side of his mouth: "See you in court, Your Honor." Sewell began to swagger slightly, caught himself, and straightened himself at the shoulders. The courtroom carpet protected against the sound of his tromping feet.

Judge Murray sat dazed.

The supreme court's order left him naked, dangling dead on the tree of innocence. The court had just adjudicated that he was guiltless, but at the same time, it took him off the case and left him to the mercy of Sewell, who would call him to the witness stand and, with other poisoned questions, chop him to bits, until there'd be nothing left but his parched old tattered hide. And this new judge, this Homer Little, was known across the state as a nice but lily-livered jurist who, on his best day, could never handle the likes of Sewell—not for a fractured minute.

The judge looked over at Lillian Adams. She started toward him. But Timothy Coker stepped in front her and said, "You can't talk to anyone, much less Judge Murray. He's now going to be called as a witness against you."

CHAPTER 32

THE JUDGE CALLED Betsy from Cheyenne. She was hysterical. "Where are you? What did they do to you? The sheriff's office won't tell me. I tried to call Tim Coker. I couldn't find him. Are you all right? Why didn't you call me? Have you eaten?"

He couldn't answer her questions fast enough. He couldn't answer them at all. He couldn't remember what he'd told her. He found his way to his pickup, and "the old hunk of junk," as he lovingly called it, proved to be eager to get home again and started right off. He scratched aside a small opening through the frost on the windshield, stuck his nose up to the glass, peered as best he could through the peephole, and put his foot hard on the accelerator. If he was going to die, well, a man should die at home.

Somewhere down the road, he entered into a zone where the voices sounded like Chief Justice Beasley's, and then like Sewell's, and the voices echoed back and forth across the crumbling walls of his mind, and he couldn't make sense of them.

Finally, he pulled the pickup over by the side of the

road and slept—for how long, he didn't know. He wakened to an aching, shivering body. His old bones felt brittle and breakable, like icicles hanging from a roof. His hand shook uncontrollably as he tried to turn the ignition key. Eventually, he got the pickup started, then pulled it back onto the highway.

A couple of hours later, a deer crossed the road. He slammed on the brakes and his foot missed the pedal, but the deer somehow escaped. Everything and everybody was out to get him—Sewell, the judges, the law, even the deer. The snow on the road had turned to ice.

You have no choice, he said to himself. You must fight Sewell with everything you have.

The old truck rattled on.

And now that his decision had been made, he felt resolved and at peace. He sensed a momentary return of his strength. Yet more than once he'd caught himself nearly driving off the road, and from time to time he had to pull the old truck to the side and let sleep take over. Hours later—he couldn't remember how long—and after an interminable wrestling with the invading ghouls, he turned into the lane leading to his cabin.

A porcupine waddled across the road. He slowed nearly to a stop and let it cross. He knew one thing. A certain truth had risen to the top of his madness: He could trust no one in the judicial system. His courthouse was a whorehouse. All had their agendas, and they'd sell themselves to achieve them. The only persons in the world he could trust were Betsy and Hardy Tillman, and, yes, he could trust old Horatio.

When he drove up to the cabin, Betsy came rushing out of the front door. She helped him out of the truck. The walkway was slick and his legs wobbly. Horatio was wiggle-wagging at the judge and pushing at him with his wet nose. The judge put his arm around Betsy's strong shoulders and, one step at a time, they finally made it into the kitchen. He collapsed into his chair next to the stove.

"You look awful," she said. "My God, what did they do to you down there?"

He didn't answer.

She tried to feed him some chicken soup, but he was too tired to eat. She helped him to the bedroom and off with his boots and his suit and pulled the covers over him. He was unable to get up for supper. The next morning, he was able to take half a bowl of oatmeal, and he drank a few sips of hot chocolate.

When he was finally able to tell Betsy what happened, her response was predictable. "That son of a bitch, Sewell," she said. "I ought to kill him myself. He's not going to do that to you or to Lillian."

He slept the rest of the day.

The following morning, Betsy coaxed the judge to eat a boiled egg and a slice of toast. The thought of returning to the courthouse, where he'd have to face all the courthouse hens, intimidated him. But a man had to face his fear. Such is the definition of courage, and in these, his last days, he thought he must be courageous.

The work had piled up on his desk—motions to be heard, orders to be drafted, lawyers playing their games—it was all a game. The courthouse crew would be watching him, a judge who'd been thrown off his case by the great judges in Cheyenne, and a judge who'd soon be shredded into particles of raw flesh by the prosecutor, Sewell.

On his way to court, he stopped at Hardy's. As was his habit, the judge flopped down into his old ripped-up chair. He could hear the air hoses popping, the sound of men wrestling with the steel rims of tires, the laughter of workingmen, and Hardy's shrill yeoman's voice barking orders. Too early to drink, but he needed strength. He pulled a Horace Adams out of the old refrigerator and opened it. He propped his feet up on a couple of old tires and took a long draw on his beer. When Hardy opened the door, he examined the judge like a doctor searching for symptoms.

"I hear them judges in Cheyenne threw your ass off the case." He pulled out a beer for himself. "Jesus," he said. "What the hell's the matter with them old petrified stumps down there?"

"They said I didn't do anything wrong."

"Well, you kept putting the boot to Sewell, an' he finally got ya. I always said you should never kick a fresh turd on a hot day. But I ain't criticizing you none." The judge took another swig and slumped farther down in his chair. They were silent for a while. His bottle empty, the judge got up to go.

Hardy walked over and patted the judge on the shoulder, which was as close as Hardy Tillman could come to expressing such an uncomfortable emotion as affection. "I wish I knew whose ass to kick, and I'd do it for you." He took the last swig of his own beer. "Maybe I'll start with that sack a moldy donkey shit, Sewell."

That night, the judge was in bed and asleep in the cabin when a little past midnight the phone began to ring. He stumbled over a footstool, smashed his shins against the coffee table, and screamed into the phone, "Who is it?"

It was Hardy. "You'd better come down here and get me out. They got me in here fer something I never done. All I done was defend myself against your friend Haskins Sewell—"

"Don't say anything more, Hardy. They're recording

whatever you're saying. I'll be down as soon as I can get my truck going."

Twenty below. The old truck ground away and begged to be left alone, took a last feeble, frozen breath, and quit. The judge stumbled through the snow, and from the kitchen, with Betsy's help, he strung out the battery charger cables, opened the hood, found the battery, checked the polarity, and hooked up the alligator clamps. Betsy put some wood in the stove and brewed a pot of coffee. When he finally got his truck going and arrived at the jail, it was past three in the morning.

He was still the judge. He ordered Hardy released on his personal bond and waited for the night clerk to process the paperwork. At about five in the morning, the jailer, Gilbert Prosser, a retired postal worker, ambled down the corridor with his prisoner. "Here's your friend, Your Honor," he said.

Without preface, Hardy said, "These retarded peckerheads got me charged with something I never done."

"We'll talk later, Hardy," the judge said.

They climbed into the judge's truck. The Big Chief Café was just opening. They stopped for a cup of coffee.

"All I done was go down to the sheriff's office, looking around fer Sewell. He hangs out there all the time. I seen his car parked out front, and I waited in my car until he come out of the sheriff's office, and I just sort of walked up to him friendly like to have me a little conversation with him."

"Like what, for Christ sake, Hardy?"

"Well, I says to old Sewell, 'I'd like to tell you a little story.' And he is trying to walk past me, and I says, 'Just don't be such an impolite bastard. You're a public servant, and I got me a little story to tell you,' and he stopped in his tracks and give me a dirty look, like I was nothing but pure dog shit."

Hardy took a swig of black coffee and continued. "I says, 'Once there was a DA who thought his shit didn't stink, an' who got too big for his britches. And you know what happened to him?' Old Sewell jus' stood there, and then he tried to push me out of the way. Now note," Hardy said with all due emphasis, "he pushed me. I never touched him. So when he pushed me, I had no other way to go except to kick his ass in self-defense. So that there is just what I done."

"Jesus Christ, what did you do to Sewell, Hardy?"

"Like I told you, I kicked his ass. I reached up and grabbed hold of his ear, and then I led him around real easy like, him following me like a pup on a leash, and when his ass was to me, well, I gave it a good hard kick."

"And then what, for Christ sake?"

"I just turned him back around, and he was looking real scared, and he starts running back to the sheriff's office. But I caught him because I had to defend myself, you know. A guy like him might be going for a gun or something. Anyway, I stops him, and I grabs both ears, and I pulls him up close to me, eye-to-eye, and I says, 'Now, you walking prick with ears, if I hear anything more about what you're doing to a certain friend of mine whose name I shall not mention, I am going to kick yer ass up so high, you'll have to take your hat off to shit, you understand?' An' I jerked both of his ears real good so he'd understand. That there is all I done, and I done it hundred percent out of self-defense, as you can plainly see."

CHAPTER 33

IT WAS NEARING five in the afternoon. Finally, Jenny Winkley tapped on the door to his office, and when there was no answer, she hit the door with her fists, and when there still was no answer, she hollered, "Are you all right in there?" He'd locked the door and fallen asleep on the old couch after his long night with Hardy.

"I'm ready to kill," the judge finally muttered.

"What's the matter with you?" she harped. "What did you eat for breakfast?"

"I am speaking metaphorically," the judge finally heard himself reply.

He sat up and ran his fingers though his hair. He was more exhausted than ever. He realized he was in his chambers. Yes, he was the judge, and he had duties—his cancerous docket had continued to grow and threatened to consume him. The supreme court had stripped him of his powers but not of his duties.

"What are you doing in there?" she demanded.

He didn't answer. If it wasn't Jenny Winkley, it would be some other member of the courthouse gang. All were his enemies. One way or another, they would get him.

When he finally struggled to his feet and opened the door, Jenny thrust the newspaper at him.

JUDGE MURRAY REMOVED
FROM ADAMS CASE

Today the Wyoming Supreme Court removed Judge John Murray from the Lillian Adams murder trial. Judge Homer Little of Platte County has been appointed by the court to sit in his stead.

The story reviewed the history of the trial, repeating Sewell's allegations that more than a passing relationship existed between the judge and Lillian Adams. The judge threw the paper down without finishing the story.

"You got good press," Jenny Winkley said, still smiling. He'd never noticed before: She reminded him of a Rhode Island Red hen—her henna red hair, her skinny legs, the puffed-up middle, and the chicken's beak. "You never finished reading it," she clucked. She picked the paper up from the floor. "Look! Right here." She jabbed at the last paragraph of a story that covered the entire front page of the paper. "It says that the state supreme court found you didn't do anything wrong. That should help a lot." Her smile creases were foreign to the scenery of her face. "I'm going to clip this out and put it in your scrapbook. This will stop all that courthouse gossip."

"All they'll remember is that this licentious old coot, me, had a relationship with a woman charged with murder in his court, that she is more than thirty years his junior, and that the old bastard, me, ought to be impeached. That's what they'll remember."

"No. The clerk said he knew all along you weren't a . . . you know what he called it."

"A cockhound, I suppose."

"Something like that," she said. "And Martha Stern-houser over in the county clerk's office said she knew you had a lot of chances at women, and you never fell. But then, none of them was as good-looking as Lillian Adams, I'll say that."

"So a man is only innocent of philandering in direct proportion to the beauty of the woman involved. I'd have to be a pedophile to get involved with Lillian."

"She isn't that young."

Why shouldn't she suspect me? he thought. And the more he protested, the more they'd believe he was a rotten old pussy chaser and had been from the beginning.

"Well, I know you're innocent if the Wyoming Supreme Court found that you were. I had my suspicions for a while." She seemed happy, even light-headed.

He felt a flood of self-hatred. He'd always been repulsed by those old toads who had no libido left except in their bony fingers and their coated old tongues. How could anyone love his old sack of hide and bones? Such is Betsy's major fault, he thought.

He fought for his breath, thinking he must be on the brink of a heart attack. So this was the way he'd cross the river Styx and take that endless dive into eternity. He wasn't afraid of death. It would be the wondrous, dreamless sleep that Plato predicted. If the heart attack was coming, let it come. Hurry and be done with it. But he wanted to die at home.

He got to his truck, reached up to adjust his rearview mirror, and felt something foreign. He pulled the mirror around, and staring him in the face was a tiny microphone neatly attached there with electrician's tape.

A new wave of fear immersed him.

What had he said aloud in his truck? Had he been talking to himself, for Christ sake? How long had that microphone been there? Had it been there that night after court when Lillian Adams was waiting for him in the pickup, when she'd said those uninvited words: "I'm so sorry, Judge Murray, for all the trouble I've caused you. I killed Horace because—"

He felt raped. And he felt sudden anger. How dare they bug a judge! He would order a hearing immediately, and throw all the bastards in jail! Yes, he would call in the attorney general and have him appoint a prosecutor pro tem. In the morning, he would interrogate both of them in his chambers, Sewell and the sheriff, one at a time, the cowardly, sneaking sons of bitches.

When he arrived at the cabin, there stood the sheriff's white Chevrolet parked in front of his door, a fog of exhaust rising from the engine. Undersheriff Jim Bromley, along with a deputy he didn't recognize, got out of the car. Bromley swaggered up to the judge's truck and yanked open the door.

"Good evening, Judge," he said in an injuriously hard voice. "You know Deputy Bill Hannery here? We've come out of duty, Judge. You wouldn't want it any other way. We have a warrant for your arrest. Hand the judge the warrant, Bill," he said to the deputy, who was wearing his new uniform.

The judge sat frozen in the seat of his pickup, both hands gripping the steering wheel.

"Get out of your truck, Judge," Bromley ordered. The young deputy grabbed hold of the old man's arm and pulled at him. He started to fall, but Bromley caught him, snapped the cuffs on the judge, and led him to the sheriff's car. He protected the judge's head with his hands to prevent him from smacking it against the car's roof until the judge was safely seated inside. Then Bromley slammed the door and crawled into the passenger side, the young deputy in the driver's seat.

It was then that Betsy came running out of the house, wielding the judge's shotgun. Old Horatio ran ahead of her. She ran toward the sheriff's car as it pulled out of the yard, the shotgun at her shoulder swaying back and forth with each step.

Old Horatio charged after the car, barking. As the patrol car slowed to make the turn onto the main road, Bromley rolled down the window, leaned out with this .357 Magnum pistol, and fired at Horatio. The old dog let out a surprised yelp when the bullet entered his chest. He fell. Then Bromley fired a second shot and the dog slumped into a pile on the snow, shaking from postmortem fibrillations, the snow strained crimson where he lay.

"What did ya do that for?" Hannery said to Bromley. "The dog wasn't hurting nothing."

"Self-defense," Bromley said.

"You dirty, rotten son of a bitch," the judge hollered. "I'm going to kill you if it's the last thing I do."

Betsy had stopped running. She raised the shotgun. It was too long and too heavy, and the shot went awry. Gasping for breath, Betsy ran to where the old dog lay lifeless. She stood for a long time staring down at the pile of bloody fur in the snow. Then she ran back to the cabin.

Wild with anger and screaming beyond the limit of his old lungs, Judge Murray continued to threaten the officers from the rear seat of the sheriff's car. Bromley turned their radio up to high blast, so that the car was drowned in loud disharmony. Then he hollered at the judge, "Shut up, you old fart."

"You rotten bastards," the judge hollered back, "how could you shoot a harmless old dog?"

"If you hadn't shot that crazy cur, he'd have tore us

apart," Bill said. "And that old lady of his had her shotgun on us. We had to get the hell out of there in a hurry, or she would have killed us both." They both laughed.

"Women are goddamned nuisance and are good for only one thing, and you know what that is," Bromley said. "I had three of them, and there wasn't one of them worth a shit."

"That's because you don't know how to pick them," Hannery said. "Them's who can cook usually can't do nothing else, if ya get my meaning."

"You're a whole lot smarter than you look," Bromley said.

At the courthouse, Bromley jerked the judge out of the car. The old man felt like a trapped rat. He found himself looking for avenues of escape. He'd been a respected member of society all his life, but now he'd been reduced to a felon, separated from the community by a piece of paper called an arrest warrant.

He tried to force the idea of escape from his mind. He was a judge, not a criminal. Besides, he couldn't run. He clutched the warrant in his cuffed hands. The officers pushed him into an elevator, which landed him on a floor where Deputy Huffsmith met them at the door.

Huffsmith looked sad. "Sorry to meet you here under these circumstances," Huffsmith said to the judge. "Now I got to search you." He pushed the judge gently to the wall, spun him around, removed the handcuffs, and then began patting him down.

"Now would you empty your pockets?" He put a tray on the counter in front of the judge.

The judge took out his billfold and dropped it in the tray. It contained two one-dollar bills, his driver's license, and a picture of Betsy.

"Now the watch and the ring, Judge."

The watch was a cheap thing he'd bought at the drugstore, plastic band and big numbers so that he could read it without his glasses. The ring was his wedding ring, which Betsy had put on his finger at the altar, love in her eyes, her happy voice saying that they would remain one "until death do us part." He gave Huffsmith his watch.

"The ring, Judge."

"Can't give you the ring," the judge said. "Betsy put this on me when we were married, and we promised never to take our rings off. You'll have to cut my finger off before I'll take it off."

The deputy called to the undersheriff. "The prisoner wants us to cut his finger off," Huffsmith said.

Undersheriff Bromley stomped into the room, showed the judge his crooked brown teeth and red gums. "You know what can happen by accident to prisoners who want to give us a lot of trouble."

"I'm still the judge in this county, and I order you to leave my ring on my finger. It is not dangerous to anyone, and it's sacred to me. Do you understand, Undersheriff?"

"Yes, I understand, Judge. So are ya going to give us the damn ring, or do we have to take it off of you?"

When the judge didn't answer, Bromley nodded to Huffsmith, who came up behind the judge and grabbed him under the arms. Then Bromley took hold of his feet and they laid the old man on the floor. His head jarred against the concrete.

"Bill," Bromley hollered to Deputy Hannery, "get me that bar of soap in the can." When the deputy came back with the soap, Bromley spit on the soap a couple of times, then coated the judge's finger with the lather and pulled off the ring.

"Now that wasn't too bad, was it, Judge?" Bromley said. His breath was full in the face of the judge, and foul. "Ya see, if ya cooperate with us, things go easier."

The old man struggled to his hands and knees. He tried to stand up. Huffsmith reached down and, with his hands under the judge's armpits, lifted him. "Now take your shoes and socks off."

The judge felt embarrassed. His toenails were too long.

Huffsmith said, "Step over here now. Stand up against the wall."

He took the judge's picture.

Then the deputy took the judge's fingerprints.

"I want to talk to a judge about bond."

"This here is Friday, as you may remember," Huffsmith said. "And it's past five o'clock. You got to wait until Monday to get your bond set."

"That's unacceptable."

"Well, everybody works five days a week now'days. And there ain't no other judge around since you got crossways with the law. Besides, you think we're supposed to make this jail run for the convenience of the criminals?"

"I told you, I am not a criminal."

"Then what are you doing here if you ain't?"

"I'm here because a bunch of other criminals conspired to put me here."

"You want to make a call before I lock you up for the night?"

"My wife will hire a lawyer."

The deputy handed the judge some canvas shoes with rubber soles, a toothbrush, a small tube of toothpaste, and a small black plastic comb. When he was finally dressed in his new jail clothes—a short-sleeved slip-over blue cotton top with a V-neck and a pair of blue cotton pants—Deputy Huffsmith led him like a well-disciplined child to his cell.

CHAPTER 34

EACH DAY AFTER court, often late into the night, Coker worked with Lillian, preparing her to testify. Coker and Lillian agreed: Tina's involvement in Horace's death, whatever it was, would not be part of their defense. Coker argued that the jurors would hate Lillian for blaming her child. Lillian would hate herself for the same reason. Besides, despite Tina's insistence she had shot her stepfather, Lillian remained steadfast that Tina was innocent. Horace had intervened to end his own life. That, Lillian insisted, was the defense and the truth.

Still the question hung heavy over the case: Could Coker convince a jury that Horace had killed himself in the face of that questionable suicide note? People on the ragged edge of psychosis sometimes suffered a change in their handwriting. Coker would argue that Widdoss's testimony was provided to Sewell in exchange for the payment he received from the prosecution. Pure business.

Would Lillian fold as a witness under the fire of Sewell's cross-examination? Ordinarily, she could hold her own in any argument. But Coker had his doubts. She could take shelter behind the Fifth Amendment and not testify. But Coker knew that most jurors would think, Don't try to fool me with that Fifth Amendment bullshit. The Fifth is for crooks and killers. Yet the more Coker tried to prepare Lillian as a witness, the more his provisional decision began to solidify. He thought she would likely wilt or detonate on the stand. Either would do her in.

Each day, Tina was becoming more erratic. Believing that Mrs. Houseman and the nurse, Mrs. Clemmins, were conspiring with Sewell to kill her, Tina pulled a butcher knife on Mrs. Houseman and the nurse, and both ran out of the house. Mrs. Houseman called the sheriff's office as well as Lillian, who'd been working with Coker after court. When Deputy Huffsmith responded to the call, he found Tina standing in the kitchen in her pajamas, the butcher knife still in her hand.

"Put that knife down," Deputy Arthur Huffsmith ordered. "I'm here because your mother sent for me." Lillian had arrived almost simultaneously and was standing next to the deputy.

Tina looked at her mother. "Yes, Tina, put the knife down. I'm here. Mrs. Houseman and Mrs. Clemmins are here. Deputy Huffsmith is here. We are all your friends." Only then did the girl hesitantly lay the knife on the table.

"Now we're going to have ourselves a little talk," Huffsmith said to Tina. He motioned to a chair he'd pulled out from the kitchen table. "Sit down," he said in a commanding voice. Her eyes darted in panic around the room, and at last, concluding there was no escape, she obeyed and eased slowly into a chair at the kitchen table, her hand close to the knife. Then Deputy Huffsmith, Lillian, and Mrs. Houseman also took chairs around the table. Mrs. Clemmins stood against the wall near the back-door entry hall. Tina stared at the deputy, a mask of fear fastened to her face.

"Now, Tina, I am your friend. I am a friend of your mom here."

Lillian nodded.

"I am a friend of Mrs. Houseman. We are all your friends. Your enemies are not in this house," Huffsmith said. "Everyone here is your friend, and everyone wants the best for you. Do you understand?"

Tina watched the deputy like a cornered animal.

"Now, you are in control of us. We are not in control of you. Do you understand?"

She remained silent, her eyes wide and unblinking.

"Yes, you're in control," he said again. "Because if you decide to be good and peaceful and cooperate, you can keep bad things from happening to you. You get in control by controlling yourself, do you understand?"

Her eyes were still wide with terror.

"But if you act crazy and pull knives, and make Mrs. Houseman call me, then you ain't in control of yourself, and you can't control nobody else. Do you understand?"

No response.

"So you want me to be in control of you, or do you want to be in control of yourself?"

Tina didn't answer.

"Tell me if you're hearing me."

A slight nod.

"Is there something you ain't saying that you want to tell me?" Huffsmith asked.

He waited.

Finally, in a high, childlike voice, Tina said, "I'm in control."

"Okay," Huffsmith said. "If you're in control, then hand the knife here to Mrs. Houseman and tell her how sorry you are for acting like you did. She cares about you, and you hurt her feelings. If this happens again, and I have to be in control, I will take you away from here, and you won't be able to come back. You wouldn't like that, would you?"

She shook her head no. Tina lifted the knife by the blade and offered it to Mrs. Houseman, who took it and returned it to the knife drawer.

"Now how did it make you feel, Mrs. Houseman, for Tina to pull that knife on you?" Huffsmith asked.

"It scared me. Tina and I get along very well, and we like each other."

"What do you have to say to Mrs. Houseman, Tina?"

"I'm sorry," Tina sobbed. Mrs. Houseman went to the girl and put her arms around her.

"You see there, you are in control," Huffsmith said. "When you are in control, you treat people right, and they treat you right. Do you understand?"

"Yes," Tina murmured.

Lillian walked with the deputy to the door. "How did you know what to do?"

"My brother has mental problems," Huffsmith said. "I learned this the hard way. He got violent because he thought people was going to kill him. He read a lot of them murder-mystery books, and we had to keep 'em from him."

"What happened to him?"

"He's better now. He lives with us. Long as he's on his meds, he's pretty good. He's a couple years older than me. He does yard work in the summer to help out. He's a good man." Huffsmith's eyes got cloudy, and he turned away.

CHAPTER 35

THE FOLLOWING MORNING, the judge once again heard the flat, tuneless voice over the loudspeaker: "You have a visitor, Murray."

Jenny Winkley greeted him with a reluctant smile in the jail's visitor's room.

"You look like something dead that the dog drug in." She handed the judge a note from Betsy:

Honey, I buried Horatio in my tulip garden. Next spring he'll come up as a bouquet of red tulips.

I'm going to L.A. to hire Marvin Grimes to represent you. You said he is the best. But he's also very expensive. The cabin is clear. We can borrow on it. Marvin Grimes will save us. Next to you, he is the best.

Love,
Betsy

"Betsy told me to get the mortgage papers on the cabin ready for you to sign," Jenny said.

"You find Betsy," the judge said, trying to maintain his composure, "and you tell her that I'm not guilty of anything, that I do not need the best lawyer in the West, and that I am not going to sign any papers on our cabin. Tell her that if I go to prison, she's at least going to have a place to live."

"I thought that's what you'd say," Jenny said. She handed him the morning paper with its headline story.

JUDGE AND FRIEND JAILED
ON CONSPIRACY CHARGES

Judge John Murray and his longtime friend Hardy Tillman were both arrested and jailed yesterday following charges filed by Haskins Sewell, Teton County prosecutor, alleging that the two had conspired to obstruct justice.

The charges arise out of an alleged assault by Tillman against Mr. Sewell. A person close to the prosecutor's office, on the condition of anonymity, said that the assault was an attempt by Tillman, on behalf of Judge Murray, to intimidate Sewell in his prosecution of Lillian Adams, who is presently being tried for murder in the Teton County District Court.

Judge Murray was removed from the case by order of the Wyoming Supreme Court. That court found that the enmity between Sewell and Murray was of such a nature and degree that a fair trial could not be conducted with Murray presiding.

Jenny watched the judge as he read the news story.

"The bastards," the judge said. "Hardy didn't do anything."

"They arrested him because of your case," Jenny said.

"But now we have to worry about you. What do you want me to do? I'm still on your payroll—but for how long? One might wonder."

"Tell Betsy I'll be out of here soon, and see that old Horatio is taken care of," the judge said. Then suddenly, he realized Horatio was dead. He didn't want to tear up in front of Jenny Winkley. He turned away and bit his lip until it bled.

CHAPTER 36

JUDGE HOMER LITTLE from Platte County, newly appointed by the Wyoming Supreme Court as the presiding judge for the murder trial of Lillian Adams, mounted the three steps to the bench. He settled in Judge Murray's old chair.

The Widdoss testimony was Judge Little's first order of business. Over Coker's objection, Judge Little made his ruling: "Although the theory of handwriting analysis might not be tested in a manner that satisfies the defense, and although standards may or may not exist for applying the technique, nevertheless, I will allow Mr. Widdoss's testimony for whatever assistance it may be to the jury."

"You mean as it may assist the jury to arrive at a wrong conclusion, like convicting an innocent woman?" Coker asked.

"Counsel, your reputation for insolence toward the court has preceded you," Judge Little said. "I'll be making note of your comments for further reference if that is indicated."

Judge Little turned to Sewell. "I've read the transcript taken when Judge Murray was presiding and accept the foundation you laid at that time. Proceed, Mr. Sewell, with your presentation."

Once again, Hamilton Widdoss took the stand. He testified he'd been provided copies of Lillian's checks, which the sheriff had seized after serving a subpoena on the bank. He had also examined other exemplars of Horace's handwriting.

"So what is your conclusion?" Sewell asked.

"I am able to say with reasonable scientific probability that the so-called suicide note, Exhibit five, was not written by the deceased, Horace Adams the Third, and that this forgery was likely written by his wife, Lillian Adams."

Stunned silence smothered the courtroom.

Lillian Adams clutched at Timothy Coker's arm and whispered wildly into his ear.

"May I have a short recess?" Coker asked Judge Little.

"We'll recess for ten minutes," the judge said with a patronizing nod and his standard mechanical smile.

"Timothy, you have to break him down. He's a horrible liar. I did not write that note!" Her anger melted into tears of frustration.

"Well, okay, you didn't, and so the son of a bitch is lying to earn his fee. These experts lie all the time," Coker said. "Those who tell the largest lies usually charge the most. But I will get him on cross."

When court resumed, Coker retrieved the notes he'd scribbled during the recess and began his cross-examination in a weary voice. "Mr. Widdoss, how much are you being paid for your testimony here today?".

"I am receiving one hundred dollars an hour for my testimony."

The plumber let out a soft whistle. He had to muck through a lot of vile stuff, and in the worst case never earned a fee like that.

"That's more than some folks make in a month," Coker said. "You certainly intend to earn your fee here, don't you?" He raised an inquiring eyebrow.

"Argumentative!" Sewell cried.

"Hold it down," Judge Little said to Sewell. Then the judge sustained his objection.

Coker continued: "Mr. Widdoss, you don't think Mr. Sewell would pay you such a fee for your testimony if you were going to tell this jury that the note was genuine, and that Lillian Adams had nothing to do with it?"

"Argumentative!" Sewell objected.

"Move on, Mr. Coker," the judge ruled.

"Very well," Coker replied. "This man did not write with great handwriting flourishes, isn't that true?"

"Yes."

"His was a rather ordinary hand?"

"In that context, yes," Widdoss replied. "As a matter of fact, his writing was quite, shall we say, boring."

"His writing reflected his personality, didn't it?" Coker said.

"I'm told he was not the most charismatic individual."

"Now what was the difference between Mr. Adams's writing style and the style you examined in the suicide note?"

"The questioned note reflects a significant spacing between the words. I've seen hundreds of known samples of his writings, and I've not found a single instance in which he wrote with the wide spacing we see on Exhibit five, the so-called suicide note."

"Well, isn't that interesting?" Coker said.

Widdoss continued: "And you will observe that the end letters of the words often drag down in the questioned suicide note, while the end letters of his known writing samples always end up."

"Well, yes, I can see that," Coker said.

Coker continued: "You've testified previously that writing habits can be altered if the author is under the influence of drugs or alcohol, isn't that true, Mr. Widdoss?"

"Yes, I've testified to that proposition."

Coker continued leafing through the papers on his desk, one page at a time. At last, he pulled a paper from the stack. The page was merely a note from Coker's bookie giving him "the inside scoop" on an upcoming race at Churchill Downs. Coker appeared deeply focused on the paper. "And have you previously testified the reason that the spacing may be farther apart and that the end letters may drag downward is because the writer's control over his pen is diminished when he's burdened by the influence of drugs or alcohol?"

"I suppose I've said that."

"But forgive me. Of course, there was no evidence in this case that the deceased, Horace Adams the Third, was drunk or otherwise under the influence of drugs."

"None that I know of."

"I take it that the prosecutor didn't bother to tell you that Mr. Adams's blood was tested after death, and that he threw a blood alcohol of point two—enough, if the test was accurate, for most men to pass out?"

The witness looked as if he'd just taken a lethal belly blow. "I wasn't told that."

"Were you told that an almost empty bottle of scotch was found at the scene?"

"No, I wasn't."

"Your testimony is only as good as the information you're provided, isn't that true?"

"If you say so."

"Well, Mr. Widdoss, this whole business of handwriting analysis can sometimes lead to serious and fatal false conclusions, isn't that true?"

"I don't know what you mean," Widdoss said, failing to disguise that he knew exactly what Coker meant.

"You, of course, know that a world-famous handwriting expert, indeed the father of handwriting analysis, has admitted that both he and other purported experts in his field have been dead wrong?"

Widdoss looked over to Sewell for help. Sewell pretended to be busy thumbing through a pile of documents.

"So the best in the business can make serious mistakes, isn't that true, Mr. Widdoss?"

"I suppose."

"No, Mr. Widdoss, I asked, 'Isn't that true?'"

"Yes, we can all make mistakes, but—"

"Do you consider yourself to be the best in the business?"

"Objection. This is sheer insulting argument," Sewell complained.

"It is argumentative," the judge ruled.

"Now, Mr. Widdoss, you charge one hundred dollars an hour for your testimony?"

"That's been asked and answered," Sewell objected.

"Sustained," Judge Little ruled.

"Well, I will not take more of your time, because we taxpayers in this county can't afford you."

Laughter in the gallery. The judge struck his gavel.

"I have no further questions," Coker said.

Sewell rushed to repair his torn witness. "Mr. Widdoss, I take it that the science in the early days was rather crude, and that there have been many improvements since that date."

"Many," Widdoss said.

"That's all I have," Sewell said, sitting down.

Coker spoke while standing at his table. "Well, Mr. Widdoss, for you to charge one hundred dollars an hour, there must be a whole hell of a lot of improvements. Could you name one?"

Widdoss looked at Coker, ostensibly in deep thought. At last he said, "There have been many improvements in the use of better microscopes and other instruments."

"Did you use a microscope?"

"It wasn't necessary."

"Did you use any other instruments not heretofore used by handwriting experts?"

"No."

"Thank you, Mr. Widdoss. No further questions."

At counsel table, Lillian Adams grabbed Coker's arm. "You just saved my life," she whispered.

"Don't count on it yet," Coker whispered back. "That son of a bitch," he said, nodding toward Sewell, "is just getting started."

Then Sewell, acting as if the annihilation of his handwriting expert had been only of passing interest, announced, "The state calls Sylvia Huntley for further questioning."

CHAPTER 37

SHERIFF LOWE HAD secured Hardy Tillman in leg shackles and handcuffs, and half-dragged, half-pushed Hardy into the interrogation room of the Teton County jail. The lights were hurtfully bright and directly in Hardy's face. Undersheriff Jim Bromley made up the threesome. Bromley paced back and forth.

"You know what we want," Sheriff Lowe began from the opposite end of the table. "We want to make it as easy on you as we can, Hardy. But this is a two-way street. You can't expect us to pat you on the head for what you done to Haskins Sewell without giving us a little help." He gave Hardy Tillman his best campaign smile.

"Well, I never seen you so shy, Sheriff. What the hell do you want from me?"

"I want you to tell me the truth."

"No, you want me to lie. The truth ain't going to do you no good. Now why don't you take these cuffs off of me?"

Undersheriff Bromley chimed in, still pacing the

floor, "We can't take the cuffs off of you. You're classi-fied as an extreme risk."

"How come? All I done was kick Sewell's ass in self-defense."

"We know you assaulted him because Judge Murray asked you to," Lowe said.

"That there is so much bullshit. The judge would have never asked me to do no such a goddamned thing. I done it on my own." Then he realized he hadn't added the critical words and did so: "And I done it in self-defense."

Bromley shoved his face into Hardy's face. "Well, are you gonna cooperate or not? I am losing my patience."

"You never had none in the first place. You're too dumb to have any patience."

"So what do you say about our deal, Hardy?" Sheriff Lowe asked.

"I say, kiss my ass, Sheriff, and if that ain't enough, you can kiss it twice."

When prosecutor Sewell called Sylvia Huntley back to the stand, she glanced at the jurors, her teeth set and her jaw jutted out in defiance. Sewell bowed slightly to the jurors and got right to it.

"I think, Ms. Huntley, when we left off, we were about to discuss a conversation you had with Mrs. Adams at the drugstore the night Mr. Adams died. Do you re-member?"

"Yes, I remember."

"She talked to you about her husband?"

"I told you before in your office, I told you before in this courtroom, and I tell you now: What she said to me was personal and private and I will not reveal it."

Coker rose. "I object. This is the same dirty trick—"

"Hold on, counsel," Judge Little said, interrupting. He excused the jury and ordered the lawyers, along with Lillian Adams and the court reporter, into the judge's chambers.

Sewell began in a surprisingly quiet voice. "Rather than petitioning this court to hold this witness in contempt, I ask the court to recognize Ms. Huntley as a hostile witness. I should be permitted to cross-examine her. In doing so, I may be able to avoid the contempt issue altogether."

"I object," Coker countered. "This prosecutor refused, even in private, to identify for the Wyoming Supreme Court who his alleged confidential source was who supposedly heard Mrs. Adams say, 'I should kill the son of a bitch.' Once the jurors hear Sewell ask that question, and they hear Ms. Huntley refuse to answer, they can only conclude that Mrs. Adams said those words, and that she promptly returned home and murdered her husband."

"I've heard enough," Judge Little said. "I've read the transcript of Ms. Huntley's testimony when she was a witness before this same jury, with Judge Murray presiding. I disagree with his ruling. I find that the witness is hostile. You may proceed with your cross-examination, Mr. Sewell."

"But Your Honor—" Coker began.

Judge Little hit his gavel. "I have to say, gentlemen, this is far too elementary for further argument. Mr. Sewell is an officer of this court, and I will take his representation that all questions he asks in cross-examination have a good-faith basis."

"Just a minute, please," Coker said in a last-ditch effort. "If he has a good-faith basis for asking this poisoned question, then he has the duty to reveal who his witness is."

"Exculpatory evidence—facts supporting the innocence of Lillian Adams—must be revealed," Sewell argued. "No such evidence exists here."

"I agree," the judge ruled.

Back in the courtroom, Sewell focused his anger on Sylvia Huntley.

"Concerning your conversation with Mrs. Adams in the drugstore—"

Sylvia Huntley interrupted: "I am not going to answer any questions about our confidential conversation."

"At that time and place, Mrs. Adams told you that, and I quote, 'I should kill the son of a bitch,' isn't that true?"

Cocker stormed to the bench again. "There's the poisoned question I have been objecting to," Coker bellowed. "Is there no decency left in this world? We have as much right to believe that Mrs. Adams was discussing her private sex life with Ms. Huntley as anything so venal as murder. Counsel is using his own concocted poisoned question to inform the jury of a conversation that never happened."

"Answer the question," the judge said to Sylvia Huntley.

"I refuse to answer," she replied. She bit at her lower lip.

Sewell started toward his table, but then Sylvia Huntley said, "I've changed my mind. I will answer the question. But please repeat it."

"Yes," Sewell said. "I shall. This defendant"—he pointed at Lillian—"told you that she 'should kill the son of a bitch,' referring to her husband, Horace Adams the Third, isn't that true?"

"No," she said. "My answer to that question is no, it isn't true."

"Really," Sewell said.

"Really," Sylvia Huntley echoed.

"So, pray tell, what did you talk about that was so private?"

"I refuse to answer that question."

"She said she 'should kill the son of a bitch,' didn't she?"

"No. I said it once. I will say it again. My answer to that question is no. She said no such thing."

"You don't want to tell the jury the truth because you don't want harm to come to your friend, isn't that true?" Sewell demanded.

"I don't want harm to come to Lillian because of your filthy lies, but she did not say that."

Sewell turned to Judge Little. "I ask the court to order the witness to answer my question."

"The witness answered your question," Judge Little said. "She said that Mrs. Adams didn't say what you claimed she said."

"She won't tell us what she claims they talked about," Sewell said.

"Show me its relevance and I'll order her to answer," Judge Little said to Sewell.

"How can I show you its relevance if she won't tell me what they talked about?" Sewell said, his frustration mounting.

"Didn't your confidential source tell you what they were talking about?" Judge Little asked.

Sewell looked up at Judge Little. "I have no further questions," Sewell said.

"Very well," the judge said to Sylvia Huntley. "You may step down, and you are released from your subpoena."

The next morning, Huffsmith was at the judge's cell door. The deputy helped the judge to his feet and led him slowly, carefully to the interrogation room.

Gradually, the judge saw the pain etched all too clearly on Huffsmith's worn face.

"How's your son's leukemia?" the judge asked.

"We don't know. The doctors don't know neither." Huffsmith glanced back at the judge and then as quickly away. "Also, the bank changed the terms on our new mortgage, and we got the foreclosure notice from the bank today."

"What!" the judge exclaimed. He felt a surge of life. "They can't get away with that!"

"Maybe, but I can't take no help from nobody who's in our jail," Huffsmith said. "It's against the rules."

"I don't know of any rule against taking a little advice from a jailhouse judge," the judge said. "Now just where is your house located?"

"You know, it's that old brown house next to old Abberly's bank," Huffsmith said. "My brother Stevie and me got it from our pa when he died. It took me and my wife twenty years to pay off Stevie, but me and Ruthie owned it free and clear until our boy, Ted, got sick."

The judge nodded and listened.

"Old Abberly's been trying to buy it for the bank's parking lot, but we don't want to sell it. Where would we go? I grew up there, and so did our kids. And that's the only place that Ted feels safe in, and besides, we don't want the old house torn down—like tearing down what your pa put up, or something."

The judge nodded.

"But we needed the money to pay Ted's bills, and we borrowed from the bank." Huffsmith caught himself. "I ain't here to talk about my problems. We all got problems, Judge. Mine ain't as bad as some. But could you help me a little by not being so stubborn and agree to tell the jury the truth?"

"How much did you borrow?" the judge asked.

"Twenty-five thousand."

"How much are your monthly payments to the bank?"

"We had to pay two hundred a month. Of course, I only make a little more than that, so we couldn't make our payments. We paid all we could. Old Abberly said it was okay if we just paid what we could."

"I see it all now," the judge said with sudden clarity.

"We was paying a hundred a month. We sold our fishing boat, and we sold our old jeep, which I used to take to the mountains, and we cashed in our pension and all. I ain't supposed to talk about this, Judge. You know that."

"So how far behind are you?"

"Six months. And old Abberly says he's foreclosing, and he is sorry but there ain't nothing he can do about it—the bank examiners are on his ass, he says. So he put the notice of foreclosure in the paper. He says he already give us six months and that he can't give us no more time."

"Sounds like he's a really caring man," the judge said.

"If you think nobody cares if you're missing, well, try missing a couple of house payments to the bank," Huffsmith said. "They'll find you every time."

"So what do the powers that be offer me for my testimony?" the judge asked.

"The powers that be want you to plead guilty to obstructing justice. I mean, it won't hurt you none, because this here is your first offense, and they'll recommend probation. That way, the whole deal will be cleaned up and you can go home."

"You tell the powers that be that I am thinking about their deal—thinking about it real hard. I'll give you an answer tomorrow."

CHAPTER 38

HARDY USED HIS one permitted call from the Teton County jail to phone whom he referred to in his most refined litany as "the baddest two-eyed fancy-assed legal gorilla in the whole goddamned world, and I mean bad. Real bad!" He told the jailer, "Put me in a call to that Melvin Belli fella in San Francisco." Later, the jailer reported that he couldn't get through to Belli, but the jailer's attempt to connect with Belli used up Hardy's one allowed call. Afterward, Hardy did a lot of hollering, threatening, beating at the bars, and other demonstrations with his accompanying colorful language, which was fully predictable to those who knew the first little thing about Hardy Tillman.

The next morning, Deputy Huffsmith once again led the judge down to the interrogation room. "You're getting me into a lot of trouble, Judge." Huffsmith held his hat in both hands.

"How's that?" the judge asked.

"Well, the big boys say I'm being too easy on you. They say that if I can't get you to plead, they'll find someone who can. Now, I been here all these years, and

I probably can't get me another job, at least not one with any benefits. And so I was just wondering if I could get you to change your mind and testify?"

"What's going on with the bank's foreclosure on your house?"

"Like I told you, I ain't supposed to talk to you about that."

"Go get me some blank sheets of paper and a pen," the judge said.

Huffsmith jumped up and headed out of the interrogation room. "Be back in a minute. Like I told the big boys—if I was patient enough, you'd finally see the light and do the right thing and give me your confession. I told them you was one that always told the truth, and I was right."

When Huffsmith returned, the judge took the pen and began to write in clear, careful, easily read words:

In the Circuit Court of Teton County, Wyoming,
Tenth Judicial District
Arthur Huffsmith and Ruthie Huffsmith,

Petitioners
vs.
Jackson's First Bank and Trust Company,
and Peter Abberly,

Respondents
Application for Restraining Order

Huffsmith was looking over the judge's shoulder as he wrote. "What are you writing there, Your Honor? I thought you was going to give me a confession for Sewell and the sheriff."

"We'll take care of things as they come up," the judge said. He continued to write:

The petitioners state that the above bank loaned us money to pay the medical bills incurred on behalf of our boy, Ted, who is suffering from leukemia. The loan was handled for the bank by its president, Peter Abberly.

The note we signed required us to make payments in the amount of two hundred dollars a month. This was in excess of our ability to pay, which we told Mr. Abberly at the time. He said the note was only to satisfy the bank examiners, and he agreed that we could pay what we could afford—a hundred dollars a month, which payments we have timely and faithfully made. After six months the bank began foreclosure on our property.

The bank, through Abberly, has been trying for many years to buy our property for a parking lot. We have steadfastly refused to sell our property. The loan was fraudulently made and empowered the bank to foreclose on our property and obtain our property in the foreclosure, when we had previously refused to sell it.

We ask the court to enter a temporary order restraining the foreclosure, to set a hearing, and thereafter to permanently restrain this foreclosure on our property.

Signed:

Arthur Huffsmith
Ruthie Huffsmith
Petitioners

The judge handed Huffsmith the paper: "Now you

make me two copies, and you and Ruthie sign them before a notary, and bring them back in the morning."

Huffsmith shook his head like an obedient child and plodded out of the room.

The following morning, the judge was out of his cell the moment the lockdown was lifted.

This time, Huffsmith snapped the handcuffs on the judge and escorted him into the interrogation room.

"So are you going to sign a statement for me or not?" Huffsmith began. He was no longer holding his hat in his hand.

"Give me a piece of your blank paper."

"Just happen to have some here, Your Honor." He reached into the bottom drawer of the desk in the corner of the room and pulled out some paper and a pen.

"Take the cuffs off of me." Then in longhand the judge began to write his temporary restraining order.

By its terms, the bank and its officers were prohibited from foreclosing the mortgage on the Huffsmith property. A hearing was set for February 27, at nine o'clock in the dayroom of the county jail before Judge Murray, at which time the bank and its president were ordered to show cause why this temporary restraining order ought not be made permanent.

The judge signed the document and looked up at Huffsmith with a small, satisfied smile. "Now I have something here I'll give you in exchange for the papers you and Ruthie were to sign yesterday. Did you sign them before a notary public?"

"Yes, sir," Huffsmith said. "I told Ruthie we couldn't do this, that I'd lose my job for sure, but she said that maybe the Lord was going to look down on us after all, and that we didn't have no other way to go, so we took them to old Ben Holiday at the real estate office, and we signed them. He's a notary, you know. I got the papers here." He reached into his coat's inner pocket and withdrew the folded documents.

The judge quickly examined them, handed two copies of the papers back to Huffsmith along with his order temporarily restraining the foreclosure. "You go make three copies of these. Then have one of your deputy buddies serve them on the bank president, Sir Abberly. They get one set. You keep one. I keep one. You understand?"

The deputy read the judge's order. "I don't understand," he said. "You going to have the bankers in here?"

"Of course," the judge said. "I know of nothing in the law that prohibits a duly elected and qualified judge from holding court anywhere he chooses. We held court in the high school gym once on Law Day in front of the whole school."

"Yes, sir. But what about giving me that statement we've been talking about? The big boys . . ."

"I am still the judge here," he said. "That I am incarcerated in this ungodly hole does not strip me of my judicial powers."

"Well, with all due respect, Your Honor, some of the inmates here claim this is the best jail this side of the Mississippi as long as you cooperate with the sheriff an' are okay to do a little work for the sheriff on the side, if you know what I mean. But the big boys—"

"You tell the big boys that you are making good headway here and that you expect a breakthrough soon."

Hardy finally got out of jail on a thousand-dollar cash bond.

CHAPTER 39

SHERIFF LOWE WAS taken by surprise when Peter Abberly, president of the local bank, in his banker's navy blue pinstriped suit and with his coal black hair slicked down, along with the bank's attorney, Marcus Krause, appeared at the sheriff's office.

Krause was slender, dressed in a light checked suit, and in his early fifties. A lawyer, he had never tried a major case in his life.

Krause represented the Cheyenne bank, various insurance companies, the Union Pacific Railroad, and a handful of oil companies. His partner, Harry Mayes, however, did most of the work.

Still, Krause possessed enormous prestige. He was the past chairman of the Frontier Days Rodeo in Cheyenne, and every year in the rodeo parade he rode a beautiful palomino gelding with a black silver-trimmed saddle. He rented the animal and saddle from a horse farm in Colorado. He was a generous Republican donor. His wife was the treasurer of the DAR; he was past president of the Cheyenne Rotary Club, and he was the state's delegate to the American Bar Association.

"Do you have a place in this, ah, establishment known as the dayroom?" Krause asked the sheriff.

"Right. How can I help you gentlemen?"

"We have a hearing scheduled there in ten minutes," Krause said, looking at his watch. "It's before Judge John Murray."

"What are you talking about?" the sheriff asked. "A hearing?"

Krause tried to explain—the foreclosure, the judge's temporary restraining order, and the bank's need to complete the foreclosure without delay.

"You'll have to wait until the judge gets out of jail to hold this hearing," Sheriff Lowe said.

"Quite the contrary," Krause insisted. "I've searched the books and there's nothing to prevent a judge from holding court wherever he orders."

"Excuse me," Sheriff Lowe said. "You want to have a hearing in our jail's dayroom?"

"The judge ordered it. Despite his current situation, he's still a judge."

The sheriff shrugged. "Follow me, gentlemen." He escorted them into the elevator.

"What is the ungodly smell here?" Krause asked, his nose puckered like that of a hound dog sniffing a skunk's den.

"Lysol," the sheriff said. "We got the cleanest jail this side of the Mississippi. I've always said that if your prisoners look clean and smell clean and they're living in clean quarters, some of that clean might rub off on them."

The judge, in his blue jail clothes, sat at the steel table in the dayroom. "I see the litigants are before me, as ordered. Would you please have Deputy Huffsmith join us. He's a party here."

"Huffsmith's on duty," the sheriff said.

"You may relieve him, Sheriff Lowe. Thank you." The judge offered the banker and his lawyer a seat at the round steel table. When Huffsmith appeared minutes later, the judge tapped the steel table with his fist and declared the Teton County District Court in session.

Marcus Krause stood up from the table. "I wish to file my motion to set aside this rather interesting, if not ill-advised, restraining order." He handed the judge a thick sheaf of legal-size papers.

The judge turned to the parties before him. "The issue here is whether the note signed by the Huffsmiths to the bank was an instrument of fraud. That will require a full evidentiary hearing. Moreover, because an important public interest is involved, I will order this matter continued until we can hold it in the courthouse, where the public can attend." The judge smiled at Krause and his lawyer. "A public airing is your client's absolute right, Mr. Krause. I must overrule your motion."

"I'm not sure I understand," Krause said.

"The Huffsmiths contend your clients—the bank and Mr. Abberly—slicked them, as it were, into signing a note Abberly knew they couldn't pay, that Abberly told the Huffsmiths the terms of the note were only to satisfy the examiners, and that the Huffsmiths could pay what they'd always paid on the note, which was half the amount that the note provided.

"Then after some months, the bank began its foreclosure proceedings. If this is true, it appears to be a scheme by the bank to obtain the Huffsmith property. The Huffsmiths' child is suffering from leukemia. They had no choice but to agree to the bank's terms. If their allegations are true, Mr. Krause, does that sound like fraud?"

"May I confer with my client?" Krause asked. He led

Abberly to the far end of the room. In a few minutes, they returned.

"We would like to settle this matter with the Huffsmiths if possible and save them the expense of a public hearing. We offer the Huffsmiths a cancellation of their indebtedness to the bank to settle this matter, which will free the Huffsmiths of debt but provide us with the property."

"We don't want to sell our home," Deputy Huffsmith said.

"In that event, we'll have to air this matter in a public hearing," the judge said.

"I don't think a public hearing will be necessary," Abberly said. "Surely we can find some way to satisfy the Huffsmiths. We have nothing but the deepest sympathy for them and the plight of their son. But we've already entered into a contract with the Henderson Excavating Company to take down the house and to begin the leveling and paving of the lot."

"We can still pay a hundred a month, just like Mr. Abberly said we could," Huffsmith offered.

"Well, if you folks can't agree," the judge said, "I have no alternative but to hold a public hearing and resolve the matter myself."

"In that case, Your Honor," Krause said, "I must ask you to step down from this case."

"I'm sorry, Mr. Krause," the judge replied, "but once you've filed a substantial motion before the court, and it's been ruled on, you've waived your right to another judge." The judge held up Krause's motion to set aside the judge's restraining order, which the judge had earlier overruled.

Krause and Abberly conferred again at the far end of the dayroom. On their return, Abberly produced the

Huffsmiths' original note from his briefcase. The banker struck out two hundred dollars a month and in its place wrote one hundred dollars and initialed the change on the note.

"That should settle it," Abberly said.

"Not quite," the judge said. 'It appears that there may have been fraud at the inception here. I'm wondering if, before I accept your settlement, it wouldn't be wise for the bank to show its goodwill toward the Huffsmiths by establishing a charitable fund for their son's medical care and treatment. I was thinking the bank might wish to seed the fund with about twenty-five thousand dollars and go public with the bank's generous example, asking the community to respond, as well. Nothing better for good banking business than public esteem and goodwill."

Again Krause and Abberly adjourned to the far end of the room, from which were heard the sounds of men in pain. Shortly, however, the banker and his lawyer returned.

"Done," Krause said. "We are only too pleased and honored to originate this public service that so exemplifies the benevolent heart of this bank." He bowed to the judge. "However, as you must appreciate, things must proceed in an orderly fashion."

"Yes, of course," the judge said. "Report to me in thirty days. Thank you, gentlemen," the judge said. "I congratulate you on your just and wise decision based on the munificent decision of the bank." He put on his most inscrutable judicial look. "I will enter an order forthwith permanently enjoining this foreclosure. And, of course, you will call off your demolition crew."

"Of course," Abberly said.

"Deputy Huffsmith, show these good gentlemen out of my courtroom. I'll be out of here tomorrow," the judge said. "I'm going to testify."

CHAPTER 40

THE LILLIAN ADAMS murder trial continued to attract the national media. The Associated Press sent a reporter, as did Wyoming's one statewide newspaper, the *Star Tribune*. *The New York Times* and *The Wall Street Journal* hired local stringers. *Newsweek* and *Time* did the same.

After Judge Little's second day in the trial, and possibly aware of the media's cameras, he began to slick down his hair. He also donned a new pair of rimless spectacles, and a bow tie.

Judge Little ruled that Sewell was required to give the defense at least twenty-four hours' notice of every witness that the prosecution would be calling. The media's excited "breaking news" of the day was that Sewell revealed he'd be calling Tina Ford, the teenage daughter of Lillian Adams, immediately following the testimony of Judge John Murray.

During the second day of the trial, Sewell had directed the county's Child Services Office to take Tina into custody, since Lillian, her sole guardian, had been charged with murder. Sewell claimed that the girl's welfare was at stake. When Lillian got home from court, she found that Tina, Mrs. Houseman, and the psychiatric nurse were all gone. In panic, she called Timothy Coker, who called the sheriff's office.

"You have to get her back," Lillian pleaded to Coker. "She'll decompensate under the stress of this. She could have a psychotic break. It's life and death for that child. She's seriously suicidal."

Coker obtained a copy of Undersheriff Hannery's report, and that evening he'd gone to Lillian's home and read the report aloud to her:

When I tried to take the subject, Tina Marie Ford, into custody, she physically fought me and nearly overpowered me. She is very strong. I had to cuff and shackle the girl.

On my way to the county jail she cursed me with every word she could come up with. Later, after she calmed down some, she claimed her stepfather, Mr. Adams, had the evil power of a witch.

I asked her what she meant by that and she said he mumbled strange words, and that his eyes got wild and he would look at her in a way that she knew he was trying to put a spell on her. She said he put a spell on her mother. She told me that she killed her stepfather in order to save both herself and her mother from his evil.

She insisted she shot Horace Adams III in the head with his pistol, which was lying on his desk when she came in the room looking for her mother. She said when she saw the gun, she grabbed it, stuck it to his head, and pulled the trigger.

I secured the girl in our temporary holding cell, reported the foregoing confession to Mr. Haskins Sewell, the prosecutor, who thereafter arranged for the girl to be delivered into the care of Henrietta Houseman at the Houseman residence. Mrs. Houseman and a psychiatric nurse had been caring for the girl at the Adams residence during the trial. Mrs. Houseman was instructed to remove the girl from the Adams household and to keep her safely at the Houseman residence under the direction of Child Services. Mrs. Houseman was also instructed not to permit Lillian Adams to visit her daughter without the permission of Mr. Sewell.

"Sewell is holding my daughter hostage," Lillian cried.

"You're right, Lillian," Coker said. "It would weaken Sewell's case if he returned a daughter to 'her murdering mother.'"

"I promise you," she said under her breath, "I will kill him. My father gave me his old thirty-eight Smith & Wesson. I bought fresh shells for it at the store yesterday."

"I don't want to hear any more of that, Lillian," Coker warned. "You want to add that threat to an already long list of violence in your history? You'd better settle down. Tina can be seen as violent and cause the jurors to conclude that violence runs in your bloodline."

"How can you just calmly sit there while they kidnap my child?"

In a quiet voice, Coker replied, "I've wanted to hurt Sewell more than once, but if you go crazy, we'll lose for sure. Now sit down. We have to work our way through this together."

"I am capable of killing," she said. "And you would be, too, if they kidnapped your child."

"Mrs. Houseman and the nurse will take good care of Tina," Coker said. "You're reacting like any good mother would. But if the jury convicts you, it will be all over for you, and Tina will be confined to some public institution for the rest of her life."

Coker waited for Lillian to finally calm down. Then he asked, "Why did Tina tell the undersheriff that she killed your husband?"

Lillian explained slowly. "She came on to that terrible scene. She'd threatened to kill Horace. Dr. Brady thinks she saw him lying there in all that blood. She believed she'd done it. Dr. Brady calls it 'transference.' In her hysteria, she picked up the gun. She was screaming when I came in."

"How do you know she didn't kill your husband?" Coker asked. Then before Lillian could answer him, he said, "I withdraw the question, Lillian. I don't want you to answer that question, now or ever."

When Lillian called Mrs. Houseman the next morning, she told Lillian that Tina had been a perfect lady. "I had to remind Tina how Deputy Huffsmith told her that by being in control of herself, she would be in control of everyone else," Mrs. Houseman said. "And when Mr. Sewell came by to see Tina, she was also a perfect lady."

"You let that animal, Sewell, talk to her?"

"I have to," Mrs. Houseman said. "Mr. Sewell says he has the legal right over her, and he visits Tina every evening."

"Are you present when he visits?"

"Yes," Mrs. Houseman said. "But Tina still insists to Mr. Sewell that she killed her stepfather. Mr. Sewell seems kind enough to Tina and even lets her hold his little dog. He told Tina that she is the only person besides himself whom the dog trusts. He claims his dog has an unfailing sense about people, and that spoke very well for Tina."

When Lillian told Coker how Sewell's dog passed judgment on Tina, Coker started to erupt: "Why, that silly son of a bitch . . ." He caught himself before he said more. Then he said in a more subdued voice, "Maybe, Lillian, we should have Sewell bring his dog to court for you to hold. If you pass his dog's test, surely he'll dismiss the charges against you."

CHAPTER 41

IN THAT CONCRETE hole of perpetual day, the judge's eyes were once again locked on the jail's ceiling. The fluorescent lights and the jail's camera watched him. When Sewell asked him what Lillian Adams said to him in his pickup that night, how would he answer? They had that little microphone hidden there behind the rear-view mirror.

What if he said he didn't remember?

They knew he remembered.

He'd probably be hauled up before the Judicial Fitness Committee, and they'd recommend his impeachment.

He heard himself answering the committee: "I refuse to dignify the charges of that rotten bastard, Haskins Sewell, by responding with the first word in my defense."

"What's that, Judge?" Whitey hollered in.

"He's talking to himself again," Jake said. "Better get him out of there before his brains turn to rat turds."

Deputy Huffsmith visited the judge that afternoon and told him that the big boys had instructed him to get the judge ready to testify. He'd be called as the state's witness first thing in the morning. So Sewell had decided to take a chance on what he'd say—not much of a risk considering they'd recorded his conversation, and the recording could be used to impeach his testimony if he didn't tell it straight. He could hear Sewell's stinging, high-pitched question: "Didn't Lillian Adams admit to you that night in your truck that she'd killed her husband, Horace Adams the Third?"

The judge had trouble making room for the likelihood that Lillian had killed her husband. Why would she kill him? For money? If money were the motive, wouldn't she, as his sole heir, inherit his fortune anyway? Besides, she never seemed to care much about money. More likely she was taking the blame for Tina.

If he testified truthfully, Lillian Adams would likely face the death penalty. If he lied, Sewell had it all on tape from that hidden mike in his truck, and Sewell would have an open-and-shut perjury case against him, and Lillian would still be convicted.

If he said he couldn't remember, Sewell couldn't disprove his memory loss, but Sewell had that damnable recording, and Judge Little would let Sewell play the recording in front of the jury to "refresh his memory." Sewell had checkmated him.

In the afternoon, Deputy Huffsmith met the judge again in the interrogation room. "Sewell wants me to talk to you one last time about your testimony." As Huffsmith spoke to the judge, he'd returned to his ritual of removing his hat and holding it reverently on his lap.

"And what does Sewell want?" the judge asked.

"He wants you to tell the jury that the lady confessed to you."

CHAPTER 42

PROMPTLY AT 9:00 A.M., Judge Homer Little called his court to order. Haskins Sewell announced his first witness of the day—Judge John Murray.

Deputy Huffsmith escorted the judge to the witness stand. Still in his blue jail outfit, he held his head up and looked neither right nor left as he moved down the aisle through the gawking crowd to the witness chair.

He seated himself with care. He glanced over the crowd, which was fixed on him. He saw Betsy sitting in the row behind the press. Her face was pallid, her eyes wide.

"How's my darling today?" he asked from the witness chair, as if he were talking to her from across the kitchen table.

She looked ripped and ragged and made no response.

"You're not all right," he said. "I'll be out of here today. Don't worry."

He looked up at Judge Little. His bow tie was tilted to the right. Judge Little stared at Judge Murray, his eyes expressionless, empty of emotion.

"Good morning, Judge Murray," Sewell began with a

painfully imposed half smile. "I notice you are in Teton County jail clothing. I asked the deputy to fetch a suit for your appearance here this morning."

"You want me to be seen by my friends and fellow citizens of Teton County as a disreputable old crock charged with various vicious-sounding crimes," the judge replied. "So I thought I'd remain dressed for the occasion." Somebody laughed. It sounded like Hardy Tillman.

"Well, let's get down to business, then, Judge Murray. Do you admit that you've had conversations with Lillian Adams?"

"Yes. Many."

"When was the first?"

"Years ago, when she was a child."

"I see. Have you had conversations with her since the death of her husband?"

Judge Murray made no attempt to answer.

"Judge?" Sewell said in his painfully piercing voice. "Please answer my question."

"Excuse me, Mr. Sewell, I have to adjust my hearing aid." He reached up to his right ear, fiddled with the device that was hidden by his long hair, and then nodded to the prosecutor. "Would you please repeat the question?"

"Have you had conversations with the defendant since the death of her husband?"

"I have asked the jail personnel to provide me with a fresh hearing aid battery. These batteries are like me, old, and they've about had it."

"Can you hear me?"

"Yes, if you don't shout. Shouting causes ringing in my ears."

"Can you hear me now?"

"Yes, of course."

"Did you have any conversations with—"

"Yes. Do you want a history of them?"

"That won't be necessary, Judge. Just tell us if you had a conversation with her on this February seventh in your pickup truck in the courthouse parking lot after court was adjourned on that day."

"I don't know what day it was. I don't keep a calendar of my conversations with people in my pickup truck."

"Did you have a conversation with her in your pickup after the death of her husband?"

"Yes."

"And what did she say to you on that occasion?"

"Well, I was previously the judge in this very case, as the jury knows. She was sitting in my pickup when I got out of court. I never lock my pickup. And when I got into the pickup, she threw her arms around me and kissed me—on the cheek. Her sudden expression of affection surprised me. She was saying something about how sorry she was for all the trouble she was causing me in court and all the rest."

"And all the rest?"

"She was saying other things, but she was up close to me, and it's sometimes impossible for me to hear when people are so close to me. I didn't hear what she said after that. I put my hand in front of her face and said, 'Don't say anything more and get out of my truck immediately!' Which she did."

"Didn't she say—"

"Objection!" Coker cried, interrupting. "We're about to be treated with another of Mr. Sewell's poisoned questions."

Judge Little knew Lillian's alleged confession was at issue—about how Lillian had said she was sorry for all the trouble she'd caused Judge Murray, ending with "I killed Horace because—"

The judge called the lawyers to the bench, out of the jurors' hearing.

"I'm merely attempting to refresh the judge's memory," Sewell said. "I offer into evidence State's Exhibit twenty-seven, which is a recording made of the conversation. It is self-authenticating. I offer it for the purpose of refreshing the witness's memory."

"He has no loss of memory," Coker said. "He had a loss of hearing. He didn't hear what she said, if anything. He told you he couldn't hear her because of the malfunction of his hearing aid."

"I sustain your objection, Mr. Coker," Judge Little ruled.

"But, Your Honor, I can prove what Mrs. Adams said to the judge."

"You can't prove it through Judge Murray if he didn't hear it in the first place."

"But, Your Honor . . ." Sewell's protestations were edged with mounting anger.

"This is too fundamental for further discussion," Judge Little ruled. "This witness either heard or he didn't hear. He says he didn't hear. You can't impeach the witness because he didn't hear. You can impeach him only if you can prove he heard and refuses to admit what he heard."

"I will lay a foundation with Officer Bromley, who affixed the instrument to Judge Murray's truck," Sewell offered.

"How short our memories!" Coker said. "Justice Beasley of our very own supreme court did not authorize a bug to be installed in Judge Murray's pickup. He only authorized bugs in the judge's house and office."

"That is my understanding, counsel," Judge Little said.

Sewell paused, as if in search of further arguments.

Then he walked in hard steps back to his chair at the counsel table. "The court has precluded my good-faith inquiry into this matter, so therefore I withdraw this exhibit. I have no further questions of this witness," Sewell said.

"Neither do I," Coker said. "May Judge Murray be released?"

"The witness is released," Judge Little said. "Thank you for your testimony, Judge Murray. I hope the next time we see you, you'll be on this bench in your customary black robe. You need a new chair," Judge Little said with a small smirk. "And by the way, I know a good audiologist up in my neck of the woods. If you like, I can give you his name."

It wasn't until the next afternoon that Judge Murray felt he could face Jenny Winkley and the files that had piled up on his desk. On his way to court, he stopped to see Hardy Tillman.

"How's the jailbird?" Hardy asked. "You're looking okay. They must have fed you pretty good up there."

The judge emptied a case of Horace Adams beer into Hardy's old refrigerator, which sat groaning against the wall.

"You done good as a witness. Never said shit. Now that's the test of a good witness, ain't it?" Hardy said.

"Come on, Hardy," the judge protested. "I answered the questions, didn't I?"

"Well, I got you into this jam. Never meant to. I was just looking for a chance to kick Sewell's ass—in self-defense, a course." Hardy took after his beer.

"Be careful what you say. If I take the stand in Sewell's ass-kicking case, they can ask me what we talked about."

"No problem," Hardy said. "Your memory ain't worth a shit or your hearing aid don't work." He laughed and took another draw from his beer. "I got this all figgered out. I'm going to get this over with. Like my daddy used to say, 'The easiest way to eat crow is while it's still warm. The colder it gets, the harder it is to swallow.'"

"What are you talking about?"

"I'm going to plead guilty to assault, if that sumbitch will agree to leave you alone for once."

"That's one crow you aren't going to eat," Judge Murray said.

CHAPTER 43

WHEN HASKINS SEWELL announced that his next witness would be Tina Ford, Timothy Coker flew to the bench. "Your Honor, is there no decency left in this world, in the law, in this courtroom? I cannot imagine even the most pernicious of judicial systems permitting a prosecutor to force a loving daughter to testify against her mother. If I have no legal ground to object, I wish the record, the jury, and this court to know that we consider this tactic despicably immoral."

"Your objection is noted," Judge Little replied. He smiled at the jury. "The jury is admonished to disregard counsel's remarks." The judge adjusted his bow tie, which also tilted to the right. "Proceed, Mr. Sewell."

Sewell approached the bench and spoke quietly to Judge Little. "May we adjourn to your chambers? Perhaps we can settle this troublesome matter." With Coker's agreement, the judge excused the jury until the following morning.

In chambers, the lawyers remained standing. But Lillian dropped into a chair some feet back from the judge's desk. She was suffering spasms of shivering, like one in the throes of hypothermia.

"Your case is lost," Sewell said to Coker. "If the jury finds your client guilty, and that's nearly guaranteed, she'll find herself in the gas chamber. I'm willing to accept a guilty plea if we can work something out with the judge for a lesser sentence that would provide some remaining life for her on the other side of prison walls."

Judge Little excused himself and left the room.

Coker sat silent. Without taking his eyes from Sewell, he walked over to Lillian, took her quivering hand, and gave it a fatherly squeeze.

"He wants me to admit I killed Horace?" she asked.

"That's about it," Coker said.

She looked away.

"If I agree, will they leave Tina alone?" Lillian whispered.

"The case would be over," Coker whispered back. "She wouldn't have to testify."

"Then I'm going to do it," Lillian said.

"Who will take care of Tina while you're lounging in the penitentiary for the next twenty years?" Coker asked.

"Oh God!" Lillian cried. "I keep forgetting."

She looked at him and saw his eyes were kind. "Sewell will be filing more charges against you," he said.

The next morning, all the parties appeared in court, as usual. Sewell was wearing another of his usual gray suits and usual gray ties. Lillian took her seat next to Coker, as usual. As usual, Judge Little called the court to order.

Sewell called his next witness, Tina Marie Ford. She walked in hesitant steps to the witness stand. She was two inches taller than Deputy Huffsmith, who accompanied her.

Benjamin Breslin, the clerk, said tonelessly, "Raise your right hand."

"Why?" she asked.

"To take the oath."

"I don't want to take an oath. Only those in cahoots with the devil take oaths."

Judge Little looked down at the girl. "Will you tell the truth, Miss Ford?"

"I lie to the devil."

"Will you tell us when you are lying?" the judge asked.

Tina didn't answer.

Coker said, "This witness has not been sworn, and she's not competent to testify in this or any court."

Judge Little, on the edge of his chair, looked down at Tina. "Overruled. I find that this witness is young but seems to understand the meaning of an oath. I will allow her testimony and instruct the jurors to give it such weight as they deem fit under these circumstances."

"This is clear and obvious error," Coker objected. "To permit a witness to testify without taking an oath, whether she understands the meaning of an oath or not, is beyond the pale. And nothing is before us that creates a presumption that she knows the meaning of an oath. Moreover, she appears to be mentally incompetent."

"Overruled," Judge Little said as he adjusted his tie. "If we disqualified every citizen from testifying who held beliefs in angels and devils, we would not be able to conduct a trial. We'll see where this young lady takes us."

Sewell began his interrogation of Tina by asking, "Where have you been residing?"

"You know where I'm living. You put me there," she said in a low, angry whisper.

"So, Miss Ford, you are living outside the home of your mother, isn't that true?"

No answer.

"Answer the question, Miss Ford," the judge admonished.

No answer.

"Did you hear me, Miss Ford? Answer the question."

"I don't want to," she said, and defiantly shook her head at the judge.

"It is not whether you want to or not. You are required to answer the question."

"No. I don't have to."

"Who told you that?"

"My mother."

"What did your mother say?" the judge asked.

"Your Honor ought not join the prosecution's team in interrogating the witness," Coker said. "Moreover, it's hearsay."

The judge scowled down at Coker and readjusted his bow tie.

"I don't remember," Tina said.

"You don't remember what?" the judge asked.

"How can I remember what I don't remember?"

The judge looked down at Tina and with a slow, stern voice said, "What did your mother say concerning your duty to answer questions in court?"

Coker said, "I renew my objection to the court's interrogating the witness. This has gone beyond pure preliminaries."

"Very well," the judge said. He turned to Sewell. "Mr. Prosecutor, if, indeed, I have preempted you in performing your duties, you may now proceed."

Sewell nodded to the judge and asked, "Were you advised by your mother not to answer our questions?"

"No. My mother always told me that we should make

our own choices in life, and that we should be responsible for the choices we make. I am making my choice, and I am not going to answer your questions. I do not have to talk to the devil."

"Whom are you referring to as the devil?" Sewell asked.

"You know who you are," Tina said.

"Did your mother tell you that?"

"No. My mother does not understand. She is innocent, like a little child. She thinks I am the child, but in the presence of the devil, she is the child."

Sewell took a step forward. "Do you remember being in my office today before I called you as a witness?"

"Yes."

"And didn't you tell me that your mother had problems with your stepfather?"

"You are just making all this up to hurt my mother."

A heavy, low buzz in the courtroom was interrupted when the judge pounded his gavel. "Miss Ford," the judge remonstrated. "You are required to tell the truth."

"I am telling the truth." She pointed at Sewell. "He's the devil. And I think you know that, too," she said to the judge. "He came to see me all the time at Mrs. Houseman's and brought me presents to try to get me on his side so I would testify against my mother. He thinks I am too dumb to understand that."

"Miss Ford, will you answer any questions concerning the death of your stepfather?" the judge asked.

"He's not dead. You can't kill those kind."

"I renew my objection to this testimony," Coker said. "This witness is obviously hallucinating."

"Let us be patient," Judge Little said in a kindly voice.

"Well, let's see if there are any questions you will answer," Sewell said. "Were you home on the night that your stepfather, Horace Adams the Third, died?"

Darkness fell over the courtroom like a heavy, color-less cloud. Tina didn't answer.

"You have to speak up so that the reporter can get your answer in the record," Sewell said.

"You made me shoot him," she said to Sewell. "You made me shoot him," she said again. The jurors leaned forward. Lillian grasped Timothy Coker's arm.

"I don't wish to drag you through the shock of that night," Sewell said in his most sympathetic voice, "but what time did you last see your stepfather?"

"I just got home. My friend Julie brought me home. She said I was having a spell, and anyway I was sup-posed to be in by midnight, and so it was a few minutes before."

"Why did you go into your stepfather's den?"

She didn't answer.

"I asked you, Miss Ford, why did you go into the den?"

Still she didn't answer, her face devoid of feeling.

"Miss Ford?"

"I went in there to kill him," she said in a far-off voice.

Lillian Adams let out a small cry.

"What are you talking about?" Sewell said. He started for the witness.

Coker jumped in front of Sewell, his fists tight and shaking. "Leave her be!" he hollered.

"Step back, counsel!" the judge ordered Sewell.

"That isn't what you told me," Sewell said. "You told me—"

"This is his witness," Coker objected. "He's not per-mitted to impeach his own witness."

"Gentlemen, gentlemen!" The judge was beating his gavel. "Approach the bench." At the bench, Judge Little turned to Sewell, whispering, "What is your offer of proof, Mr. Sewell? And keep your voice down."

Sewell spoke in a sharp, angry whisper. "I expected this witness to say she went into the den, looking for her mother, who often spent time in there with her step-father, and that when she got there, her mother wasn't there, and that when she saw the dead man on the floor, she went screaming though the house for her mother and her mother came to her out of the bathroom, where, we will show, she'd been attempting to get rid of the blood on her clothes." He caught his breath. Sewell continued: "I further expected this witness to say that she saw blood on her mother's clothing. I have been surprised by this witness, and I have the right to cross-examine her."

"That is totally unacceptable, and prejudicial," Coker said. "He is not permitted under the law to ask another of his infamous poisoned questions, much less attack with cross-examination this hallucinating girl who has yet to take the oath. My question to Your Honor: Why are you allowing the contamination of this record with this sick child's delusions under these clearly improper circumstances?"

"Have you forgotten, counsel? I am the judge here. I do not answer questions. I simply rule on them. I'm going to let Mr. Sewell do what may be necessary to straighten this out. We will proceed cautiously. Mr. Sewell, do I have your representation that the witness told you these facts yesterday?"

"Yes, that's my representation to the court."

"You may proceed."

Sewell turned back to Tina. "You've been under a good deal of strain these last few days, Miss Ford. But do you remember talking to me in my office?"

No answer.

"You told me then that when you came home, you found your stepfather dead in the den, that you ran screaming for your mother, and that she came out of the bathroom with blood on her clothing, isn't that true?"

"You're making that up," Tina said. Her voice was eerie and chilling. "I told you I killed him, and you know it."

"You claim I'm making this up?" Sewell asked. "What really happened is that you've decided overnight to take the blame for the death of your stepfather in order to save your mother, isn't that true?"

"I told you I shot him!" She was staring darkly at Sewell, her nostrils flared, her hands in tight fists.

"So how did you shoot him, young lady?" Sewell asked.

"With a pistol."

"Yes. What kind of a pistol?"

"I don't know. But I shot him with it."

"Where did you find the pistol?"

"He had it there on the desk."

"So how does the pistol work?"

"You pull the trigger."

"And you know how to shoot?"

"Yes," she said. "My grandfather taught me how to shoot. I am a good shot. I just walked up, put the pistol to his head, and shot him."

"And I suppose that your stepfather said nothing and did nothing while you shot him?"

"He looked at me and smiled. He knew I couldn't kill him. He's a warlock. I suppose you don't know what a warlock is." Her expression turned from hate to disgust. "It is a male witch."

Sewell went to the clerk's table and brought the pistol to her.

"I hand you State's Exhibit seven. Show me how you work this."

She grabbed the gun, cocked the hammer, and pulled the trigger.

Sewell shrugged his shoulders, as if Tina's demonstration had been valueless. He returned the pistol to the clerk's desk with the other exhibits. "What did you do after you shot him?"

"I don't remember. I just remember shooting him."

"When you pulled the trigger, what did he do?"

"He fell facedown on the desk, and started to shake all over." She gave a small, quick shaking of her body to illustrate.

"Why did you shoot him?"

"Because he was evil and ruining my mother's life."

"In what way was he ruining your mother's life?"

"She didn't laugh anymore. She always used to laugh."

"Where did the so-called suicide note come from?" Sewell asked.

"I don't know," she answered. "I told you in your office that I didn't see any note there."

"Your mother wrote a note and put it—"

Coker jumped up. "That's another one of those poisoned questions, Judge Little. There is no competent evidence whatever that Mrs. Adams wrote anything."

"That's for the jury to decide," the judge said. "Overruled."

"And how, pray tell, did Mr. Adams get to the chair from the floor?"

"He was sitting at his desk. I put the gun to his head and shot him."

"How did all those bloody drag marks get on the floor?"

"I don't know."

"You lifted a two-hundred-fifty-pound dead man and put him in his chair? You want the jury to believe that?"

"I didn't put him in his chair. He was already there."

"You and your mother lifted him from the floor and put him in his chair, isn't that true?"

"No. That's another of your filthy lies. But the jury knows. The devil always lies. Always."

"What time do you claim you shot your stepfather?"

"Just before my mother got home. She got home at midnight."

"I suppose you wiped the gun free of fingerprints? There were no fingerprints on the gun," Sewell said.

"I don't know. I told you in your office yesterday that I shot him." Her words grew harder and more resolute. She started to get up out of the witness chair.

"Sit down!" Judge Little ordered.

The girl dropped back into her chair.

"You saw your mother wipe the gun, didn't you?"

"No. She called the police."

"I'm going to ask you one more time. You told me in my office yesterday that you found your stepfather dead in the den, that you ran screaming—"

Coker objected. "This is repetitive. It has been asked and answered."

"Sustained," Judge Little ruled.

"You've decided to take the blame for your mother—"

"That's been asked and answered, as well," Coker said.

"Sustained."

"You know that if I prosecute you for the murder of your stepfather that you will only go to the girls' reformatory until you achieve the age of majority, but if your mother is convicted of this murder, she will likely be executed. Someone told you that, didn't they?"

"No," she said.

"You love your mother and want to protect her, don't you?"

"Yes. I love her very much. I would shoot you, too, if I had a gun."

"Why did you go into your stepfather's den that night, Miss Ford?"

"I had our big kitchen knife. I was going to kill him. Then I saw his gun there, and I used it instead."

"I have no further questions," Sewell said.

Judge Little called a recess.

Coker and Lillian Adams spoke in frenzied whispers at the counsel table. "Well, Lillian, before I cross-examine your daughter, maybe you and I had better have another little heart-to-heart." Coker sat back in his chair and took in his client like a father about to discipline an errant child.

"You are not going to cross-examine Tina," she said.

"I have to cross-examine Tina," Coker said. "It's not what Tina said. It's what Sewell said in his poisoned questions that the jury will believe."

"I suppose you want to make it look like she killed Horace when you ask her one of your own poisoned questions," Lillian said.

"I have to do something."

"You forget, Timothy. I'm her mother."

"It's you who keeps forgetting: If you're convicted, it will be your one-way ticket to the gas chamber and Tina's to an institution for the rest of her life. Why do you continue to forget that?"

CHAPTER 44

WHEN THE TRIAL resumed, Timothy Coker rose from the defense table and stood, intently considering Tina. Finally, he said, "Miss Ford, when you talked to Mr. Sewell in his office, who else was with you?"

"No one."

"Did he record what was said?"

"I don't know."

"You and I have never talked about this case?"

"No."

"Now, the jury's been shown what purports to be a suicide note." He retrieved the note from the clerk's desk and handed it to the girl. "Have you ever seen this before?"

"No."

"I want to make sure. That night, before the police came, did you see anything on the desk?"

"The gun." She looked at Coker as if she saw the death scene spread before her. She spoke in a near-whisper. "Maybe his journal. I used to see him writing in it, but I didn't want to read it. He was probably writing stuff about my mother. He had her under his evil spell."

"Did you see a Cracker Jack box on the desktop?"

"I saw an old cardboard box, all beat up, but I didn't know what it was."

"Now why, Tina, do you claim you shot your stepfather?"

"Because I shot him."

"You had a reason to shoot him?" Coker asked.

"Yes, I had a very good reason." The audience was enraptured. Even Judge Little leaned forward, his eyes fixed on this mere child confessing a killing.

"And what was that reason?" Coker asked.

Lillian jumped up and ran to the podium and began whispering wildly to Coker. "You leave her alone. She's trying to protect me. She doesn't know what she's doing."

"I'm beginning to see it all too clearly. You're the one who's insane, Lillian. I know what I'm doing," Coker whispered back.

Judge Little hit his gavel. "The defendant will take her seat immediately!"

"I want a recess," Lillian said in a high, frightened voice to the judge.

"I, too, need a recess, Your Honor," Coker said.

"The court will stand in recess for five minutes." Judge Little struck his gavel again and left the bench. As the jurors retired to the jury room, Deputy Huffsmith led Tina from the courtroom.

Lillian and Coker sat huddled at the counsel table. In a frantic whisper, she cried, "What are you doing, Timothy?" Her eyes were wild. "Are you trying to convince this jury that Tina killed Horace?"

"You've lost it, Lillian," Coker said. "If you don't quiet down, I'm going to ask the judge to have you examined. You don't understand what's happening. I'm trying to save both of you."

"You want to turn my child into a confessed murderer?"

"She already is. If the jury believes Tina, the jury will acquit you. If they can't figure it out, they may hang or acquit you. Don't you understand?"

Lillian looked wildly around the courtroom, like one searching for something not yet identified.

"It's our only chance to save Tina's mother for Tina," Coker said.

Lillian stared blankly at Coker, and her lips started to form words, but none escaped.

When Judge Little called the court to order, and Tina was once more stiffly settled in the witness stand, Coker began anew. "I believe my last question to you, Miss Ford, was why did you kill your stepfather?"

Tina looked over at her mother. "We used to be close, Mother and me. That was before he came along. Then things changed. I saw why. He was teaching my mother to do those things. I saw them once. He is an agent—"

Lillian jumped up again.

"Sit down, Mrs. Adams!" the judge ordered.

Lillian, as if preparing to run to the witness stand to save her daughter, remained standing.

"I said, 'Sit down, Mrs. Adams,'" the judge repeated.

Slowly, Lillian sunk into her chair.

Then Coker asked Tina, "What do you mean your stepfather was teaching your mother things?"

"I saw them. My grandfather told me that people who do that stuff should be killed, and that they are agents of the devil."

"That's objected to as hearsay," Sewell said.

But before the judge could rule, Tina continued: "He was doing those things to my mother, and she was doing it, too. It was disgusting. I told my grandfather what I saw, and he said the man should be shot."

"I have no further questions," Coker said, and sat down.

Sewell took quick, determined steps to the lectern for his redirect examination. "I suppose you know what perjury is, Miss Ford."

"Yes, it's when you lie. And you've been lying about what I told you in your office. You are a perjurer."

"You told me in my office that your mother was home when you got home, isn't that true?"

"No, that's a dirty, filthy lie, and you know it." Tina turned to the judge. "Judge, he's lying some more. I want you to put him in jail for lying, just like I'd have to go to jail for lying."

Coker rose in support of Tina's objection. "This is still another one of Mr. Sewell's poisoned questions, Your Honor. No one was present except Mr. Sewell during his interviews with Tina. He didn't record them. He's impeaching his own witness, and by that means he's testifying. I move that his question be stricken, that the jury be admonished—"

"Save your breath, counsel," the judge said. "I sustain your objection, Mr. Coker. It's repetitive. Proceed, Mr. Sewell."

"I move for a mistrial," Coker demanded. "The jury has again heard Mr. Sewell's statement disguised as a question. You can't unring that bell."

The judge turned to the jury. "Ladies and gentlemen, any inference of fact arising from Mr. Sewell's last question is to be completely disregarded, do you understand?"

All the jurors nodded except the older woman in the front row. Her arms were still folded across her bosom.

"That should take care of it, Mr. Coker," the judge said. "Your motion for a mistrial is overruled. Proceed, Mr. Sewell."

"What did you say to your mother when she got home?" Sewell asked Tina.

Lillian cried aloud, "This child has been under the care of a psychologist, and she's sick. Please order these lawyers to leave her alone."

"That's enough out of you, Mrs. Adams," the judge said, pounding his gavel.

"You are the devil," Tina said to Sewell. "You make me sick. Sick!"

"I agree!" Lillian Adams said. "You are the slimiest of them all."

The judge slammed his gavel. "Have the sheriff remove Mrs. Adams from this courtroom."

"I have no further questions of Miss Ford," Sewell said with disgust.

Deputy Huffsmith came forward and loosened the handcuffs from his belt for Lillian Adams's waiting wrists. Then he led her stumbling from the courtroom. As Huffsmith dragged her from the courtroom, she cried, "You are all sick. And you, Judge, are the sickest of them all."

Judge Little turned to Timothy Coker and slammed his gavel to emphasize that he was still presiding. "Mr. Coker may re-cross-examine Miss Ford."

Tina sat crumpled on the witness stand, her mother, her protection, now occupying the padded cell in the jail.

"My client, Lillian Adams, is entitled to be present during my cross-examination of her daughter," Coker said to the judge. "After all, she is the legal guardian of her child, who now sits without representation."

"That may be so," Judge Little acknowledged, "but your client has, by her conduct, deprived herself of her right to be in the courtroom to represent this juvenile."

"Under your ruling, the child has no guardian present," Coker argued.

"I will watch over the child's rights," the judge said.

"Are you saying that you will act as her guardian during my cross-examination, and so long thereafter as Lillian Adams is not in this courtroom?"

"I will," the judge said.

"In that case, I ask Your Honor to step down. You cannot act as the self-appointed guardian of this witness as well as the judge in this case."

The judge aimed his rheumy old eyes at Coker. Then he peered out over the spectators. "I see Mrs. Mildred Maines in the audience. She is a lawyer and an officer of this court. Will you come forward, Mrs. Maines?"

A sober, businesslike woman in a brownish suit got up from the middle of the courtroom, excused herself as she edged to the aisle past the other spectators, and walked with authoritative steps toward the bar. She'd made no attempt to disguise the gray that etched her dark hair at the temples. Her hair was in bangs and concluded with a ponytail in the back. Once inside the bar, she faced the judge, who administered the guardian's oath to her and directed her to a seat at Timothy Coker's table. She tendered Coker an embarrassed smile and sat down.

"Proceed, counsel," Judge Little ordered, withholding any suggestion of triumph.

Coker fumbled at buttoning his suit coat. Finally, he said, "Tina, you know your mother loves you?"

"Yes. She does. But he put her under a—"

"And your mother has attempted to protect you all along from the likes of Mr. Sewell, including her willingness to take the blame for your having shot your stepfather."

Mrs. Maines rose to object. "As the guardian of this child, I instruct her not to answer the question, on the grounds that her answer might incriminate her."

Tina turned to Mrs. Maines. "I'm old enough to say 'Go to hell.' So I say, you can go straight to hell!"

Sudden silence in the courtroom. The judge acted as if he hadn't heard.

"Do you have any further questions of this witness, Mr. Coker?" the judge asked.

"Yes, I do." He turned back to Tina. "You remember when you tried to stab your stepfather with a butcher knife?"

She nodded her head.

"Why did you try to stab him?"

"He was doing that with my mother. I saw them through the transom on the roof."

"I have no further questions," Coker said.

Sewell approached the witness cautiously. "Miss Ford, it's true, is it not, that your stepfather attempted to do that same thing to you, and you told your mother about it?"

"No, it is not true. You are such a filthy, lying beast."

Coker jumped to his feet. "When do these fictional, groundless, poisoned questions end? The prosecutor obviously has no foundation whatever for that question. It is just Sewell stating his own concocted fictions to this jury."

"I agree," Judge Little ruled. "The jury will disregard the prosecutor's last question. Any more of this, counsel, and I will have you removed from this courtroom, as well. Do you understand?"

"Yes," Sewell said. He offered the jury a knowing look, as if to suggest that even the judge had been captured by Lillian Adams. "I have no further questions."

"The witness may step down," the judge ordered. And with that, Tina Marie Ford exited the courtroom, accompanied by a deputy, who'd been instructed to return her to the care of Mrs. Houseman and the psychiatric nurse, Roberta Clemmins, until further order of the court.

Haskins Sewell rested his case, and Timothy Coker

moved the court for a directed verdict, on the grounds that the state had offered no competent evidence by which Lillian Adams could be found guilty of first-degree murder. Judge Little found that the evidence, taken in a light most favorable to the prosecution—as was the standard test—was sufficient to go to the jury.

That evening, Hardy Tillman called Judge Murray. "I been in court all day, Judge, and just to keep you up-to-date, they throwed Lillian's pretty ass into jail for raising hell in the courtroom. She went plumb nuts."

When the judge told Betsy the news, she said, "My God, you have to go get her out of jail."

"That's the safest place for her right now," the judge said. "She can't do her case any more harm than she's already done it. Timothy knows that."

"I know Lillian is innocent." She turned to the judge. "She is, isn't she?"

He saw the deep, tired worry in Betsy's eyes. "Yes, honey, she's innocent."

But the judge understood one simple truth: that mothers are governed by the same natural impulse as the goose that will fight off the coyote or die in her attempt to save her goslings. Then the judge asked himself the overriding question: How can mothers be held to the law of man when the law of nature is in supreme command?

CHAPTER 45

THE JUDGE DIDN'T want to get out of bed. Finally, he
found his way to the bathroom, and as he passed the mirror, he refused to look at himself—"to behold the face of
an old liar" is how he put it to himself.

He'd lied to the jury about Lillian's confession to
him when she'd been waiting for him in his pickup. He
abhorred perjury. If witnesses felt free to lie under oath,
the entire judicial system would be reduced to a meaningless charade, and he'd sentenced more than one convicted
perjurer to prison for a substantial term of years.

Yes, Sewell habitually lied. For Sewell, lying was a
customary weapon. But what if Lillian had killed her
husband out of compassion—to save him from the pro-
tracted hell of his lost mind, wounded by the onset of
senile dementia? Or what if Horace, in a passing moment
of clarity, had killed himself, and both Tina and Lillian
were innocent?

The judge staggered back to bed, and stared at the
ceiling for a long time. Finally, he saw a woman take
form in his mind's eye.

She wore a plain cotton dress and her hands showed

traces of fresh soil. Her arms were strong. He saw her breasts as she leaned forward to loosen the dirt around a climbing tomato plant. Then she came up close to him, and he could smell the scent of earth and growing things. She expanded like fog, and her arms spread around him, and after that there were no boundaries between them. She disappeared into the fog, and when she returned, she picked a tomato and handed it to him.

"These are delicious," she said. She held it up for him to taste. "If there's a God, it's in a vine-ripened tomato." He held her close to him, and felt her strength, and her youth. Then he said, "Betsy."

"You called, honey? Your breakfast is getting cold."

Timothy Coker announced that Deputy Arthur Huffsmith would be his first witness. The deputy trekked to the stand and pulled himself up straight like a schoolboy about to be admonished by the teacher. Without his sheriff's cowboy hat, his bald head was exposed and white. His deep-set eyes shifted from side to side and his jaw was clenched. His stomach protruded, covering his wide cowboy belt with the letters *ART* carved next to the buckle. He shifted nervously in the witness chair like a bull rider getting settled for a dangerous ride. With both hands, he protected the brown expanding file on his lap.

"You were the deputy who first arrived at the death scene?" Coker asked.

"Yes, sir." Small beads of sweat appeared on the man's temples.

"Did anyone accompany you?"

"No."

"Other than receiving evidence from you, did Mr. Sewell ever talk to you about this case?"

"No."

"Do you find that strange?"

Sewell objected. "This is irrelevant."

"He may answer," the judge ruled.

"Kinda, because I was the first at the scene. I figured he'd wanna talk to me."

"What were your duties as the first officer at the death scene?"

"To secure the area."

"What did you do in that regard?"

"I first asked Mrs. Adams and her daughter to leave the room. They was crying. Mrs. Adams was shaking all over. I asked her what happened. She couldn't speak except to say over and over, 'Oh, Tina. Oh, Tina.' She was holding on to her daughter and both of them was crying. I asked them to leave the room. Then I waited until the other officers come."

"Did you do anything else?"

"Yes, I had the camera I carry along. It ain't my job, but I usually take a few shots of my own because it makes it easier for me to write up my report."

Coker asked Huffsmith to produce the photos he'd taken that night, marked them as exhibits, and offered them into evidence. Sewell objected that the photos had not been shown to him twenty-four hours in advance, which was the court's rule. Coker responded that he hadn't been apprised of their existence until the evening before.

"Let's see where this takes us," Judge Little said.

Coker continued, "So, Deputy Huffsmith, you took these photographs before anyone else arrived?"

"Yes, sir."

"I call your attention to Defense Exhibit A, your photo. Does this accurately reveal what you saw on the desk at the time you first arrived?"

"Yes."

"Do you see any paper there, any writing, any so-called suicide note?"

"No."

"Are you saying that you found the corpse of Horace Adams the Third at his desk, and that you found no suicide note there?"

"Yes, sir; that there is exactly what I am saying."

Coker went to the clerk's desk, retrieved the supposed suicide note that had been examined by the handwriting expert, Widdoss, and handed the note to Huffsmith. "Have you seen this note before this moment?"

Huffsmith took the note, held it as far away from his body as possible, as if it were contaminated, but examined it carefully. "No, sir, I ain't never seen this before."

"Do you know where it came from?"

"No, sir."

"You say you were the custodian of the evidence in this case?"

"Yes."

"But this is the first time that you've seen this note?"

"Yes, sir. Sure is."

Coker continued: "In the upper-right-hand corner of Exhibit A—your photo of the scene when you first arrived—there appears to be a Cracker Jack box, and something that looks like a cigar stub. Do you have those items in your possession?"

"Yes, I do."

"What do you make of those two items?"

"Don't know," Huffsmith said. "They was on the desk when I found him. The Cracker Jack box was old and beat up and empty." He pointed to the cigar stub. "That there was a toy cigar—just brown paper. They used to put a toy in every box, along with the caramel popcorn."

"Did Mr. Sewell know you had custody of the Cracker Jack box and the toy cigar?"

"Yes, I told him."

"Who next arrived at the scene?"

"Sheriff Lowe, and Undersheriff Bromley was the next to arrive, and then Sergeant Illstead. After them, Mr. Sewell come."

"Did you ever discuss the so-called suicide note with them?"

"Yes, I did. After I heard about this note during this trial, which was the first I heard about it, I asked the sheriff about it. But he said he figured I had the note all along with all the other evidence I took that night."

"What other evidence did you take into your possession that night?"

"The pistol, and Mr. Adams's journal. That's about it."

"What can you tell us about his journal?"

"Well, I found his journal there on the desk. You can see it here." He pointed to a notebook clearly visible in his photograph. "I took it along with the pistol."

"Do you have the journal?"

"No. I delivered it to Mr. Sewell."

"What are you talking about?" Coker asked in surprise.

"Mr. Sewell come to me about a week after the killing, and before he charged Mrs. Adams, and asked me for the journal."

"And you gave it to him?"

"Yes. He signed a receipt for it." Huffsmith reached into his folder and extracted a paper. "Here it is," he said, holding up the paper.

"Have you seen the journal since?"

"No. I asked him for it before I come to court today."

"What did he say?"

Sewell objected. "This is irrelevant and hearsay."

Judge Little: "Overruled."

"I must object, Your Honor," Sewell continued. He

was rushing to the bench. "This is totally irrelevant and is taking us astray."

"You may answer the question, Deputy Huffsmith," the judge ruled. "What did Mr. Sewell say when you asked him for the journal?"

"He said he was in charge of the evidence now and to mind my own goddamned business. Them was his exact words." Huffsmith looked sheepishly at Sewell, as if he'd betrayed a family secret.

Sewell moved silently back to his table and sat down.

"Mr. Sewell," the judge said in a low, nearly inaudible voice, "during the noon recess, will you kindly produce the journal so that we may dispose of this matter?"

"Yes, of course," Sewell said, as if he were speaking to no one.

"I call your attention to Defense Exhibits B and C. What are these, Deputy Huffsmith?" Coker asked.

"These here are photographs I took at the den, where I found the body."

"Can you see the floor in these photographs?"

"Yes."

"I call your attention to State's Exhibit nine. You see that State's Exhibit nine is a photograph of the same area as is shown in your photos, Defense Exhibits B and C. Do you discern a difference in what is shown here?"

"The photographs speak for themselves," Sewell objected.

"You may continue," the judge ruled.

"Yes. There are bloody-looking drag marks in State's Exhibit nine. There isn't any blood on the floor in the pictures I took, and I was the first there."

"Where was the body of Horace Adams the Third when you took these photographs of the floor?"

"He was at the desk, where I found him. He hadn't been moved yet."

"I see." Coker offered Exhibits B and C into evidence and, with the court's permission, showed them, along with State's Exhibit 9, to the jury.

"So do you have any idea how these bloody drag marks got on the floor?"

"Yes, sir. I helped remove the body. We couldn't get the gurney behind the desk, so Sheriff Lowe and I dragged him up to the gurney."

"Was Mr. Sewell present when the body was removed?"

"Yes, he was. He seen it all." Huffsmith looked at Sewell out of the corner of his eye.

"So where did this so-called suicide note come from?"

"You'll have to ask Mr. Sewell," Deputy Huffsmith said. "I wouldn't have no idea."

CHAPTER 46

AFTER THE NOON recess, Haskins Sewell approached Judge Little's chambers with quick, menacing steps. He handed Horace's journal over to the judge.

The judge thumbed through the pages, pausing to read here and there. Finally, he handed the journal to Coker. Coker remained intent on the pages for more than half an hour. Sewell made three trips to the men's room and twice attempted to engage Judge Little in conversation, although unsuccessfully. At last, Coker looked up with a vague smile on his face. "I think there can be little doubt that this journal is relevant."

"I agree," Judge Little said. "I'm going to admit it into evidence."

Turning around, Sewell stamped out of the judge's chambers.

When the trial resumed, Coker handed the journal to Deputy Huffsmith. "Deputy Huffsmith, is Defense Exhibit D, this journal, the one shown in your photographs?"

"Yes, it is."

Coker turned to the jury and began to read aloud to the jurors from the journal:

December 25
I am losing my mind. I couldn't remember what we were doing. I asked Lillian and she said, It's Christmas, Horace. We are opening our packages.

January 1
We had a party here. I couldn't remember the people. I asked Lillian who they were and she told me their names. I have already forgotten. I am losing my mind, like my father did. Damn his genes. I am too young for this.

January 13
I have periods when I can remember, and at times I can't remember at all. I cried with Lillian. She told me how much she loved me. I told her all I wanted was her love. I made her promise that she would never tell anyone how I was losing my mind. She promised, and she is one to keep promises.

January 25
I am told I may have little clearheaded time remaining. I am like my father was. I have clear days, when I understand all that is happening. By my will I have left fifty million dollars to my darling, Lillian.

I do not want her to return to work after my death. We have agreed to organize and operate a charity—the Fate Fighters for homeless women. I want her to manage it. We have already hired an executive director, but she will need the creative skill and passion of Lillian to make it successful.

*I have provided that the balance of my estate will
go to our Fate Fighters charity. I do not want to die
without having done something worthy with my life
and my assets. And it all began with my darling,
Lillian. It was her idea.*

January 27
*My periods of clearness are growing farther apart.
Tina does not understand what is happening to me.
She thinks I am dangerous. I have tried to be kind
to her, but she is repelled by me. I will never be the
burden to Lillian that my father was to me. I will
never do that to my darling.*

Coker turned back to the witness, Huffsmith. "Five
days after the last entry I just read to the jurors, you
found him dead in his den?"

"Yes," Huffsmith said.

"I have no further questions," Coker said, and returned to his table.

"Well, I have some questions," Sewell said, hurrying
to the podium. "Deputy, you claim you never saw the
suicide note before you took the stand today?"

"That there is correct, sir."

"That's a lie, isn't it? Or did you just forget that you
gave me that suicide note along with his journal?"

"No. I never seen no note."

"And you had me sign a receipt for the journal, but ap-
parently you overlooked including the note in the receipt
you had me sign, isn't that true?"

"No, sir. There was never no note." Huffsmith's voice
was on the rise.

"Hamilton Widdoss, a renowned handwriting expert,
says that the note is a forgery and that it was written by
Mrs. Adams. Did you know that?"

"That's a misstatement of the evidence," Coker objected. "The jury heard it as well as I. He said his opinion was that it was probably written by Mrs. Adams."

"The jury will remember," the judge said.

"So how do you explain that?" Sewell demanded.

"Well, I know one thing. That guy was right. It was a forgery, because there never was no note, and I was the first there. Who forged it, I don't know."

"And about the smears of blood on the floor that you say weren't there when you arrived? Well, Deputy, I hear you're a photo buff."

"I like to take pictures."

"You know that photos can be altered by even a novice."

"Yes, but I never done nothing to them photographs."

"Of course not," Sewell said with sweet sarcasm. "I have no further questions."

Huffsmith stepped down and started out of the courtroom, when Sewell turned to him and said, "I'm sorry, Deputy, but I do have a couple more questions." Huffsmith, surprised, stood motionless for a moment. Then he turned back to the witness stand.

"Deputy, your home was mortgaged to the bank?"

"Objection. Relevance," Coker said.

"I'll tie it in," Sewell said.

"Proceed, counsel," the judge ruled.

"The bank was foreclosing on your property during this trial, isn't that true?"

"Yes."

"And that foreclosure was somehow mysteriously stopped during this trial."

"Wasn't mysterious. Judge Murray stopped it. Had a hearing and the bank fixed it so's I could pay."

"I see," Sewell said. "I see. Well now, where was that hearing held?"

"In the jail."

"You mean the bank officials came into the jail, and the judge held a hearing in the jail, where the judge was incarcerated as a material witness in this case?"

"That's what he done."

"You didn't find that unusual?"

"Well, I never seen nothing like that before."

"And somehow the foreclosure was stopped?"

"Yes."

"Did you pay the bank any money to stop it?"

"No."

"Do you know who did?"

"No. Nobody did."

"So you have a hearing in the jail, and the bank stops the foreclosure and no one pays anyone anything?"

"Yes, sir."

"Then you come into this courtroom and tell this jury that you never saw the suicide note when you were at the scene, and that you didn't take that note into your possession, and that you didn't deliver it to me, and that you didn't include the note in the receipt I signed for you—all of that is your testimony, Deputy?"

"That there is true. I never seen no note. It wasn't there."

"And then after your foreclosure is mysteriously halted without the payment of money, you produce for the first time these photographs that are supposed to show there were no bloody drag marks across the floor?"

"Them photographs is accurate."

"Now, did you talk to Lillian Adams during this trial?"

"No, sir."

"I will refresh your recollection, Deputy Huffsmith. The jail records here"—he picked up a sheaf of papers—"show that she went to the jail last week and that you let her into the jail."

"She come to see the judge."

"Aha. She came to see the judge—you mean Judge Murray?"

"Yes."

"And, when she came to see the judge, you, Deputy Huffsmith, had a conversation with her?"

"Not much. Just let her in. But the judge said he shouldn't be talking to her, so he never come to the visitors' room."

"Didn't you talk with Mrs. Adams about your photos at the death scene, and about your foreclosure, and about the suicide note?"

"No."

"You are quite certain of that?"

"Yes. We never talked about nothing like that."

"As a matter of fact, didn't she mention to you that she might be able to stop the bank from foreclosing on your property?"

Coker rose. "That's another of his poisoned questions. I want to know the basis for such a question."

"Answer the question, Deputy," the judge ruled.

"No. We never talked about that."

"You are under oath, Deputy Huffsmith," Judge Little reminded him.

"Yes, sir."

"Do you want to change your testimony in that regard?" Sewell asked.

"No, sir."

Sewell gave Huffsmith a menacing look. "Your choice, Deputy." He turned to the judge. "I have no further questions of this witness."

Coker slowly stood up. He turned to Huffsmith. "Deputy Huffsmith, do you know why the bank stopped its foreclosure?"

"Yes, sir. Because my boy is sick and the judge made 'em stop."

"You mean Judge Murray?"

"Yes, sir."

"Did this have anything to do with Mrs. Adams?"

"No."

"Did she pay you anything or pay anything for you?"

"No. The bank just changed the note."

"Do you know why the bank agreed to change the note?"

"I figured they—"

Sewell objected. "This witness is not entitled to speculate on the bank's reasons."

"Sustained," Judge Little ruled.

Coker walked back to his table and sat down. Huffsmith stood down from the witness stand and walked out of the courtroom with his head up and his chin out.

When the door closed behind Huffsmith, Timothy Coker asked for a recess, which Judge Little granted. During the recess, Coker sought Lillian's release from her jail cell, on Coker's assurance that she would comport herself properly. Judge Little agreed and authorized her release.

"How was your night?" Coker asked Lillian. They were sitting at the counsel table in the courtroom. Lillian had tried to "freshen up," as she put it. She looked worn. Her hair was uncombed and her dress was wrinkled.

"I couldn't sleep. All the noise all the time."

"Well, that's over," Coker said. Suddenly, his eyes grew soft. "Sewell has just about done us in. He's connecting up a bunch of false dots. And I haven't the slightest idea what Judge Murray did while he was in jail to get the bank's foreclosure stopped. Sewell makes it look like you paid off the bank, and Huffsmith suddenly claims there never was a suicide note and comes up with his secret photos that show no blood on the floor. My good Christ!"

Lillian bit at her upper lip.

"Even though we've prepared for it, I've never really planned for you to take the stand, Lillian," Coker said. "But Sewell is forcing me to put you on. How else can we hope to show the jury that his new conspiracy theory—the bank, Huffsmith, and you—isn't just more of Sewell's concocted crap? But when you testify, if the jury gets the idea you're lying, even a little, you'll be convicted."

Lillian refused to look at Coker.

"What are you going to say about what happened the night you found your husband dead at his desk?" Coker asked.

"Timothy, I can only stand to talk about it once. And you want me to tell the truth?"

"Of course."

"You won't want to hear what I have to say."

"In the end, you take charge of everything, don't you, Lillian? That just may be what does you in." He got up and left her sitting alone at the counsel table.

CHAPTER 47

JUDGE LITTLE INSPECTED the overflowing courtroom crowd and adjusted his bow tie. He turned to Timothy Coker, cleared his throat, and in a crackly, dismissive voice said, "You may call your next witness, counsel."

"The defense calls Lillian Adams."

In an unsteady stride, Lillian Adams walked toward the witness stand. Her face tendered no expression. When she raised her hand to take the oath, it shook like the hand of an old woman. With both hands, she pulled herself into the witness stand and carefully sat down. She was focused on the folded hands on her lap.

Coker watched her from behind his thick glasses. The courtroom waited. Finally, Coker presented his first question: "Mrs. Adams, why are you up here? You know you don't have to testify, and, under the law, if you don't testify, the jurors will be told by His Honor that they cannot make anything of your silence one way or another."

She didn't answer.

"Do you understand, Mrs. Adams, that you are not required to testify?"

"I know," she finally said.

"There is only one question here, Mrs. Adams. Just one. That question is, Did you kill your husband?"

"How could I kill him?" she asked in a fading voice. "I loved him. He was kind to me. I felt protected by him and loved by him."

Coker waited.

Then she turned to Sewell. "I am sorry for that man," she said. "He knows I am innocent."

Sewell was rapidly scribbling notes without removing his eyes from her.

"Are you aware that your husband's journal reveals that he was painfully, fearfully aware of his deteriorating state of mind?" Coker asked.

"Yes. Horace was so ashamed and terrorized that he was failing like that."

"You'll have to speak up," Judge Little said. "Some of the jurors can't hear you."

"He cursed his genes," she said. The jurors leaned forward to hear her. "Early senility ran in his family. He'd watched its horrid onset with his father. He couldn't bear to witness his own degeneration."

"Take your time," Coker said. "We have all day."

After a discomfiting pause, she finally said, "I saw Horace deteriorating. The doctors said he was in the early throes of an advancing and incurable senility."

"Objected to as hearsay," Sewell said without rising from his chair.

"Overruled," Judge Little replied.

"But there were times when suddenly Horace would come alive, as if he'd been off in another world, and he was like his old self again."

"I see," Coker said.

"He told me he wanted to end it, that he didn't want me to suffer what he had suffered with his father. I told him that if he loved me, he'd stay with me and let me join with him in fighting it to the end—that it was my right." She looked down at her hands again.

"How did his death affect you?"

She didn't answer, her eyes still on her hands. "Can you tell us?" Coker urged.

She finally said, "I saw him there, and the blood . . ." Her lips began to move in a silent mumble. She started again. "His face was laying . . ."

Coker rescued her with another question: "Calling your attention to the night of his death. Do you have a clear recollection of that night?"

After a long silence, she answered Coker. "Yes. I remember that night. Sylvia Huntley and I went to the drugstore, where we often met. I broke my promise to Horace to keep his deterioration a secret. I had to talk to someone. I swore Sylvia to secrecy and told her about his worsening mental condition. I needed advice."

"How did you describe your problem to her?"

"I told her I wasn't going to accept what the experts claimed was inevitable—that an early senility like his usually gets worse. I'd heard of a medical center in Salt Lake City that claimed some successes. I made arrangements for him to receive treatment there. I wasn't willing to give up. We were to leave the next day."

Coker urged her on. "What did you do?"

"I planned to leave Tina with my father and mother until I got Horace settled. When I got home that night—well, you know what I found." She began to weep. "Horace made his own decision."

"What did you see when you got into the house?"

She didn't answer.

Coker waited.

She was staring with wide, terrified eyes at Coker.

Finally, she said in ragged tones, "Tina was screaming

when I came in the door. She had Horace's pistol in her hand, the one he always kept on his nightstand, by his side of our bed."

"Yes, and . . ."

"I took the pistol from her, and she kept screaming and pointing to the den. When I got to the door, she cried, 'Don't go in there, Mama.'"

"Yes, and then . . ."

"I hurried to the den, and there he was, slumped over on the desk in a pool of blood."

She wept.

After a long pause, she said. "And I had the gun in my hand."

"What did you do?"

"I ran over to the desk and lifted his head and saw the wound in his forehead."

Coker waited.

Finally, she said, "I realized that I had the gun, and that my fingerprints and Tina's were on it."

"What did you do?"

"I called the police department."

"And then?"

"I ran to the bathroom, took a towel, and wiped the gun clean of her prints and mine and put it back on the desk. Before the people from the sheriff's office arrived, I told Tina not to talk to the police. To say nothing. Nothing. I made her repeat, 'I will say nothing.' I sent her to her bedroom."

"Why?"

"I believed Tina killed her stepfather. She'd never accepted him. She tried to keep me from marrying him. She thought he was an agent of the devil. She was very attached to me. And very jealous of him."

"Did your husband and Tina have words?"

"She was usually sullen around him." Lillian continued to speak slowly, a decibel above a whisper, the jurors leaning forward. "But at times she would just fall into some awful place and begin calling him every rotten name she could think of. And the more she yelled at him, the more he was convinced she was his first wife. By then, Horace was mostly out of it. And so was Tina. That's when I met with Sylvia at the drugstore."

"You say you thought Tina killed your husband?"

"Yes. She was screaming that the witch killed himself. Later she claimed that she shot my husband. She thought he was a witch and was going to kill us both, and she had to kill him to save us."

"Why did you try to convince me that you killed him?"

"I'm her mother. I wanted to save my child." The woman in the front row unfolded her arms. "But you wouldn't listen to me. Something about ethics—that if I admitted to you that I killed Horace, you couldn't ethically put me on the stand to deny that I had."

"I'm sorry," Coker said, his voice sad. "I don't make the rules."

"Ethics! I thought that Tina killed Horace. She had her whole life ahead of her, and I had lived a good deal of mine. I was willing to go to trial for his murder."

"But you heard Tina testify here?"

"Yes."

"You heard her say that she killed your husband?"

"Yes. She was trying to protect me. She's a very sick child."

"When did you first realize that Tina hadn't killed your husband?"

"Dr. Brady explained it to me, something called 'transference.' Tina wanted Horace dead. When she found him dead, she thought she'd killed him."

"That is totally hearsay and so much psychojabber," Sewell shouted. "I move that answer be stricken."

"It may be stricken," Judge Little ruled.

"After she came home yesterday on the leave that Judge Little granted her, we were able to talk about it for the first time," Lillian continued. "She goes in and out of her delusions. With her testimony over, she seemed clear for a change. She found Horace dead in the den, saw the gun, and didn't know why she picked it up. She said she didn't remember picking it up. She didn't remember anything after that."

"That is hearsay, and should be stricken," Sewell objected.

"I will admit it, not for the truth of the matter, but to provide a background for the testimony of this witness," Judge Little ruled.

"What about the long smears of blood on the floor?"

"I never saw any. All the blood was on the desk."

"How did you get gunshot residues on your hands?"

"I had the gun in my hand before I put it back on the desk."

"How did you get blood under your nails?"

"I lifted Horace's head off the desk. It was all bloody. I saw the bullet hole." She was hanging on the edge of collapse.

"Do you want a recess?" Judge Little asked Coker.

"No, thank you, Your Honor. We need to get through this pain as quickly as possible."

Lillian forced her words, as if they were stuck in her throat. "I washed my hands before the police arrived, but there were probably traces left under my nails. I felt very sick."

"What about the suicide note. Did you write it?"

"No."

"When you saw your husband slumped over on the desk, was there a note there?"

"No. If there'd been one, I would have seen it. I would have read it."

"Who wrote the note?"

"You will have to ask that man over there."

Coker said, "Let the record reveal that the witness was pointing at the prosecutor."

"It may so reflect," the judge ordered.

Coker turned to look at Sewell, as if waiting for his admission. Hearing nothing, he said, "Some other issues have arisen here, Mrs. Adams. Did you ever have a conversation with Deputy Huffsmith about this case?"

"No. He was the officer who let me into jail, but we never talked about this case or anything else."

"Did you know that his home was being foreclosed by the bank?"

"No."

"Did you ever talk with the banker, Mr. Abberly, about Mr. Huffsmith, his mortgage, or about any other thing?"

"No. I have not spoken to Mr. Abberly except on a social basis, and that was months ago—I believe at a dinner to raise money for disadvantaged children."

"Did you talk to Judge Murray about Deputy Huffsmith's foreclosure problem?"

"No. I didn't know the deputy's home was being foreclosed."

"Why did you go to the jail to talk to the judge?"

"I wanted his advice—but he refused to see me."

"I have no further questions," Coker announced.

Sewell walked up to Lillian with fast, hard steps. "This is all very pretty, Mrs. Adams. It all fits together so very neatly."

"Objection," Coker said. "This is grossly insulting. He's at least required to ask a question and to refrain from making his prejudicial speeches."

"Ask a question, Mr. Sewell," the judge ruled.

"I will ask a question. I take it that you tried to talk to Judge Murray because you wanted to use your obvious charms to curry favor in your case, isn't that true?"

"No," she said. "He was the only person left in the world whom I trusted and who would understand me."

"You knew you could manipulate him, didn't you, Mrs. Adams?"

"Manipulate?"

"Yes, manipulate. He's an old man. But he is a man. You waited for him in his truck that night, and you kissed him."

"It was just an impulse. I kissed him on the cheek like a daughter kisses her father. He was like a father to me."

"Then he followed you home?"

"Yes. But only to tell me not to contact him again."

"I suppose that when you embraced him in the jail's visiting room that he didn't embrace you back—that you were unable to arouse him in any way?"

Suddenly, her voice gathered life. "I consider that an insult to him and to me," she said.

"So you want this jury to believe that you and he had nothing going on while you were being tried for murder?"

"Yes, there was nothing going on between us then or ever. I admired him. That was all."

"That was all?"

"Yes. He is a wise and decent man. He is a father figure to me, so different from my own father, who is impetuous and always at war and ready to fight. He sits here in court every day and then goes home and drinks and shouts that they all should be shot, especially you."

"When did you decide to testify in this case?"

"I needed the jury to know that you lied to them."

"Really!" Sewell scoffed. "How thoughtful of you."

"Yes, you tried to make it look like I paid off Deputy Huffsmith's loan to the bank in exchange for his testimony that there was no suicide note and no blood on the floor when he arrived at the scene."

"And, of course, you deny that you paid off his loan to the bank, don't you?"

"Yes. I paid nothing to either the bank or the deputy, or to anyone else."

"You told Judge Murray that you wanted to plead guilty, and that you killed your husband. That's true, isn't it?"

"Yes," she said quietly. "I didn't want Tina to go through this nightmare of a trial, which you have now put her though. You should be horribly ashamed."

"I have no further questions of this witness." He sat down and left Lillian Adams staring out from the witness chair.

Coker rose and walked toward the jury. "I wish to read from the last page in Mr. Adams's journal. It says—"

"Objection!" Sewell cried. "Counsel can't testify."

"It is the deceased, Mr. Adams, who is testifying, Mr. Sewell," said Judge Little. "Overruled."

Coker read the passage aloud.

This one last clear day before the horror sets in again and never leaves. You have been my life and it has been beautiful. Remember, darling, I have and always will love you.

Horace

Lillian began to say something, but tears interrupted. Finally, she said, "I have something more. It's about the Cracker Jack box and the toy cigar."

"How could that possibly be relevant?" Sewell interjected.

"We shall see," Judge Little ruled.

"Horace's mother left him at an early age," Lillian said. "She gave him a box of Cracker Jacks that had a toy cigar in it. It was his most prized possession. He showed it to me once. When Horace wanted to talk to his mother, he took that box and toy cigar out from his safe. He sort of talked to his mother through the box and toy cigar, the only material things he had to remember her by. She died homeless. They found her body in the park."

"Isn't that interesting." Sarcasm saturated Sewell's words.

"Yes, it is interesting," Lillian said. "He kept the box and toy cigar in his safe. To get to it, he had to remember the combination to the safe. He must have wanted to talk to his mother one last time before he ended his life. And, as you know, the combination to his safe was so complicated that your expert safe man couldn't open it, and he had to drill it open."

Sewell glared at Lillian.

"So, on the date of his death, Horace was able to recall that complicated combination?" Coker asked.

"Yes."

"You wish to re-cross-examine on this issue, Mr. Sewell?" the judge asked.

"I think not," Sewell said. "We've heard quite enough from this woman. We don't need to endure more absurdities about Cracker Jack boxes and toy cigars."

Timothy Coker turned to Sewell. "Mrs. Adams says I should ask you about the suicide note. So I will. Did you write it?"

"You will not address each other, counselors," Judge Little said. "The court will stand in recess."

Lillian patted Coker's shoulder. "I think we won," she whispered.

"Don't be too sure. As long as the bastard's alive, he can make up another pack of lies."

Lillian nodded. "Yes, he can."

Coker walked past Sewell's table, and out of the side of his mouth, he said, "Don't you think you should dismiss this stinking case before it destroys you?"

CHAPTER 48

JUDGE LITTLE LOOKED unassailably proper as he sat on his bench and read the instructions that every judge reads to every jury in every criminal case. He instructed the jurors about the presumption of innocence and the burden of proof that rested on the state, and that nebulous concept of "beyond a reasonable doubt."

What was reasonable? Judge Murray asked himself. That which was reasonable to one juror would likely be unreasonable to another. And every living soul, including himself, carried around his or her own junk pile of prejudices, most of which were unreasonable.

Judge Little instructed the jurors: "While motive may be relevant, it is not an element of the crime of murder, and proof of a motive is not necessary for a conviction. The prosecution is only required to prove that Lillian Adams intentionally killed her husband with what the law calls 'malice aforethought'—meaning she had planned the killing and intended to kill him." The judge turned to Sewell. "You may present your opening final argument."

Sewell stood and stared at the jury. He began by pointing a finger at Lillian. "Ladies and gentlemen of the jury, she has an excuse for everything. She has an excuse for the blood under her nails. She has an excuse for the blood on her clothing. She has an excuse for the gunshot residues on her hands. And now her lawyer even claims that the forged suicide note had been forged by someone other than Lillian Adams. Well then, who forged it? We have proven Lillian Adams did it.

"And the bloody drag marks." He lowered his eyes as if in prayer and moaned in mockery. "I'm sorry that such an individual as Arthur Huffsmith, a deputy with a previously unblemished record, should try to foist upon this jury the trickery of his photographs. Why did Deputy Huffsmith keep these photographs secret all of this time?

"Why is he part of this devilish conspiracy to cover a murder? Deputy Huffsmith's house was mortgaged, and the mortgage was being foreclosed. Suddenly, the foreclosure proceedings ended, and Lillian Adams had nothing to do with that? She was a woman about to gain fifty million dollars if she was acquitted of the murder. Can we now understand why Deputy Huffsmith claims—and for the first time—that the suicide note was not present when he arrived at the scene?" He paced in front of the jury.

"We have a woman here who stands to gain fifty million dollars—*fifty million*—if we close our eyes to her vicious crime." Sewell's lips grew whiter and thinner and his eyes were squinted nearly shut in his effort to restrain his mounting fury. "We have here the base effrontery of Sylvia Huntley, who, under oath, refused to tell the jury the simple truth. Who are these agents of the devil!"

"Objection!" Coker cried. "Your Honor, I move once more for a mistrial. Yet again this prosecutor has stepped over the permissible boundaries of propriety when he refers to one of our citizens with such prejudicial language."

"I'll hear you in chambers, counsel," Judge Little said, and called a recess.

In chambers, Coker in slow, carefully chosen words said, "Hopefully, we're not returning to the Dark Ages. This prosecutor's reference to 'agents of the devil' would be appropriate only in the infamous inquisitions of medieval times. The last we heard of 'agents of the devil' in this country was the infamous Salem witch trials, which left their shameful scars on the history of America."

"Yes, I agree," Judge Little said. "I will instruct the jury to disregard any reference to 'agents of the devil' as made by Mr. Sewell."

"With all due respect," Coker said, "how can the jury disregard such reference when you, Your Honor, will be republishing those forbidden words when you tell them to disregard the prosecutor's words 'agents of the devil'?"

Judge Little examined his desktop, as if the answer would be revealed there. Without saying more, he ordered the parties to return to the courtroom. He spoke to the jury in a stern judicial voice. "Ladies and gentlemen, any reference to that certain entity of evil in any form or in any connection is forbidden in this case. You will not make reference to it, discuss it in any way, and you will abolish it from your minds. Mr. Sewell, I admonish you for this misconduct, and warn you that any further violations of this kind will be dealt with severely by the court. Do you understand?"

"How, Your Honor, does one abolish something from one's mind without bringing it to mind in order to abolish it?" Coker asked.

After another long pause, Judge Little said, "I will

further advise the jury that they may take Mr. Sewell's improper remarks concerning a certain entity of evil as evidence of a weak case. Your motion, Mr. Coker, for a mistrial is overruled."

"The devil made you do it," Coker said with unclothed sarcasm.

Little instructed Sewell to continue, "being cautious to stay totally within the bounds of a proper final argument."

Sewell looked up at the judge, nodded, and, acting as if the judge's instructions were of little consequence, began anew by saying, "Sylvia Huntley did not tell the truth. Deputy Huffsmith did not tell the truth. The girl, Tina Ford, did not tell the truth. This defendant did not tell the truth, and, I am loath to say, Judge Murray, held in jail as a material witness, conveniently hid the truth with the clever device of his faulty hearing aid. Oh, how clever!" he hissed. "What a feast of lies we have endured!

"Truth is calling to you. Listen!" Sewell waited as if Truth were plainly audible. "It is a clarion call for justice. Bring justice back to Teton County. Let all within the sound of my voice know that justice is ours only if we discover it, have the courage to demand it, and embrace it. Otherwise, we live on the borders of hell."

Haskins Sewell bowed slightly to the jury and sat down.

As if searching for assistance, Timothy Coker slowly peered through his thick glasses from one juror to the next. He pulled his suit coat together and struggled to button it over his escaping paunch. He would have been more comfortable in a battle with bare fists. But this was a battle in which the weapons were words. And he'd win or lose the war depending on the words he chose to penetrate the armor of the jurors' prejudices.

He began like a tired father speaking to his children at bedtime. "I want to tell you a story. It's a story about an ambitious prosecutor with all the power of the state behind him. You've met him." The jurors followed Coker as he walked with a perceptible limp toward Sewell's table. He looked at Sewell. A foreboding dusk seemed to settle into the courtroom. Coker turned back to the jurors' blank faces.

"This prosecutor is just that—he's a prosecutor. What does he seek to gain by this heinous false case? What does he hope to accomplish by disparaging a decent and honorable member of the sheriff's department when he charges Deputy Huffsmith as a liar without a sliver of evidence to support it? I'm not permitted under the law to give you my opinion about Mr. Sewell's motivations. But we must remember, he is the only person in Teton County with the power to prosecute innocent people. On the other hand, there is only one person in this case who's presumed under the law to be innocent, and it is not Mr. Sewell. It is Lillian Adams."

Coker spoke as if addressing his own thoughts. "There is a conspiracy here all right. It's a conspiracy to convict Lillian Adams. This forged suicide note"—he lifted it from the clerk's desk and held it up—"could never exist without a conspiracy. Sheriff Lowe had to know that no such note was ever in the possession of the sheriff's office. He was at the scene when the evidence was gathered, and he was never called as a witness. Why? *Why?* Not a single witness testified that the note was at the scene. No one has explained where it came from. It just mysteriously floated down on us from Mr. Sewell.

"But one telling fact cannot be hidden in this case. If it had not been for Deputy Huffsmith, Mr. Adams's journal would never have been discovered. It, too, was in the secret possession of Mr. Sewell. Let's ask ourselves, 'Why did the prosecutor and the sheriff hide that journal from us?' Isn't the answer clear—that they didn't want us to hear Mr. Adams telling us the reason he ended his own life?"

Coker waited. Still he saw only the jurors' empty faces.

Coker waved the alleged suicide note at the jury. "This putrid piece of paper. It doesn't stand as a forgery by Mrs. Adams. It stands for something unspeakable, something planted in this case by this prosecutor through the testimony of a high-priced witness, Mr. Widdoss." As if he'd touched something vile, he dropped the note on Sewell's desk and faced the jurors once more.

"Why did this prosecutor try to frame Lillian Adams with that obviously forged suicide note? And who forged it? I think you know the answer to both of these questions." He waited.

The clerk of court sat mute and stony.

Judge Little peered down from his bench mute and stony.

Finally, one juror, the blacksmith, cleared his throat as if to speak, but he remained silent.

"We've witnessed how easily the innocent can be converted into the guilty." Coker took in the jurors one at a time. "This prosecutor had Mr. Adams's journal in his secret possession during this entire trial. He knew, as we now know from reading Mr. Adams's journal, that he took his own life. So how can Mr. Sewell make honest, intelligent jurors doubt that truth?

"First he hid the journal from us so we couldn't know that Mr. Adams took his own life to save his beloved wife from the horrors of his advancing senility. Then this prosecutor provided a phony suicide note, hired the alleged expert, Widdoss, to tell us it is phony, and that

Mrs. Adams wrote the note to cover the murder of her husband. And thereby that prosecutor"—Coker pointed to Sewell—"converted suicide into murder, and a grieving wife, Mrs. Adams, into a murderer."

Sewell tipped back in his chair, closed his eyes, and sighed audibly, as if what Coker was saying was not worth a withering whit.

Coker began anew: "Let us consider another piece of his fakery. We discovered that the smears of blood on the floor came from the officers dragging the body to the gurney. The sheriff knew that truth because he helped remove the body. Other officers in this case knew the truth, as well." Coker pointed at Sewell. "That prosecutor knew the truth. He was there. But he called none of these officers as witnesses to testify to the truth. Instead, he knowingly presented and argued fake evidence to us."

Again Coker took in each juror, eye-to-eye. Was he speaking to a choir of mummies? Had the dead taken over the courtroom? He looked up at the judge, who peered down with empty eyes.

"The great American safeguard—that the accused must be proven guilty beyond a reasonable doubt—was not only given to us by our founders to protect the innocent against a prosecutor such as this one; it was provided to protect each of you. You as jurors!" Coker began to pace. "Our founders gave us reasonable doubt to save each of you from staring at the ceiling in the dark in bed and wondering, Did my decision convict an innocent person?"

Coker's face was sad, his anger worn away, his voice tired but firm. "This is not a case of reasonable doubt. This is the prosecutor's totally failed case. Worse, it is his fake case. He knows it. Give it back to him!" Coker's hands gathered up an imaginary bundle and threw it in the direction of Haskins Sewell.

"Under the law, the prosecution is given the last word. When I sit down, my lips will be sealed forever here. Please remember as he argues again that if I were given the chance, I could answer every one of his fabrications with the truth. I will be silenced by the law. But justice is not silenced, because each of you has the last word, not Mr. Sewell. In my absence, I ask you to answer Mr. Sewell's arguments in the jury room, as you know I would have answered them had I been permitted to do so."

Coker's voice was as if a weary friend were speaking confidentially to a gathering of friends. "This prosecutor has enormous power. Under the law, we are all presumed innocent. It is as much, yes, even more, his duty to fight for our rights as it is to charge and convict the guilty. When the people elected prosecutor Sewell, they trusted him to perform those duties faithfully and to protect them. But he has done the opposite. He is charging one of us with a crime and dragging her before a jury to face false charges. But he is attempting to destroy one of us. We elected him to save us from the ravages of crime, to prosecute only the guilty and to protect the innocent. Such is his sad betrayal of our trust."

Once again, Coker engaged each juror slowly and thoughtfully. "We have choices to make in our lives, and we live by our choices. And the choices we make define who we are." In a near-whisper, he said, "When the facts of the prosecutor's case are scattered across the table of truth like pieces in a puzzle, and none fit, the prosecutor argues that there has been a vicious conspiracy of liars. We can choose to believe that the prosecutor and his handsomely paid handwriting expert are the only truth tellers here. We can believe that the other witnesses, one and all, are liars including a faithful judge who has served us for nearly forty years, and an honest deputy who broke from the prosecutor's gang and came forward with the evidence they hid from us. This is your choice. You can choose to believe that Horace Adams the Third was murdered for whatever motive was Mr. Sewell's motive of the moment, or you can believe that Mr. Adams loved his wife, provided for her, and removed himself from her life as his final act of love. We have the choice to believe in love and compassion or in the lies that feed hate."

Again Coker waited for his words to settle on the jurors.

Finally, he said, "I have this vision. I see us walking out of this courtroom together, you, and Lillian Adams, and, yes, I will walk with you. We will be celebrating the immortal vision of our forefathers, who gave us the jury to protect us against the power of the state. We will be rejoicing that you, as jurors, have once more thrown your arms around us to protect us against the unrelenting, hideous, self-serving power of the likes of Mr. Sewell."

Coker looked across the courtroom as if he could see into the past. "The greatness of our system is that each of you, alone, by simply saying no to Mr. Sewell, has the final power to save us from the betrayal of justice in the hands of this ambitious prosecutor."

Timothy Coker gave Lillian Adams a fatherly, apologetic smile and started slowly to sit down.

Sewell rose before Coker was settled in his chair. He began, "You have just heard so much emotional defense-lawyer fancy talk. If juries listened to that sort of folderol, no murderer would ever be convicted. Speaking of duty: We have a dead man here." He waved the photo showing Adams facedown on the desktop, his head sur-rounded by the large pool of blood. "He was one of our citizens. If people can kill and get away with it because of the fancy talk of a clever mouthpiece, none of us would be safe."

Sewell's voice rose in ringing, righteous indignation. "Coincidences do occur. We all know that. But things are just too neat here. We have a very crafty woman. She sits there in tears. Are those tears for her dead husband, or tears for herself?"

Sewell checked his notes. "Ah, yes, I see. I am asked to explain the supposed suicide note. I, of course, went home and forged it, right after the murder, brought it to court, hired the best expert in the business to tell you that the note was forged, and had the county pay him thousands of dollars to say so as part of a conspiracy. Then Deputy Huffsmith tells us that nothing in his rec-ords revealed the existence of the note. Do tell!" Sewell puckered his lips and squinted his eyes cynically. "Can we in law enforcement no longer trust our own officers? Are we but barnacles on a sinking ship? How can we protect the citizens of this county when we can no lon-ger trust our own officials?"

He walked a step closer to the jurors. "I agree with Mr. Coker on one thing. You have choices to make here, and you must live with them. They do define who you are. You have either found the truth—that Mr. Adams was murdered and his murderer sits right here"—he pointed to Lillian Adams—"or you will be taken in by the likes of Mr. Coker and give a murderer a free pass. I have more faith in you than that."

The sound of his leather soles and heels laid a confi-dent beat back to his table. He closed his file and nodded to the jurors.

CHAPTER 49

THE JURORS ELECTED James Smithson, the bank's youngish vice president, as foreman. He wore a banker's clean white shirt and a different tie every day; his black pointed-toe shoes were shined and his fingernails polished. He was chubby, but his tailored, well-pressed suit coat nicely covered his girth. He was pale and wore his blond hair in a short cut, so that his ears protruded slightly, but all in all, he exhibited an air of credibility. He spoke in a confident tenor voice.

"Do we need to read the judge's instructions again, given that we've just heard them?" He looked from juror to juror.

"Let's take a vote and get this thing over with," the rancher, William Witherspoon, said in his rough, splintered voice. "I got chores to do and a bunch of cattle loose on my neighbor's land. He don't like my cattle eating his grass. Grass is money, you know."

The jury took its first secret ballot, after which Smithson carefully unfolded each piece of white paper the jurors had used for voting—seven to five for conviction.

Witherspoon said, "I don't know who voted to convict that lady, but whoever you are might need a little head examination yourselves." He was sitting on the edge of his chair and inspected each of his fellow jurors with a challenging look.

"Everyone should try to be civil, Mr. Witherspoon," foreman Smithson said in a voice edged with the authority he'd been awarded. "I can always call the judge if this sort of conduct continues."

"You look like the type who'd go running for mama if everything didn't go your way," Witherspoon said. "I suppose you voted to convict her."

Smithson turned his head away. "This was a secret ballot," he said. "And since I am foreman here, I think it improper for me to reveal my vote, because it might influence others on this jury."

"Well, I know how you bankers operate," Witherspoon said. "You can tell a man what he's got to do, because a man's got to have your money in hard times."

"This deliberation isn't about me, but your conduct here doesn't measure up to—"

Witherspoon interrupted him and stood up. "If you're passing your banker's judgment on me, we can have us a little talk outside this jury room."

"Well, we've all gotten along pretty well here," Margaret Reed Smith said. She was the grandmother who worked as a volunteer at the hospital. "This is a very important case, and we must consider it like adults."

"Well, ma'am," Witherspoon said with a nasty twang, "if you don't mind telling us, how did you vote?"

"I voted for conviction," Margaret Reed Smith said. "To cover her lies, she did a lot of crying. I know women of her type."

"I suppose that everybody who's ever lied is a

murderer," Witherspoon said. "If that's the case, I should get the hell outta here on account of I am surrounded here by murderers."

"Well, I'll put in my two cents' worth," Amos Rogers, the blacksmith, said. His back pain caused him to slump in his chair. "That Sewell is wanting the judge's job. Everybody knows that. And he kept that journal away from us because he knew it would show that the old boy killed himself."

"I'm sick and tired of listening to Timothy Coker," Helen Griggsley, the piano teacher, said from behind her sunglasses. "He's always getting some scummy individual loose so that now a person is afraid to go out after dark in this little town." She stopped to catch her breath. "And I know that Haskins Sewell is a God-fearing man. He goes to my church every Sunday, where I play the organ. I see him there praying, and he supports the Women's League with a solid donation every year and—"

"I don't recall any of that being in the evidence," Witherspoon interrupted. "And I don't remember that when you were being selected for jury duty that you said anything about you knowing Sewell."

"Nobody asked me," she said.

"The judge asked if there was any reason why you couldn't fairly try this case," William Carter, the mechanic, said. "You damn sure heard that."

"I can be fair. Just because I know that Mr. Sewell is a God-fearing man doesn't disqualify me. Mr. Sewell isn't on trial." Helen Griggsley gave Carter a quick, victorious nod and sat up a bit straighter.

"Let's get back to the evidence, shall we?" foreman Smithson said. "I don't know what her motive was for sure, but Judge Little said we didn't need to know her motive to convict."

Harmony Biernstein, the real estate broker, said, "I

agree." She was wearing her blue business suit. A small gold cross hung across her front on a thin gold chain. She wore low-heeled black patent-leather shoes. "Everybody knows Lillian Adams. Her reputation isn't so, shall we say, spotless. She's been married a few times. And she is wild, or so I hear, and I mean wild."

"Yeah," Witherspoon said. "She's capable of taking away your man or, for that matter, any other woman's man. A woman gets to hating a woman like that."

"You men are all alike," Mary Lou Livingston, the waitress, said. "You see a pretty face and a pair of legs, and you forget everything else."

Witherspoon snorted. "You women are all alike, too. You see a pretty face on another woman and a pair of good legs and you immediately go into your killing mode."

Finally, foreman Smithson said, "Well, I shouldn't say this, but I happen to know that Lillian Adams was writing checks on his account, forging his name and all."

"Horace was losing his mind," Witherspoon replied. "Somebody had to write the checks to pay the bills. And you shouldn't be revealing confidential information like that. As soon as this case is over, I'm going to take my money out of your bank."

"Yeah," Tom Mosley, the pawnbroker, said, looking squarely at Smithson. "You told Coker under oath during jury selection that you knew nothing about the finances of the Adamses. You were under oath and that is perjury."

"That's perjury all right," Witherspoon agreed. "So we got us a perjurer for a foreman, and he's voting to convict the lady. How do you like that?"

"Well, I haven't said how I voted," Smithson said.

"I know one thing," said Bertie Hartnett, the school district's secretary. She wore rimless glasses and a black sleeveless dress, exposing her thin arms. Her hair was graying and cut short. "The Adams woman admitted killing her husband both to Sylvia Huntley and to Judge Murray himself. That old devil! I've known the judge and Betsy for years. Just goes to show you: You can never trust a man. Not even a judge!"

"None of that ain't been said." It was the plumber, Manuel Ortega. He wore his customary bib overalls. "The judge, he has bad ears, no? You remember?" He shook his head and laughed. "And I remember another thing. Judge Little says we decide this case on the evidence, and for me, well, I seen sewers all messed up, and you no can follow them nowhere—and this case is like a plugged-up sewer. And that there is reasonable doubt."

"You got something there all right," Witherspoon said. "But that journal. Sewell hid it because it showed it was a suicide. If it hadn't been for old Huffsmith, we would have had to convict her! Are we supposed to believe somebody like that, who holds himself out as an honest prosecutor?"

Manuel Ortega said, "You could tell he's fightin' to keep his lights on. And if that ain't so, why was that Sewell tryin' to hide his journal from us? There's something down there that's cloggin' things up, if ya know what I means."

Suddenly, Helen Griggsley said in a voice that was faintly romantic, "If he loved her like everybody says, he would have written something like, 'Darling, I love you. It's better this way,' or something loving. Like Mr. Widdoss said, somebody else wrote that note for sure."

"He did say he loved her. It's right there in black and white in his journal," William Carter said.

"It ain't easy to write lovey-dovey stuff," Witherspoon said. "I been married forty-two years, and me and my wife are pretty close. She can pull a calf as good as any hand I ever had. And she can shoot a coyote from a couple hundred yards with open iron sights, and put up the rhubarb for them pies she makes, and when it comes to our anniversary, I can't ever figure out what to say except to tell her . . ." And he started to tear up.

The jurors waited.

Witherspoon finally began again, this time with a holler. "But that doesn't make me a killer on account of I don't wear my heart on my sleeve. And if a guy's about to shoot his own head off, he might have trouble thinking about something sweet to write."

"I agree with you there," Mary Lou Livingston said. "You can't tell anything about what a man thinks, especially if he's in the mood to kill. And if this was a suicide, well, he was in the mood to kill."

"Maybe he was going to kill his wife, and she shot him in self-defense," Josephine Heller, the unemployed art teacher, said. "Maybe she wrestled him for the gun or something. I'm not necessarily voting that way, but maybe . . ."

"I never thought of that," Mary Lou Livingston said.

"She never claimed it was self-defense. She said he shot himself," Margaret Reed Smith said. "She said it in open court."

Witherspoon spoke up again. "Well, one thing: All along she was trying to protect her daughter. I don't know how you mothers can forget that. Even an old cow will lay it all down for her calf. Especially an Angus cow. But I will grant you, them Herefords—"

Tom Mosley interrupted. "Well, Deputy Huffsmith said the note wasn't there when he got to the scene. And he was the first there."

Helen Griggsley said, "I know Mr. Sewell, and I'm sure he had nothing to do with forging a note."

"Those churchgoin' kind are the first to lie," Wither-spoon said. "If they weren't such thieves and liars, they wouldn't have to go to church so often to get forgiven."

"That is the most horrible thing I have ever heard said. Mr. Sewell should sue you for slander," Helen Griggsley told him.

"That is Sewell's privilege," Witherspoon said. "They tell me that truth is a defense to slander."

"I haven't said much to this point, but I'm under oath," said William Carter. "So I'd better come out with it." He was looking at Helen Griggsley. "I happen to know you had a house party for Sewell when he ran the last time."

"And how would you know anything about my personal life?" Helen Griggsley asked.

"You probably don't remember," Carter said, "but you'd been raising hell because your car wasn't working, and I came by your house when your party was going on. I saw Sewell there with my own eyes."

"I never get into politics," Helen Griggsley said. "It was a church affair. Covered-dish supper. Mr. Sewell's a member of my church. Any member of the church could come."

Finally, Smithson said to Helen Griggsley, "I'm a little surprised about this party thing with Sewell. I think we should ask the judge about it. After all, I am the fore-man, and it's my responsibility to see that our delibera-tions are not tainted in any way."

"You can do whatever you like," she said. "I've done nothing wrong. And I am perfectly willing to discuss this case as if I had never met Mr. Sewell. In fact, I hardly know him."

Witherspoon said, "That suicide note came popping up just in time to make a case for Sewell. He had the journal, too, and plenty of time to phony up old Adams's handwriting."

"I think she killed her husband because he was molesting her daughter," Helen Griggsley said.

"There was nothing in the evidence about that," Smithson said. "You are making that up."

"Well, she couldn't admit she killed him for that reason," Helen Griggsley said. "After all, it might be the right thing to do, but the law doesn't permit us mothers to protect our daughters, and nowadays the law doesn't protect our daughters, either. So what's a mother supposed to do?"

"That girl, Tina, is nuts, and tough," Witherspoon said. "But I say her mother was lying to protect her."

"Yeah, and I never trusted that handwriting expert," Tom Mosley said. "Nobody's handwriting is the same all the time. Sometimes I'm in a hurry. Sometimes I got a different pen."

Silence took over. Finally, Amos Rogers said, "Judge Little told us the Adams lady doesn't have to prove anything. It's Sewell's job to do the proving. Old Sewell was just raising questions he should have answered. And he didn't. How come? He could have put the sheriff on the stand to contradict Huffsmith when he said he and the sheriff dragged Adams across the floor and that's where the bloody drag marks came from. And he didn't."

William Carter said, "There's a lot of doubt here. I think she may have been covering for her daughter, and I can forgive a mother for doing that. Might even be the right thing to do if you're a mother. I think the law of mothers trumps the law, period!"

"That's what I've been trying to say all along," Josephine Heller said.

"Well, I knew Tina before I went to the bank. I was teaching chemistry at the high school," Smithson said. "She threatened once to shove a hot test tube up the rear end of Clint Black, our left tackle on the football team, and he backed off. She probably could have."

"There we go again," Mosley said to Smithson. "Coker asked you if you knew any members of the Adams family, and you said no."

"Well, Tina is not a member of that family."

"I have a stepson, and he is a member of my family," Mosley said.

"Maybe we should take another ballot," Smithson suggested. "It's getting late."

The vote was nine for acquittal and three for conviction.

"I say we go have dinner on the county and come back with a full stomach," Witherspoon said. "I always say that important decisions should never be made on an empty stomach."

They ate at one long table in the back of the Emery Hotel's dining room, where the Rotary Club met every Tuesday at noon. Witherspoon ordered a whiskey and water.

Helen Griggsley spoke up. "It is not proper for a juror to drink on the job."

"Who said so?" Witherspoon asked. "I never heard nothing in the judge's instructions that said a man couldn't have a drink before dinner, and I been having a drink of good whiskey before supper for thirty years. It's good for your heart." He lifted his shot glass up as if to make a toast.

"In that case, I'll have a glass of red wine," Harmony Biernstein said.

"I will, too," Smithson said, and after that everyone except Josephine Heller and Helen Griggsley ordered wine.

They talked about how cattle prices had gone to hell, and about the mountain-climbing guide who fell to his death on the Grand Teton and took a tourist down with him, which inspired Witherspoon to order another shot of whiskey.

Carter wanted to take after the Republicans, and Witherspoon wanted to criticize "them lily-livered liberals that hang around Washington making out with each other like a bunch of hot steers," but Smithson said that politics was a forbidden topic.

Witherspoon hollered to the waitress for the dessert menu. When he read the menu, his lips moved. "Is that peach pie hot?"

"Yeah," the waitress said. "At least it was this morning."

"Give me a piece of that, honey," he said with a good-natured wink. "And some vanilla ice cream on top."

Back in the jury room, Smithson started the discussion anew. "Now I've been thinking. And that is dangerous." He gave his fellow jurors a wink and a smile. "Now, justice is to do the right thing. And I've been thinking that old Adams was losing it. He must have wanted to die. He would have been a terrible burden on his wife and on everyone else. And losing your mind is a terrible thing. I know. My father didn't know who he was or where he was when he finally died." He looked down when he spoke of his father.

Then Smithson went on. "The facts do not always define justice. And the law doesn't, either. It was not just that my father lived about ten years too long and near broke my mother and all us kids. It was horrible. I don't know if Lillian Adams killed her husband or not. She might have. But I am thinking that maybe he killed himself to save her the misery of living with a man who is slobbering and raving and lost like my father was. Adams knew he was slipping bad. His journal said so. I am beginning to think he killed himself out of mercy for her, which, as I see it, was the right reason."

Helen Griggsley answered him. "If he killed himself, she probably talked him into it, and that makes her as guilty as if she killed him."

"I know," Smithson said. He gave her his kindest banker look. "But don't you have a reasonable doubt about this? I mean, she could have killed him. Her daughter could have killed him. He could have killed himself. She could have talked him into killing himself. The note could have been forged. She could have forged it. Sewell could have forged it. A 'could have' case is a reasonable-doubt case."

"I do not think there is any doubt, much less a reasonable one," Helen Griggsley replied. "One way or another, that woman is guilty of murder."

Witherspoon piped up. "Now maybe she did kill her husband. But I'll tell you one thing: If a man has a good horse, and the horse gets old and can't make it no more, a decent man don't let the horse die a little at a time until the coyotes eat him alive."

Smithson said, "Now, Mr. Witherspoon, we are not going to get into a debate about euthanasia."

"I suppose that's one of your fancy words for mercy killing," Witherspoon said. "But if the lady shot the old boy to put him out of his misery, I, for one, am not about to send her off for the rest of her life to a bunch of hot cows in some woman's prison, or, worse, let them lock her in a gas chamber. Takes brass balls to do a mercy killing."

Smithson said, "Sewell didn't prove that Tina didn't kill him. The girl said she did kill him. Remember?"

"I didn't believe the girl," Helen Griggsley said. "She wasn't that crazy, if she was crazy at all. Her mother is one vicious woman. You could see it the way she looked at Mr. Sewell, who I know is an honorable—"

"But he didn't prove that the girl didn't kill him and—"

Tom Mosley interrupted Smithson. "Well, the blood's been bothering me. The sheriff and Sewell had to know that the bloody marks on the floor were from them dragging the body out. They were there. They lied to us."

"That Sewell is a great guy all right," Witherspoon said. "But if God had wanted him to actually convict Lillian Adams, he would have given Sewell a better hand to play."

Suddenly, Helen Griggsley asked, "What happened to the Cracker Jack box and the toy cigar? Why would that Cracker Jack box and toy cigar just happen to be there on the desk when Huffsmith found him, but we haven't heard of that since?"

"Yeah, why didn't Sewell tell us about the Cracker Jack box?" Amos Rogers asked. "It had been in Adams's safe, and only he knew the combination. So he knew what he was doing that day, or he couldn't have opened the safe, that's for sure."

"Yes, and the Cracker Jack box and toy cigar were all he had of his mother, which goes to show you he was talking to his mama before he shot himself," Witherspoon said.

"A mother's love coming through in a Cracker Jack box and a toy cigar," Helen Griggsley said in a tiny child's voice. "Oh, dear Lord!"

Foreman Smithson said, "Maybe we should take another vote."

And on the next ballot, the jury returned its unanimous verdict, acquitting Lillian Adams.

CHAPTER 50

JUDGE JOHN MURRAY felt that light, airy, uplifting feeling in the heart area when Lillian walked free. Too often he'd seen juries' verdicts ricochet from the facts like a bullet bouncing off case-hardened steel. Too often prejudice, rather than the law and the facts, captured the case. But this verdict was spot-on.

He took in a breath of life as if he'd never breathed before. Moreover, there was a personal reason that he and Betsy could celebrate: The "evil bastard," as Betsy called Sewell, had been exposed. He'd hidden Adams's journal, and he must have forged the suicide note, or knew who did. He should be prosecuted. Maybe he'd at least lose his license to practice law.

The judge traveled to Hardy Tillman's garage to help him drink up the last of the brew stored in his refrigerator. Hardy had a head start on him and greeted the judge with a pat on the back and his hoarse laugh. "One thing you got to say: Letting the cat out of the bag is a whole lot easier than putting it back. Old Sewell should have knowed that."

They toasted the jury, and they toasted Coker, and after that Hardy toasted "the pretty ass of Lillian Adams that just got saved."

For reasons not clear to the judge, Sewell dropped the charges against Hardy and the judge for the ass-kicking Sewell got from Hardy. Maybe public sentiment reigned. Some of the townsfolk were saying they wished they'd have been the ones giving the son of a bitch an ass-kicking. Hardy was becoming a local hero.

The judge raised his bottle to salute his old friend.

"Old Jacobs from the paper called me and asked me if I had any statement to make," Hardy said.

"And . . ."

"I tells him, 'I ain't got nothing to say except I kicked old Sewell's bony butt in self-defense.' And he says, 'Is that all you got to say?' and I says, 'Yeah, a closed mouth gathers no foot.'" Hardy began to laugh again, and he laughed until his laughter turned into fits of coughing.

They downed a couple more beers, and after all the hilarity, the two old men discovered they had nothing more to say. A rare embarrassment settled in.

The judge knew the jury's verdict in Lillian's case didn't acquit him. He'd lied. Worse, he'd lied again, because he'd never told Betsy that he'd lied. The judge struggled to get up out of his chair, but Hardy opened another round. "I'll say one thing, Judge"—Hardy lifted his bottle—"and one thing only: You are a sly old bastard."

The judge frowned his "What are you talking about?" frown and took a long draw on the bottle.

"They had you cold and you squeezed out of it. You didn't even have to say 'I don't remember.'"

"So who's saying that besides you?" the judge asked.

"Everybody. They all know with yer hearing aid on ya can hear a pin drop on a pile a shit."

"She was too close to me for me to hear," the judge said. He had no choice but to lie again.

"Right," Hardy said, smiling his disbelief. "I wish she'd have got that close to me—within ten inches!" Then he added, "Ten and a half if it's early of a morning."

"I have to go home and feed my birds," the judge finally said.

Twenty-seven days following the acquittal of Lillian Adams, Haskins Sewell charged Judge John Murray with two counts of perjury. The judge was charged in Count I with having lied under oath when he told the jury he hadn't heard Lillian Adams say "I killed Horace because—" and in Count II, that he lied again when he claimed his hearing aids failed him.

On the same day, Undersheriff Bromley arrested the judge at his cabin and confiscated his hearing aids as evidence. Betsy, frantic, called Timothy Coker, and Coker, in turn, petitioned Judge Little, who immediately ordered the release of Judge Murray "on his own recognizance," after which Coker traveled out to the judge's cabin for a conference.

Judge Murray nodded silently to Coker. Betsy was pale and silent. Coker took the judge's chair by the fire.

"He will never make this stick," Coker said. "Not in a lifetime."

The judge was wearing his old hearing aids, which Betsy had stuffed in the bottom drawer of their bureau, along with a ring of old keys and a pair of scratched sunglasses.

"Sewell knows he can't make those charges stick," Coker said. "What you hear and what you can't is like what you remember and what you can't—it can't be proven. Besides, he can't prove that your batteries weren't dead. There will always be doubt, and Sewell knows it."

"He'll never give up," the judge said.

"It's part of his scheme to finally take over your judge-ship," Coker said. "You're supposed to file for reelection pretty soon. He comes out with these groundless charges before it's time for you to file. Win or lose this case, he thinks the people won't vote for a judge under indictment."

Betsy was squeezing her hands together, her knuckles white.

Coker continued: "This is also a clever way for him to explain why he lost the Adams case. He'll argue that Lillian admitted the killing to you and that you lied. Otherwise, he would have convicted her. He'll claim that Lillian got off on your perjured testimony."

"I should kill the evil bastard," Betsy said. "And I will. I swear I will."

"Don't waste your time thinking thoughts like that, Betsy," Coker said. He offered a small, sad smile. "I'll take care of Sewell. Don't worry."

Then Betsy walked out of the room.

Up to the last hour, the judge and Betsy had worried over his filing for reelection. "I don't want to be judge anymore," he said. "I've had enough of it, and I'm not as sharp as I used to be. I have those spells, you know, and I'd like to do something different with what little of my life remains."

"Like what?" Betsy asked. "You're as sharp as you ever were. And if you don't file, people will think you're guilty, and that rotten rat bastard will take over the county, and none of us will be safe anymore."

"You have no choice," Coker argued. "If you don't run, people will think you're guilty, and Sewell will win by default."

At the last minute, the judge filed for reelection.

The following evening at about 6:15—it was dark by then—Haskins Sewell was shot to death as he was about to enter his car, which was parked in the courthouse parking lot. The wound in the center of his forehead left a powder-burned entry lesion typical of a contact wound. The killer had put the gun against Haskins Sewell's forehead and pulled the trigger.

CHAPTER 51

THE FOLLOWING MORNING, before the ravens had visited his feeder, Judge Murray got a phone call. "Jesus Christ, I just heard on the news that . . ." The judge couldn't understand the rest—the fast, wild yelping of the caller. It was Hardy Tillman.

"You hear me, Judge? They just found old Sewell. He has a pretty little bullet hole in the middle of his forehead."

The judge made no reply.

"Somebody shot the bastard." Hardy laughed a high, hysterical laugh. "That shivering little dog of his he called Honeypot was trying to get into the back door of the courthouse. Huffsmith found the dog damn near froze to death, and then old Huffsmith started looking for Sewell, and that's when he found the bastard in the parking lot by his car, dead as a blowed-out tire."

"Hardy! Don't talk about this to anyone. Not anyone! I'll be there in a little while." He hung up the phone.

Betsy grabbed the judge's arm as he sat frozen on the edge of the bed. "What is it?" she asked. When he told her, she started to say something.

"Betsy," he said, "do not talk to me about this. I am not going to talk to you. They can't make you testify against me—our husband-wife privilege—but if I'm charged along with Hardy, they might try to make you testify against him."

"I don't understand," she said.

"Neither of you has an alibi, nor do I," he said. "You were coming home from school and the grocery store about six, right? The clerk at the grocery store can only testify you were in town about the time of the murder. You could be a suspect, crazy as that seems. And I was still at the courthouse, but I don't recall seeing anyone there. They'd all gone home."

Suddenly, the reality of the moment came thundering into the judge's consciousness: Yes, Sewell had been murdered! He'd tried not to hate the man, but he'd failed. Hate was a poison. Still, he felt a forbidden sense of triumph over the man's death.

Yes, he'd fantasized killing Sewell. But that didn't make him a killer. What man didn't kill his enemies in his own safe dream world? Such was the function of fantasies—to test reality—to follow the good and reject the bad. Dreaming was healthy. Although Sewell's murder had provided a fleeting sense that a greater justice had been served, the judge also felt guilt creeping in. And more frightening, once again he found himself struggling with what was mere dream and what was reality.

Sewell must have been a lonely man. He had no family. Only that little yapping lapdog. He had no one to love him. How could he give love back? Yes, the judge thought, I have survived my archenemy, Sewell. But had he won? He knew there'd be trouble, because hate enjoys an eternal life and is transferred from the dead to the living like an incurable plague.

He didn't remember if he'd slept the night following

Sewell's murder. He didn't remember getting dressed. Betsy put his bacon and eggs in front of him. Then quietly she said, "John"—she rarely called him John, usually she called him honey—"I was scared, so I went to the closet to see if our pistol was there. It's gone." She waited for his response. He cut into the egg, and the yoke was softer than usual and ran across the plate. "What did you do with it?"

"I told you, Betsy, we can't talk about this."

After Betsy had left for school, the judge gathered enough energy to feed the ravens. They were talking to him. What did they know that he didn't? They only wanted to be fed, he assured himself.

He drove to town, met Hardy at the tire store, and told his old friend that they couldn't be friends anymore, at least not until the Sewell murder was solved and the killer charged and convicted. If either of them was charged and either was called to the stand, that person might be required to testify about what the other had said. "And remember, we never had this conversation," the judge said to Hardy.

"My mouth is clammed shut as tight as a donkey's ass in fly time," Hardy replied.

Before the week was over, the governor appointed a special prosecutor to take over the duties of the late Haskins Sewell. The governor's appointee was an ambitious young assistant district attorney named Robert Headley, Jr., thirty-seven, from Laramie County, who, by reputation, had collected far too many convictions for a prosecutor of his age and experience.

Headley came storming into Jackson with an unconditional commitment to dispose, in a timely manner, those who had had anything to do with the murder of a fellow prosecutor. He stood well over six feet and was blond, with cold blue eyes that could focus on a subject like a spotlight at midnight. He wore alligator cowboy boots, a big silver-gray Stetson, and a western-cut suede jacket, no tie, but a bolo with a large hunk of mounted turquoise on the slide. If he'd been born a century earlier, he'd have been wearing matched ivory-handled Colts.

The morning following his arrival in Jackson, Headley met with the local paper. "I'm here on a sacred mission," he began, reading from his prepared statement. "The good people of Jackson Hole should know that their reign of terror is over. I'm here to bring back the safety of law and order to this county. We will find whoever is responsible for this heinous crime. I will prosecute, and I will see that justice is done—to the maximum." He set his right hand on his hip, as if genetic habit demanded that he reassure himself that his six-guns were loose in their holsters.

"Mr. Headley, do you have any suspects?" the reporter asked.

"There are more than a few persons of interest whom we will examine. This was a brazen, arrogant killing by a killer or killers who knew what they were doing. Let me tell you this much: A single shot killed prosecutor Sewell. The shot was placed precisely and expertly, and he died instantly."

"Do you suspect the Mafia?" the reporter asked.

"In Wyoming? Hardly!"

"Do you have a scenario for the motive?"

"Yes, the killer or killers obviously were not happy with Mr. Sewell."

"Do you suspect that the killer or killers intended to stop the prosecutor from exposing criminal activity in the county?"

"No comment."

The next day, Headley empaneled a grand jury, and Judge Little was appointed by the Wyoming Supreme Court to preside over all judicial aspects of the investigation. Once more, the press, in a noisy, pushy mob, descended on the small town of Jackson. The sheriff's office was flooded with calls from citizens offering help.

A mechanic from the local Chevy garage called, claiming that on the night of the murder he saw a black Cadillac with a driver and three passengers who didn't belong in Jackson Hole. They turned in to the courthouse parking lot just about six the evening of the murder. The mechanic said he'd earlier stopped at the tavern for a couple of beers and was on his way home when he witnessed the car.

A teacher at the high school called the sheriff's office, saying he knew about a bunch of kids who'd been prosecuted by Sewell, and one of the kids, Roger Moore, son of the local Baptist preacher, owned a pistol and was a crack shot. Sewell had sent one of Moore's buddies off to the boys' reformatory as a result of his second shoplifting conviction. The caller said he'd personally heard the kid threaten to kill Sewell.

The sheriff's office received scores of calls from citizens whose neighbors were suspected of various crimes, ranging from kid-kicking to kidnapping. Every citizen who'd ever been prosecuted by Sewell was automatically a suspect. But the special prosecutor had his own scenario, and he was quick to lay it out for Sheriff Lowe.

"I always look for the obvious first," Headley told the sheriff. "People, including law enforcement, read too many *True Detective* magazines, where the least suspected comes up guilty. We are not here to beguile the media or impress the public. We're here to solve this outrageous crime."

Lillian Adams was called to the grand jury as

Headley's first witness. The only other persons in the room were Headley; his assistant, Jimmy Friedman, an assistant district attorney from Laramie County who'd been sent along to help Headley, if, indeed, he should require any; the court reporter; and twenty ragtag grand jurors whom Undersheriff Bromley had gathered at random off the streets of Jackson. As is the standard rule in grand jury proceedings, no judge remained in the room to officiate, and as a consequence the prosecutor was free to employ any tactics he might choose—proper, intimidating, unjust, or otherwise.

The special prosecutor was a man guided by simple rules. "Delay," Headley asserted, "aborts justice." Without introduction, not even a "Good morning," he began his questioning of Lillian. The sound of his voice was accusatory. His presence was powerful and threatening, his patience virtuous.

"Mrs. Adams, you harbored a great deal of enmity against Mr. Sewell, isn't that true?"

"I would like my attorney, Mr. Coker, present," she replied. She looked worn, but her voice and appearance were steady.

"You are not permitted to have your lawyer in a grand jury hearing."

"I find that unacceptable," she said. "I'm an American citizen. I'm entitled to a lawyer."

"I see that Mr. Coker is waiting outside. You can leave this room and obtain advice from him as is reasonably needed. But he will not be present for your testimony. That happens to be the law."

"In that case, I refuse to answer any of your questions."

"On what grounds, Mrs. Adams?"

"I don't have to have grounds. I just refuse to answer."

"Do you want to be held in contempt?"

"Do what you please. I'm an American citizen, and I have rights."

"Yes," Headley said coldly. "I will ask His Honor, Judge Little, to come in."

Shortly, Headley's assistant, Jimmy Friedman, returned to the room with Judge Little in tow.

"You refuse to answer a question put to you by Mr. Headley?" Judge Little asked Lillian Adams. He was still wearing a bow tie, and he was not smiling.

"I want my lawyer present."

"What you want and what the law provides are two different things. You perhaps do not know this, Mrs. Adams, but it is the universal law across the land that a witness is not entitled to representation inside the grand jury room. Do you understand?"

"In that case, I refuse to answer."

"What are your grounds?"

"How do I know what my grounds are? I'm not a lawyer. But one thing I know: You are a part of this ongoing witch hunt that is intended to destroy the lives of innocent people."

"I have heard quite enough from you, Mrs. Adams," Judge Little warned. "I would not rely on escaping the law a second time. Are you going to answer Mr. Headley's question or take leave to ask your attorney's advice?"

"I want my lawyer here. You can throw me in jail. That's what you've wanted from the beginning. Now you have the power. I have no doubt you will use your power as you and Mr. Sewell have attempted in the past."

"Call the sheriff," the judge said.

Within minutes, Undersheriff Bromley entered the grand jury room. "Take this woman," Judge Little ordered. Promptly, Bromley grabbed Lillian's arm and, without apologies, locked one handcuff to her wrist and the other to himself. Then he dragged her from the room.

Coker had been sitting in a chair close to the jury room door, to be handy if Lillian needed him. As Bromley passed by with Lillian in handcuffs, Coker stepped in front of the undersheriff. "What's going on here?"

"This lady has been held in contempt by Judge Little," Bromley said. He sounded on the outskirts of a grand hurrah. "She won't answer any questions, and she refuses to talk to you about it."

Coker whispered in Lillian's ear. Then he turned to the undersheriff: "She's ready to talk. Take her back to the grand jury."

Once more in front of Judge Little, Lillian Adams looked up at the judge with disdain and said, "I refuse to testify on the grounds that my testimony might incriminate me."

"Release the witness," Judge Little ruled. "You see, this is still America, despite what you may think, Mrs. Adams. You have stated proper grounds for not testifying, which I find particularly interesting given the testimony I've heard in your case. However, my comments are ad hominem."

"What's that supposed to mean?" she asked.

"Ask your lawyer," the judge replied. "You may go."

By noon, Headley had gone through twelve witnesses, most of whom proved to be of little interest to him. However, his first witness after lunch was Henry Green.

"Mr. Green, you called the sheriff's office to report that Hardy Tillman had made certain threatening statements against Mr. Sewell?"

"That's right," Green said. "Sometimes Hardy has coffee with the boys, and that time when he was charged with an assault on Sewell, he said, 'I should have killed the son of a bitch instead a just kicking him in the ass in self-defense.' I distinctly remember him saying that."

"Yes?" Headley said, as if asking for more.

"I know one thing for sure," Green said. "Hardy hated Sewell. He is Judge Murray's best friend, and he was raising all kinds of hell about how Sewell had charged him and the judge with obstructing justice, and when Sewell charged the judge with perjury, Hardy went plumb bananas."

Headley had subpoenaed Hardy. He entered the jury room as Green was leaving. Without preliminaries, Headley hit Hardy with a volley of questions. "Mr. Tillman, have you ever made any threatening remarks against prosecutor Sewell?"

"I suppose that retarded peckerhead, Henry Green, told you I did."

"I asked you a question. Have you ever made any threatening remarks against Haskins Sewell?"

"That there is none of your business," Hardy said.

"It is my business to determine such facts," Headley said. "Please answer my question."

"I ain't in the habit of talking about my business to strangers," Hardy replied.

"Answer my question, sir."

"Well, I ain't talking," Hardy said.

"Do you refuse to answer?"

"What do you think?"

Headley stuck his head out of the jury room door and hollered, "Call the judge."

Judge Little appeared, and Hardy assured the judge that he was not about to answer any questions "for that nosy blond pipsqueak punk," whereupon the judge found him in contempt and ordered him confined to jail. Undersheriff Bromley cuffed both of Hardy's hands behind him and led him from the jury room.

"When I get out of here," Hardy hissed over his shoulder at Headley, "I'm gonna have a little meeting with you, and you're going to look like a turtle. Nobody is going to be able to tell where your head starts and your ass ends."

As the undersheriff led Hardy past where Coker was still sitting just outside the jury room, Coker hollered, "Tell them you take the Fifth, Hardy. That's your ticket out of jail."

"I take the Fifth," Hardy hollered back, whereupon Bromley led him back to the jury room. Hardy took the Fifth on the record and was immediately released by Judge Little.

As Hardy walked out, Jim Mortensen, Lillian's father, walked into the jury room. He, too, took the Fifth, after which Mortensen turned to the grand jurors and said, "Any good citizen doing his duty would have killed that no-good bastard. I fought in the war to save us from those kind. And now look what we got! Lying no-good bastards like that Sewell, who was supposed to be protecting our rights, not shitting on 'em—excuse my language."

Late that same afternoon, Judge Murray was called to testify. The judge took the stand and was slow and stiff in sitting down. "Judge Murray, I'm sorry to meet you under these circumstances." Headley's hostile eyes belied his sentiments. "I have always been a great admirer of yours. But I have to ask you some questions. You've been waiting to go to trial on perjury charges that were brought against you by Mr. Haskins Sewell, is that true?"

"Yes," the judge said.

"That must be extremely troublesome to you."

"Of course."

"And to your wife." Then Headley came out with it. His eyes were fixed on the judge as if the judge's reaction to his next question would settle it once and for all.

"Did you kill, arrange for the killing, or agree to the killing of Haskins Sewell?"

The judge, stunned, stared back at Headley for a long time, trying to determine how to answer the special prosecutor. If he answered any part of the question, there would be an endless volume of additional questions: Where had he been that night? Who could attest to that? Others would be drawn into his inquiry, including Betsy. He would be asked about his conversations with Hardy, and his relationship with Lillian, as paternal as it was.

"I refuse to answer on the grounds that my answer might incriminate me," the judge said in as strong a voice as he could muster.

A week later, the special prosecutor announced that the grand jury had indicted both Judge John Murray and Hardy Tillman for the murder of Haskins Sewell. The charges carried the death penalty.

CHAPTER 52

Spring arrived in Teton County and the early arrowroot balsam turned the lower hillsides yellow. The Canada geese were nesting, and the quaking aspens were budding. Already, here and there the rose-colored wild geraniums were popping into early bloom, and the alpine buttercups, already half past bloom, held on, as if they knew it was their last chance.

Once more, Judge Murray's springtime view was gray concrete and dark bars. Most of the time he refused to eat.

Betsy daily visited the judge. She tried to buoy his spirits, and he smiled at her and tried to talk about the pond, and the geese and their nests, and about the birds at his feeder.

Betsy reassured him that she was feeding his birds. The ravens were in charge, but sometimes she shooed them away so the chickadees and the white-breasted nuthatches could slip in for a seed or two. Some claimed ravens knew the secrets of death, but she kept that superstition to herself.

"Don't worry, honey," she said. "I talked to Timothy,

and he says you'll be out of here soon. He says the prosecution is stalling but that he's going to get you a trial right away or move for a dismissal."

Coker had asked Judge Little to let Judge Murray out on reasonable bond.

"I let him out without bond the last time," Judge Little said. "And we ended up with a prosecutor dead and Judge Murray indicted for his murder. We could run out of prosecutors if I don't put a stop to it."

"He's presumed innocent," Coker argued.

"Even serial killers are presumed innocent under the law," Judge Little said. "No, Mr. Headley represents to me that his case against Judge Murray is strong. I have reviewed the grand jury transcript, and I so find. Your application for bond is denied."

Late one afternoon, Deputy Huffsmith announced over the loudspeaker that Judge Murray had a visitor.

When the judge arrived at the visitors' room, there sat Lillian in old jeans and a loose woolen sweater. She looked years older, half-kempt, her fresh beauty wilted.

"I thought we had a deal, Lillian," the judge said. "Every time you come to see me, it creates another set of problems." He began his inventory. "You got me thrown off your case by that little visit you made to me in my pickup, and I had to defend myself before the Wyoming Supreme Court. Then the state claimed I perjured myself to save you. Now I'm in jail, and I've been waiting for fourteen weeks for a trial in which I'm charged with the murder of the man who prosecuted you. If I see you one more time, I will be assured of the death penalty. Maybe that's for the best." He hollered for Huffsmith.

"I know you're innocent," she said.

"How can you be so sure?" he asked. He put his finger to his lips to hush her.

"I know," she whispered. "Tina said she skipped class

that afternoon and waited until Sewell came out of the courthouse. She said nobody saw her. She walked up to Sewell and she said, 'Hi, Mr. Sewell. I have something for you.' She said she had the gun behind her back, and when he stopped, she walked right up to him, put the gun to his head, and before he knew what was happening, she pulled the trigger. She said, 'He fell like in the movies, but he jerked around on the ground quite a bit, just like grandpa said they did.' It was my father's gun."

"Why didn't you tell me before this?" He could barely get the words out.

"I didn't know what to do. I'm her mother. I have the duty to protect her, even if she's a murderer."

Speechless, he stared at her.

"I realized I had to tell you sometime," she said. "You're being charged with something you didn't do. I couldn't stand it. What if you were convicted?" Tears came, and she turned away from the judge. "One day I knew I had to tell you," she said. "And I knew I had to get help for Tina."

He put his finger to his lips again and tried to stop her.

"It's too late," she said. "If they're listening, they're listening." The judge started to call for the guard. "You can't stop me," she said. "Not now. And you need to hear all the facts. That's what you always say. You need all the facts."

"Let me tell you some facts that I know," the judge said. "Sewell didn't forge the suicide note. You did. You sneaked the note in behind Huffsmith's back." His pause gave her time to deny it.

She stared at him, her gaze steady.

"You saw the gun in Tina's hand, and you thought she'd killed Horace. So you staged the suicide."

She continued to stare at the judge.

"Then, young lady, you forged the note. You'd had a lot of practice forging his signature after his mind wandered off. You thought Tina killed him. She had the motive all right. She hated him. What you didn't realize was that Horace killed himself."

Shock grabbed at her face.

"What about Tina, that poor girl?" the judge finally asked.

"She'd been getting better, and her attending school seemed to be beneficial, just as Dr. Brady said. I even let her drive her car to school like a normal kid. But that night she came home and told it all to me the minute she walked in the door. The first thing she said was, 'Mama, I had to kill that Sewell. He hurt you, Mama. You should kill people who hurt your family. Otherwise, you don't deserve your family.' She sounded exactly like my father. Then she said, 'And he hurt Judge Murray, and that Sewell should be killed, because Judge Murray is a good man and he loves us. You always said he was the best man you ever knew, Mama, so I killed him.'" Lillian's eyes squinted against the tears and her lips grew tight. "My God, how did all this happen to us?"

"She must have been suffering another of her delusions," the judge said.

"I've talked it over with Dr. Brady and with Sylvia. You're in here for something you didn't do, and I know you won't take care of yourself."

"How do you think you're going to prove to anyone that Tina killed him? They'll just claim she's hallucinating again."

"There's an eyewitness to the shooting," Lillian said.

"Really? Who would that be?"

"Deputy Huffsmith saw it all."

Without explanation, Robert Headley, Jr., dismissed his case against Hardy Tillman. Some thought they'd made a deal, and that Hardy was ready to testify against the judge. Others said, no, that Headley didn't want to face all the distracting noise Hardy would make in a joint trial with the judge. They thought that the judge was Headley's main target, and he wanted to eliminate any potential distractions.

CHAPTER 53

THE SPECIAL PROSECUTOR walked to the jury box and greeted the jurors with a small, sad smile. He was about to deliver his opening statement, which would outline his case against Judge Murray. Headley was tall and immaculately handsome in black alligator boots, his black suit, and black shirt with a turquoise slip tie around his neck, and he wore his thick blond hair slicked back. He took in the jurors with uncompromising blue eyes and spoke in a matter-of-fact voice, like one reading irrefutable truths carved in stone.

"Judge Murray is a murderer, I am sad to tell you. He was the law in Teton County for many years. Only Haskins Sewell stood in his way. Even after nearly four decades, prosecutor Sewell would not crumble under Judge Murray's distorted and often unlawful emasculations of justice. At last, unable to subdue the prosecutor, the judge resorted to violence. I will prove that tragic fact beyond a reasonable doubt with eyewitness testimony." With an uncompromising nod of the head, Headley sat down.

As had recently become his habit, Coker reserved his opening statement.

The special prosecutor called Sheriff Howard Lowe as his first witness. The sheriff, now obviously entering the venerated realm of the aged, had won reelection term after term and had become a minor local celebrity. On the stand, he offered a long, rambling history of the enmity that began between the judge and Sewell even before Sewell had been elected prosecutor—how the two men first met at the lily pond when Sewell lawfully shot a goose the first day of the season, and how the judge had verbally attacked him for doing what Sewell had a perfect legal right to do.

Much of the sheriff's testimony was unbridled hearsay and inadmissible. But when Coker tried to object, Judge Murray stopped him. "Let him speak," Judge Murray said.

The sheriff told how Sewell's first case as a beginning prosecutor had been defended by John Murray—the Ezra Mills hay-stealing case. "That man," Sheriff Lowe declared, pointing to the judge, "was always eager to represent criminals of the worst kind. After he beat Haskins Sewell for the judgeship—by only a vote or two, mind you—we had to fight not only the criminals but the judge himself, who sat on their cases."

Several times, Coker started to object to the sheriff's testimony, but Judge Murray stopped him.

The sheriff pressed on. "How we managed all these years to keep the good people of this county safe under such intolerable conditions speaks to the caliber of the dedicated lawmen we have provided the citizens. Lillian Adams—you know her—she lives up there on the hill and was recently in this very court for murderin' her third husband, a filthy rich beer manufacturer—well, she was like a daughter to Judge Murray and his wife, but did he take himself off her murder case? No. And Mr. Coker over there got her acquitted—"

"Objection!" Coker cried. "Objection! This is preju-dicial and—"

Judge Murray reached over, grabbed the tail of Cok-er's suit coat, and pulled him down.

Judge Little intervened. "This is pure argument, Mr. Headley. And so far as I can see, totally irrelevant. Please hold your witness to proper testimony." Headley nodded.

The sheriff continued, "Well, this all goes back to the time when Lillian Adams was a mere slip of a girl, sixteen years old, and she nearly beat her new husband to death with a brass vase. Put him in the hospital. Did the judge here," he said, pointing to Judge Murray, "send her off for some instruction to Wyoming's reform school for girls? No. He gave her a pat on the head and sent her home."

Attempting to elicit an objection from Coker, Judge Little interrupted. "Mr. Coker. What do you have to say about this?"

Coker whispered to Judge Murray, "We have to stop him. He's killing us. Even Judge Little sees it."

"Let him make his point," Murray replied.

Coker turned to Judge Little. "At this time, I am re-serving my objections."

"Counsel, you know better than that. You must make your objections at the time or they're waived."

Coker remained silent.

Sheriff Lowe hastened to tell how Lillian had stabbed her second husband with a pen. "I have already testified how she was charged with the murder of her third hus-band, which case was unfortunately lost by prosecutor Sewell when justice went awry, to the danger and dis-grace of the people of this county."

Judge Little ordered a recess and ordered the parties to his chambers. He scowled over at Coker. "Are you feeling all right, Mr. Coker?"

"Not exactly," Coker said.

"What's the problem?" the judge asked.

"The sheriff is running wild with his testimony, and Judge Murray won't let me put a stop to it."

Judge Little turned to Judge Murray. "Why are you interfering with your attorney? I know him to be competent, and I know he wants to protect you from improper testimony."

Judge Murray said, "A trial is a search for justice."

Headley joined the fray: "The sheriff's testimony is totally proper. It sets the background for the crime with which Judge Murray is charged."

"I caution you, Mr. Headley," said Judge Little. "There is something in the law known as 'fundamental fairness.' If those boundaries are breached, you may suffer a mistrial or, on appeal, a reversal."

"Of course," Headley said. "I am fully aware of the law."

Back in the courtroom, Sheriff Lowe began where he'd left off. "There was always a feud going on between prosecutor Sewell and Judge Murray. It got so bad that Judge Murray found Sewell in contempt of court and sent him to jail, not once, but twice. You can imagine the bravery of prosecutor Sewell, who spent those times in jail as the price he was willing to pay in his futile attempt to preserve justice in Teton County."

Coker was peering at Judge Murray in obvious alarm, but the judge sat calmly, silently by.

"What happened next?" Headley asked.

"Well, finally prosecutor Sewell had no other choice but to petition the Wyoming Supreme Court to remove Judge Murray from presiding in Mrs. Adams's murder trial," the sheriff said. "And only after the supreme court prohibited him from taking any further part in the case was the state given the gift of an impartial judge, Judge Little, who presides here."

Judge Little looked down and straightened his bow tie.

With a voice reflecting his most ardent respect, Sheriff Lowe told how Sewell had courageously filed a series of charges against Judge Murray for his arrogant perjury when he denied under oath that he had heard Lillian Adams admit to the murder of her third husband, Horace Adams III. "We had it all right there in a recording we made in his pickup. Not only that; we had a witness who saw her kissing the judge in his pickup, but he"—Lowe nodded in Coker's direction—"talked a jury into turning her loose."

Judge Little looked over at Coker, waiting for his objection. Coker started to object, but Judge Murray pulled him back down again.

"Prosecutor Sewell fought like the shades of Billy Hell to preserve law and order in Teton County. And what Judge Murray couldn't get done as a judge, he finally finished with a bullet through the head of Haskins Sewell as he was peacefully leaving the courthouse to go home. Prosecutor Sewell laid down his life for justice."

Coker had jumped up to object, but Judge Murray restrained him. When Coker rose to cross-examine the sheriff, Judge Murray grabbed his coat sleeve and whispered, "Let him go."

"He's killing us," Coker said. "No, he's already killed us."

"Let him go," Judge Murray repeated.

Coker, confounded, slowly sat down. "You're trying to commit suicide," Coker said to Judge Murray.

The judge looked straight ahead and didn't answer.

The special prosecutor then called the Teton County coroner, Dr. Roger Norton, to testify concerning the wound in Haskins Sewell's forehead, the powder burns, the star-shaped blowout around the entry wound, and his conclusion that the shot had been fired at point-blank range. Headley showed the jury the bloody photos, and again Judge Murray would not allow Coker to cross-examine.

Finally, Headley called his star witness, Deputy Arthur Huffsmith. Huffsmith walked to the witness stand. He spoke in a distant monotone. He related that on the night of the shooting he heard what sounded like a shot, and within seconds how he had rushed to the window of the sheriff's office on the third floor of the courthouse to look out.

"What were you doing at the courthouse at that time of the night, Deputy Huffsmith?"

"I was processing a couple of drunks that give me a hard time."

"On the night of Mr. Sewell's murder, did you have occasion to see the defendant, John Murray?"

"Yes, sir."

"What time did you see him and where?"

"I seen him down in the parking lot."

"And the time?"

"About six in the evening.'"

"Did you hear anything unusual?"

"Yes. I heard a gunshot."

"What did you see?"

"I seen the judge here," he said, pointing to Judge Murray. "Something in his hand. I figured it was a gun. Yeah, it must have been a gun for sure. I never seen him walk that fast before. He was almost runnin' to his pickup."

"What did he do after that?"

"He got in his pickup truck and drove off."

"No further questions," Headley said.

As Coker jumped up to cross-examine Huffsmith, Judge Murray tried to stop him. Coker pushed past Judge

Murray and rushed to the podium. With a vengeance, Coker released a rapid flurry of questions to Huffsmith.

"Didn't you and I talk about what you saw when I visited you at your home three weeks ago?" Coker asked.

"Yes, sir."

"Deputy Huffsmith, didn't you tell me that you saw Tina Ford, the teenage daughter of Lillian Adams, there that night, and that you saw her with a gun in her hand?"

"Yeah, I said that."

"You are lying about Judge Murray, aren't you, Deputy?"

"I owed the judge a lot. He saved my house, and he helped to save my boy, and then—"

"Answer my question. You are a liar, aren't you?"

"Yes, sir." Huffsmith's lower jaw began to quiver. "Mrs. Adams, she told me right off that Tina done it, that her daughter admitted killing Sewell, and that they was going to put her daughter in the hospital, so I figured that I'd go along with that. Wouldn't hurt nobody. Tina was going to go to the hospital anyway, so I just as well save the judge. He's a good man. And Sewell—"

"And Sewell, what?" Coker asked, interrupting him.

"Well, some say he should have been shot a long time ago."

"So you've now changed your statement as to what you saw?"

"Yes, sir."

"To your knowledge, did anyone else see what happened that night?"

"No, sir."

"So you were willing to lie to me, and to let Mrs. Adams lie to you about her daughter, but you are not lying now to these jurors? How can we tell when you're lying and when you're telling the truth?"

"Well, I got me a sick boy of my own, and I know what it's like to worry about your kid. I got to thinking about Tina, and if she got okay, well, I didn't want her to grow up believing she was a murderer when she wasn't."

"So will you tell the jurors how they can tell that you aren't lying right now?"

"That there is up to them. But I am telling you the truth. That's all I can say."

Headley rested his case, sat down, and adjusted the turquoise slip tie around his neck. Then he cocked his head and looked slowly over at Judge Murray.

Coker asked for a recess. He sat at the counsel table with Judge Murray, and neither spoke for a long time, both peering into nowhere like two lost souls looking for a landmark.

Finally, Coker said in a quiet voice that carried the strained sounds of his decision, "I can still win this case on reasonable doubt. A lot of people in town don't believe you did it. Some may be on this jury. Huffsmith lied. Twelve citizens aren't going to convict you when the only eyewitness is a confessed liar. I can at least hang this jury." He hit the table with a decisive thud of his fist. "And I'm not going to put you on the stand."

"I want to take the stand," the judge said.

"You never killed anybody, and you know it. A false confession under oath is perjury."

"Yes, perjury," the judge said.

"Your life is at stake, Judge. Don't you understand that?"

"I have always said one must trust the jury."

"You're having another one of those spells, Judge."

The judge's eyes were closed, and he was rubbing his forehead, as if in deep thought.

Coker stood with his hands on his hips, searching the judge's face.

Judge Little returned to the bench. "Call your first witness, counsel," he ordered.

Judge Murray labored to his feet. Coker jumped up to stop him.

"I'm going to testify," the judge said. He walked with faltering steps to the witness stand. He was wearing his blue jail coveralls. Judge Little administered the oath and gave Judge Murray a quick, anemic smile and looked away. The judge settled stiffly into the witness chair and waited.

Coker looked as if he were witnessing the dead walking. Finally, he took refuge in his standard preliminary questions. "Judge Murray, you know that under the Constitution of the United States you are not required to testify here. Why are you testifying?"

"I want the jurors to know the truth. Jurors don't often get the whole truth."

"What do you mean?"

"I mean that by the time the lawyers get through with a witness, it's often hard to sort out what's true from what isn't." His voice was clear but distant.

"You heard Deputy Huffsmith say he saw you at the scene of this homicide just seconds after he heard the blast of a gun?"

"Yes, I heard that testimony."

"Was that testimony the truth?"

"Yes, it was."

Coker, smashed back in profound shock, finally half-recovered and said, "You must have misunderstood me, Judge Murray. I asked you if Deputy Huffsmith's testimony was true—that he saw you at the scene just seconds after he heard the blast of the gun. And what is your answer?"

"I have never known the deputy not to tell the truth as he sees it."

Coker picked up a file and pretended to read something while he desperately grasped for his next question. Under oath, his client had just admitted to murder. The case was over. John Murray's life was over. And Betsy's.

Finally, Judge Little interrupted his silence. "Do you wish a recess, counsel?"

"No, Your Honor. Judge Murray has these spells. Mr. Breslin, the clerk of court, has witnessed a number of these from time to time, as have I." The clerk nodded his head in vigorous agreement. "How are you feeling, Judge Murray?"

"I feel just fine."

"Where are you at this moment?"

"I am on the witness stand in my courtroom."

"Why are you on the stand?"

"To see that justice is done."

"You previously pled not guilty to murder. Have you changed your mind?"

"Are you listening carefully?" the judge asked.

Coker heard himself ask, "What caused you to change your testimony?"

"Deputy Huffsmith was right," Judge Murray said. "Tina might get well. She shouldn't be blamed for a crime she didn't commit."

Coker heard himself mutter the ultimate question. "Did you kill Haskins Sewell?"

"Of course," the judge said matter-of-factly.

"Indeed!" Coker could think of nothing else to say. Finally, in shock that had invaded all reason, he heard himself ask the "why question" that every first-year law student is taught never to ask. "Why did you kill him?"

"It was the right thing to do."

"How can you say that murder is the right thing to do?"

"Sewell was the incarnate of evil. He was the devil's agent, and he could not be stopped."

"You are utterly delusional," Coker was finally able to say. He turned to Judge Little. "Please, Your Honor! Judge Murray is obviously a very sick man. I ask that he be examined immediately."

Judge Little sat frozen, his eyes wide, his lips tight white lines.

Without a further question, Judge Murray continued, "For nearly forty years I watched that man destroy innocent people. I saw him take sadistic pleasure from crushing helpless families. After he had me arrested for everything in the book, he was about to become our judge—a position that would have brought untold misery and injustice to Jackson Hole. I had no choice."

"Come now, Judge," Coker pleaded. "I've known you for decades. You wouldn't even kill a mouse."

"I protected the people from him as best I could," Judge Murray said. "When he charged me with perjury as a common criminal, he destroyed my reputation and the people's faith in me, and I could no longer protect them."

"They were false charges. Everyone knew that," Coker said.

"No. Everyone did not know that." His eyes had taken on a strange light. "The people have been taught that the prosecutor keeps them safe from crime. Sewell's charges turned me into an inveterate criminal in their eyes and left me powerless to protect them."

"You have been through too much. You're an old man, and you've been in jail all these months. You are—"

Judge Murray interrupted him. "Sewell was running against me for the judgeship and would have won. It was all over—for me and for the people."

"Yes, but . . ."

"After he became the judge, who would save the people? They are my people."

"Judge Murray, you are quite ill. You've been taken over by one of your spells."

"Yes, I am ill," the judge said. "I never thought I could kill any living thing." His voice cracked, and he looked as if shaken, his bones would scatter across the floor. "Now you need to haul me off as the law provides and dispose of me."

Coker looked to Judge Little again. "Judge, please. This man is delusional."

Judge Little was transfixed by Judge Murray.

"Judge, please," Coker implored.

Coker turned back to his witness. "Judge Murray, you were sworn to uphold the law. You have always upheld the law."

"Yes, the law too often fails to do right, and when it failed, I, as a judge, failed, as well."

"Do you realize what you're saying? How can you testify to such nonsense?" Coker threw his words at the judge as if to awaken him.

"Justice must find ways to trump the law."

"After these nearly forty years, you're now claiming you are above the law? That is utterly insane."

"No," Judge Murray said. "Insanity in the law is when one doesn't know the difference between right and wrong. I know the difference. It's the law that is insane. The law doesn't recognize the difference between right and wrong."

"You are truly insane," Coker said in a near-whisper.

"When the law fails us, our responsibilities are not diminished," the judge said.

"Well then, listen to what you have repeatedly ruled over your whole life—that no one is above the law, that were it otherwise, we would become a lawless nation." Coker turned again to Judge Little. "You see, Your Honor, he is very ill."

The jurors were leaning forward in their chairs, some with eyes wide in apprehension, some with eyes squinted in dismay. The woman in front on the far left was holding on to the railing. Some, with nothing else to grasp, clenched their hands tightly.

Judge Murray spoke again in a low, far-off voice. "The law has a moral duty to protect the people, failing which the people must protect themselves."

Coker said, "I have heard quite enough, Judge Murray. You have forgotten who you are. You are a judge."

"It is one thing to be a judge. It is quite another thing to be a human being."

Judge Murray then got up from the witness chair and walked back to the counsel table and sat down. Coker sat down beside him and gazed at the table's top, his jaw slack, his eyes downcast.

Finally, Judge Little came alive and hit his gavel to get Coker's attention. "Do you have further questions, counsel?"

"No," Coker said in a barely audible voice, his head still down.

Headley rose slowly, tentatively, to cross-examine. He took in the judge as if to assure himself that the man hadn't descended into some kind of dangerous, irretrievable madness. Finally, he reached out with a careful question while Judge Murray was still seated next to Coker. "Judge Murray, did I hear you correctly, that you intentionally killed Haskins Sewell?"

"Yes, you did," the judge said in a clear, convincing voice.

"When did you decide to do that?"

"I had been thinking about it for some time."

"You want this jury to convict you?"

"I want them to do their duty."

Betsy Murray hollered from the front row, where

she'd been seated, "He's sick! Can't you see he's sick? He's very sick."

"Sit down," Judge Little said to Betsy. He slammed his gavel.

"I'll never sit down," she said. "He's sick! Can't everyone see that?" She started to run up to her husband, but before she was able to clear her way past other seated spectators, both bailiffs moved in to stop her.

The lawyers' final arguments were the shortest in the annals of Wyoming jurisprudence. Headley began and ended by saying, "I have no argument to make. I join the defendant, Judge John P. Murray, in asking you to do your duty."

Coker got up. He didn't approach the jury as was his habit. Instead, he stood behind Judge Murray and made his statement to the jurors with a hand on each of the judge's shoulders.

"I have my hands on a great man. I am humbled to represent him. I have never known him to bring injury intentionally to anyone. I have only known him to do the right thing even when he could have benefited by doing the wrong thing. We cannot believe his testimony here. By his conduct, he has shown us how ill he is. I wish I could ask you to love him as I love him." Timothy Coker sat down, grabbed the judge's hand, and held it like a son holding the hand of a father who was in mortal danger.

The courtroom emptied.

After the verdict, members of the press interviewed some of the jurors. Several thought that Haskins Sewell had had it coming, no matter who had killed him. Some thought that Deputy Huffsmith was an unreliable witness, that he had changed his story for reasons of his own, and they couldn't convict anyone whose story bounced around as Huffsmith's had.

Others thought that the judge was protecting someone he cared about—most thought it was the girl, Tina—that she was young and had a possible life in front of her, while the judge was old and near the end of his.

One juror argued, "That Tina was like a granddaughter to the judge. Everybody knows that. And she is one crazy bitch." Another juror chimed in, "Yeah, and she hated Sewell. And yeah, the judge would have took the blame. I say, sometimes a man's got to take care of his family, no matter what."

Most believed that the judge was innocent but was doing the right thing, as he always had, that it took courage for him to martyr himself for the right reasons. They all agreed that a guilty man would never take the stand and admit his guilt. Guilty men always say they're innocent. And one juror reminded the others that Huffsmith never claimed he saw the judge shoot Sewell. Huffsmith just said he'd heard the shot.

One juror argued, "The judge was right. We all know that Sewell was about to take the county over, and none of us would have been safe after that. If he done anything, he done what he done to save us."

Although a couple of jurors thought the judge was having one of his well-known spells, most believed that with the death of Haskins Sewell, Jackson Hole would be a safer place. After three hours of deliberation, the jury returned their verdict of not guilty.

When Betsy heard the verdict, she was unable to speak. She and the judge walked out of the courtroom together. They didn't speak. She couldn't stop crying. At the turnoff to the cabin, he kept on driving. "Where are you going, honey?" she was finally able to ask.

"Thought we could drop by our pond. Maybe our geese have come back," he said. "It's spring again."

ACKNOWLEDGMENTS

I AM GRATEFUL for the good work, kindness, and patience of Bob Gleason, my editor, and for the eagle eye, sharp tooth, and rock-solid judgment of Junius Podrug, whose guidance from time to time during the writing of this manuscript has been invaluable both as an editor and a dear friend.